LOVE ON THE OUTSKIRTS OF TOWN

ZOE YORK

ABOUT THIS BOOK

Matt Foster has never met a woman he couldn't seduce into his bed. But when he meets Natasha Kingsley, there's just one little problem—she's not alone. Her three-year-old daughter wants a pony ride, an ice cream cone, and help to reach the highest rungs of the climbers at the park. Before he knows it, he's spent all day with the Kingsley girls, and for the first time in forever, finds himself wanting more.

Tasha doesn't realize who Matt is related to until he gives her his number at the end of a perfect day. Turning down his request for a second date—with both her and her daughter—is the hardest thing she's ever done. But her history with his brother, and her firm commitment to living a drama-free life for her daughter, means she can't flirt with, sleep with, or dream about Jake Foster's younger brother.

Not even if he makes her daughter laugh.

Not even if he seeks her out again and shows her just how interested he is in every part of her life. Because there's no such thing as a truly secret affair—and Tasha's done with being anyone's guilty pleasure.

WELCOME TO PINE HARBOUR

Tucked into a hollow half-way up the Bruce Peninsula, on the eastern shores of Lake Huron, **Pine Harbour** is where cottage country meets northern living. For generations, the Foster family has been a rock in the community. All the Foster men serve in the local Army reserve unit and the youngest adult generation is no exception.

Meet the Foster boys: **Dean, Jake, Matt** and **Sean**. A cop, a contractor, a paramedic and an adventure racer. All soldiers. None of them looking for love, but it's coming!

Their best friends are the Minellis: **Zander, Rafe, Tom** and **Dani**. A full-time soldier, a cop, a park ranger and a paramedic. Dani's the only girl in the entire bunch and she's not sure how she feels about that. When Rafe got married, she was thrilled to have a sister–and even though he and Olivia have split up, Dani's not giving up that bond. (And neither is Rafe, for that matter).

The other books of Pine Harbour

Love in a Small Town
Rafe and Olivia
Six years. Two break-ups. One divorce. They should be over
each other…

Love in a Snow Storm
Jake and Dani
Never fall in love with your best friend's little sister…

Love on a Spring Morning
Ryan and Holly
Duplicity. Desire. Denial. They were doomed from the start.

Love on a Summer Night
Zander and Faith
Sometimes saying goodbye is just the beginning.

Love on the Run
Dean and Liana
She needs a bodyguard. He needs a job. But there's nothing
strictly professional about their attraction.

Love in a Sandstorm
Sean and Jenna
It was supposed to be a fling. Two weeks in the south of Spain
before they returned to war. They weren't supposed to fall
in love…

www.zoeyork.com

Everyone should have a Big Dream Plan, and people in their corner who tell them to go for it even when it feels impossible

For Kristi

PROLOGUE

Six months ago
March

MATT FOSTER PULLED on his favourite pair of winter gloves and tapped the button on the wall to open the huge garage door of the Tobermory EMS station.

His partner, Owen Kincaid, drove their ambulance out into the blowing snow, then Matt hit the button again and ran for the passenger door. They were eight hours into their shift and had just received their next call.

"I'm looking forward to the automated doors at the new station in Pine Harbour," Owen said as he eased the rig onto the highway.

Matt smirked. "I'm looking forward to rolling out of bed and being at work ten minutes later."

"Take a damn shower, you animal."

Matt laughed. "That's with a shower. Unless I have a friend to wash my back, then I'll need a full hour. Like this morning, for example."

"Do you ever sleep alone?"

What a crazy question. "Not if I can help it."

"Have you always been this intolerably cocky?" Owen laughed and shook his head. Of course he didn't get it. He was long divorced, bitter, and raising a teenage daughter mostly on his own. He probably hadn't been laid in ages. Months at least, maybe even a year. An unbearable length of time, no doubt. Which was an extra shame because he was still relatively young—almost forty, fit as fuck, and covered in tattoos.

Matt didn't have shit-all to be bitter about. His life was fan-fucking-tastic. "You love me, admit it."

"You definitely make shifts go by quickly, that's for damn sure."

"You're going to miss this, admit it." The older man was getting a promotion. Trained as both a paramedic and a fire-fighter, he'd be the Fire and Emergency Services supervisor at the new station. This was one of their last shifts together.

"Besides, I'm in the process of moving. My life is in boxes, so it's only smart to sleep in other beds as much as possible."

Since the new station was about to open in Pine Harbour, he was moving back to town so he'd be right around the corner. Nobody could say he wasn't a reliable paramedic.

He was a rock star with rock star habits, right down to the late night parties and parade of pretty girls leaving his apartment.

What wasn't to like about his life?

"All right, Romeo," Owen said as he tapped the computer between their seats. "We've got a job to do. Hit the lights and pull up the details on Fred Carleton."

Fred was a regular pick-up for them because of his chronic obstructive pulmonary disease—in his case, bronchitis that never went away. A veteran, he was probably ten years older than Matt's father, but life and the military had been hard on him. He was a big, barrel-chested man who hated every single intervention into his life, even as they prolonged it. He'd called in and told dispatch that he hadn't been keeping up with his treatments and he was having trouble getting his breathing under control.

Matt confirmed the address, then checked in with dispatch, who still had Fred on the line.

If they needed to transfer him to hospital, it sounded like they'd be heading south, all the way down the peninsula to one of the bigger medical centres, which would keep them busy for a couple of hours.

The roads were clear and they made it to Fred's quickly. The lane at the old farmhouse hadn't been plowed or driven on recently, though, so Owen had to slow down to make it up the lane.

"We should get the Legion involved here for snow removal," Matt said.

Owen snorted. "Sure. Good luck finding a way to convince Fred he needs help."

Shit. Good point.

Maybe he could just borrow his older brother Jake's truck, since he had a plow hitch, and come out and do it himself.

"First things first," Matt said when they parked. "Let's get him breathing more comfortably. Then I'll find a way to get him to let me do him a solid."

Inside they found him on a recliner in the living room, still on the phone with dispatch.

"Tell them we've got it from here, Fred," Owen said with a big, friendly grin. "And Matt had a hot date last night, so we bring good stories to entertain you as well."

"Sure did." Matt snapped on a pair of gloves, then quickly took the man's vitals as Owen made easy chatter. So much of being an EMT was establishing a good rapport with patients.

Fred's pulse was elevated and his pulse oximetry was low

—his baseline was already low, so the big guy didn't have a lot of room there before he got in distress.

"Let's give you a bit of oxygen, my man." Not too much. That was a risk, too. Matt just wanted to bring his levels up enough to be safe. He hooked up a mask. "Keep breathing. That's good. Owen's going to mix you up a sweet cocktail in a nebulizer that's going to help you. How you feeling otherwise? Any nausea or pain?"

"No. Sorry to have you kids come out…" Fred tried to cough and his entire body strained with the effort. "On such a…shitty day."

Kids. Matt grinned at that. "Ah, we were fine. Love the snow, don't we, Owen?"

His partner gave him a look that said he was being too obvious and he should get back to talking about the woman he spent a few hours with last night, but lingering on those details wasn't Matt's style.

Charm got him further than most, and it was going to work on doing Fred a solid here with his driveway, too. "You know what I do for fun sometimes?"

Fred weakly lifted one shoulder. "Two girls at once?"

Owen guffawed out loud.

Matt rolled his eyes. "I use my brother's plow attachment and make a giant snow hill for the kids in town."

"Long time…since I went sledding."

Matt grinned. "You see right through me. After the kids are home for the night, I'm sliding down that thing myself. Or with a friend."

That got him a weak, wheezing laugh.

"Hey, next time I do that, would you mind if I swung by and plowed your drive?"

Fred shook his head. "I do it…myself. Sorry 'bout today."

"Nothing to be sorry about." Matt let it drop as Owen

administered the bronchodilator.

Fred's breathing eased a bit, but he still looked unwell. Once they were in transit, Matt could administer other drugs which would kick in later at the hospital, but this was the most they could do for immediate effect.

Really, Fred needed to not be alone in a farmhouse, but recommending the vet move to a retirement home was beyond Matt's scope of practice.

Owen went over the options, making sure Fred was the one who made the decision to pack up and head to the hospital, even though it was a pretty obvious choice given his circumstances.

"My bag is…in the closet."

Matt nodded gently. "I'll grab it. Smart to have it ready to go."

Painful that after a life of independence, the man had to be constantly ready to be admitted to the hospital at any time.

Matt took Fred's bag and their gear back to the rig, then came back inside and helped Owen get him standing. They wrapped a blanket around him to keep him sheltered from the bitter cold, then carefully moved as one, three men stepping in unison.

"Just like in the army, eh, Fred?"

The older man didn't reply until he was carefully settled in the back of the ambulance. Matt clipped the pulse oximeter on Fred's finger, took another set of vitals, then started to prep the other meds he could deliver.

"Are you still parading with…the infantry in Wiarton?"

"Sure am, sir."

"Don't call me that," Fred said with a smile. "Never made Warrant."

"Yeah, well, neither will I, so you're in good company."

"What rank are you now, son?"

"Just made sergeant. And will be forever, I think. Hard to take the time off from this for the courses I'd need to progress further. Besides, I'm thinking of doing some advanced training for paramedics, like Owen did. Except cooler. Maybe I'll be one of those people on the helicopters who do trauma response, yeah? I'll get all the girls that way."

"Rumour has it you…get all the girls…now."

Matt smiled. "I do okay."

They talked army shop-talk the rest of the way to the hospital, and the drive was uneventful. Owen got the direction to head all the way into Owen Sound, so they did that, and by the time they pulled up at the Emergency department, Fred's oxygen levels had lifted a bit and he was breathing more easily.

"You're going to have a good night here," Matt promised as they wheeled him in the side entrance. "I made sure they'd have the prettiest nurses on shift for you."

"Can't say that anymore," Fred whispered, his eyes drifting closed.

"Sure you can," Matt said, winking at the nurse and doctor who approached. "You just gotta read the room first. Always good if you can encourage them to make the first move. Consent is sexy, Fred. Just remember that and you'll go a long way with the ladies."

"Never had any problem there."

"I bet not." Matt shifted gears and gave a quick, thorough report to complete their handover to the ER staff. "Okay, we're out of here, Fred. You have a good one."

Instead of heading outside, where it was damn cold, Matt and Owen ducked into a side room to complete their paperwork on the call. As they were finishing up, a code blue was called over the overhead announcement system, to a location just around the corner.

The hospital had a code team to respond, but that didn't stop Matt from sprinting out the door.

That wasn't just any location, that was where they'd wheeled Fred to.

Owen was right behind him, not that it mattered. By the time they were in the corridor, there was a nurse and a doctor working on the retired vet, with two others in support. Owen dragged Matt out of the way, holding him against the wall as they watched for twenty agonizing minutes as the team tried to bring Fred back to life.

But the old guy wasn't having any of it.

He was gone.

When the doc called time of death, Matt heard himself almost protest. *No.*

Instead, he stalked back to the room where they'd left their gear.

"What did we fucking miss?" he asked when Owen closed the door behind them.

"Nothing. It was just one of those things."

"Fuck that. That's—" Matt turned and kicked at the nearest thing, which happened to be a chair that went flying. "Jesus."

His chest was tight, like his uniform was suddenly too small, and he couldn't breathe.

"Come on," Owen said quietly. "It happens. We know that."

Yeah. It happened. It happened when they saw it coming, when it was a code four out of the gate. He knew how to manage a trauma call.

This was...*Jesus Christ.* The last thing he'd said to the man was advice on how to pick up women.

Matt's phone vibrated in his pocket.

Blindly, he shoved his hand at it and silenced it.

A few seconds later, it went off again.

Yanking it out, he glared at the screen. He'd missed a couple of texts from his older brothers—one from Dean, two from Jake.

Dean: Call Jake when you get a second. Urgent.
Jake: Need to talk ASAP.
Jake: Can I call you?

Shit.

He scrubbed his hand over his face and pulled himself together. "Sorry," he muttered in Owen's direction. "Gotta call my brother for a sec."

"No worries. I gave dispatch the heads-up that we'd probably stay off air unless needed. We're fine."

Matt dragged in a rough breath, then called Jake, who answered immediately. "Matt."

"Hey, what's up? Now's not a great time."

"Where are you?"

"Owen Sound hospital."

"Are you with a patient?"

"Nah. Just with Owen in a break room." His mouth was dry. He needed water. He needed to sit.

"Are you— Can you talk?"

"Not really." He sighed. "Look, we're pretty much at the end of our shift. Can I call you back later?"

"Uh…" Jake groaned. "No. This is shitty, but it's really time sensitive. Is there any way we can pick you up there?"

"We? Who's we? What's going on?"

"It's Sean." Their youngest brother was serving a tour of duty in northern Iraq. A captain, he was officially there in a training capacity. Unofficially, they all knew otherwise.

The corners of Matt's vision turned dark and a dull roar started in the distance. "What happened?"

"He's hurt. That's all we know." Jake's voice cracked. "Dean was at the armouries when the CO got the call. It's being kept under wraps…"

The roar got worse. Matt heard individual words. Investigation. No media alert. *Dad.* "What was that?" he asked hoarsely.

Jake repeated himself. "Dad pulled rank and got Dean cleared to meet Sean in Germany." The American medical base. Holy fuck. But it also meant Sean's injuries couldn't be treated by the medical teams on the ground.

The room spun angrily, and Matt tried to suck in air.

No.

No.

"Tell me he's okay," he said hoarsely.

There was a long pause. "I don't know. We don't know anything yet. Dad's working on getting us more information." Their father might be a hard-assed, bitter motherfucker, but he'd also been a colonel in the Canadian Forces, and that changed things. For once, Matt was grateful for that advantage. "Fuck, I'm sorry, bud."

"I'm with Owen right now," Matt repeated, feeling dumb. They were already off air, he didn't need to do anything, but he was in the middle of a hospital. And he wasn't sure what he could tell his partner if there was a media blackout and his father had to pull rank just to get a family member at his brother's side.

"Tell him you have a family emergency. Dean's flying out of Toronto first thing tomorrow. I'm driving him to the airport."

"I want to go with you. I'll be waiting here." He hung up the phone. "Fuck."

Owen didn't miss a beat. "What do you need?"

For the first time in his entire life, Matt had no idea.

CHAPTER ONE

DOWNTOWN PINE HARBOUR was still quiet as Matt did his third gruelling climb up the hill from the glittering blue waters of Lake Huron into the main stretch.

He'd never been a die-hard runner before Sean was hurt. There was no keeping up with the youngest Foster brother, who'd always run like a gazelle, effortlessly and forever. They all tried anyway, to support him and be good brothers. But Jake was the only one who ran all the time. Dean and Matt did it with protests, because it would be so much more fun to hit something, lift anything, or climb hand over hand until every-thing screamed.

Now Matt craved all of that *and* the hard pounding of his feet on the pavement.

He regretted never being more into it while his baby brother was a world-class athlete.

Bile rose in his throat and he churned his legs faster, like he could outrun guilt if he just trained hard enough. Before and after shifts and always alone. He liked these pre-dawn runs the best. In the darkness, with blood thumping in his ears, there was no room for the feelings that plagued him when all was quiet.

And he worked.

He worked himself to the bone, happy to take extra shifts, long patient-transfers, whatever filled the coffers. He'd made noises before Sean got hurt about getting more serious about his career, about advanced training. *Time to grow up*, he'd said.

He hadn't known shit.

Still didn't.

He worried about why he hadn't figured anything out, and he ran even faster.

On his arm, his phone vibrated from a special pocket in his shirt. He slowed at the top of the hill and dug it out.

Even though it was early, his youngest brother was already up. It had been a long, brutal summer for the entire family—his baby brother particularly—but after months of rehab, Sean was solidly on the road to recovery. And with a gorgeous wife at his side.

Sean: Did Jake talk to you about my mug-out?

Matt hated how nobody in his family thought he was reliable enough to remember things like the date of the regimental party marking Sean's retirement from the military. He swallowed that frustration and typed back a more enthusiastic response.

Matt: I've booked the night off work. I'll be there with bells on.
Sean: I can't drink too much.
Matt: No worries.

He didn't need the reminder that those days were behind all of them. Sean had been a steady wingman, always up for a night of clubbing or hitting a house party, and the thought of either of those things just wasn't the same without his brother. At first, they'd been sidelined by Sean's injury, and now, even though his brother was recovering, he only had eyes for Jenna, and zero interest in being anyone's wingman.

Matt's party style had been altered—permanently.

Sean: What are you doing up this early, anyway? I thought I'd get a response in a few hours.
Matt: Getting ready for work.

It wasn't a lie. He had a shift starting in an hour. Getting his run out of the way was step one in having a good day.

Step two would be saving as many lives as he possibly could.

Nine hours later, Matt was back at the station after three back-to-back calls. He had a date with a meatball sub, and nothing was going to stand in his way.

Except apparently Owen, who was leaning his big, broad frame against the fridge, his tattooed arms crossed over his chest. "How's it going?"

"I'm starving, and if you don't move, I might kill you."

"Seems like an over-reaction HR might object to. Listen, I need a favour."

"Personal or professional?"

His former partner thought for a moment. "Bit of both. Let's say I'm asking as your supervisor, but the details are friend-to-friend."

Matt groaned. "Can I eat while you ask me?"

The chief EMT chuckled and stepped out of the way. "Sure.

I'd like you to go to Port Elgin day after tomorrow for a three-day training course on electronic patient records."

Fuck. "I'm on the schedule all week." Matt grabbed his sandwich and a can of sparkling lemon water, and threw himself into a chair at the big table.

Owen sat across from him. "I've found people to cover those shifts."

"Without asking me?" Matt wanted to protest again, because he loathed the idea of taking a course right now. There was a lot of sitting around, a lot of downtime.

A lot of silence for his thoughts to take over and wreak havoc.

But something in the big guy's face stopped him. "Were you going to go on this?"

Owen lifted one shoulder in a resigned shrug. "Yeah. My ex can't take my daughter after all, so..."

Ah. And that wouldn't be something he'd tell just anyone. Owen was fiercely protective of his daughter, who was sixteen going on twenty-five.

Having been the asshole kid who took advantage of parents being away to sleep with his fair share of classmates back in high school, Matt couldn't blame his friend for not wanting to go away.

Shit. It looked like he was stuck in a classroom for the week. "All right. Count me in."

"It's at a conference centre and they've got rooms booked for all participants for the entire week. There's a mixer tomorrow night with local politicians and allied health part-ners, but you can skip that."

Yeah, Matt would find something better to do.

Or someone.

Except that wasn't who he was anymore. The old him—before Sean got hurt—would have had a field day with being out of town and having a hotel room. No strings attached sex was his favourite kind.

Really, his only kind. But something inside him had shifted and now he only had a vague, muscle-memory instinct to use this opportunity to get laid.

He'd been off his game for six long, dry months.

That needed to change, because he hated the restless, uncomfortable feeling he got when he didn't have anything to do with his hands. There were only so many overtime shifts he could sign up for, only so many projects to start with his brothers, before people started to look at him weirdly.

Maybe he should head to the Green Hedgehog in Lion's Head after work. No reason to put off getting laid to tomorrow.

But he didn't go out to the pub. He finished his last patient transfer, passed the rig over to the next team, bade his partner, Will, a good night, and went home.

Netflix and chill with his right hand seemed to be all he could manage lately.

He fell asleep to the news quietly flickering on the television, and woke up at the crack of dawn, driven out of bed by familiar and unwanted dreams. After a punishing run, he had a quick shower, then threw clothes for a few days and his toiletry kit into a duffel bag. The only thing worse than feeling restless was dealing with that discomfort inside the quiet box of his Spartan apartment.

He grabbed a coffee and breakfast sandwiches to go from Mac's, the diner on the edge of town, then rolled down his windows and soaked up the bright morning sunshine as he drove south.

Pine Harbour sat halfway up the Bruce Peninsula, overlooking the glittering blue of Lake Huron. Cottage country to some, home to others. Where he'd been born and raised.

Further north, at the tip of the long, narrowing stretch of land, sat Tobermory, where Lake Huron met Georgian Bay. South of him, southwestern Ontario stretched wide, small towns and farm country neatly divided in a way the bedrock of the peninsula didn't allow.

Wiarton was the dividing point, the town where the peninsula met the rest of the province. He knew it well—his military unit was based there, and as a paramedic, it was the nearest hospital. Sometimes they'd have to transport further south, to the bigger towns of Owen Sound and Port Elgin, but more often than not, Wiarton was his destination. It was also where he banked and grocery shopped, but today he was driving straight through.

He was on a mission now. Get to the conference hotel, figure out where he needed to be tomorrow morning, then find a soft body to get lost in for a few hours. Ha. Wishful thinking, but maybe it could happen.

The change of location could be good, too.

His whole game had shifted. He didn't understand the new rules, that much was clear. But he didn't know where to start in figuring them out. And thinking about that—about the restlessness, about the confusion and chaos deep inside him— made everything worse. So he cranked the music, rolled down his window, and stepped on the gas.

At the conference centre in Port Elgin, he gave the check-in clerk his trademark winning smile as she handed over his room key. Pretty, blonde. She was cute, friendly—definitely his type. "Where would you recommend for dinner tonight? I'm looking for something casual but fun."

She pulled a printed map out from under the counter and circled a pub right in the heart of town. "Bailey's is probably the best option. Good wings, great music. Pretty young crowd."

"Sounds great. You ever go there?"

"Sometimes." Her eyes twinkled. "With my boyfriend."

Swing and a miss. "I'll have to check it out myself sometime this week, then. How about during the day? Anything you'd recommend to kill a few hours?"

She pointed to a bulletin board in the library off the lobby. "There might be something posted there. And there's always the Saugeen First Nation Amphitheatre. The gardens are lovely, and there are paths down to the river."

"I've been there before, yeah. Good rec, thanks again."

He didn't have high hopes for the bulletin board, but a bright pink flyer right in the middle caught his eye. A weekly series of cooking classes at rotating restaurants in town. Today's class was cake decorating at a bakery, and when he punched the address into the map app on his phone, it was only a short walk from the conference centre.

He wasn't particularly interested in piping sugar roses onto a birthday cake, but hell, a daytime cooking class might be a great place to meet women.

———

EVERYONE ELSE HATED MONDAYS, but for Natasha Kingsley, they were magical. After a weekend of working too much and not sleeping enough, the start of everyone else's week was the beginning of her weekend. And once she got her niece and nephew off to school, she had six hours with her daughter, Emily, to do whatever they wanted to do—watch a movie, go to the park, cuddle, or search for new treasures at the thrift store.

Mommy and Millie time, Emily called it, with all the wide-eyed innocent joy a three-year-old could pack into four words.

Natasha knew, given her circumstances, she was lucky to

get as much time with Emily as she did. They got all day together, just the two of them, all week.

And on Monday, Natasha got to put Emily to bed, too.

Her heart ached that she didn't get to do that the other six nights.

It was paying off, though. Because they were living in her sister and brother-in-law's basement, she could save all her earnings as a bartender at Bailey's, except for the necessities she needed to buy for Emily. At one point, she'd been saving toward her Big Dream Plan of having her own inn. Now her dreams were more practical. A house of her own, a nine-to-five job working in someone else's hotel, maybe. Hard to find, though, so in the meantime, she worked with what she had and was always mindful that she had a lot to be thankful for even though her life had drifted well off track from her original hopes and aspirations.

And she made sure she gave back to Meredith and Dan as good as she got. She happily did the before-and-after-school childcare, prepared dinner, and did all the grocery shopping.

Happily. It was a weird word. Was she happy?

She was grateful.

And she found ways to eek out a bit of selfish pleasure here and there. Like this morning, she was taking Emily to the new bakery on the outskirts of town for a cake decorating workshop. It was part of a series of cooking classes she'd latched on to.

It wasn't quite using her hospitality and tourism degree to the max, but beggars couldn't be choosers when it came to professional development.

She'd thought she'd have time to get serious about jobs later.

Then Emily happened.

Now her every waking minute was scheduled around the

needs of the most perfect three-year-old in the entire world, and any real professional development would be later. Way later. Like…in a decade, maybe.

You could move to the city.

Except the thought of the noise, the traffic, the concrete…it all made her want to cry. She'd done it twice and then spent countless weekends there after moving away, returning for time in David's bed, going out for fancy dinners and to the best clubs.

It wasn't for her. No, deep down she knew the small towns of Bruce County were where her heart was happiest. Where she'd imagined building a business one day, and now where she saw herself building a life for Emily.

Because it was an understatement to say that David hadn't been enthusiastic about the accidental pregnancy—he'd wanted nothing to do with the future baby, so when her sister had poured a big pot of tea and told her the basement was hers for as long as she needed it, it was a no-brainer decision.

She'd traded her nomadic life and a pile of dreams in for regular childcare she didn't need to pay for, because there was no way she could afford full-time daycare on her own.

Now cake decorating was what she had.

It would have to be enough because it was the only thing on offer.

"Mommy," Emily said as they locked up the house.

"Yes?"

"What's your favourite kind of cupcake?" She asked it with all the solemnity such an important question deserved.

Natasha grinned. "Vanilla with chocolate icing."

"Mm."

"You don't agree?"

"I like pink cupcakes."

"Pink isn't a flavour."

Emily frowned as she climbed into her car seat. "Yes it is."

"Not really, honey."

"I love pink."

"I know, but—"

"It's my favourite kind."

"Right. Okay. Well, I guess it is a kind, even if it isn't a flavour."

"Will they have pink icing today?"

Natasha sure as heck hoped so.

Her phone vibrated as she put the key in the ignition. Her neck burned hot at the sight of her least favourite person's name on the screen.

David: We need to talk.

It had been a month since they'd done that last, and that conversation hadn't gone well because he'd asked her to make Emily be quiet.

Natasha: You and me? Or you and me and Emily?
David: You and me.
Natasha: Unless you want to talk to your daughter, I'm not sure you and me have anything to talk about.
David: I don't mean it like that. Of course I want to talk to her, it's just hard.

She didn't have time for this right now. Yes, talking to a three-year-old on the phone was an exercise in patience. So was raising one every single God-damned day.

Natasha: We're about to drive across town. Do you want to talk now?

David: Going into a meeting. Soon, though. I thought it would be polite to give you a heads up.

She rolled her eyes and tapped back a quick reply that any time that afternoon would be fine. There was a slim-to-none chance he'd actually call in a timely fashion, though.

It doesn't matter. She repeated both mantras until her pulse calmed down, then said them again in her head with more confidence. His actions weren't within her control, so she needed to let go of how much they frustrated her. They may be tangled together forever because of Emily, but she didn't have to let David mess with her head. And if he opted out of active parenting, that was his choice. But damn it, she hated how he gave almost nothing, over and over again—no time, the bare minimum financial support, very little contact—and then imperiously waltzed back into Emily's life. At this point, her daughter only knew her father from photographs and a handful of visits over the last two years, all at Natasha's urging.

That was what bothered her about today's text messages. What on earth did David want to talk to her about? She shoved that thought away and put her car in gear. *It doesn't matter.* Maybe one day she'd actually believe that.

When they arrived, the bakery parking lot was crowded. She recognized some of the cars from regulars on the cooking class circuit. She looped her bag over her shoulder, then went around to get Emily out of the back seat. "Careful," she reminded her daughter. "Hold Mommy's hand in the parking lot. Got it?"

"Got it."

Nobody warned her that parking lots were the scariest part of parenting. Parking lots and fevers.

Inside, the decorating class had taken over the eat-in part of the bakery space, with all the tables rearranged with chairs on one side, facing a raised demonstrator table with a tilted mirror above it. Normally Natasha liked to grab seats at the perimeter just in case Emily got bored, but every table close to the exit was already filled. There was one at the back, though, so she pointed to it. "Let's grab those seats, okay?"

Emily nodded and tugged her hand out of Natasha's grip just as another class regular, Mrs. Cargill, tapped her on the shoulder. "Nice to see you both again," the older woman said.

Natasha gave her a warm smile. "And you, too. I hope Emily won't be too distracting today. She's pretty excited about the icing."

"She's never a distraction. It's a joy to see her—and look, she's made a friend."

What? Natasha twisted around just in time to see Emily slide onto a seat next to a man. A stranger. A hot stranger, which wasn't really the most important thing to take note of right now, although…*damn.* His cut jaw and broad shoulders were the kind of grade-A masculinity that used to get her purring without hesitation.

She motored over just in time to hear Emily introduce herself, full name and age. "Are you here for cupcakes? Do you like pink?"

The stranger glanced around, and when Natasha stopped beside them, he gave her a kind smile. "Hi," he said. "Apparently I stole your table."

"I said, do you like pink?" Emily pushed herself up to her full, but still tiny, height, and propped her hands on her hips.

"I sure do," the man said blandly, like a small child hadn't just gotten up in his face about the colour pink.

Natasha's cheeks flamed bright red. She knew where her daughter got that hands-on-the-hips exasperation. It was a perfect mirror of Natasha's own behaviour. *I said, did you brush your teeth?* "Emily, manners." She glanced around, but now all the other tables were filled. Okay. She took a deep breath. "I think it's our table to share now," she said apologetically. She slid into the chair on the other side of Emily. "I hope you weren't planning on using any of the pink icing," she muttered under her breath as the instructor stood up at the front of the room. "Because the tiny dictator between us has laid advance claim on it all."

He chuckled. "It's all hers."

Emily gave them both a frustrated look. "I can share."

That made Natasha laugh. "Yes, I know. You try very hard."

"Mommy, shhh." But then Emily gave her the sweetest, most angelic smile, and pressed her own lips together, and… sigh. They'd work on not being totally precocious tomorrow.

Out of the corner of her eye, she caught the handsome man grinning, but they were all looking ahead now. Officially. Unofficially, she was mentally cataloguing all the ways he was totally gorgeous as her lady parts were reminding her it had been four years since she'd had a chance to roll around naked with someone.

Oh, shut up ovaries. You've done enough for one lifetime.

CHAPTER TWO

———————

MATT WAS CONVINCED the universe was punking him. Of course the hotel clerk had a boyfriend. That was fair. But a gorgeous, willowy brunette was attached to the toddler who'd arrived at his table at the same moment he did? Clearly, he wasn't going to get laid in Port Elgin.

At least he'd have cupcakes and an hour of amusement.

The hot mom didn't have a wedding ring, not that that necessarily meant anything. *Eyes off the mother, Foster.*

Had he ever slept with a mother? Not that he knew of, although he didn't always get into life stories.

You aren't sleeping with her today. Or ever. His lizard brain would hang on to this as off-limits fantasy material for his right hand, though. The mature, functional rest of him could shut that off. Which meant he could shift into safe, easy flirting, which was almost as much fun, just without the mutually satisfying ending.

He looked down at Emily Kingsley, proudly three-years-old, and she smiled up at him. He returned the grin. She held her finger up to her lips. *Shhh.* Yep, he got that rule.

At the front, the instructor was talking about different kinds of icing. Swiss meringue, buttercream, fondant. Today they were going to use buttercream, apparently, and as she said that, volunteers started to bring around pre-filled bags of icing. Each tray had three bags, but the mix of colours was varied around the room.

Matt watched as the volunteer came down their line. There was one tray that was chocolate heavy, and another with more pastel colours. The latter was handed to the table next to them, and he quickly leaned across the gap between the tables. "Sorry," he whispered, sticking out his arm. Thank God for having a long reach. "We're going to need the pink."

He zoinked the tray for their table, setting it carefully in front of Emily.

She gave him a solemn look. "Mommy likes chocolate."

Oh. He glanced past her to her mother, but the pretty woman shook her head with a small smile. *I'm good,* she mouthed. *Thank you.*

Emily poked at the ice packs on either side of the icing bags. "What are these for?"

"They keep the icing cold," he said.

"Why?"

"So it won't melt."

"Is it ice cream?"

"No, but you don't want it to be too warm or it won't hold the shape when you pipe it out." He pulled a piece of waxed paper between them and lifted the pink icing bag. He didn't actually know what he was doing with them, but he'd watched enough cooking shows in the last six months to pretend he did, and as long as the little girl was looking at him like he was a baking god, he'd do his best to answer her question.

Besides, the instructor was still droning on, and this was more fun.

He handed her the bag, then carefully set his hand at the top, where he could control the pressure without taking over. "Squeeze a bit out."

She squared her shoulders and pressed on the bag. He helped, and they drew a line of icing down the paper.

"Okay, put that back now," he whispered, and she stowed the icing bag back on the tray with the freezer packs. "And while the lady up there is talking, watch the icing. It's not going to melt like ice cream, but it will soften. Ready? Your job is to watch that super carefully."

She nodded and hunkered down, bringing her chin level with the edge of the table, and she glued her gaze to the bubblegum-pink line of icing.

He sure as shit hoped that icing started to melt or something, or he'd look like an idiot to a three-year-old.

When he straightened up, he realized her mother was looking at him with a curious look on her face.

"I'm Matt, by the way," he murmured. "Total icing novice, but don't tell her."

She laughed. "Natasha. And your secret is safe with me. Thanks for giving her something to do."

He nodded and turned his attention back to the demonstration. He still felt the warmth of that careful look, though, and he was pretty sure if he looked back at her, he'd catch her eyes.

He didn't glance back.

If she wanted to look her fill of him, that was fine. He was a stranger talking up her kid. She had every right to be wary.

And if she liked to look at him for any other reason, that was a-OK, too.

Ever since he was little, Matt had gotten a certain zing out of pleasing women. At first that meant charming the same teachers he aggravated or winning over the endless parade of babysitters before his brothers could rat him out for just being a normal, boisterous kid.

As an adult, sometimes that meant taking women to bed—definitely his favourite way to make someone happy. But it also meant being a handsome face, a strong set of arms, or a steady shoulder. He knew he was good looking. He knew he sometimes used that to his advantage, and so far, no harm, no foul, as long as he kept the balance right. He tried to be a good guy, a good friend, and always set really clear expectations.

Look at me all you want, Natasha. He should probably make sure there was no Mr. Natasha before he went whole hog on the sexy mom fantasy, though.

Emily watched the icing—and secretly ate just a little of it—through the rest of the introduction. The practice part of the class was more fun. They did roses and leaves, and a fun squiggly line technique that turned Emily's cupcake into a pink monster right out of Sesame Street.

Matt turned his cupcake into a bad version of a potted fern, but it made Emily laugh. Natasha decorated the rest of the half-dozen cupcakes they'd been given to practice on. Each one was a minimalist design, with a bottom layer of icing carefully smoothed out, then the same colour piped on top in a careful single bloom.

As she worked, and he practiced his piping skills making monster faces for Emily, he found out she wasn't a baker. She'd worked in hospitality her whole adult life, and now that she was home with Emily during the day, they did these cooking classes together. "It's not the same as going back to school or anything like that, but it helps me keep a toe in the food world."

"You could probably teach one of these classes."

She laughed, but then she nodded, surprising him. "Yeah. I mean, not now, but I do like that kind of thing. How about you? Are you an aspiring chef?"

He shook his head. "Total amateur hour for me. I'm a paramedic. I stumbled across this class after I arrived at the conference centre today."

Emily looked up. "What's a paramedic?"

"Do you know what an ambulance is?" She made the siren sound, and he nodded. "That's right. I'm the guy in the back of an ambulance. If someone has an emergency, I can help get them to a doctor really fast."

"Are you a superhero?" she asked earnestly.

Hardly. He gave her a gentle grin. "Only on Halloween."

The volunteers returned with takeout boxes as they were talking, and Matt took his cue from Natasha as she started to box up their cupcakes. He only had his one, so he waved off a box and stood up. "I'll eat this on my way back to my hotel room."

Emily grabbed his hand and tugged on his fingers. "Can you come to the park with us?"

He jerked his gaze to Natasha, who was busy not looking at him. Definitely an awkward, unwanted invite. "Gotta take my cupcake back to my room, sorry."

Natasha nodded quickly, still not making eye contact. "Emily, we need to take our cupcakes home so the icing doesn't melt."

"But Mommy…"

"Emily."

Matt knew that tone, and he respected it. "I really do need to get going," he lied, dropping down to a squat so he was at eye level with the little girl. "Thank you for teaching me how to make cupcakes."

She giggled. "I didn't teach you."

"Someone did. Wasn't that you?"

More giggles. "No."

"Huh. I'm sure it was someone about this tall…" He held his hand up above her head. "And very bossy."

She made a squeak of recognition, like yes, that must have been her after all. "I'm bossy!"

That made him laugh.

"Mommy says I should listen."

"She's right." He leaned in. "Moms are always right."

That got him a solemn nod in agreement.

"Okay, I have work to do, so I'll go do that, and you can take your cupcakes home." Why he was repeating that information, he wasn't sure. He should just do that. Stand up, leave, and let the Kingsleys move on with their lives.

Emily wasn't buying that he needed to go anywhere, though. "And then we'll meet at the park?"

He glanced at Natasha, who looked a bit exasperated with her precocious daughter. He really didn't mind Emily's attitude, though, and thought he could offer a reasonable compromise. "Can I walk you out to your car instead?"

Emily shrugged. "Okay. My mommy has a Jeep. It's red."

"Nice!"

"Do you have a car?"

"I have a truck."

"Is it pink?"

"No, it's blue."

"That's okay." But the seriously disappointed look on her face said it wasn't, and he chuckled as he stood up.

They walked outside, and he stood beside Natasha's car as she buckled Emily into the backseat. He was just waiting to say goodbye, he told himself. He could hear the words in his head. *That was a lot of fun. Thanks for sharing a table with me.*

That was the right thing to say. He definitely shouldn't ask if she had a husband, or boyfriend, or anything that might stop him from kissing her. Because he didn't do entanglements, and it wasn't like he could propose an afternoon hook-up to a mom with a kid.

"Thank you," Natasha said as she turned around and shielded her eyes from the sun. "That was a fun hour. You were very good with her."

"Probably the other way around."

"I think you're underestimating how exhausting she can be."

"Now it's definitely the other way around."

Her eyes flared wide.

He hadn't meant exhausting in a dirty way, but— "Sorry."

She laughed. "It's fine."

"Are you really going to a park?" Those weren't the words he'd prepped in his head. *At all.*

She hesitated, which meant the answer was no. He'd already guessed that, and he shouldn't have asked. He was drawn to her, there was no denying that, but he liked her caution as much as everything else—her bright eyes, her dry humour, and the way she was with her daughter. And all of that was exactly why she should turn him down. He wasn't the guy for a beautiful, wary single mom.

"Never mind." He took a step back and raised his hand. "Thank you. That's what I should have said. I had a lot of fun too."

Her head bobbed in a slow nod as she searched his face.

He took another step back. *Give her space.* He was—just not quickly.

When she exhaled, a rough sigh, he stopped. And he grinned, because he liked to make women happy even when it was a bad idea. "What can I say here?"

Another laugh. "Say you understand that it's weird that my child just invited a strange man to the park?"

"I get that."

"You don't claim you're not strange?"

"Can't do that. As a first responder, it's my job to educate the public on stranger danger, not *be* the stranger danger."

Her lips twisted as she looked at him long and hard. Then she nodded. "Right."

"So this is goodbye?"

"It should be." Her lips fell apart and her cheeks turned pink. "I mean, yes, it is." She glanced down at his feet, not moving.

God, he wanted to flirt with her so badly. Maybe he already was. Maybe this was how his fifteen years of intensive training rolled out with a single mother. "Is there a reason why I shouldn't suggest I could meet you at the park?"

"Is that your way of asking if I'm single?" She asked the question without looking up at him.

"Yeah."

She didn't answer at first, and when she did, it wasn't exactly an answer to the question. "There's a mini fall fair happening today. Pre-school level of activities. I'm not sure it'll be fun for you."

Heaven help him, but he was certain it would be. "I don't have anything else to do. I'm all yours today."

A surprised look flitted across her face. "Well, it's…" She turned, pointed toward the centre of town, and described how to get to the park. "We'll be there in half an hour."

He shouldn't be looking forward to that. There was no sex to be had in the park. But he still grinned at her. "Then I'll see you both in thirty minutes."

NATASHA SPENT the next twenty minutes trying to convince herself Matt wouldn't show up. She needed to lower her expectations, pronto.

He was officially too good to be true. Sweet, funny, *hot*. There was something about him that made her immediately comfortable, like they already knew each other. But that was only one layer, an unexpected base level of comfort she rarely felt around men.

This man, though…

One afternoon. That's all you get. No, she knew that. But the fantasy was nice. Very nice. Smoking hot level of nice.

She made Emily eat a healthy lunch to make up for the icing-overdose, then encouraged a just-try, just-in-case pee break before they packed a bag of snacks and water and spare clothes, and headed out to the park on foot. It was right next to the school where she'd have to pick up Noelle and Logan in a couple of hours, so they'd spend the entire afternoon at the mini fair.

With Matt.

Maybe.

If he showed—

"Matt!" Emily streaked away from her, her hands waving in the air as she caught sight of their new friend striding along the edge of the mini fair.

So he showed up. That wasn't reason enough for her insides to flutter. She was smarter than that now.

Natasha watched, a lump forming in her throat, as Emily raced around Matt in a tight circle, then grabbed his hand and gestured toward the fenced-off area for pony rides.

He looked over, seeking permission.

"Sure, let's do the ponies first," Natasha said, lifting her voice. "I think the ticket stand is just on the other side."

"I can get those," Matt offered when they met in the middle of the grassy expanse.

Emily bounced off the end of his arm.

"We took the bulk of the cupcakes home. I can't let you buy my daughter a pony ride, too, but thank you. Emily, stop bouncing. Please."

"I want to get in line!"

"We need tickets first."

"Mommy!"

"Emily," she said, a low warning. "Best behaviour, right?"

Matt slowed down as they passed the ponies. "You can see us from the ticket line," he said quietly. "If you want me to wait with her?"

It was a nice offer, but…

Before she could say no, he picked up the pace again. "Or we can all get tickets together. Besides, we need to find out what else they have here, don't we?"

"Okay," Emily said.

Natasha rolled her eyes. "Well, now that we're all in agreement…"

Matt chuckled, warm and low.

Once Emily was astride a pony, and they were both watching from the other side of the fence, he bumped his arm against hers, a gentle nudge with his elbow. "Thanks for the invitation, by the way."

She gave him a solid, suspicious side-eye.

He grinned. "A guy's gotta do what a guy's gotta do to get his mini fair fix."

"I'm glad we could help you with that." She couldn't help but smile. "So you're just in town for a couple days?"

"Yeah. There's a regional training thing at the conference centre. I was strong-armed into attending by my boss, but I'm not complaining now." The look he gave her, like the nudge with his elbow, was just right. Warm and interested, an obvious opening for her to take the next step, but not pushy.

Natasha knew this routine. This was her routine, although she was rusty at it. She let her smile grow as she looked back and forth between Matt and Emily. On the third slow swivel of her head, his gaze darkened, turning hot and incandescent just for a moment.

Oh, yeah, she knew this routine well.

Her breath caught in her throat. She let her lips part on her next exhale, her eyelashes fluttering against her cheek as she dragged in a ragged breath. *You affect me*, her body language screamed. And it felt good to admit that, even if they couldn't do anything about it.

It had been too long since she'd flirted with someone. She used to do it at work all the time, but since having Emily, she'd morphed her bartender persona into a tougher, no-nonsense friend. She liked that role, too.

But it was nice to be wanted as a woman.

Really nice.

"What's next?" he murmured, and none of the answers that sprang to life fully formed were even remotely acceptable.

She turned around, scanning the other activities. "The inflatable corn maze, probably. We'll have to go through with her, though. Despite all evidence to the contrary today, she's pretty shy."

"Emily Kingsley, age three? Defender of all things pink?"

"Yeah, that was…something. She doesn't usually like strangers."

"That's smart," Matt said, and something in his voice dragged her attention back to his face. God, his eyes were dangerous. Hot and bright and way too clever. "But maybe I don't need to be a stranger."

"That's—"

Before Natasha could set the record straight, Emily was hurtling towards them again, her pony ride over. "Mommy! That was fun!"

"Yay! Do you want to do the corn maze next?"

Her answer was a gasp, then she bounced back and forth between them all the way to the maze, and through it—twice.

Next they went to the ice cream truck. They carefully ate miniature ice cream cones at a picnic table and Natasha tried not to replay Matt's words in her head. *Maybe I don't need to be a stranger.*

What was happening?

"All done, Mommy." Emily beamed at her. "Can I show Matt my new shoes?"

"Sure," Natasha murmured. *Focus.*

Her daughter pivoted all her attention to their new friend. "I have new running shoes."

Matt grinned, a shallow dimple popping in his right cheek. "They look fast. Are they fast?"

She took off, running in circles around the table.

"Sugar high," Natasha said. "I'm sorry."

"Don't be. She's adorable. It's a good age." There was something in the way he said it that made her curious, and he met her inquisitive gaze with a boyish grin. "I'm a newish uncle. My nephew Calvin is almost one. And my younger brother is newly married, too, so I hope there will be a baby there soon enough."

"Sounds like a big family."

"Not as big as some around here, but yeah, we make a lot of noise at holiday dinners."

She laughed. "I just have one sister. We're close—Emily and I live with her family—but it's never mayhem, even with our three kids all sharing a space."

He gave her a look that made her heart jump. "So it's just the two of you?"

He'd essentially asked if she was single earlier, but she'd sidestepped the topic. Now he was curious again, and damn it, there was only so much curiosity a girl could take. And something about him weakened her usual resolve to keep all of this tightly private. "Yeah. Always has been. Her dad lives in Toronto." And never wants anything to do with her, except today, maybe, but who knows because he hadn't called back.

"Mommy, can we go on the climbers?"

Natasha flashed a quick glance at her watch. "Yep. We have another half hour before we need to go over to the school to pick up your cousins."

The next twenty minutes were spent circling the climbers, with Matt being called upon frequently by Emily to help her reach the highest rungs—and then be immediately rescued.

He was endlessly patient, constantly amused, and managed to give Natasha a delicious chunk of his attention even as he entertained her tiny, demanding spawn.

Her pulse thumped in her neck. Time was getting away from her. She needed to find a way to say goodbye.

Or…not. Or something, the details of which she couldn't bring herself to guess at. She hadn't tried dating in years—hadn't had the energy to play the games, and wasn't comfortable introducing Emily to anyone yet.

Ha. Joke was on her. Emily had done the introducing for them.

When her daughter crawled under the play structure, Matt made his way back to Natasha's side. The way he looked at her, his gaze hot and piercing, she was pretty sure his thoughts were in the same place.

She wasn't wrong.

He leaned in. "Like I told you, I'm in town until Thursday night. If you two are free for dinner…"

Crap. "I work every night."

He gave her a regretful smile. Right. So that would be the end of that.

"Today was nice, though," she heard herself saying. "Very nice. Thank you for entertaining both of us."

"Thanks for letting me tag along. Maybe we can stay in touch." He pulled out his phone. "Can I have your number?"

Can I get your hopes up? But they'd really had a good day together. She didn't need to be cynical and shoot herself in the foot, even if this didn't turn into anything. Maybe he'd go home and realize, wow, that was a dead-end way to never get laid. Or…maybe not. "Sure," she finally said, and he laughed.

"Hard decision to make?"

"Well, you know, I guess I'll take pity on you," she said softly, not meaning it at all. Flirting still felt good, felt right with him. "Gotta throw hot guys a bone every so often or they'd never score another amazing playground date."

"You know it. We're hard done by, for sure." He grinned. "Is it Kingsley? Like Emily?"

She nodded and spelled out her phone number for him.

He tapped the screen, and her phone started ringing. She pulled it out and answered the call. "Hello?"

He grinned at her. "Hey, Natasha, it's me, Matt."

"Oh, right. Icing novice. I remember you."

"That's right. Remember how much fun we had at the park?"

Her heart skipped a beat. "Yeah. I do."

"I was thinking we should do that again sometime soon." He held her gaze as he spoke into the phone. "I'd love to see more of you and Emily."

She didn't respond. She couldn't breathe. How was he this perfect? She forced herself to inhale, her breath hitching at the top. "Are you for real?"

"Yep."

She laughed and nodded. "Yes, we'd love that."

She was still shaking her head as she ended their call and tapped on the number to add it to her phone book. First name, Matt. Surname…

"I should put you in here as Mr. Too Good To Be True, but what's your last name?"

"Foster."

Her thumb froze over the keyboard. *No.* Not Foster. Anything but…

She didn't want to look up at him. Didn't want to see that sharp jaw, those bright eyes, the dark brown hair that fell over his eyes just like his brother's.

The man she'd wanted to be the father of her baby.

The man who hadn't been, and who'd broken her heart a little.

It had been almost four years since she'd seen Jake, but now she knew with sickening certainty that's why Matt had seemed comfortable and familiar to her.

Heat swarmed her face. She kept her head down and hit save without adding his last name.

Matt.

That's how he'd live in her phone book. Just Matt. And if he called, she'd have to dodge him.

She forced herself to smile as she closed her contacts app and stuffed her phone into her bag. "Okay, we need to go." She lifted her voice. "Emily! Time to go pick up Noelle and Logan from school, baby."

Her daughter came racing across the playground and

threw her arms around Matt's legs. "Bye," she said. "See you later."

They wouldn't, though.

Today had been yet another episode in the ongoing saga of Natasha's terrible luck with men. They would never see Matt Foster again.

CHAPTER THREE

MATT COULDN'T WAIT to see Natasha and Emily again.

Gone was his interest in hitting a bar tonight. Instead, he ordered room service for dinner and replayed the conversations from the afternoon in his head.

He'd been off his game for too long. Or maybe he didn't have the right game to date a single mother. He frowned at that thought because, damn it, he liked her.

"So it's just the two of you?"

"Always has been. Her dad lives in Toronto."

What kind of man would abandon this woman? That child?

He pulled out his phone, not for the first time, and clicked on her contact information. It was too soon to text her. He was here for three days. He'd reach out tomorrow and see if they wanted to grab lunch since she worked at night.

Yes, he'd like to see her again. And Emily, too. He knew they came as a package deal, and the fact that didn't scare him at all? Surprising didn't touch it.

Huh.

Matt Foster and a gorgeous single mother.

Stranger things had happened, of course. He'd hit a dry

spell for the first time in his adult life, although right now he was wondering why he'd ever lost faith in the pursuit of women. Because Natasha was all woman, and he was very interested in pursuing every inch of her. It wouldn't be his usual modus operandi, but maybe that had been the problem.

Maybe he could try something a little more serious for once in his life. A friendship.

And they could see where that might lead.

Or not. That would be her call, and for the first time in ages, Matt had to face the reality that he might not measure up. Oh, they had chemistry, there was no doubt. But more than once this afternoon he'd seen wariness in her eyes.

If she was reluctant to trust someone now, it might be that she'd had her trust broken before.

He was out of his depth. He thought about his brothers, his circle of friends, and wondered who he could call, who might be able to advise on how to handle this. When you grew up in a small town, your siblings were your best friends. He was the second youngest of four boys. They'd grown up around the corner from the Minellis, four boys and a girl. Matt was the same age as Tom Minelli, and of the entire crew, Tom was his closest, oldest friend.

But Tom was also the responsible one. The serious one.

He definitely would know the right way to woo a single mother, but that advice would also come with a dose of hard reality about how Matt wasn't the right kind of guy for a woman like that.

He didn't want to hear that nonsense.

On the other hand, Tom's oldest brother Zander, who was the same age as Matt's oldest brother Dean, had married a single mother. A widow named Faith with a little boy. Eric.

And Zander had been a confirmed bachelor before he met Faith.

In the end, he chickened out and called Sean instead.

His younger brother answered on the second ring and sounded tired. "Hello?"

"Did I wake you from a nap?"

"Nah. I was just stretching out on the couch a bit before dinner."

"Jenna home tonight?"

"Yeah." In a single syllable, his brother went from tired to happy. "She pushed me out of the kitchen because she's just reheating some soup."

"Sounds good." It sounded perfect. And for the first time all day, those thoughts he hated threatened to close in again.

Matt had thought he knew what it was to be happy.

He'd been wrong. And he'd spent the last six months painfully aware of the yawning deficit in his life, but hadn't known where to start in rectifying the problem.

"Do you want to come over for dinner?" Sean asked.

"Nah, but thanks. I'm actually in Port Elgin for a couple of days." He exhaled. "Last minute work thing. I'll be back Thursday night."

"I'm going to the Search and Rescue training site Friday morning to put Tom through his paces if you feel like being punished."

He huffed a laugh. "I might need it after this week."

"That bad?"

"That something. The course will be whatever it'll be, but honestly, I—" *I met someone.* The words died on his tongue. "Yeah. Something. Anyway, I should go."

"All right, man. See you Friday."

"Good deal."

He stared at the phone after he ended the call. Wondered why he hadn't told his brother about Natasha. About the warmth in his chest, a new and interesting feeling that made the generalized worry that plagued him seem less scary.

But of all the Foster brothers, Matt was the last one anyone would think to have feelings of any kind—and especially not sensitive ones about a single mom. Sean might get it. Jake and Dean wouldn't. Like Tom, they'd have reservations about the harm he might do.

Would they be wrong?

Fuck, he didn't know. And he didn't want to dig into that question, because what if they weren't?

———

NATASHA TOOK her time putting Emily to bed. It was a bittersweet cuddle for reasons she understood too well but didn't want to name. She didn't want to give them power in her head. This was enough. This was perfect.

When she got up, she thought about going straight to bed herself, but she could hear her sister moving around in the kitchen. She went up to offer help and found Meredith putting the last of the dishes away.

"Sorry," she said, but her sister waved her off.

"Dan's fallen asleep reading Logan a story," Mer said. "I thought maybe you'd done the same with Emily and I had the television all to myself tonight."

Natasha half-laughed, half-sighed. "I did think about an early night."

Her sister twisted around and gave her a searching look. "Is everything okay?"

"Yeah."

"Do you want tea?" That was Meredith's way of saying she didn't believe nothing was wrong.

"Sure."

"So much detail, don't overwhelm me all at once."

Natasha shook her hands, wiggled her arms, and rolled her shoulders before taking a deep breath. She didn't want to get all the way into it, but she'd learned her sister was a good listener, and always had her back. "I was thinking about regret. Not a healthy place to dwell, so now I want to shake that off."

"Fair enough. Do you want to talk about it?"

No. Yes. Sort of. "We met someone today. At the cooking class series."

"A guy?"

"Yeah."

"And he was a complete monster."

She laughed. "No. He was really nice."

Meredith didn't say anything.

Natasha sighed. "We had to share a table. Emily demanded pink icing and he made that happen for her."

"That *is* nice."

"Right? What kind of guy gets that when a three-year-old demands something, it's not rude, it's just…they're little and they don't know that the world is not their oyster just yet?"

Her sister snorted.

"But he didn't blink. He just clicked with Emily, which was nice, and then…" She trailed off. *And then.* Her chest pulled tight.

"You're not ready to date yet." Maybe if her sister had phrased it in the form of a question, she'd have corrected that misunderstanding.

She was ready, in a guarded kind of way. She missed sex, although the thought of having sex and the very real consequences that can come from it also terrified her.

Maybe she just missed third base. Second base was pretty good, too.

Matt would round the bases like he had all the time in the world because he'd knocked it clear out of the park.

Yeah. He would.

With someone else.

"Yeah," Natasha said quietly. "I'm not prepared to handle all of that."

The truth, even if the real question was different. Was she ready to date? Maybe, yes. Was she ready to date a Foster? No, never.

Meredith squeezed her arm. "You got burned, and more than once. But not all people are like David and Jake."

They rarely talked about Tasha's most humiliating period in her life, when she chased after Matt's older brother when he wasn't interested and had made that clear.

She didn't want to start talking about it now, either, but maybe she needed to get it off her chest. Process it, four years later. "Yeah, I know that. David is a special kind of narcissist." She told her sister about his text. "If it's so urgent that we need to talk, why didn't he call today? But I can't let him manipulate me like that, I can't care about it too much, because he doesn't care at all. And Jake..." Natasha winced. "That was just a mistake all around. One I need to forgive myself for and move on, but that's easier said than done when it's the biggest mistake of my entire life."

"Wow, that's not just a little bit of regret."

"Bah. I know. But...shaking it off, see?"

"Good." Mer looked like she wanted to say something else, but decided better of it. Instead, she made tea, and they drank it in the living room while they watched a reality singing show and booed the judges together.

Sleep was a long time coming when Natasha crawled into bed.

The next morning she kept Emily busy with finger-painting

and creative laundry folding, but by the time lunch rolled around, she was all out of distractions.

And it didn't help that Matt had sent a text mid-morning.

Matt: Are you and Emily free for lunch?

Nope. Not free. Not available. She closed the messaging app without replying, doing her best to ignore how good the question felt low in her gut.

Emily bounced in front of her. "Can we go back to the park today, Mommy?"

Natasha gave her a knowing smile and ignored the pang of regret that reverberated through her insides. "Are you hoping to see Matt again?"

Her three-year-old did a surprisingly good job at looking innocent. "I like the park."

"Mm-hmm." She dropped to her knees and pulled Emily in tight. "He's not going to be there. Remember? He said he's working today. He was just there for one day. He won't be back."

How many times would she have to repeat that?

As many as it took to convince them both. "We won't see him again, but that was a really nice day yesterday, wasn't it?"

Emily's head bobbed against Natasha's neck. "I like him," she whispered, and pain lanced through Natasha's chest.

"I know, baby. I liked him too."

Emily sighed, then pulled away. "Can we watch a TV show instead?"

That was how to get over the disappointment of a hot man being unavailable, one hundred percent. "Sure thing. A Mommy show?"

That made Emily giggle. "No! A Millie show."

Natasha mock-groaned. "Come on! Let's watch a Mommy show about *cooking*. Long and boring."

More giggles, then a tickle attack that ended up with Natasha sprawled out on the couch and Emily perched like a princess on top of her while they watched *My Little Pony*.

After two episodes, they went to the grocery store before collecting Logan and Noelle at the school. The kids helped her make cupcakes for dessert, so she could practice her piping skills learned the day before, and then they went out to the backyard while Natasha started dinner. When her sister and brother-in-law got home from work, they all sat down to eat as one big happy family.

She was lucky. Maybe she wasn't getting laid, and maybe she was a bit lonely in the quiet minutes before she fell asleep each night, but their life could be a lot harder than it was. They were blessed.

"Icing doesn't melt," Emily announced as she wiggled her cupcake at Noelle. "Right, Mommy?"

"Pardon, baby?" Natasha heard the words filter into her head a little too late and only realized where Emily was going after she'd missed her opportunity to change the subject.

"Matt said icing doesn't really melt. It *softens*. Right?" Emily looked at her expectantly.

So did Meredith.

"Right," Natasha said, her cheeks heating up. "We learned that yesterday at cooking class."

"I like Matt," her daughter continued.

Meredith cleared her throat and took a long sip of her coffee. Dan looked back and forth between the sisters, and Natasha willed him not to ask what was going on. She failed.

"Who's Matt?" her brother-in-law asked.

"Nobody," Natasha said at the same time as Emily beamed. "He's my new friend. He played with Mommy at the park."

Oh, sweet baby Jesus. She lifted her eyes to the ceiling. "He's someone we met at the cooking class. Nice guy. Doesn't live around here, though. Not a big deal."

There was a pause, then Dan made an appreciative statement about the cupcakes and the girls started talking about icing colours.

When Naasha dropped her gaze back down from the heavens, her sister was grinning. *Nice guy*, she mouthed. *Named Matt.*

Yep. But he'd been a single day's fantasy, and now she really needed to move past him. Permanently.

After dinner, Noelle dragged Emily off to play with dolls, and Meredith shooed Natasha downstairs. "I won't ask anything about *Matt*, but at some point, I want to know more. Now go take a few minutes for yourself before you head to work."

At some point like four years down the road. That seemed about how long it took Natasha to get over awkward feelings.

She took a long, hot shower, then dried her hair, blowing it out smooth before carefully putting it up in a ponytail. She got dressed in her work outfit of dark jeans and a black t-shirt, then made up her face. Back upstairs, she found Emily dancing toy ponies over the headboard in Noelle's room.

"Mommy's going to work, baby. Gimme a kiss?"

Emily launched herself into the air and Natasha caught her.

"Love you so much," she murmured into her daughter's hair. "See you in the morning."

CHAPTER FOUR

three-and-a-half years earlier
Valentine's Day

BARTENDING while pregnant was a special kind of hell, but the customers at Bailey's tipped well, and Tasha could use all the extra income she could get right now. For car repairs and savings, too, because she was a complete dummy.

A complete dummy who was going to be a mother in four months, give or take a week. She'd only known she was pregnant for a few weeks—and just how pregnant she was? That was even newer information.

Another reason she'd volunteered to help Malcolm, the owner, tonight was because she could use the ego boost, and she was a damn good bartender. She'd seen on Facebook that he needed an extra pair of hands behind the bar, and she'd leapt on it. Malcolm hadn't asked why she was so easy to cover the Valentine's Day shift, but he did poke a bit at her when she came in early.

"Don't you want to visit with your sister while you're in town?"

Nope, she thought. *Because she might find out that I'm preg-nant and have no clue what I'm going to do, and I can't handle that. Not this week.*

At some point, she'd have to deal with the inevitable fact she was going to have a baby.

Alone.

"They're doing a thing with the kids tonight at the community centre, so I'm all yours," she'd said brightly.

Now, seven hours later, midnight was around the corner.

Her last Valentine's Day that she would spend alone for the next eighteen years. She pressed a hand to her belly—still not really showing, just a thickness to her middle, thanks to being long-waisted. *Just you and me, kiddo.*

It was a Friday night, and Malcolm had gone all out to make Valentine's at Bailey's a fun night for everyone, single or coupled or complicated. So the last hour before they closed, technically into the next day, was jammed with people wanting one or two more before they stumbled into the cold night.

Tasha remembered what that was like. That had been her life just a year ago. Party girl, nomad. Always up for hitting the club when she went to see David in the city.

David.

After she cashed out the bar, she checked her phone. No messages. If she'd had any doubt about his resolve to not have anything to do with the baby, his silence tonight spoke volumes.

There would be no Valentine's love note. No happy-ever-after ending for her and her child's father.

She shoved her phone into her bag and looped it over her arm before taking the cash drawer back to Malcolm's office.

He shook her hand. "Thanks for coming in tonight."

"You know I've always enjoyed Bailey's when visiting."

"If you ever decide to stick around here longer than a weekend or two at a time, I'd be happy to have you come work for me full-time. You're the quickest read of any customer I've seen in a bartender, and that kind of thing keeps people coming back."

Not men, she thought. To them, she was just a pretty face.

Except for Jake. He'd always been nice to her. And then she'd gone and fucked that up by sleeping with him, which was so not what he wanted from her.

He'd offered friendship, though.

"Who knows," she heard herself saying. "Maybe I'll move down here."

It had already occurred to her that she might need to ask her parents or her sister for help. The thought grated, but she had to be realistic. It would be hard to do it all on her own.

"If you do, you get in touch, okay?"

"Will do."

She grabbed her coat and boots, dressed for the winter, and headed outside to her Jeep. Her expensive Jeep, which she'd driven into a ditch in a snow storm last month. Right after finding out she was pregnant.

Once again her thoughts spiralled to David. To Jake. Comparing them.

Jake wasn't the right guy for her. She knew that. But he was maybe her only friend in the entire world right now.

She was going to head home in the morning. Drive up the peninsula. Maybe he'd be up for having breakfast or something.

Before she could think twice about whether or not this was a good idea, she pressed the call button.

Each ring ramped up her heart rate. *Hang up the phone*, she tried to tell herself.

She didn't listen.

"Hello?" It was short, curt, and not welcoming in the least.

"Jake?" This was a mistake, but she couldn't hang up now. He'd already have seen that she called and would think the worst of her if she hung up.

"What's wrong?"

"Nothing. I'm fine."

"It's the middle of the night."

"I'm in Port Elgin at my sister's, and I'm driving home tomorrow. Thought maybe we could have breakfast." The words spilled out of her so fast she wasn't sure they were comprehensible.

He heard them—and rejected them soundly. "I've got plans."

Crap. *Hang. Up. The. Phone.* Instead, she opened her mouth again and poor-me-itis spilled out. "I talked to David. He's not thrilled. About the baby."

"I'm sorry to hear that." He sighed, and his voice softened. "I can't be a stop on your way north and south anymore, Tash."

She'd fucked this up. Lost her chance to have something decent for once. "You were so good, in the hospital—"

He cut her off. "You shouldn't have called me tonight. Or in general. I mean, if you were in a real bind or something… no. There have to be other people in your life that you can turn to, people you haven't slept with."

"I thought we were friends."

"Well, I thought so too, but this conversation has me thinking otherwise."

"Oh."

He sighed. "I wish you well, I really do. But you can't call me in the middle of the night, okay?"

"Shit." She started to cry, which she really didn't want to do.

"Can you talk to your sister?"

She would have to, sooner than later. But she wasn't ready for that yet. She sniffed and cleared her throat. "Yeah. I just…I don't want anyone else to know how much I've fucked up, ya know?"

"Jesus, Natasha. You haven't fucked up."

"It doesn't feel like that from here. I didn't even know I was like five months pregnant. What the hell kind of mother am I going to make?"

He laughed gently. "Probably an average one. No, a great one. Listen, go wake up your sister and tell her all of this. She's going to be a better support to you than I can be."

He wasn't wrong. She should have told Meredith what was going on as soon as she arrived instead of trying to cling to denial like a life raft.

She hated that, and she started to cry harder, but it was silent, and somehow, deep inside, she found the strength to swallow that and wipe her eyes. "God, how much do I suck that I needed to have someone else tell me that?"

He didn't reply to that, which was good, because she needed to get off the phone and never speak to him again. Jake was a good guy, but he wasn't her guy, and she needed to go. She mumbled an apology before ending the call.

Well, it was official. She hated Valentine's Day.

She turned her car on and, as the engine warmed up, she stared out the window at the darkened Bailey's sign on the side of the building.

Maybe she should take Malcolm up on his offer. For a few months, at least. Move to Port Elgin and have her baby close to her sister. She wouldn't stay long. A year at most.

And then she'd get her life back on track.

CHAPTER FIVE

Present Day again

MATT WATCHED the clock tick painfully slowly toward five o'clock. Before he'd arrived, he'd have argued there was no way this course needed to be three days long. The integration between emergency services and the hospital network seemed pretty straightforward to anyone who could intuitively use a computer, but it turned out that was only a small subset of people involved in healthcare delivery.

And he had another sixteen hours of listening to the instructors patiently explain—over and over again—how to do a basic records search.

At ten to five, one of the instructors said, "Okay, so that wraps up today's material." Matt was halfway out of his seat before she continued. "And now we have a ten-minute peer debrief session."

Fuck. Fine. He took a deep breath and dutifully buddied up with the two people closest to him.

One of them was obviously a goody-two-shoes. She'd sat,

ram-rod straight, and taken detailed notes on the entire day. Four pages of notes.

He was quite certain she already knew how to use the system, but one of their jobs was to take this knowledge back to their home EMS stations and act as a subject matter expert. He supposed notes might be helpful in that regard. Probably better than his preferred plan to sigh loudly when people didn't just fucking get it. *That's the spirit.*

He scowled at himself and quickly scrawled the key take-away points for the day on his blank notebook. Then he turned to the other guy in their debrief triad who still looked confused.

Matt took a deep breath. "So, got any questions?"

It turned out the other guy had made the classic error of overthinking it, and between Matt and Ms. Goody-Two-Shoes, they got him up to speed, but it was five-thirty before they broke up.

"What are you two planning for dinner?" the guy asked.

Anything but more of this. "Uh…" Matt cracked his neck. "I need to call home. I'll probably go grab something in town after that." He held his breath until the other two agreed to grab food together in the restaurant on site. "All right. See you guys tomorrow, then."

And he was on his own for fifteen hours. Not something he'd have been thrilled about a day ago. Not something he was thrilled about now, either, although…

He looked at his phone. Still no text message from Natasha.

Go out. Forget her. But it wasn't that easy. Yesterday had been something interesting. Something new and different.

She was magnetic on a brand-new level. He couldn't stop thinking about her.

He shoved his phone into his pocket instead of messaging

her again. If she wasn't sure, that needed to be okay. He'd give her time and space.

He'd go out tonight, grab some fries and a beer. See what else the universe had on offer.

But he wouldn't forget her.

It turned out, that was never a risk. When he stepped through the door of Bailey's, the pub recommended by the hotel clerk, Natasha was behind the bar, pouring a drink for the customer in front of her.

Thank you, universe.

He strode toward an empty barstool, a grin growing on his face. But as soon as she looked up and saw him, her expression froze.

Ah. Shit.

His steps faltered, but he drove himself forward.

Him walking into her bar was a sign. Or something. Whatever, he was taking it.

"Hey," he said softly. *Easy.*

"What can I get you?" She asked it carefully, plastering a polite smile on her face. *I'm a bartender, you're my customer. Got it?*

He got it, even as wildly inappropriate hope fired inside him. He leaned against the bar and nodded toward the bank of taps. "What do you have that's local?"

She listed a couple of craft breweries. "I like the Neustadt lager, myself."

"I'll take a pint of that." He scanned the room. Most of the tables were big, and it was pretty busy. He'd be an asshole to take zone for himself, but he wasn't in the mood to make friends, either. At least not any new friends beyond the one behind the bar. The same one who was surprised to see him, and maybe not in the best way. Damn it, his usual skills were suspect. Better to do an honest check-in. "Do you mind if I sit here?"

She shot him a quick glance from where she was pouring his beer. "Sure. It might get busy, though."

"I won't stay long." Lie. He'd stay as long as he could without making her uncomfortable.

She set a tall glass in front of him on a coaster, and he slid a ten-dollar bill across the gleaming wood.

"Do you want a dinner menu?"

"I hear you've got good wings."

"Where you'd hear that?"

"Clerk at the hotel."

She gave him a tight smile. "Yeah, they're good. You just want those or do you want to see a menu anyway?"

"I'll take a menu."

She moved back to the other end of the bar and, after grabbing his menu from the rack, took a quick drink order there before dashing it back to him.

He could watch her work for hours, he'd guess. And he just might, because once she took his order, she made a point of being elsewhere. Of being busy.

Watch me work, her body language said, *but don't expect anything else.*

Okay. Message received. But he didn't understand why.

———

NATASHA POURED Matt his third drink of the night, this one a cola.

He hadn't tried to talk to her yet, but she could feel it coming. She was relieved when one of the waitresses came to take over for her at the bar so she could take her break.

"Take fifteen," she said. "Malcolm's working on a new soup in the kitchen if you want to be a taste tester."

"Thanks," she murmured. "I'm going to grab some fresh air first."

It was a mistake as soon as she'd said it, though. She felt Matt look up from the remnants of his dinner.

Fine. She probably owed him some explanation anyway. Or maybe she didn't owe him anything, but she wanted to be alone with him for a minute.

Either way, this would be the end.

"If you need me, I'll be in the alley out back," she added to her boss.

She headed straight down the hallway, past the bathrooms and the kitchen, to the heavy metal door to the quiet space behind the bar.

Matt pushed through the same door thirty seconds later. "Funny running into you here," he said as she gave him a half-wave.

"It's a small town."

"Mmm." He grinned.

"So…"

"Yes?"

"You sent me a text today."

"And you didn't reply."

"Yeah. About that…"

He walked a few paces closer and leaned against the brick wall. "Too much?"

"Too complicated."

"It's just a meal. Everyone has to eat, so we could do it together. Lunch was one idea. Dinner on your night off might be another."

She dragged in a deep breath. It was hard to think when he

pinned that easy, warm gaze on her. "I use up a hundred and ten percent of my babysitting favours from my sister for covering my shifts. I can't ask her to watch Emily while I go on a date."

"Then let's go out the three of us."

"I can't." This time she didn't bother to throw out an excuse. It was the truth, and anything else might muddy it.

He searched her face. "Why am I getting the feeling that there's another reason?"

She didn't want to lie to him. He'd been kind to her daughter and sweet to her. Hurt welled up in her chest and jammed into her throat. She nodded roughly. "There is."

"What is it?" His gaze bored into her, and there was no more hiding.

"The county is a small place," she whispered. "We have a shared past I wish I'd realized sooner." Before she'd gotten carried away by imaginary promises, easy smiles, and the gentle way he played with her daughter.

"Look, if you know someone I've hung out with in the past, that's all that is—the past. I'm a friendly guy, but I never promise anything beyond a good time. And it's been a while since I've done that, too."

"What? No, it's not…" She waved her hand. "I don't know anyone you've dated." Quite the opposite, in fact.

"Okay…and there's something here between us, isn't there? Something more than a good time?"

There was definitely something between them. That's what made this so hard. *Tell him about Jake,* her inner conscience said. *Get it over with.* She didn't say anything.

He leaned in and braced his arm against the wall beside her head, and pitched his voice lower. "I was thinking we could have a romantic picnic for three. Pink lemonade for Emily, hard lemonade for us, and a bonfire if it gets cold."

Her heart squeezed. No, not a smart idea. "I'm not a solid bet for a good time, what with the three-year-old chaperone."

"Maybe my idea of a good time is shifting."

"I slept with your brother," she blurted out, and even though her heart was pounding a mile a minute, she didn't miss the shock and disbelief that rolled across his face. She sucked in a shallow, desperate breath and forged ahead because it needed to be said. "I didn't put two and two together at first, but when you gave me your last name, I realized you're Jake's brother."

"Jake." He gave her a slow, searching look. Confusion now instead of disbelief. "Jake's happily married."

Wow. Yeah, he would be. Time marches on, and he'd made it clear that he'd fallen in love with someone. But it still hurt a little to know he had the happy relationship she'd wanted and never managed to hold on to. She shoved that feeling away and nodded. "Before that. Before…Emily, too." She swallowed hard. "I used to work in Elliot Lake, at a hunting lodge he'd come up to."

Matt's eyes went wide, and she could see him put the pieces together.

Had his brother ever talked about her before *the incident*? The hot piece of ass at the hunting lodge who flirted shamelessly for tips? They'd had a casual flirtation that stretched over a year, whenever she was in an off-again phase with David. But it never went anywhere until one night he'd shown up unexpectedly. A friend had died, another was in the hospital, and he'd been out of his mind with grief.

She'd mistakenly thought he might want to do it again, but she'd been wrong.

Then she found out she was pregnant. And for a hot minute, she'd wondered if maybe there was a way it could be Jake's child.

"You're…" He huffed a short, disbelieving laugh and stepped back. So he did know about her. Great.

"His needy knocked-up friend? Yeah. That's me."

Matt frowned. "That wasn't what I was going to say."

It was the truth, though. She'd known that David wouldn't want the baby to be his, so she'd let herself hope it might be Jake's, even though the chances weren't nearly as good.

Jake Foster had been a friend when she needed one, but that kindness came at a cost—when everyone found out that Jake had a female friend who was pregnant and in trouble. She hadn't known he'd already moved on to another woman, a woman he loved with his whole heart. Natasha had just wanted her child to have a father, so she'd latched on to the fact that Jake was a good man and forgotten for a short period of time that he wasn't the *right* man.

His rejection of her had been embarrassing and public.

When she'd pushed her luck and reached out again, Jake had been less than impressed. "It's what your brother would say if you asked him."

Matt's jaw flexed, and his eyes darkened, but he didn't retreat further. "I hope that's not true." He moved in closer again, his dark gaze liquid as he searched her face. "And I don't care about what he thinks."

"I didn't know that you were his brother," she whispered. "If I had, I never would have invited you to come to the park with us."

"We didn't do anything wrong." He dipped his head like he might kiss her, and oh God, she wanted that.

She wanted that so much it hurt.

But they couldn't. She planted her hand on his chest and pushed. He moved back immediately, giving her some space, and the look on his face matched the twisted ache in her chest.

"I need to get back to work." She ducked her head and stepped past him.

He didn't reach out to stop her, and that hurt, too. She wanted him to grab her and push her against the wall. Wanted his hands on her body, his mouth on her skin, like a demand. *I can't give myself to you. Take what you will.* But he wouldn't.

He closed in behind her, catching the door so he could hold it open. She stepped back into the warm, noisy hall at the back of the pub and took a deep breath.

When she turned around to say goodbye, he was right there, and she was in his arms.

Big, strong, solid arms. Wide, sure hands pressed against her back.

Her heart hammered in her chest as she leaned into him. She couldn't, wouldn't kiss him. But a hug…friends hugged, right? She could sink into the broad strength of his chest for just a second.

"I only have one regret about yesterday," he murmured. "I don't regret meeting you, or spending the afternoon together, or even giving you my last name." Her heart pounded in her chest as his lips brushed the curve of her ear. "I'm sorry we didn't use the chocolate icing."

She pulled back, lifting her face in surprise. "Why?" she found herself asking, even though what she should be saying was *stop* or *enough*, even though it would never be enough and she definitely didn't want him to stop.

He brought his hand to her cheek in a gentle caress. "Because you deserve some things to be just for you." He rolled his lower lip through his teeth and shook his head. "I know you need to go back to work. But if things were different, I'd be kissing you right now."

She could feel how it would be, too. His lips on hers, soft at first, then more demanding. "It would be good."

"Are you kidding? There's no point pretending I don't have a ton of experience in this area. It would be great."

She laughed. "I know. I'm missing out."

His gaze dropped to her mouth, then dragged back up her face. "Nah. I'm the one who's missing out. Tonight, anyway. I'm not sure this is as much of a deal-breaker as you think."

It had to be. She wanted to curl up into a tight ball of nothing when it came to Jake Foster and his perfect life. "It's too weird for me," she whispered. Not the whole truth, but close enough.

Matt gave her a soft look. "Ah, Natasha." So much was loaded into those two words. "I hope you reconsider. I like you a lot."

"Thank you," she whispered. What else could she say? She still had complicated, messy feelings when it came to his brother? That could only be misinterpreted badly.

"Have a good rest of your shift, okay?"

"Yeah."

This time when he stepped back, it was for good. She watched him duck back out the door to the alley, removing himself from her life exactly as she'd asked him to. The door clicked shut with a definitive, painful click. She took a second to mourn the lost opportunity of a kiss that didn't happen and a friendship that wouldn't get a chance to bloom.

Then she smoothed her hands over her jeans. *Okay. Back to real life.*

CHAPTER SIX

MATT DROVE HOME THURSDAY NIGHT, wrote a long email to Owen Kincaid so he wouldn't forget the key points from the course, then racked out hard. On Friday he woke up early and swung past Mac's for coffee on his way to meet Sean and Tom for the as-promised punishing workout.

But when he walked into the diner and saw Jake and Dani sitting in a booth with their baby boy, he regretted making the stop.

What was there to say? *So, funny story…I met a woman this week, and it turns out, you've already banged her and left her heart bruised, so she thinks she's off-limits to me.*

It wasn't funny.

He also didn't think she was actually off-limits.

On the other hand, he didn't have the best track record to bring to the table as a loyal and understanding boyfriend. Or any kind of boyfriend, for that matter.

But he couldn't shake the feeling of Natasha in his arms, and he wanted that again.

Just as that thought clanged through his head, his brother looked up. "Matt!"

Fucking hell. "Hey," he said, his steps slowing as he approached their booth. "I'm just grabbing coffee and heading out."

"How was the course?" Dani asked. She was a first responder, too, and if she weren't on maternity leave right now, she'd probably have leapt at the opportunity to take the course.

She was good like that.

Matt liked Dani a lot. As a friend, as a colleague, and as a sister-in-law.

He liked his brother, too.

But for the first time in a long time, he looked at them now and saw their goodness, their wholesome happiness, in a new light.

Everyone in town had been aware of their relationship exploding, seemingly out of nowhere, into something serious. And then, just weeks after they started dating, there was another woman. A friend, Jake said, who'd been in a car accident and needed a place to stay for a few days because it turned out she was pregnant.

Not by Jake.

But there had been some question there. And for a few days, Matt's straight-laced older brother had been the subject of rumour and intrigue, torn between two women. The one he'd slept with and the one he'd loved for years, from afar.

In the end, that had faded fast, because Jake wasn't torn at all. When it came to love, there was only Dani for him, and everyone knew it.

Nobody had given two thoughts for where that left Natasha. She was gone and forgotten, not a part of their happy ever after.

And whoa, was it weird that Matt was suddenly thinking about happy ever anything.

Emily Kingsley, three years old, and her love of all things

pink. That's what had gotten under his skin. *Natasha Kingsley and her bright, fierce gaze.* That, too. There was something sweet about the two of them, something he'd never taken the time to see or value before.

Something he wanted, suddenly, with a clarity that kind of scared him.

Dani's question echoed in his head. How was the course? Matt laughed, a little too harshly. "It was something," he finally said. "Weird week."

As he said it, a weight settled on his chest. It wasn't the right answer. It didn't feel good.

I met someone amazing, he wanted to say. Instead, he gestured to the counter and muttered about his coffee.

His brother and sister-in-law turned back to their baby, who was giggling through bites of toast. They were good people, Matt reminded himself. They didn't know.

But he knew.

And something inside him started to burn.

By the time he got to the provincial park north of town, where the SAR team trained, he was ready to let off some serious steam.

It didn't take long for Tom and Sean to notice. They warmed up quickly, then his brother gave them a quick interval cardio set to jack their heart rates up. Alternating push-ups and jump squats. Back and forth, back and forth, pushing hard and never quite catching their breath.

Four minutes had never felt quite so long, and when Sean's timer beeped, Matt staggered over to his water bottle. "Excellent," he rasped. "What's next?"

"Rope climb," his brother said calmly. "But take a minute of rest first."

Matt prowled like a caged animal until Sean let him go, and then he sprinted for the climbing tower. Up he went, hand over hand, his shoulders burning in protest, his legs swinging heavily beneath him.

From the ground, Tom swore at him. Something about being unnecessarily competitive. Matt laughed. He wasn't competing. He was excising demons he didn't even know he had.

The last few pulls were agony, and when he got high enough to throw himself onto the platform, he was gasping for breath again.

It took another half-minute before Tom joined him, his friend stretching out on the top of the wooden platform.

"What's gotten into you?" Tom finally asked.

Matt shrugged as he looked up at the sky. "Eh. Dunno."

"Your brother is supposed to be kicking my ass, not you."

"I guess I needed this more than I thought I did."

"Maybe we should go out tonight. Burn off a different kind of energy."

"Yeah, maybe." For a wild, reckless second, he thought about suggesting they make the drive to Port Elgin. He knew a fun bar with a young crowd and a gorgeous bartender who wanted nothing to do with him, except when she was in his arms.

But he wasn't ready to share Natasha yet. First he had to convince her they might be good together.

"We could just go to the pub."

Matt nodded. Yeah. The Green Hedgehog in Lion's Head was their usual place, although he hadn't been there in ages since it was where women knew to look for him if they wanted a good time. He wasn't that guy anymore. He'd traded good times for nightmares and sweaty runs at dawn. Guilt now ate at his insides the way lust once had.

"It's been a while." Tom said it levelly.

Matt still jerked his eyes up to meet his friend's curious gaze. "Yeah."

So Tom had noticed.

He scrubbed a hand over his face. Fucking hell, if his friend knew he wasn't himself, he needed to rein in his emo bullshit. He was fine. "Let's go out tonight. It has been too long."

The weird burn in his gut sparked back to life.

———

FRIDAY NIGHT at Bailey's was a steady hum of groups at the tables and regulars at the bar. Natasha heard her phone vibrate from its perch next to the cash register, but she ignored it. When the next call rang out loud, that meant it was a repeat call from the same number—and at ten at night, it might be Meredith.

She held up her finger to tell the next customer she'd just be a minute, but the call wasn't from her sister. She rolled her eyes as she looked at the screen. "Malcolm," she called out. "Can you cover the bar for a minute?"

Her boss stuck his head out from the kitchen. "Sure."

She took a deep breath and answered the call as she hustled down the back hallway. "David, I'm at work. What do you need?"

"I called to say goodnight to Emily." First time ever without a direct invitation. Maybe fifth time total in three years.

She rolled her eyes. "It's ten o'clock, and I work Friday nights."

"Is ten too late?"

"She's three. Yes."

"Sorry." But he said it flippantly, like he wasn't at all, and she had to swallow her outrage.

"Do you want to call her tomorrow during the day?"

"Tomorrow's jammed." He hesitated. "I need to have more contact with her, though."

No shit, Sherlock. "Well, that's hard when your days are, as you say, *jammed*, and I work six nights a week. I've emailed you my schedule in the past, but I can forward that again. I'm home with her all day, every day, until five, and Monday nights, but she goes to bed at eight. That's…" God, the mental math made her head hurt. She slammed through the door to the alley and blessed quiet. "Like eighty plus hours a week where you could have contact with your daughter, but you've chosen not to."

"Come for a visit." David's voice was louder in her ear now that she was out of the bar. Louder, and more persuasive. Ugh.

She pressed her eyes shut and bit her lips to keep from howling in outrage. *I just finished telling you I work six nights a week, jackass.* "That's not easy to do right now. You are always welcome to make the drive up here."

"Fine. If you're going to be difficult, I'll be the one to do the travel."

"I don't want this to be confrontational," she said with a sigh. "Why don't you email me? It's easier to work things out in writing."

"I wanted—" There was a murmur in the background, a woman's voice, then silence. Ah. Of course this sudden need to have contact with Emily wasn't driven by David himself, even if he was the one parroting the words right now. "She's my daughter, Tasha."

"Yep. Fully aware of that fact. Are you being prompted by someone to make this call? Does whoever that girl is know that ten o'clock is far too late to call a three-year-old?"

"Nobody prompted me to make this call."

"Sure thing, Romeo." Oh, damn it, now she was on a roll. *Hang up the phone, Natasha.* Too late. "Look, I don't mind talking productively about co-parenting, but it would be better if we document everything in writing. Also, you can't interrupt my work shifts like this. So I'm going to hang up and email you my understanding of this phone call, okay? And you can tell your friend there that you did your best and now she can blow you with the full confidence that you aren't actually a deadbeat dad."

As soon as she angrily ended the call, she regretted losing her temper.

Mostly.

Like, she seventy-percent regretted it, and thirty-percent was giving herself a high-five.

She fired off a quick text. **Sorry. (Really). Email might be best for this, but I will always do my best to accommodate your relationship with our daughter.**

God, being the bigger person was a challenge.

She scrolled through the photos on her phone and picked a recent picture of their no-longer-a-baby baby and sent that, too. He may be a jackass, but he was the jackass who'd given her the most beautiful child in the world. She'd find a way to be civil to him, and hope for even more.

"Sorry," she muttered as she took her spot behind the bar.

Malcolm poured her a shot of tequila. "I've never known you to be a drama queen, Natasha. Everything okay?"

Well, at least she'd done a good job of rehabilitating her reputation. She tossed back the shot and winced. "Yep."

"You want to talk?"

"Nope." She grinned. "Thanks."

"Good. Get back to work."

———

FOR A FEW YEARS, Matt had lived in Lion's Head mainly so he could walk to The Green Hedgehog, the best pub anywhere on the peninsula. Then he'd moved back to Pine Harbour, which didn't have a bar, good or otherwise, and now he had to be more responsible about his nights out.

Or find a bed to sleep in, although that hadn't happened since he'd moved.

The pub was crawling with tourists tonight. At the pool table next to theirs was a group of women up on the peninsula for a bachelorette weekend. In between friendly trash-talking, Tom had found out the women were staying at a cottage just outside town.

Matt knew how to play this game. Easy smiles, enough questions to find out which of them were single, and which of those were looking for a good time.

He was Mr. Good Time.

"Your turn," Tom said, snapping his fingers in front of Matt's face.

"Yeah." He shook his head and refocused on the table. Fucker hadn't left him with any clear shot, but there was a combo that he might be able to make from the far side, closest to the bachelorette party. He prowled that way, flashing a grin at the two women closest to him. "You ladies don't mind if I use this side of the table to kick Tom's ass, do you?"

"If you win, maybe I should play you next," one of them said, flipping her hair.

Bingo. Wide open invitation to get to know her better.

"Sounds good," he heard himself say, but it didn't. He squeezed his cue. "Winner of this game definitely gets to play you next. Deal?"

Even before he took the shot, he knew he'd flub it. Let Tom have the chance to brush hips with this woman.

"Damn," he said as the cue ball glanced off Tom's ball. "Bad luck."

From beside him, the flirty woman didn't miss a beat. "Maybe I'll have to play with your friend, then."

"I guess so." He straightened up and winked, unable to help himself from still stealing a little of her attention. "My loss, for sure."

"The game could still turn." She gave him a sweet smile that went all the way to her eyes, but he felt nothing.

"We'll have to wait and see what Tom—"

The crack of the cue ball against the ball right beside Matt's hand broke their conversation up. They turned in time to watch that ball sink into the pocket, and the cue ball bounce back across the table to nudge in the one Matt had scratched on.

And that was the game.

Matt laughed. "Bested by the best." He handed the woman his cue. "Good luck."

She spun on her heel and gave Tom the full force of her sweet smile. His buddy gave him a curious look, and Matt just shrugged. *Not tonight, man.*

As they racked up the balls, he took a seat at one of the tall bar tables along the side of the room and pulled his phone out of his back pocket. He tapped on Natasha's contact information, but he didn't know what to say to her. She'd made her concerns known.

He needed an excuse to talk to her again.

No, not an excuse. Fuck, he couldn't think of her like that, as a conquest or a game. He needed to be sure…

And that was the problem.

He wasn't sure of anything.

A dark, anxious thought clawed at the back of his mind, and he shook it away.

He needed a reason to see Natasha. A real one, within the parameters of the fact they couldn't date.

He couldn't pursue her.

Maybe there was a way he could make a case to her that they could be friends. Deep down inside, he knew it was all he was really capable of anyway. All he could offer and all she'd be willing to accept.

So what if he found her mouth captivating? He knew all about boundaries and could respect the hell out of them.

As a friend.

Who maybe wanted to learn more about cooking.

He did have a genuine interest in it. *Nothing wrong with a man developing a new skill set.*

He was on night shifts for Saturday and Sunday, then he had a day off before shifting to days. He tapped into his calendar to double check.

Yeah, Monday was wide open.

Now he just needed to figure out where the next cooking class was. He did a Google search for the conference centre in Port Elgin and clicked on the phone number.

"Hi, I have a weird question I hope you can help me with," he said to the clerk who answered the call. "There's a poster on your community bulletin board that I'd like some information from…"

CHAPTER SEVEN

IT TOOK Natasha ages to wind down that night, and in the end, she only tossed and turned for a few hours before it was time to get up.

Meredith gave her a worried look as they waited for the coffee maker to finish brewing. "You were up late last night."

"David called." She told her sister about the woman in the background.

"Are you jealous?"

"What?" Natasha made a face. "No. Whoever she is, she's welcome to his mess. Maybe she'll straighten him out, which would be good for Emily. Just…I don't know what it means."

Meredith sighed. "Sorry."

"There's something about this whole situation that is freaking me out. He's so consistently been a non-factor in our lives, and now…this is different. I don't like it, but I shouldn't have lost my temper."

"I don't know, I think he got exactly what he deserved from the sounds of it." Meredith grabbed two mugs from the cupboard. Extra big ones, because it was that kind of a Saturday. "Listen, there's something else I need to talk to you about, but I don't want to stress you out."

That didn't sound good. Natasha took a deep breath. "Too late. Shoot."

"Dan's had an interview for a new position. He was head-hunted, actually, last month, and we didn't think anything would come of it, but now they want to bring him in to meet some people." Meredith's face tightened up. "The job sounds amazing. But it's in Ottawa."

All the way across the province. Her heart plummeted. "Oh."

"He may not be offered the job."

But Meredith wouldn't have said anything if it wasn't a possibility. "That sounds exciting," Tasha said, which was the truth. "So, they're flying him there for an interview?"

"Yeah." But her sister still didn't look thrilled, and Natasha hated that any worry about her might be clouding a very good thing for their family.

"Oh, honey." She moved over and wrapped her arms around Meredith. "It's okay."

"It may turn out to be nothing…"

The unspoken *but* was crystal clear. "Are you interested in moving? For you?"

Her sister squirmed, looking guilty. "Yes," she finally admitted. "I'd like to live in a bigger city. It would be a big adjustment for the kids, of course. We're still talking it over."

"They're both outgoing kids, they'd probably take to new schools no problem."

Mer lifted one shoulder. "More variety, too," she said quietly. "There are some advantages to living in a city."

She grabbed Mer's hands. "Then I hope it's perfect for him, and you guys, and I don't want you to worry about me. Deal?"

"Deal." Her sister gave a sheepish look. "Is it terrible that I really want to be within driving distance of a Starbucks?"

She shook her head. "Nope." It wasn't for her, but she got it. She'd had that once. It had come with a painful side-effect of not being enough to hold all of David's attention, but it had been fun while it lasted. "Okay, while we still live on the same side of the province, what should we do with the kids today?"

———

THE WEEKEND SPED BY, working at night and cramming as much sister fun as possible into the days. By the time Monday rolled around, Natasha found herself needing the normalcy of seeing her sister and brother-in-law off to work, then walking the kids to school, and finally—blissfully—having alone time with Emily.

They cleaned up the kitchen, then talked about the cooking class that afternoon. "This one will be mostly talking, baby. So you'll want to bring a book and some crayons, okay?"

"No pink icing?"

"None."

"Boo."

"I feel your pain, kiddo."

"Will Matt be there?"

Ah, crap. Kids never forget anything. "He doesn't live near here. Remember? Last week was his only time coming to the lessons."

"Boo."

Despite her best efforts to forget him, Natasha had to admit she felt Emily's pain on that point, too.

"Mommy?"

"Yes?"

"You like cooking." Emily said it like the statement it was, not a question. The wisdom of a three-year-old.

"I do."

"Okay."

Natasha smiled to herself. If only everything could be as simple as that. *You want to have an inn. I do. Okay.*

You want to go back in time and never sleep with men who didn't value you enough. I do. Okay.

But life wasn't that easy; wishes and wants didn't just come true. She had to live with her past decisions, which was okay —they'd made her smarter, wiser, sharper.

"Mommy?"

She jerked her attention back to her gorgeous daughter. "Yes, baby?"

This game could go on forever. Emily never tired of getting her attention. Her eyes sparkled. "I love you."

As Natasha sank into the sweet, soft-armed hug, she reminded herself that it wasn't just wisdom she'd gotten out of her past decisions. She'd also got this. Pure, unconditional love. She buried her face in Emily's hair. "I love you, too."

Which was an important thing to remember three hours later when she was willing herself to not grump at Emily for fidgeting at cooking class.

They were at the Chinese restaurant today. Mrs. Chan's class was called **Cook Dinner in Under an Hour!** and promised prep tips and tricks from a chef. No pink icing, no cupcakes.

Her adorable three-year-old was grumpy and wanted everyone to know it. When Mrs. Cargill stopped by their table to say hello, Emily scowled before quietly whispering her response.

Mrs. Cargill just smiled. "Having a rough Monday, are we?"

Emily opened her colouring book and grabbed a crayon.

Natasha took a deep breath and nodded. "Little bit."

The older woman sat in front of them, and the tables quickly filled up, but maybe everyone could sense Emily's mood because nobody sat in the chair at the end of their table.

Mrs. Chan called the class to order promptly at the top of the hour, launching into an overview of the objectives. She was about to give her first tip when the door chimed, and everyone turned to see who the straggler was.

Not a regular, that was for sure. A big, broad body stood in the doorway, backlit by the afternoon sun. Someone who shouldn't be here, because he didn't live here, and last week was a one-off. Or something like that.

Natasha felt her eyes go wide and her mouth drop open as Matt Foster gave the room a sheepish wave. "Sorry I'm late. I'll just, uh…" He pointed to the empty chair next to Emily, who was beaming at him, and dropped his voice to a stage whisper. "Is that spot free?"

Emily gave him the world's biggest grin and nodded her head.

She doesn't know Matt is off-limits.

And neither did most of Natasha's rioting body parts, either.

He gave them both a quick smile as he sat down. Once again they were sharing a table with Emily in between them. Again Natasha was doing her best to not look at him even though she was completely, utterly aware of every inch of his six-foot-plus deliciousness.

Most of all, she couldn't stop seeing the hint of a blush along his cheekbones.

God damn it, if he was a little nervous, that would just melt her heart. She wasn't prepared for heart-melting. She wasn't prepared for any of this.

She'd told him it was complicated and pushed him away. Why had he come back?

From the counter, Mrs. Chan gave Matt a disapproving look before continuing with her tips on getting organized before you begin. "Really, the true secret to cooking dinner quickly is having a clean kitchen from the previous meal. If you have a wide open counter space with lots of room to do your prep, everything will go faster."

That was true. Bailey's had a small prep space, and it meant that Malcolm spent more time doing that work and cleaning up in between, rather than waiting for the dishwasher to come in.

In her fantasy future inn, she'd have a big farm kitchen with a giant work space in the middle. In reality, she'd probably be working as a bartender for the rest of her life and doodling kitchen drawings when she was fifty, an empty-nester who worried that her daughter was making a big mistake by not going to medical school. Or something. God, she didn't want to fall into the same trap her parents had.

Whatever Emily wanted to do with her life would be just fine.

And Natasha's Big Dream Plan was fun to think about.

Plus it was an excellent distraction from the Big Hot Hunk on the other end of her table—who was taking notes.

Notes.

He'd brought a notebook.

She gave up pretending that she wasn't aware of him and turned her head, giving him a brow-pulled-together curious look before shooting a glance at his notebook. *Taking notes?* she mouthed.

Very interesting, he silently responded. Then he grinned.

She turned her attention back to Mrs. Chan, who'd moved on to a comparison of cooking techniques. "Obviously, I am biased toward the stir-fry," she said, leaving room after that for a round of weak laughter. "But anything with high heat and small pieces of meat is sure to cook quickly. Big pieces of meat and slow heat? Those are for Sundays. Or when you are retired, so for some of you, why are you here? Go home and make a roast."

From the table in front of them, Mrs. Cargill muttered something about having better things to do with her time because she was old, not dead, and glanced meaningfully at Matt.

He grinned at her, too. Free and loose with those smiles, the Big Hot Hunk was.

Mrs. Chan sighed. "Moving on. When time is short, it's smart to choose recipes that can be accomplished in much less time than you have. Whatever time it says on a recipe, double it. That's how long it will take."

The tips continued for the next ten minutes, all common sense but most not applicable for Natasha. She already knew how to cook for a family and in a hurry. She was here for the hands-on part of the class—a salad prep race.

The little things in life amused her. Racing senior citizens for the fastest vegetable chop in town would usually be the highlight of her social life for the week. Now Matt was at the end of the table, and she was very distracted by his mouth.

His smile, not his mouth, she tried to tell herself.

Definitely not the promise of a kiss she couldn't have.

She wanted to ask him what he was doing here, except she knew the answer would almost certainly be dangerous.

———

MATT LIKED the way Natasha kept looking at him. He couldn't keep his eyes off her, either.

She had a notebook in front of her, covered in neat writing, organized into stacks of words. Somehow she managed to sneak looks at him, give the presenter her full attention, and keep an eye on Emily, too.

The young Miss Kingsley was colouring right now, but she kept fidgeting. Each time she got restless, Natasha would pull out something to redirect her attention. A little plastic pony, a sheet of stickers. Sometimes she just flipped the page of the colouring book to give Emily something new to focus on.

He couldn't blame the three-year-old for being bored. This class had nothing on cupcake decorating.

If Natasha wanted to concentrate on the lesson, though, he could at least help keep Emily occupied. He hunkered down, bringing his head to her level. "Can I colour with you?"

She gave him a blue crayon. "Here. You can do the sky."

He did, and then he was tasked with filling in a tree while Emily did the rainbow in alternating pink and purple stripes.

"I told Mommy you would be here," she whispered.

Ah, shit. He could imagine how that would have gone with Natasha. "I can't always come to cooking class. But I liked last week."

"Me too." She pursed her tiny mouth and scribbled harder.

He switched out green for brown and coloured the trunk of the tree.

Emily didn't say anything else, and he wondered why she was so different today than last week. But she kept giving him colours to use, and smiling when he did her colouring-related bidding, so he didn't worry too much about it.

Maybe she was trying to be good for her mom, who was taking the most diligent notes.

Matt was quite glad he'd decided to bring his own pad of paper. They could bond over food prep. It might be the start of a beautiful friendship.

After the lesson wrapped up, the hands-on task was a salad-assembly race. There were only eight trays assembled, so people needed to group up. Natasha gave Emily a nervous look, and Matt cleared his throat. "Uh, how about I hang out with Emily, and we colour, while you join a group? We're good here, I swear."

She looked at the red flower he'd just finished colouring in. "Yeah?"

"Promise. Go slay a head of lettuce."

Emily turned the page and handed him the green crayon again. "Now this other tree."

"Yes, ma'am."

He got back to work as the class grouped up. Natasha wasn't that far from them, and he could hear her taking the lead with their plan as the small Asian woman in charge gave them a two-minute warning.

Once the whistle went, she leapt into action, taking on the chopping, while the older women on her team made the dressing and ripped lettuce. By the sounds of it, there were three necessary steps, and Natasha was keeping track of all of it, even as she focused on her own task.

And she made time for good-natured smack talk to the other teams, too. He grinned as she raised her voice to comment innocently on the size of the onion slices at the next table. She was fierce, although her competitiveness had a distinctly kind edge to it.

The other table grabbed another onion and this time their slices were more consistent.

He caught her gaze with his knowing one. *I see you.*

She pinked up as she undoubtedly realized that he knew she'd just helped them a little, although now they were behind. So she'd helped her team, too.

Afternoon cooking classes were more cutthroat and entertaining than he'd ever have thought.

"Is Mommy winning?" Emily asked.

"It looks like she is," he said, finishing his treetop with a careful line around the curved edge.

"Mommy likes cooking."

"Yeah?"

"Yeah."

"What's your favourite thing she makes?"

"Pasghetti."

"Nice."

"Do you like pasghetti?"

"I do. With extra sauce."

The three-year-old gave him a sideways look and echoed him. "*Nice.*"

He laughed out loud.

Of course Natasha's team finished first, everything tidied up and the salad up to the exacting standards of the chef. For their efforts, they got praise and first dibs on the fortune cookies. Natasha grabbed three and brought them back to the table.

"Thank you," she murmured as she sat down and handed him a cookie, then gave one to Emily. "Did you have fun colouring with Matt?"

"Yep."

"Good."

Emily turned to him. "Can you come to the park with us?"

"Uh…" He looked up at Natasha's face, but her expression was carefully neutral. "You'll have to ask your mom if it's okay first. I can't stay long today, though. I worked last night, so I need to get back home and grab some more sleep soon, because I'm working again tomorrow morning."

"On the ambulance?"

"That's right."

"Okay."

Natasha laughed. "Life is simple when you're three. Okay is her new answer for everything."

"I like it."

She nodded. "Yeah, me too. It's like, a reminder that some things just…are. Anyway, we don't want to keep you."

"Mommy, can Matt come to the park?"

Natasha laughed. "Okay, one of us wants to keep you a bit longer. Do you…?"

"Going from a night shift to a day shift is weird, but I've got twenty-four hours to re-arrange myself. Gotta stay busy for the afternoon anyway." Which wasn't exactly honest, but he'd driven an hour to come and see her. See both of them. He wanted to squeeze as much as he could out of this time, because he wasn't sure if he'd get another chance. "If you don't mind me inviting myself along."

She shrugged, then grinned, a wide, unexpected smile he felt in his chest. "Sure. Why don't you follow us over there."

They made their goodbyes and he did just that, driving the short distance to the park behind the school. Today they had it all to themselves, and Emily sprinted ahead of them toward the climbers, scampering up the stairs and zooming down the slide before they stopped at the edge of the wood chip ground covering.

"I was surprised to see you today," she finally said.

"Is it okay that I showed up?"

"Better to beg for forgiveness than ask permission?"

"Story of my life."

She laughed. "Really? That's honest."

He grinned and tried to remember he'd had a noble purpose today. Okay, a noble-ish purpose. Come to the cooking class and give her a chance to feel comfortable around him in public again. Just as a friend, no pressure.

"Of course it's okay you came," she said before he could

respond. "Although I'm surprised Mrs. Chan didn't take you down for being late."

"That would have been awkward. But worth it."

Before she could reply to that, Emily ran over and tugged on his hand. "Can you lift me up?" She pointed to the monkey bars.

He looked at Natasha, who waved her hand.

"Sure."

The three-year-old was light as a feather as he hoisted her into the air, arms wiggling to grab the metal bars. But even when she had a good hold, he wasn't sure if he should let go. Loosening his grip, he waited to see if she had it, and he'd been right to be cautious. She let out a nervous yip, and he squeezed her sides again. "I've got you," he said. "Get your legs up."

She shifted back and forth until her legs were securely hooked over another bar, but then she couldn't move on her own.

"It's hard to figure out," he told her. "Want to go up on top?"

"Yes!"

So they did that next, then they tried hanging again. Finally she figured out how to pull herself up between the bars, and slowly started to move back and forth on top.

The whole time, Natasha silently watched, her gaze locked on her daughter.

He leaned against the climber, keeping one eye on Emily as she scampered along the monkey bars, but also turned part of his attention back to her beautiful mother. "So, what's next week's class?"

Natasha burst out laughing. "Don't you know? How did you find it this week?"

Ah. He scuffed his heel against the wood chips under the

climber. "I called the conference centre and had a clerk go and find the flyer for me on the bulletin board. I thought I'd be pushing my luck to ask for all the dates over the phone. I can stop there on my way out of town and take a picture."

She held his gaze for a long, poignant beat, then pulled out her phone, waving her hand at Emily at the same time. "Watch her."

With a deep inhale, she flicked her thumb across the screen, and a moment later his phone vibrated. He reached for Emily. "Come on down from there, Miss Monkey. I have an important text I need to check."

She sprinted off to the slide again, and he looked at his screen.

A text message with a link.

"The schedule is online, too," Natasha said, and he looked up in time to see her smiling at him. Laughing with him.

He gave her all of his attention now. "I'll ask in advance this time. How would you feel if I showed up next week?"

"Mmm. My answer's kind of complicated." Her eyes softened and she gave him a smaller smile. "How's that?"

"Sounds honest."

"It is."

"Good."

Emily called his name and he turned to watch her go down the slide with a big squeal.

Natasha drifted closer. He glanced at her next, and found he couldn't look away.

"You're staring at me," she finally said, her voice a low murmur.

But he could hear it because she was right next to him, and damn, he liked that a lot.

"Do you want me to stop?"

Another deep inhale. "No," she finally said. "But I don't know what you're hoping to find."

You, he wanted to say. He brushed his knuckles against the back of her hand instead.

She exhaled and swung her hand, touching him back. Each brush of her skin against his made it hard for him to think straight.

"I told myself I could come today if I were focused on just being your friend," he said under his breath.

She smiled as she looked straight ahead. "Really?"

"Yep."

She bumped her shoulder against his and grinned. "Come on. You aren't usually this sweet, are you?"

"No." He took a deep breath and winced. "Wait, I shouldn't have said that."

She laughed. "Yeah, you should have. It's good. Honesty is good. We've got a healthy communication theme going on, it's refreshing."

Well, if they were being honest…

He gestured at Emily zooming down the slide for the dozenth time. "I've never dated a single mom before."

"We're not dating."

"Fair point. But last week, I was…" He laughed. This was such a mistake. "You know what I was looking for? A hook-up. I thought, cupcakes in the middle of the day. Gotta be a single woman there."

She stared at him, her eyes wide and her lips parted.

He kept going. "I haven't had a great social life lately, to be honest, which is not something I'd tell you if I was trying to hook up with you. It's actually not something I've told anyone else. I know that's a weird thing to admit to a woman I'm trying to impress, but I want you to know that I may not have been looking for friendship, but as soon as I saw you, I wanted to know you. And anything else on my agenda immediately disappeared."

"Just like that?"

"Yeah." He let out a short laugh. "Surprised the hell out of me, I gotta say."

"What about when I told you…I know Jake?"

He shrugged. "That didn't change how I feel. It really couldn't, because you're not the only one with a history. I don't care about yours, and I hope you could look past mine. I've made a lot of choices in the past you might not like, but they're done now. That might not be the right thing to say, but—"

She reached out and took his hand, her fingers cool and small against his. "I don't care about the right thing to say, Matt. I've dated players. I've had men say *all* the right things to me, and mean none of them. I'm not interested in that ever again."

He squeezed her hand and then let it go. Too soon to linger, no matter how good it felt. "Then I'll do my best to blunder my way through this."

"This," she whispered with a small laugh. "What exactly is this?"

He couldn't say dating. She'd already shot that down. Wooing her, seducing her…none of that worked, either. "Truly no clue," he admitted. "But I like it, whatever this is."

That got him another smile. "Me too."

He wanted to put an endless stream of those on her face. "So I'll see you next week?"

"That sounds really good."

"What if I showed up at the bar one night? I'm not working this weekend." He knew he was pushing his luck, but he couldn't help it.

She screwed up her face, then dragged in a tortured breath. "I thought I'd never want to see a Foster ever again."

"Damn." But he couldn't help grinning. "And yet...?"

"And yet..." Did she know how beautiful she was when her feelings skittered across her face like that? "Yeah. Sure, if you want to come by the bar this weekend, I wouldn't mind that. As a friend, right?"

"As a friend."

"I'll be working," she warned him.

"I'll be good. A paying customer."

"Okay."

It's a date, he wanted to say, but he'd pushed his luck far enough for one day.

CHAPTER EIGHT

THAT NIGHT, Natasha lingered in Emily's room after her daughter fell asleep. It had been a big day, a long day, and they'd butted heads over dinner.

Sometimes it was exhausting being the only parent, the only one to put her foot down. Meredith would back her up of course, but it wasn't the same. So after two stories, she'd curled up and just held her daughter as she softly drifted into slumber, grateful for the gentle reconnection and a restoration of peace.

When she finally disentangled herself and headed upstairs, she found Meredith sitting at the kitchen table.

Waiting.

Her phone was in her hands.

Dan had flown to Ottawa that morning for an in-person interview.

Everything was happening so quickly, so naturally, it seemed like an inevitable turn of events she should have predicted long ago. Of course they couldn't stay like this forever, a safe little refuge of communal living.

And yet…

Natasha took a deep breath. "Did you talk to Dan?"

Her sister nodded. "They offered him the job."

Oh. "Wow."

"Yeah." Meredith's face crumbled, and as one, they burst into tears.

Meredith stood up and Natasha leaned into her. "It's going to be okay," she said. "This is great news."

"I know. Why am I crying?"

"Because we'll miss each other, you dork."

"Right." Meredith squeezed her tight. "We're not going to move until Christmas, so I don't want to you to freak out. He's going to work remotely until we find a house there. And this doesn't mean we're necessarily selling this place. You guys can stay here if you want," she said, her voice hitching. "We could rent it to you…"

Natasha shook her head. No, she didn't want to get into a complicated rental relationship. And Ottawa houses were expensive enough that she knew they would need the equity from this place if they wanted to buy there. "It'll work out." She hugged her sister back. "Emily and I will be fine."

Hopefully.

God, her stomach twisted at the thought of house-hunting. She'd have to do that, too. She'd have to make a lot of changes —both her and her sister were losing their childcare arrangements. "We'll be fine," she repeated, this time making her voice firmer. They would be. She'd spent more than three years building a nest egg for just this kind of thing.

David will want you to move to the city.

Not happening. She couldn't afford a house anywhere near the city. But up here, there was a chance she might find something.

A place for her and Emily to make a home of their own.

The training wheels period of being a single mom was over. No more protective sister, no more rent-free basement.

It was time for her to show Emily they were going to be just fine. Better than fine. They were going to be *amazing*. Just the two of them.

———

MATT WOKE up before his alarm early Tuesday morning. He crawled out of bed and tripped over his running shoes.

Glancing at the clock, he decided he had time for a quick run. Fast, hard, punishing.

After he showered the sweat off, he grabbed his duffel bag and headed to his truck. It was a short drive to the new station, and he was grateful to be posted there. It beat the hell out of driving up or down the peninsula like he used to, like he still did for the army.

Like he'd happily do to go and see Natasha, he realized.

But that was different.

He rolled into work with at least three minutes to spare before the start of his shift.

Maybe even four minutes.

"I'm here," he said as Owen mock-glowered at him from the door of the supervisor's office.

"Cutting it close."

He grinned at his boss. Owen knew Matt always made it in, if sometimes by the skin of his teeth. And usually more than that. If he spent the night with a woman, he'd roll in early, because work was a good excuse not to spend the *whole* night. Always best not to linger.

Owen turned and nodded toward the break room. "You've got a ride along today."

Shit. "O-kay." Owen's brows hit the roof and Matt heard

the insolence in his voice a second too late. "Got it. We'll make it a good one."

"See that you do."

He found the student, a bright young woman he'd met a few times before named Shawntelle, and had her come with him to do the prep work, checking over the rig.

It ended up being a good shift to take a student on, too. Two calls, the first an in-home assessment with lots of communication modelling, and the second a complicated leg fracture from a motorcycle crash with an equally complicated patient move from the accident site—a steep ditch—to the ambulance. They'd had to form a human chain to pass the patient on the backboard up the ravine, which was a first for the student. After they got the patient to the hospital, there was a lot for her to process as they prepped to go back on-air.

"How often does that kind of multi-ambulance response happen up here?" Shawntelle asked as they used antiseptic wipes on the gurney post-call.

Matt thought about it. "Once a month, maybe? Sometimes there aren't other paramedics available, and we use the cops or firefighters instead."

"I wasn't sure about doing a rural placement. I wanted to work in the city, but…" Her cheeks pinked up.

Matt shrugged. "I didn't get my first choices for placements in college, either. I always left my applications to the last minute."

Her flush deepened. "Yeah."

"We'll make it good for you. And there's a lot to be said about rural emergency services. You get to know people in the community more."

Before he could add anything else, Will interrupted them from the front of the ambulance where he'd been doing the paperwork for the call. "Done. Let's get back on the road."

They got the gurney in the back, then they hopped in. Matt gestured to the radio. "You do the honours, Shawntelle."

She grabbed the handset. "Two-zero-three-four, on the air."

They didn't get another call, though, and an hour later, they were back at the station, the shift over.

Matt sat down with the student to complete his post-shift placement report, then went to find Owen.

"How'd it go?" the supervisor asked, barely looking up from his own pile of paperwork, twenty-times deeper than theirs. Never in a million years would Matt want Owen's job, although the guy was a single dad with college tuition looming in the near future. It was probably worth the extra pay for him.

"Pretty good." Matt gave a quick summary of the shift. "We'd take her out again any time. She was helpful."

"Good."

"Hey, there's something I wanted to ask."

Owen lifted his head, giving him his full attention. "Shoot."

"I was hoping to get the next few Mondays off. I'm already off this coming Monday, but I'm on the schedule the week after that."

Owen frowned. "You already have Wednesday nights protected as off so you can parade with the army."

Matt frowned right back. "I will take literally all the other shifts. I can come in at the last minute if you need me."

"Sure." Owen crossed his arms. "Plus you're close to maxing out on overtime and we still have three months left in the year. Don't think I haven't noticed you cramming your schedule as full as possible."

"So is that a no to Mondays?" If he was taking a lot of over-time, shouldn't that mean giving him a day off would be easier, not harder?

Owen shook his head. "Not a no. Just a… Is everything okay?"

"Yeah, sure. I was just asking about the schedule."

Owen pointed at the door. "Can you close that and sit down?"

Whoa. Matt rolled his shoulders, suddenly uncomfortable, like he'd stumbled into a planned conversation he knew nothing about. "My shift's done."

"Yeah, but you walked in here, and now we've got an opportunity to talk, so we're going to talk."

"About what?"

"Close the door."

Shit. Owen wasn't in the military anymore, but he'd been infantry for ten years. He still had a decent NCO bark, and friends or not, former partners or not, Owen was pulling rank.

If his supervisor wanted to have a chat, they'd have a chat. Matt knew how to play this game. Deep breath, nod, say "yes, sir" as many times as needed until the talking-to was finished.

After shutting the door, he sat where Owen pointed.

"Relax."

Matt laughed, even though it sounded a bit hollow to his ears. "I'm a pretty chill guy."

"Not so much lately." Owen raised his eyebrows, as if to say, *want to argue that point?*

No, maybe he didn't. "We all get jaded."

"Yeah. Is that it?"

Matt shrugged. "Sure."

"Anything overwhelming you?"

"I'm fine."

"For now. But I'm seeing some early warning signs of workplace stress."

"What?" Matt shook his head. "No. You're reading this all wrong. I promise I'm fine."

"You're juggling a lot more than you used to. Now you're adding something on Mondays, and your personal life is none of my business, but—"

"The Monday thing is personal. It's not another job."

"Okay." Owen rocked back in his chair. "I want to be clear, I don't have any concerns about your performance on the job—yet. But I'm starting to see some fraying at the edges. I know your family has been through a lot. And I know a thing or two about being tough, about being strong. Pushing stuff down deep."

"That's not what's going on here."

"It can be innocuous at first. Change in habits."

Matt opened his mouth to protest, then his eyes went wide. "This is about the extra shifts I've taken on?"

Owen shrugged. "It's out of character."

Matt laughed. "Yeah. I get that. Shit, man. I'm growing up, how is that a problem?"

"I don't know." Owen scrubbed his jaw. "Look, as your friend, I'm worried about you. As your former partner, I know how you used to be on the job and now you're not that guy anymore. Something happened."

"Yeah, my brother got blown up and barely came home in one piece. I'm trying to be a better man now."

"I see that. God, Matt, I know it's been rough for you all."

"Not really for me," he said, tense all over now. Fuck, he didn't need Owen feeling bad for him. His life was *fine*. They'd dodged a real bullet, and his family had a lot to be grateful for. And now that he was really figuring out what mattered, it was going to only get better.

"Okay, look…you're an easy-going guy, so your breaking point isn't going to be as clear to see as someone else's. I gotta do my due diligence and touch base."

"Over a schedule change request."

"Yeah."

Matt shook his head. "All right. Thanks for the talk. I'll keep your words in mind, how's that?"

"Come see me in a week or two, let's talk again."

"Sure thing. I'll bring you cupcakes. I'm perfecting my icing techniques, you know."

"Get the hell out."

Owen grinned.

———

Matt: How's your Tuesday night going?

Natasha: Slow pub night. But might be able to close early, so that's okay.

Matt: I'm crawling into bed. Half shift tomorrow at the crack of dawn.

Natasha: Yikes. Sleep tight. I'm so not a morning person.

Matt: No?

Natasha: Well, I can't actually sleep in anymore— thanks, Emily—but if I had to choose...

Matt: LOL @ thanks Emily

Natasha: Are you a morning person?

Matt: My sleep is so messed up because of work I'm honestly not sure anymore.

Natasha: LOL

Natasha: Well, I meant what I said. Sleep tight. And sweet dreams.

Matt: Thanks. You too. And maybe I'll text you again sometime soon...

Natasha: I'd like that.

SHE'D LIKE THAT A LOT, and boy, wasn't that a weird feeling. That thought stuck with her as she headed home.

But when she crawled into bed, she didn't sleep tight. She didn't sleep at all. Her mind spun with to-do lists and worry lists and an ever-growing collection of possibilities.

A bed and breakfast for the twenty-first century. A new twist on her dream of having an inn, or maybe a first step in that direction. Like Lorelei Gilmore but with less coffee, more whiskey, and better taste in men.

Although if she met a real-life Luke, she'd drink all the coffee in the world until he noticed her.

Maybe her taste in men was just as bad as Lorelei's.

She rolled over and bounced her forehead against her pillow. *Go. To. Sleep.* Easier said than done.

Something she learned in those early days with Emily was that lying in bed when she couldn't sleep was an exercise in frustration, so once she admitted to herself that her brain was working too hard to drift off, she got up. She went upstairs and quietly put the kettle on.

Perhaps a cup of tea might help. If it didn't, she'd toss back a shot of whiskey as a chaser.

While she waited for the kettle, she grabbed her laptop off the shelf and opened it up. No new emails, nothing on social media…she really had no choice but to go and look at the real estate website again.

There wouldn't be anything in her price range, though. There hadn't been either of the last two nights.

She looked again anyway, with a tight chest and a dry mouth, because now that her sister was moving and she was being pushed out of the comfortable nest in the basement, she wanted to do this right.

She didn't want to rent. Didn't want to make the best of a tiny one-bedroom apartment over a grocery store.

And she definitely didn't want to go hat-in-hand to her parents up in Tobermory, either. She'd lived with them off and on until she got pregnant—then she wasn't welcome, not with "the choices she had made."

Like Emily was something to regret.

Never.

"What are you looking at?"

Natasha jumped at the unexpected sound of her sister's voice. She shook her head as she glanced over her shoulder. "Nothing."

Meredith stepped closer and Tasha waved her hands in front of the computer screen, but her sister just knocked her fingers out of the way. "That doesn't look like nothing."

"You are so nosy. It's just something that might work for step one in my Big Dream Plan."

"Ah, the capital-P Plan! I remember that." Meredith grinned and pointed to the kettle, now whistling. "Shall I make tea while we house-hunt together?"

Tasha groaned. "It's a futile effort. Everything is so expensive. And I don't want that to be on your mind, either." She swallowed hard. "Tomorrow I'll start looking for rental places."

"Is that what you want?"

"I want a long-lost relative to bequeath me a rambling mansion I need to share with a Chris Hemsworth look-a-like who's always losing his shirt. Reality demands some compromise on what I want."

Meredith didn't say anything to that. She made them tea, then shoved a steaming mug of something herbal in front of Natasha. "Move over. Let's do some dreaming."

They didn't find anything that night, but the next day, Tasha didn't call any rental agents, either. She felt something —the edges of a dream, maybe—percolating deep inside her, and when the bar slowed down, she let her mind wander.

The next morning over breakfast, she showed her sister the apps she'd found. Three of them, all very popular, featuring short-term vacation rentals.

"If I found the right place, a house split into two or three apartments, Emily and I could live in one and we could list the other two on these websites."

Meredith scrolled through the apps, chewing on her lower lip. She didn't say anything. Her silence didn't do anything to dampen Natasha's enthusiasm, though, which was a good sign.

"That's not the whole of the plan," she whispered, the corners of her mouth twitching up in a smile. "That's just phase one."

"How many phases are there?"

"Three at least. Maybe four."

The kids bounced into the kitchen, and the conversation paused.

They picked it up later that night when Meredith was still awake when Natasha got home from the bar.

"I've been thinking about your plan all day," her sister confessed.

"Me too."

"It's risky."

"Yeah. I'd need to keep another job, for sure. But it's a way to maybe help offset a mortgage I'm going to need to carry anyway. And it's also a way to test out if I want to get back into hospitality and innkeeping."

"I was wondering about that." Meredith poured tea that Natasha hadn't asked for but gratefully took. "I remember you wanted to have an inn when we were kids."

"I think it was from watching *White Christmas* every year."

Meredith laughed. "So from the very beginning, you knew it was a lean business model."

Tasha nodded. "Yep. I guess so. And I don't think I have unrealistic expectations. I just want...something of my own." She took a deep breath. "And I've found a couple of potential houses. Really more just to give me an idea of what duplexes and triplexes go for. None of them are in the right towns or right price range. But they're not out of the realm of possibility."

"Show me."

So they opened up the computer again and poked through real estate listings. They took turns running searches, and when their cups were empty, Meredith made more tea.

Halfway through that second cup, one of them expanded the search further north, and a listing caught Natasha's eye. Her pulse ratcheted up. There was no way...

She clicked into the listing and scanned for the words that would make it a no-go. *As-is. Septic tank. Former grow-op.* None of those were listed. It even had central heating. Sure, it needed a new kitchen, new floors, new windows, new... almost everything. But the bones were outstanding. And it was already sub-divided into three apartments.

"Is that the price for the entire house? Not an apartment inside it?"

Natasha groaned. "The entire house. Don't you dare get excited. I can't afford it."

"It's so pretty." Meredith clicked through the gallery of photos, and Tasha rubbed her chest, trying not to get excited. "It needs a lot of work, though."

"Yeah. But it sounds like a steal."

"Stop it. This is not a good idea." And not just because it was so far north it was definitely inside Matt Foster territory.

That should make her run scared in the other direction.

It didn't.

Her sister grinned. "We should go and see it."

"No."

Meredith winked, and Natasha groaned again. "Maybe."

"Email the real estate agent. See if we can get an appointment to view it. I'll book time off work so we can go together."

"This is crazy."

"I know. That's the best kind of way to start an adventure." Meredith propped her elbow on the table and leaned on it. "Seriously, though… When Dan told me about the job in Ottawa, he wasn't going to apply for it. I told him he needed to do it, just to see what might happen. Let's see what happens here. If it's perfect, we can help you with the mortgage. I know you'll want to carry it yourself, but we can co-sign the loan. It's seriously the least we could do after booting you out of this place."

Natasha nodded. It wasn't going to be perfect, so it didn't matter.

ON WEDNESDAY NIGHT, Matt grabbed a ride into Wiarton with his brothers. It was their regular Army training night, but it was also the commemoration of Sean's early retirement from the Forces. Jake drew the short stick to be the designated driver.

When they arrived, a fellow Pine Harbour resident and reservist, Ryan Howard, was waiting for Matt outside the orderly room.

"What can I do for you, Sergeant Major?"

Ryan grinned. "Your choice tonight." He held up a shiny gold loonie. "Since the senior NCOs are being invited to the officers' mess for your brother's mug-out tonight, we want to contribute to their bar." The officers' mess would be well-stocked with all the wrong things. Bringing their own beer was a good idea.

"You'll need more than a buck."

"We're going to flip on who goes to pick up the booze from the liquor store. You can call heads or tails."

"And what does the loser get to do?"

"Give the Mental Resiliency talk to the recruits."

Matt groaned. He grabbed the coin out of Ryan's hand and flipped it between his fingers before tapping it back into Ryan's palm. "I'll get the booze."

"That's not how it works." But Ryan still handed over the purchase order and told him to drive the MILCOTS in the yard.

At the liquor store, Matt had to wait a few minutes, so he headed back to the beer section to see if there was anything else he wanted to grab. The first thing that caught his eye was the local craft beer section—and the Neustadt beer Natasha had recommended to him.

He grabbed a six-pack of it. Everyone else could drink what was ordered in advance. Tonight, he was going to get a little tipsy and give some serious thought to what he wanted, who he wanted it with, and what the cost of that might be.

———

TRAINING DRAGGED when he got back to the unit. Matt couldn't shake thoughts of Natasha—and Emily. Of his brother and that winter storm when Jake's "friend" was in a minor car accident and she'd called him, because she was pregnant and needed a place to stay. Matt's brother had had a lot of explaining to do in this very armouries to Dani's brothers.

Probably a hell of a lot more explaining to do to Dani.

And once again he burned at the painful reality that Natasha had been discarded in the aftermath.

Nobody had given her a second thought.

Matt hadn't, that was for sure.

Would he still be twisted up like this if he'd met her then? Would he have felt that zap of awareness for her when she was pregnant, when she thought it might be his brother's child?

Across the parade square, Jake laughed at something his LT was saying, and Matt swung his attention toward his brother.

Do you ever think of her? Probably not. Matt didn't think about the trail of women he'd left in his own wake—a trail of carefully constructed one-night stands that right up until the minute he met Natasha he wanted to resume.

Would he use and discard her, too?

Maybe I don't deserve her.

But he wanted someone to deserve her. He wanted her to find some happiness, that was for damn sure.

After training ended and Matt had dismissed his troops, he fell in step with his older brothers as they headed to the officers' mess. As non-commissioned members, they usually went to the Sergeants' Mess, but tonight they'd been extended an invitation upstairs because their baby brother was having a proper send-off from the Canadian Forces.

Sean was the only officer among them, the only one of the four brothers who had followed their father's footsteps into commissioning. The other three had all enlisted, happy to be grunts. Happy to take a different path than that of their cold and distant father, who had provided the bare essentials of life after their mother died of cancer, but never more than that. Never love, not really.

Sean's ambition had outweighed any resentment. He'd wanted to go far in the Forces, but that career path had been taken from him in a single, brutal explosion.

They were lucky to have him alive. Standing, albeit with the aid of a cane. Smiling, too—although that was mostly credited to Jenna, the woman he'd secretly married right before his injury, the unexpected wife who had shown up in Pine Harbour while he was recuperating.

They were lucky to have Sean, and he was lucky to have Jenna.

Lucky, yes, but that didn't change the fact that their baby brother was saying goodbye to the military far sooner than he'd have liked.

There were the usual toasts from the commander of the unit and Sean's fellow officers, but once the formalities were over, Dean grabbed them all for a private toast, just the four of them. "To our baby brother," he said. "Full of surprises and capable of anything."

"I'll drink to that," Jake said, lifting his glass, and Matt did the same, finding himself choked up.

When they were younger, they'd been close in a blood-relations way. Responsibility bound them more than commonalities. But over the last few years their friendships had been tested and strengthened, and now his brothers were his best friends.

And you're keeping a secret from one of them.

"You guys have been…" Sean shook his head, looking a hell of a lot older than his twenty-seven years. "I'm beyond grateful," he finally said. "For all the ass-kicking, and driving, and food and shelter and beer."

"Speaking of ass-kicking and shelter," Dean said, changing the subject to the new house Sean was building for his bride. "Jake pushed the calendar appointment to my phone this afternoon. Construction begins in March?"

Sean nodded, but before they could get into that conversation, Dean pointed to the door, where their father stood. "Hey." Their dad was long retired now, but as a former member of this very mess, as a former CO of the unit, he was always welcome. But Matt was pretty sure none of them had known he was coming tonight.

"Yeah," Sean said gruffly. "I invited him." He looked at them all. "What?"

"Nothing." Dean raised his voice. "Over here, sir."

"Sons," the Colonel said as he approached. "I see you're bringing your beer-guzzling ways into the Officers' Mess."

Seriously? Matt sighed. "Only way to do a mug out, Dad. Mug. Of Beer. Well, I'd do a mug out with gin, too, but I don't think you'd approve of how that would end."

Jake groaned. "Don't say it."

Matt crowed as he lifted his beer in the air. It felt good to cut loose. "Pants off, all the way."

Their father ignored that and turned to scan the crowd. "Good turn out tonight."

Sean cleared his throat. "How about you and I go have something that's served in a proper glass?"

Matt couldn't hold back his reaction, and from the look on his brothers' faces, they were surprised that Sean was giving their dad the time of day, too.

Sean pointed at him. "Matt, make sure your pants stay on until you head back to your own mess."

He lifted his glass in a sober mock-salute. "Yes, Captain."

A year ago, he'd have zero intentions of obeying that order. Now, he didn't really need the reminder to behave.

"Where'd you go?" Dean nudged his arm and Matt looked up to see both of his older brothers frowning at him, their brows furrowed.

He tipped back his glass. "Nowhere."

Jake opened his mouth to say something, but they were saved when his phone started ringing, and he excused himself.

When Matt looked back at Dean, the oldest Foster brother was staring at him.

"What?"

"Are you mad at Jake about something?"

"No."

Dean didn't look convinced.

Matt sighed. Fuck. "Do you remember that whole thing

that happened around the time he finally admitted he had feelings for Dani? With his friend from up north?"

"The pregnancy scare? Yeah, I don't think anyone will forget that." Dean's frown deepened. "What made you bring that up?"

"Nothing." Matt took another long swallow of beer. "So much for you and Jake being the responsible ones, right?"

"How did I get lumped in there?"

"Never mind."

"Is this about Sean wanting to build a house and start a family?"

Matt choked on the next sip of beer.

Dean misread his reaction. "What did you think, he wants to build a five-bedroom house so he has extra rooms for his shoe collection?"

No, that wasn't what Matt thought, but he wasn't about to correct his brother. He drained his glass. "I need another drink."

"Before you stumble off into tonight's friendly warm bed, I want to talk to you guys again."

Matt's head started to buzz, and not in a good way. This point he would correct. "There won't be a friendly…whatever. I'm not that guy anymore."

"Since when?"

"Seriously? Since Sean came home with his brain scrambled."

Dean made a surprised face. "Huh."

Matt wasn't sure why he was making a point of that. The only person he wanted to know that, actually, was Natasha. It didn't matter if anyone else thought he was still sleeping around, but it rankled at him that his brothers had all been so wrapped up in their own lives they hadn't noticed he'd changed.

You've hidden a lot from them, though. Maybe it wasn't just one secret he was keeping, and not just from one brother.

"What do you want to talk about that you need all of us together, anyway?" As soon as he asked the question, Matt knew the answer, and he felt like a heel. Damn it. He was just as guilty of not paying attention. "You've set a wedding date."

His brother grinned. "Yeah. Now that Sean is in a good place, it's time. We're thinking early spring. Something casual at our place that will still somehow take six months to plan."

"Well, shit, man, that's exciting." Matt stuck out his right hand. "Congratulations. You've waited long enough."

Of all of them, Dean had taken on the bulk of Sean's care when he'd been released from the hospital. Which meant that all of Dean's newfound happiness with Liana, the country music singer he'd fallen for when he worked as her bodyguard on tour, had been put on hold so he could nurse their bitter and broken brother back to health.

Dean gave his fingers a quick squeeze, then clapped Matt on the shoulder. "I guess now I can tell Jake and Sean individually."

Matt nodded. "And I guess I can get back to the best part of a mug out."

"I wouldn't expect anything less, bud."

Of course he wouldn't. And Matt was doing his best to live up—or down—to his brothers' expectations tonight.

He headed for the bar anyway. The next two beers went down quickly, but the one after that he drank more slowly, and then he switched to Coke. Just because it would be easy to be that guy again didn't mean it was who he really was. Or something. He was pretty sure he was drunk.

It had been a while, though.

And from the looks of it, he wasn't the only one. Sean was leaning pretty hard against the wall, and his cane.

Matt weaved his way over to his younger brother and waved off an offered glass of brandy from one of the retired officers. "Thank you, sir, but I've had enough tonight." He waited until Sean had also declined a drink, and when they were alone, he gestured to his lower body. "Pants are still on."

Sean grinned. "Miracle."

"We all have to grow up sometime."

"Afraid so," his baby brother said with a laugh. "Sorry, man."

Jesus. Until he'd been injured, Sean wouldn't have been one to razz Matt for his choices. Hell, Sean would have been right there with him, living it up and not worrying about the consequences. Now even his baby brother saw him as lacking. And Matt couldn't be bothered to argue, so he just shrugged. "I'm in no rush. Growing up is highly overrated."

Which was a stupid thing for him to say when he didn't really feel that way anymore. Maybe hadn't for a while. But it seemed like what his brothers would expect from him.

"I don't know about that. Life is short. I told Jenna I wanted to fill all the bedrooms with babies."

Matt scuffed his heel as he rolled that around. Dean had already said as much, but it was something else to hear it from Sean directly. "What did she say?"

One corner of his brother's mouth curved up in a satisfied smile. "That's between me and my wife."

Matt nodded. "Well…good for you. Jenna's great. You're lucky. And kids are great."

Had he just said great twice? He frowned. He meant it sincerely.

Beside him, Sean chuckled, then sighed. "I can't drink like this anymore."

"You aren't missing anything." Matt made a face.

No, it was him who was missing something. Not that anyone would ever notice.

He grabbed the last bottle of his Neustadt lager to take home with him. His brothers filled the truck with noise so he didn't have to participate, and by the time he was dropped off at his apartment, all he could think about was texting Natasha and saying goodnight.

That's not exactly what he typed, though.

Matt: I've been thinking.
Matt: Hi.
Matt: Are you still up?
Matt: I wanted to say goodnight again. Ignore the part about me thinking.

It took her a few minutes to respond.

Natasha: Hi. I'm at work, but it's dead. And thinking sounds dangerous.
Matt: Maybe.
Natasha: What are you doing?
Matt: Just got home. Drinking a bottle of that beer you recommended.
Natasha: Nice.
Matt: You're nice.

He was making a hash out of this. He should just say goodnight and then turn off his phone.

That's not what he did.

Matt: Hear me out.
Natasha: LOL, I'm listening.
Matt: I like you.

Natasha: I like you too.
Matt: See? That's a good first step.
Natasha: Or just a fun anecdote in the story of my life.
Matt: I've been thinking about that.
Natasha: You have?
Matt: Yeah.
Natasha: This is a weird conversation to text about.
Matt: Can I call you?

Instead, she called him. His screen lit up, and he greedily tapped to accept the call. "Hey."

"You sound drunk."

"I'm something."

"I kind of got that impression from the texts."

"I was thinking about you. And about other stuff."

"You said that."

"Right." He took a deep breath. "I don't want to be an anecdote."

"That was glib," she said softly. "I'm sorry. We had fun on Monday. It was nice to see you again."

"Really?"

"Yes, really."

"Good."

"We probably shouldn't—"

"—I'm looking forward to next week," he said at the same time, cutting her off.

She sighed. Then she laughed, and that was when he knew he had her. Maybe just a tiny bit of her, but it was the opening he needed.

"And Saturday," he said quickly. "I'm looking forward to any little slice of time I get with you." And now he needed to beat a hasty retreat before he lost any traction. "All night long,

I looked forward to texting you good night. The rest sort of spilled out, but that was what I really wanted to say."

"Okay," she whispered. "Good night."

She ended the call.

That was for the best.

He finished the beer, then turned on the TV. Netflix-and-complicated-thoughts-about-Natasha didn't have quite the same ring to it as Netflix and chill or even Netflix and his right hand, but as far as Wednesday nights went, it wasn't really that bad at all.

CHAPTER TEN

———————

ON FRIDAY, Dan had a vacation day to burn and volunteered to watch Emily, so Meredith and Natasha could see the house in Wiarton.

It was totally perfect.

Damn.

Natasha prowled around the main floor again, looking for any reason to hate it. She couldn't find any.

Sure, it needed a lot of work. A ridiculous amount of work. The two small studio apartments on the back of the house were complete gut jobs. The photos hadn't shown any of that, and their realtor—who Meredith had quickly become best friends with—was apologetic about the condition of the space.

Natasha didn't really care, because the main unit, where she and Emily might live, was in better shape—relatively speaking.

On the main floor, only the living room was habitable. The kitchen needed to be completely gutted. Same with the bathroom on the first level. But upstairs had an old but perfectly functional tub and toilet, so she could move right in and do the renovations herself.

"What do you like?" Meredith asked under her breath as they passed each other on the stairs.

Everything. "Not sure yet."

"Liar."

"Shut up." Natasha shook her head as she climbed the last few stairs. She couldn't really do this. It was—

She stopped in the front bedroom.

No, she wouldn't shut herself down like that. Just like she wanted Emily to grow up thinking she could do anything she wanted, she needed to live that for herself.

Because yes, actually, she *could* do this.

It would be hard.

It would be stressful.

But the old Natasha wouldn't have shied away from the challenge. She would have grabbed on with two greedy hands and made this house the best little inn Wiarton had ever seen.

You don't even know what the market is like here for this kind of thing.

It didn't matter. That was one thing she'd learned over the years. You didn't try to horn in on an already crowded part of the tourism market. You made your own space and then hustled hard to convince people it was too good to pass up.

You got people to go out of their way for you.

She'd lost sight of that, too. Hell yes. She could do this. She could do this like a freaking boss.

Maybe not this house, though.

But one just like it, and soon.

Apparently her sister didn't get the *maybe one just like it* memo, though, because when Natasha got back to the main floor, she found her sister saying the most outrageous thing to the realtor.

"We might make an offer," her sister said, ignoring the

wide-eyed *stop it* message Natasha was trying to send her. "But we'd have a long list of conditions."

"The owner isn't in a position to make changes to the property," their agent warned them.

Meredith beamed. "Excellent. Then they must be in a position to negotiate the price. Let's start at twenty percent below asking. What do you think?"

The agent laughed. "I think you're a force to be reckoned with."

"You have no idea," Natasha muttered. Oh. God. She lifted her voice and gave her sister a pointed look. "We aren't in a position to make an offer today. Sorry."

"Don't be sorry," the agent said. "You've got my card, and I've got your numbers. I'll let you know if I hear of any movement on this place."

"Call me," Meredith said, waving her hand at Tasha's protest. "I mean, call both of us. Of course."

The agent laughed. "Of course. And before you leave town, make sure you check out the new school. It's an easy walk from here. Everything in town is walkable, really."

He was right. They set out on foot, and after walking past the recently renovated school, Meredith steered them towards Tim Horton's.

"You need tea," she said.

"Tea is not a cure-all!"

Meredith just smiled.

"Fine. And get me a cookie, too."

As they waited for their order, Natasha fiddled with her phone, but her mind was racing too fast to concentrate.

She took a deep breath, then let it out slowly and scanned the coffee shop and then out the window. An ambulance pulled into the parking lot, and her heart rate sped up. But when the paramedics hopped out, neither of them were Matt.

Her relief felt a lot like disappointment, and she squirmed.

"This is a nice town," Meredith said once they'd found chairs.

"Yep."

"How do you feel about moving in this direction?" North. Closer to Pine Harbour. Meredith didn't need to spell out the rest of her question.

The little hospital here in Wiarton was where she'd been taken by Jake's girlfriend, now his wife, when Natasha had been in a car accident. Where he'd come running when she called him. Where she'd fought with her inner demons for hoping beyond hope that maybe he was her baby daddy.

This was a place she'd run away from four years ago.

Why had she fallen in love with a house here?

Why indeed.

"It's fine. That was all a long time ago." If she kept telling herself this, maybe she'd start to believe it. "Drink your tea."

The conversation shifted to the pros and cons of a smaller town. Meredith tsked about the school being combined elementary and secondary, but since Emily was only three, that hardly seemed like a driving decision-making factor.

"And really, if I want to buy a house, I need to look outside the bigger towns," she murmured, trying not to feel weird about what that meant.

She was officially a low-income single parent. That came with limitations that would affect her daughter. But the rundown house in a small town was only phase one in Natasha's Big Dream Plan. Maybe by the time it mattered what kind of school Emily went to, they'd live somewhere else.

"What are you thinking now?" Meredith asked.

"There's not enough parking." Natasha wriggled her nose as she looked at the single car driveway. "Which isn't a problem in the summer, because street parking is plentiful. But in the winter, when the snowbanks are sky-high and crazy wide..."

"Is that a deal breaker?"

She shook her head. "I don't know. Really, the long-term value in this property would be as a flip." Which made her stomach do exactly that because the risk was enormous. She pressed her hand to her belly. "Renting out those units to tourists would ease things significantly. At least in the summer."

Her head was already spinning with numbers—and they didn't all add up. It would take months to get the units rentable. She wasn't sure she had enough savings to put a down payment on the house and float the necessary renovations, too. That conclusion didn't help the stomach gymnastics at all.

"Come on, let's keep walking and see what you can offer big city folk who are looking for a country getaway."

They strolled up to the main drag, where they turned toward the centre of town. It took just a few minutes to pass the coffee shop, a grocery store, a gas station, all before hitting the main shopping strip—that was exactly one block long.

But it had everything a tourist might want. An outfitters, a dollar store, a bank, and a couple of restaurants. It even had a thrift store, which made her so happy because the one in Port Elgin had been a lifesaver over the last three years.

And then right when her guard was all the way down, she spotted Matt Foster, hopping out of a bright blue pickup truck in front of said bank. Damn it. She'd used up her Matt-antici-pation earlier on the red herring ambulance.

She stumbled to a stop and Meredith turned around. "What's wrong?"

Which clearly was a clarion call for a first responder, even across a street, because Matt stopped and looked across at them.

Tasha didn't move.

Neither did he.

Meredith took a slow, curious turn and followed Natasha's gaze, then twisted back, questions and amusement written all over her face. Tasha glared at her sister, who continued her streak for the day of totally ignoring important, pointed looks. Mer's eyebrows hit the sky and she pivoted sharply again. Matt grinned and waved before strolling slowly up the stairs of the bank.

"Stop looking at him," Tasha said, yanking on her sister's arm. "You're a married woman."

"And you are not. Who is that?"

"That's…Matt."

"*Matt?* The guy who was really nice to Emily? *Why didn't you mention he looked like that?*"

"It's complicated."

Meredith gasped. "He doesn't look *complicated*. He looks like a really good idea."

No kidding. "He's…"

"He's what?"

"Jake's brother." Natasha lowered her voice and let all the secrets spill out. "His name is Matt Foster, and I slept with his older brother, and then really wanted him to be Emily's dad. Okay? So it's complicated. Because he is also, in fact, really nice. Yeah."

Meredith stared at her. Then she took a deep breath. "Okay, you need time to wrap your head around how to make it work. I get that. That'll make for awkward family dinners, but I'm thinking he's worth it."

Tasha did not like how her sister said that. It was indecent. "Based on what, exactly?"

"Six-foot-three-inches of hold-you-against-the-wall sex."

"Shut. Up."

Meredith laughed. "Tell me you're not imagining that right now."

"I'm not speaking to you. Let's head back to the car."

"He looks like he could toss you over his shoulder and hike up a mountain." Meredith paused. "Where you'd then find a cabin to have monkey sex in."

"I think you and Dan need a weekend getaway without the kids. Someplace with walls and maybe a sex swing."

"We totally do," Mer sighed. "I miss sex."

Natasha gave her an alarmed look. "How long has it been?"

Her sister screwed up her face. "I don't know. Like…three weeks, maybe?"

"Oh, screw right off. It's been four years for me, so you can take your three weeks and shove them where the sun don't shine."

At least her sister had the good grace to blush at that.

Tasha sighed. "How about I take all three kids to a movie on Monday night?"

Meredith's face lit up. "That would be amazing."

And now she was a sex agent for her sister, with little chance of that being reciprocated any time in the near future. She was a martyr to the cause. "I really need the realtor to call right now and distract your dirty mind, thank you very much."

"Come on, I'm having so much fun. We're sister bonding."

"You were there when Emily was born. I almost broke your hand. I think we've bonded enough for life."

Meredith slung an arm around her shoulders. "I'm going to miss you so much when we move, you know that?"

Suddenly it was hard for Natasha to swallow. "Yeah." She

stopped her trundle across town and leaned into her big sister. "I'm going to miss you too, you pervert."

———

IT WAS dinnertime before they were back in Port Elgin. Meredith didn't bring up Matt again on the drive, although it was clear she wanted to. They picked up pizza on their way into town and rescued Tasha's brother-in-law from a three-kid pile-on by walking in the door with everyone's favourite.

"How did it go?" Dan asked, wrapping his arms around Meredith.

Tasha rocked back on her heels. "Eh. It went. I'll keep looking a little closer to home."

"Sorry it wasn't perfect." He clapped her on the shoulder.

Oh, but it is perfect. That's the problem. She wanted things she really shouldn't have. A perfect house she just couldn't quite afford. A perfect man she couldn't quite handle.

None of that mattered, though. She had Emily, who was clinging to her leg. She looked down at her daughter, more perfect than anything else. "Hello, baby."

Emily climbed up and held out her sweet little arms for a hug. "Miss you, Mommy."

"Always. Shall we cuddle while we eat pizza? Because Mommy needs to go to work soon."

"Okay." So simple. So sweet.

She soaked up the love, and by the time she needed to leave, Emily was ready to go and play with her cousins anyway. Tasha said a small prayer of thanks for the easy goodbye on a day when they hadn't spent much time together. Then she headed to work, laptop tucked into her bag just in case she had some downtime to search real estate listings.

But it was a busy night, and she didn't have a chance to

check her phone, let alone daydream about house stuff. By the time her first break rolled around, which she took in Malcolm's office, curled up with a cup of coffee, she couldn't even look at her notebook.

"Tired?" her boss asked her.

"Mmm." She closed her eyes. She liked working at Bailey's. If she found a babysitter who could take Emily overnight, maybe she could keep everything exactly as it was. She could rent an apartment and keep working here, and nothing had to change.

Her phone vibrated, then again a minute later.

Malcolm cleared his throat. "Are you going to check your messages?"

She sighed. "Shh, I'm sleeping."

"Emily wore you out today, huh?"

"No, my sister and I went on a bit of a road trip."

"Fun."

"Yeah." She opened her eyes and tugged her phone out of her pocket.

Her cheeks immediately heated up. Matt's name was on the screen.

She glanced up, but Malcolm had gone back to his ordering.

Hiding behind her mug of coffee, she clicked into the messages. There were two of them.

Matt: It was nice to see you today.
Matt: Even if it was from a distance.

She didn't know how to reply to that. She finally settled on the truth.

Natasha: Same. Hi.

Matt: Was that your sister?
Natasha: Yep.
Matt: You look alike.
Natasha: LOL thanks. We like to pretend we're twins,
but she's older and smarter.
Matt: You're pretty smart.

That shouldn't make her feel giddy. Of course, she shouldn't be texting with him, either.

Natasha: I need to get back to work. Busy night.
Matt: K. I'm working tonight, too.

She watched bubbles appear on her screen as he typed something else. But instead of a text, the next message was a photo: Matt, leaning against a concrete wall, the dark blue collar of his paramedic uniform at the bottom of the frame. He was smiling enough that the corners of his eyes crinkled.

It was an exceptionally good-looking selfie. Of course it was. Of course he had good selfie game.

Meanwhile, she was curled up in a whiny ball in her boss's messy office.

"I'm just going to step outside for some fresh air before I get back to work," she muttered, not that Malcolm cared about the excuse. He didn't even look up as she unkinked her limbs and stood up.

Except outside was dark now, so that wouldn't be good.

The washroom had terrible lighting, and also, a selfie in the bathroom was painfully cliched.

She turned in a slow circle in the hallway, irrational panic rising inside her.

She wanted to send a picture back, a quick, oh-yeah-this-is-how-I-totally-look-right-now-without-effort kind of selfie, but it had to be a good one.

Finally, she turned her camera on and held up her phone. She felt ridiculous all of a sudden, even though she took selfies all the time, but they were with a three-year-old.

For this, she needed to look hot.

Somehow this picture needed to say, *Please come and see me tomorrow night.*

It took three tries for her smile to look natural, another two to get one where her eyes were open just the right amount.

Fucking hell, flirting was complicated all of a sudden. When did that happen?

Fingers shaking, she hit send.

His reply was almost instantaneous.

Matt: You're beautiful.

What was she supposed to do with that?
Swoon, clearly.

Matt: I'll let you get back to work now. See you tomorrow night. I'll be the guy at the end of the bar practicing pick-up lines on the pretty bartender.

She couldn't wait. Any denial about how he made her feel was abandoned now.

The next question was, how could she juggle that with what she'd done in the past?

CHAPTER ELEVEN

THE WEEKEND BROUGHT A COLD SNAP, and the leaves started falling. Meredith and Dan took the kids outside to rake a big pile, and Natasha threw herself into cleaning the main floor so she could pretend she wasn't excited about seeing Matt that night.

She was just finishing the kitchen when David called.

"We'd like to have Emily visit next weekend for Thanksgiving," he said, ruining her good mood.

"There's so much to unpack about that statement," she said, closing her eyes. "Like, who is *we* and what do you mean by *visit*? That's just a week away, and we already have plans. Do you mean overnight?"

He'd never had Emily overnight. And it had been a year since he'd taken her for any one-on-one time at all.

"I would like to have Emily for part of the holiday weekend, is that better?"

"Changing the phrasing doesn't erase my questions about the first version of it." She took a deep breath. "I think it's an abrupt change to go from infrequent and limited contact to overnights. Is that something we can work up to?" She bit her tongue to keep from adding, *Like, maybe over a decade?*

He sighed in frustration. "The distance makes that a problem."

"Well…" She screwed up her face, hating what was about to come out of her mouth next. "How about you come here for Thanksgiving?"

"To your sister's house?"

"Yep." And they wouldn't talk about the fact that she was moving out. That was strictly on a need-to-know basis, and right now, David was up to something, which meant he definitely did not need to know. Yet.

"Could I bring someone?"

Ah, the mysterious other part of the aforementioned *we*. She pantomimed crushing something in the air—her phone, his neck, she wasn't sure which would be better—and made another face before replying as sweetly as she could, "Of course, bring a date. If there's someone who is going to be spending time with Emily, it would be great for us all to get to know each other."

It was a miracle she didn't gag on the kindness.

Another miracle was David ending the call after a gruff thanks.

She sighed and went outside. "Hey."

"What's up?" her sister asked.

"So…David is coming here for Thanksgiving. With a still-unnamed girlfriend. If it's okay with you, we've got an extra two for dinner."

"Of course."

From the other side of the leaf pile, Dan muttered something less charitable, which made Tasha laugh a little. "Well, it could be worse. He wanted to take Emily for the weekend."

"No!"

"Yes."

"Jackass."

"I know. I told him that was too much of an abrupt shift, and he accepted that. For now. But he won't be put off forever. At least this way, I'll know the girlfriend before she has a sleepover with my daughter." She grabbed another big armful of leaves and savagely shoved them into the bag. "Argh."

Emily ran over, and Dan scooped her up. "Want to go to the park?" He glanced at Tasha. "Let's leave your mommy and Aunt Mer to finish with the leaves, okay?"

"Okay." Emily spun around. "Nollie! We can go to the park!"

Tasha held it in until the kids were gone, then the hot, angry tears fell. Meredith dragged her inside, away from the leaves that didn't matter, and poured them each a glass of whiskey.

"No tea?" Tasha asked as she tossed back the drink.

"Sometimes tea, sometimes the hard stuff. It's an expert call."

"You called it right." She groaned. "Sometimes I hate him. And sometimes I don't care. I wish I didn't care more, and hated less, because hate feels suspiciously like caring, you know?"

"I know."

"I really don't care that he has a girlfriend." Much. She didn't care much. God, she was pathetic.

"But you care that someone else can get him to be invested in his kid when you couldn't."

"Ouch." Tasha scowled at her sister. "You wound me. Accurately, but still."

Meredith refilled their glasses. "Can I ask you a terribly personal question?"

"When have you ever held back before?"

She got a raspberry for that. "What's really going on with you and Matt Foster?"

"I don't know." She took a deep breath. "He's coming to the bar tonight."

Her sister's eyebrows hit the roof. "Yeah?"

She could feel a tentative smile pulling at the corners of her mouth. "Yeah. I warned him I'll be working, and he promised to be a good customer. I mean, I've warned him about all sorts of things, and he knows we can't really be more than friends, but..."

Meredith snorted. "We'll see how long that lasts."

"I don't want to rush into anything. Actually, I *can't* rush into anything."

"Regrets," her sister said, her voice softening. "That's what you were thinking about when you met him."

"What?"

"The night you told me about him—before I knew he looked like *that*, before I knew who he was. You said you met a nice guy, but you were really sad, too. You said you were trying not to dwell on regret."

"I guess so, yeah. Kind of a constant theme in my life." She scowled as she picked up her glass. "Obviously, David wasn't a mistake, regardless of how our relationship was broken, because he gave me Emily. But Jake was entirely avoidable and completely regrettable. He didn't want me when he slept with me. He was deep in grief, I was a warm body, and we both knew it. But then I made it awkward and uncomfortable, and now, four years later, I've met this awesome guy. Hot, kind, funny... but it's a non-starter because I banged his brother once and then clung for dear life when I found out I was pregnant with a deadbeat's kid."

"Hey, nothing wrong with a pregnant woman clinging to anyone she can find."

Natasha shook her head. "Nope. Lots wrong with that. That's how hopes get dashed."

They sat together in silence and finished their drinks, then headed back out to the leaf pile.

"It's possible that buying a house might be a bigger mistake than making a fool of myself over Jake," Tasha said in a falsely bright voice. "So there's that."

"Stop it, that's not true."

"You don't think it's a mistake to tie everything I have in real estate I probably won't be able to unload?"

Her sister laughed. "No."

"You sound so confident."

"I am. I have confidence in you and your Big Dream Plan."

"Why?" Her sister's steady belief was much stronger than her own.

Meredith leaned on her rake and gave Tasha a serious stare. "Because I don't think you make mistakes. I think you live life to the fullest and that sometimes means you bump into the jagged edges. And Jake was particularly pointy, maybe. Sharp enough to cut you."

"Deep enough to scar."

Mer shrugged. "Chicks dig scars."

Well, Tasha had loads. "I should try dating women, then."

That got her an eye roll. "I bet Matt digs scars. He looks like he lives life to the fullest too."

"You have no way of knowing that."

"I know how you look at him. That was some kind of thing you guys had across the street. I took one look at your face, and I knew you weren't thinking, *gee, I'd rather play it safe.*"

No. That wasn't what she really thought about Matt. He lit up all sorts of things inside her, made her feel alive in a way she'd thought was long buried. Alive in the most dangerous way. "I don't like my instincts. They can't be trusted."

"Well, I like them just fine. You have a wealth of experience and an amazing daughter. You are going to conquer the world. Why not have the company of a sexy man at the end of a victorious day?"

"Because it's not that simple."

"It's how you used to live your life."

"And look at what happened! I went from carefree and reckless to cowering in my sister's basement."

"Temporarily doing your sister a major childcare favour while you regrouped."

"Nice spin."

Meredith grinned. "Thanks."

Gripping the rake like a weapon, Tasha attacked the errant leaves again. "I don't want to ruin Emily's life."

"Whoa, where is that coming from?" Meredith got in front of her. "You aren't ruining anything. You found a way to raise your daughter on your own terms. You managed to save enough money for a down payment on a house. You did me a solid at the same time, and without even trying, you picked up a tall, dark, and sexy firefighter."

"He's a paramedic, not a firefighter."

"Shhh. In my fantasy, he's a firefighter."

"Stop having inappropriate thoughts about Matt!"

"Why are they inappropriate if you don't want anything to do with him?"

That was not a question she wanted to answer.

So she shoved her sister into the pile of leaves.

WHEN MATT ARRIVED at Bailey's Pub that night, he found Natasha dancing behind the bar. Her back was to him, and she was swivelling her hips to a sexy Latin dance song as she replaced bottles on the back wall.

The last time he'd come in here, she hadn't been happy to see him, and concern about that wariness had taken precedence. But now he could look all he wanted, and fully appreciate just how beautiful she was. Tall with willowy limbs and a curvy torso poured into a black t-shirt and dark blue denim. Her jeans rode low on her hips, and her shirt showed just a slice of pale skin above her heavy leather belt.

He wanted to dance with her, feel her body moving against his.

Who was he kidding? He wanted a lot more than dancing, but they were taking things slow—and that was good because there was something about Natasha that unlocked some nerves low in his belly. Good nerves, better than the anxiousness he'd been dealing with since Sean came home.

More like hungry anticipation, except he didn't know when or if he'd get a chance to strip her down and make her moan. And it was strange that he didn't really mind. Whatever this was that they were doing, it was on her terms, and he was one-hundred percent okay with that. He got to hold on and enjoy the ride.

Or the show, as it were.

She reached up high, stashing a bottle of whiskey on the top shelf, then turned around and caught sight of him.

"Don't let me stop you," he said as he leaned against the bar.

She rubbed the cloth she'd be swishing through the air on the counter and gave him a warm, pink-cheeked smile. "Hey, you."

"Nice to see you again."

She laughed under her breath. "Yeah."

He glanced around. "It's not too busy tonight."

"You came in at a good time. It'll get busier again." She inhaled quickly. "How was your day? Can I get you a drink?"

So she was nervous, too. He liked that he wasn't alone in that. He nodded. "That Neustadt lager was good. What other recommendations do you have?" She shifted sideways to the taps but kept her gaze on him.

"A craft IPA?"

"Sure." He grinned. "And my day was mostly spent sleeping."

"Right, you were working last night." She set his beer in front of him, then grabbed herself a glass of water with a couple of lemon wedges. Three of them. "And you were on days earlier in the week?"

They talked about his split schedule a bit—light, small-talk-y kind of questions from her, answers that kept the conversation going from him. It felt a bit awkward, not in a bad way, just tentative. He wanted to grab on to that nervousness and name it, reassure her that he felt it too.

But something held him back. She'd told him she wasn't sure about getting involved with him because of his brother. Better to show her he wasn't worried, show her that wasn't a big deal for him, that she could trust him to be focused on the here and now.

A couple of customers came in. She broke away to help them, and when she came back, she brought a menu. "I didn't ask you if you wanted anything to eat before."

He ordered a basket of fries, and then they were interrupted again. She'd been right—he'd come in during the quiet window before the rush, but they hadn't had much of a chance to talk before she was swamped again.

She poured beer and set up shots, working quickly and efficiently. A lot of the customers knew her, and he liked watching her interact with them. None of her nervousness with him was on display there. She was flirty and professional, recommending drinks with ease as she moved up and down the bar.

"How do you know what someone might want to drink?" he asked her when she brought him his fries.

She laughed. "I don't." She relaxed against the bar, keeping one eye on the room. "Want to know the secret?"

"Absolutely."

"It's a bit of a sleight-of-hand magic trick. Part presenting the most popular options, guessing based on demographics, some remembering what a customer liked in the past, and a dash of whatever I feel like mixing tonight."

"What's your favourite?"

"Whiskey," she answered immediately.

He raised an eyebrow. "That was a fast, sure answer."

She leaned in and lowered her voice. "Rye and scotch drinkers are the best tippers."

"Is that so?" He grinned. "And beer drinkers?"

She winked. "More varied."

That made him chuckle. "Then in that case…I'll take a rye."

He liked the way her face split into a wide, amused smile. "No! Order what you want."

"I want to be your favourite customer."

She laughed gently and reached across the bar to squeeze his hand, no more nerves on display. He was feeling pretty warm, pretty comfortable, too. She gave him one last pat before she stood up and stepped back. "Do you usually drink beer?"

It took everything in him not to catch her fingers as she pulled away. He wanted to hold on to her all night, but she had a job to do. "It's a good one to nurse when you're eventually going to drive home." And he wouldn't necessarily finish it, either. "If I'm not driving, I'll drink pretty much anything. I like to try different things."

"Okay, how do you like your rye?"

With a hefty mix of ginger ale. "I'm easy. How do you like it?"

"Depends on the bottle. Neat is the best way to truly taste it." He made a face and she winked. "It's not for everyone. Or me, really. I like it over ice."

"That's still badass."

Her lips parted and the tip of her tongue peeked out the side of her mouth. Her eyes sparkled as she glanced up at him. "Yep, guys usually think it is."

"Clever woman."

"Yep." She turned slowly and, after some careful consideration, pulled down a top-shelf bottle. She set it in front of him, then grabbed a tumbler and filled it with ice.

Chink, rattle, clink. Then a subtle crack as she poured the rye over the cold cubes.

Watching her pour him a drink had an unexpected erotic appeal.

Having her slide the glass across the bar and into his hand, her fingers brushing his? Even better.

"Thanks," he murmured as he lifted the glass to his lips.

He hated hard liquor straight up. With a sharp exhale, he tipped the glass and took a long, burning swallow of the fiery drink.

She grinned at him and in that moment, he loved rye with his entire being. "Badass," she murmured.

Indeed.

"I see how that gets you good tips," he admitted. And probably a lot of numbers, too. He frowned.

She searched his face. "What?"

He went for honesty because she valued that, and he knew the truth trumped any effort to cover his feelings up. "I was thinking that probably gets you a lot of numbers, too."

"It used to." She tipped her head to the side and gave him a teasing smile. "You get a lot of numbers, too, don't you?"

She had him pegged. "I used to."

That stretched between them as she sized him up. He wanted to tell her more, that it had been months, that the only number he wanted was hers, but his mission here tonight wasn't to push hard.

It wasn't to push at all.

It was to get to know her, on her terms.

And her terms were, apparently, playful. She winked at him. "Okay, show me yours."

He grinned. "My what?"

"Your move. In a bar. You know my whiskey secret. I want to know how you pick up women."

Ha. She wanted to compare notes? He nodded slowly. "The opposite works. Women love a guy who happily drinks a Bellini with them."

"Indeed they do. Good move." She gave him a careful look. "But that's not your A-game."

He took a sip of the rye on the rocks. It burned on the way down, warming his chest. "That's harder to describe. I'll have to show you."

"I'd like that." Someone called her name and she glanced toward the other end of the bar. "Excuse me."

He watched her move away, watched the curve of her hip and the long, denim-clad stretch of her legs. She poured a tray of drinks for the waitress, then grabbed herself another glass of water on the way back. When she stopped in front of him, she lifted it to her mouth, her eyes bright as she examined him over the edge.

"What are you thinking?" he asked. Nerves had definitely been replaced by a warm, steady hum inside him.

"You don't mind me thinking of you as a player?"

"No." He paused. "Maybe."

She laughed, deep and from her belly, her eyelashes brushing against the happy curve of her cheek. "Maybe?"

"It's not the word I'd use anymore."

"Okay." Her lips twisted and plumped together as she swallowed another laugh.

He poked his tongue into his cheek as he watched her. "What?"

"How about you?" he asked, feeling suddenly…something. Turned on, he realized. This was fun. "How would you characterize your dating life?"

She gave him an innocent look. "I was a total player, too."

His mouth dropped open as she held out her glass in a cheers.

NEVER IN A MILLION years did Tasha think she'd end up talking to Matt about her history with men, but this was fun in a lovely and curious way. She'd been so looking forward to seeing him, and then David's phone call knocked her off course.

Now she was back on track. Flirting for the first time in four years. It felt…right. "Did I surprise you?"

His eyebrows pulled together just a little, an almost frown, as if he was trying to figure her out like a puzzle. "Most people —myself included, I guess—don't describe themselves like that."

"I'm not most people."

"I know." He lifted his drink in a toast. "And I'm intrigued by you more and more."

"All that is behind me now. Not because I didn't like it—I did. God, to be young and twenty-three again." She took a deep breath. Remembering, and missing a little, but also putting an important pause before she underlined the next point. "But it's different now."

"Sure, I get that. My life has shifted recently, too. We both have a lot of stuff going on. You more than me."

"I doubt that. Don't you do army stuff on top of being a paramedic?"

He shrugged that off. "Ah, the army isn't really a job. It's a way of life for my family. It's nothing like you juggling work and a three-year-old all by yourself."

She knew he meant it to be praise, but ugh, that just reminded her Meredith and Dan would be moving soon and she'd really be on her own—and she wasn't sure how she'd manage.

"What did I say?" He reached across the bar and squeezed her hand gently. "Your expression just fell."

Laughing nervously, she grabbed for the bottle of rye. "Another drink?"

"I'm fine." He leaned back, his eyes sharp as he searched her face. "Is something wrong?"

She pulled her shoulders up and squared them. "I'm not really all on my own. My sister has been a huge help."

"The sister I saw the other day?"

"Yeah. And now she's moving across the province."

Matt exhaled roughly. "What does that mean for you?"

"It's just a shift. Emily and I need to find a new place to live —and that's a good thing. It's time. Actually, that's why we were in Wiarton. We were looking at a house that I can't really afford."

"Ah. Shit, sorry I dragged the conversation there."

Before she got a chance to respond, one of the waitresses hurried over and grabbed the cordless phone as she swore under her breath.

"What is it?" Natasha asked.

"Phil Dixon is vomiting in the men's room, and it sounds bad. I'm not dealing with that."

Crap. Phil had a tendency to get pissed off and lash out and get belligerent. Tasha reached out and took the handset. "Don't call the cops."

"He deserves to be in the drunk tank."

"If he's vomiting, he's probably done for the night. Let me see if I can convince him to head home in a cab." She stepped around the cutout in the bar, squeezing the waitress's arm. "Go and get Malcolm."

Matt fell into step as she headed toward the washrooms. "I can help."

She sighed. "My boss will handle this, it's fine."

Except the waitress returned as they stopped in front of the washrooms. Malcolm had apparently headed home for a bit.

Matt set his hand on the door and eased it open, just in time for them to hear more retching. Natasha tried not to react to the smell of puke, but it was hard. Not for Matt, though. He pasted on a smile and called out, "Hey, is everything okay in here?"

She followed him into the men's room. There weren't any other customers in there, which was good, because she wasn't leaving Matt alone with an angry drunk—not that Phil was in any shape to be a threat to anyone.

He was slumped in the stall, his head on the toilet seat.

Matt grabbed a thick wad of paper towels and gingerly stepped into the small space. "Okay, buddy, let's get you moved—" As soon as he said that, Phil groaned and vomited again—and his puke was pink and streaked with blood.

Great.

"Natasha, I need you to call 911 after all," Matt said without looking away from Phil. "He needs an ambulance, not the police. Tell them we have an intoxicated man vomiting blood, unable to walk." He said it calmly, but immediately Tasha's hands started to shake.

She dialled emergency services and recited all of that to the dispatcher who answered. "Yes, he's breathing. I don't know how long he's been sick." She gave the address and explained there was an off-duty paramedic with him right now.

Matt used the paper towel to clear some of the mess off the toilet seat, then he put his fingers to Phil's wrist. After a beat, he leaned in further and touched the man's neck instead. The quick, rough exhale Matt gave as he jerked his head toward Tasha made her heart race.

"Tell them his pulse is thready. Code 4."

Oh, God. She repeated that, and the cool voice in her ear reassured her an ambulance was on the way.

Matt didn't move from his awkward crouch, his fingers pressed to Phil's neck, until the heavy footsteps of uniformed paramedics were heard in the hallway.

"In here," she called out, then got the hell out of their way as Matt gave a quick report, using alien terms and numbers she didn't understand.

He helped move Phil out of the stall and onto a board, then up onto the gurney. When they were alone again in the putrid bathroom, he turned to the sink and washed his hands.

She handed him a paper towel, then pulled open the closet door that housed all the cleaning supplies.

"I can help," he said.

She shook her head. "I've got this. Just…maybe don't go far?"

He reached past her and grabbed a garbage bag. "I'm not going anywhere. Let's do this together."

"Leaping to the aid of others is annoyingly attractive," she said with a weak laugh.

He grinned. "I'm sorry we were interrupted, because I was having fun out there, but hey, if this impresses you, I'll take it."

Once she stopped shaking, she'd have a better response to that. Right now, all she could think about was Phil and the pink vomit. "Is he going to be okay?"

He hesitated before answering. "I hope so."

Her heart sank.

"Once you're in the ambulance, you've got a great chance. He's in good hands right now, don't worry."

She did, though, her heart staying all twisted up as they cleaned the bathroom and disinfected every surface. When Malcolm arrived, taking over the last of the bathroom cleaning duties, he had an update: Phil was at the hospital and the initial word was that he was stable.

Then he gave Matt a suspicious look and left them alone in the hallway.

"That's good news," Matt said quietly as Natasha dropped her head against his shoulder, sagging in relief.

"Very. Come on, we can wash up again in the ladies' room." She bumped the door open with her hip and made sure it was empty before ushering Matt inside.

After they'd scrubbed their hands and arms, she needed some fresh air. That's what she told herself as she led him out to the alley. It was chilly and dark, but there was something cleansing about the biting cold.

But she needed something else, too. And she didn't know quite how to ask for it.

"I have to get back to the bar," she whispered. "I feel like that's a standard refrain in our few interactions."

"You're a busy woman."

She gave him a rueful smile. "Yeah." She wrinkled her nose. "I've got a lot going on right now."

"That's okay. I just wanted to hang out with you tonight."

"I have to tell you, I was in a weird place when you arrived," she whispered. "And then you had to go and be all heroic and brave."

"Nah. I just held a guy's head while he puked and checked every thirty seconds to make sure he wasn't dead." He grinned as she looked up at him.

"That was really scary."

"I'm sorry."

"I'm glad you were here tonight."

"Yeah, me too."

She was staring at his mouth now, and from the way he let the silence pulse between them, maybe he knew what she wanted next.

"Hey," he said softly, his lips just so painfully perfect as he formed the word. "Don't let that be the reason you want to kiss me."

She looked back at his eyes. "It's not the reason I *want* to kiss you," she confessed. "But it might be the reason I actually do."

"As long as it's what you really want." He gave her a gentle grin as he brushed his fingertips against her neck. Her skin sizzled under his touch. "Speaking of pulses, yours is still elevated."

She swallowed hard. "Is that professional concern?"

"Very personal, actually." He pressed a little firmer, his voice slowing down, getting huskier as he looked at her. "But you can tell a lot from taking someone's vitals."

Kiss him already. But she couldn't, so she licked her lips and kept playing along. "What does my pulse tell you?"

"You're nervous."

"I am."

"And you're brave."

"It doesn't tell you that."

"Oh, but it does. It's steady. Fast, yes, but strong. That tells me you want this, even though it scares the shit out of you."

"How can you be so sure about all of this?"

"Hey, we both know how nice it is to just hold someone, right? If you need something right now, take it. No questions, no expectations."

How many times had she done that? Offered that to others? Sex used to be her favourite way to exercise frustration, celebrate achievements, or just have fun.

Now she was stressed about a simple kiss.

But Matt was offering, and she wasn't going to turn that down.

The space between them shrank, slowly and deliberately, until she pressed against him. His hand slowly settled on her hip and it felt even better than she'd imagined. Big, solid, strong.

He blinked twice as they looked at each other, his eyelashes brushing his cheeks. *You are the most beautiful man in the world,* she thought to herself, warmth flooding her chest. *I want—*

And then his mouth was on hers, his lips soft.

Yes. *This.* She wanted this, she wanted him, she wanted more.

He smiled against her mouth and gave it. His lips teased at hers, brushing and parting just enough to invite her to take the next step.

Her tongue slid out eagerly, just the tip, to trace the curve of his lower lip. *Please,* she said with her body. *Let me take this.*

She didn't need to take anything, though. He gave himself freely, deepening the kiss as they sank back against the wall together. His hands moved over her body, up her side, from her hip to her ribs, then got tangled in her hair again as he held her head.

Their tongues surged, tasting and teasing.

It was more than a first kiss should really be. More assuming, more demanding.

It should be their only kiss, but she wasn't that strong.

"Another," she murmured when he started to pull back.

"Sure." God, he was so agreeable. And talented. He'd promised her it would be good, and from the way she was quivering inside, he'd surpassed that high bar he'd set for himself.

When was the last time a kiss had affected her this much? Never.

She breathed his name. "Matt…"

He groaned as she fisted the front of his shirt. "Yeah. You feel so good."

Their legs slid together, his heavy thigh pressing between hers, and she pushed herself right into him, so there was no more space, no room for anything but this. Lips and tongues and hands and skin.

His touch felt so right, so deliciously, distractingly good. His hand curved against her bare waist, his thumb rubbing against the bottom of her rib cage, and she wanted his fingers higher.

It wasn't until he flexed his thigh and she felt it against her clit that she realized just how far they'd taken it past a simple kiss.

With a gasp, she pushed away from the wall, then turned her back to him. "I'm so sorry. God, that wasn't supposed to happen."

He dragged in a ragged breath. Loud in the quiet night.

She had to get back to work. How long had they been back there? Malcolm would come looking if he needed her.

She turned around again, and Matt was just looking at her. Gently, even. No judgement, no pressure, and it cracked her chest open. "Too fast?"

"Too much?" She shook her head. That shouldn't have come out like a question.

"I liked it," he said slowly.

"I liked it too. Stop looking at me like you want to do it again."

"I do want to do it again."

She groaned.

He stared at her for a long, pulsing stretch.

Crap, she shouldn't like this—like *him*—so much.

"There's nothing weak about grabbing what you want with both hands," he finally said. He hooked his thumbs through the belt loops on his jeans and gave her a soft, understanding look she didn't really deserve. "And you never need to apologize for grabbing me. Kissing me. Or even pushing me away. I want to be your friend, whatever that looks like."

"I'm sorry I'm so skittish."

"Something traumatic happened and you needed an outlet for a minute. I think that's a totally acceptable exception to the 'just friends' rule." He held out his hand and she took it, letting him lead her back to the entrance to the bar.

"You weren't wrong," she whispered just before they stepped inside. "It was really good."

He kissed her temple. "It's all good. The talking, the teasing, working together to save a life. And it's only going to get better."

CHAPTER TWELVE

MATT SHOWED up on Monday for cooking class, Three Ways to Make Chicken Soup Amazing for Cold Season!, and spent the whole time colouring with Emily. Natasha wondered if anyone could tell they'd made out Saturday night, or if the scorching memory was her deliciously dirty little secret.

Their secret, really, but Matt was on his best friends-only behaviour for the entire class. Then they had to skip the park because it was raining. Tasha felt weird inviting him back to her sister's place, but Matt didn't skip a beat. He said a quick goodbye to them in the bistro where that week's class had been held and promised to text soon.

He sent his first message before she got home.

Matt: You make Mondays so much fun.

She waited until Emily had disappeared into the living room, then she leaned back against the wall in the entranceway and let herself blush.

Natasha: And you elevate the entire cooking class

experience to something…really lovely. And distracting.
Matt: Did I distract you today?
Natasha: Uh, yeah. Hello, forearms.

He sent a picture of himself, parked in his truck, with his arm flexed in the foreground.

Matt: They say hi back.

She laughed. It should be too much, too fast, like the mistakes of her past. But it only felt good and right, and she found herself taking a quick selfie to send back.

Natasha: Have a safe drive home.
Matt: Will do. See you soon.

They spent the rest of the week exchanging text messages. Definitely flirty, definitely not just friends, but zero pressure.

Which was good, because the closer she got to Thanksgiving, the more worked up Natasha got about David's sudden desire to be a part of Emily's life.

She also had a house to find, but nothing had come close to the one in Wiarton. More than once she'd thought about ways she could stretch her budget to make it work, before convincing herself that the right house at the right price would eventually pop onto her radar and the waiting would pay off.

By the time Sunday night rolled around, she'd shifted her real estate browsing to the rental listings. It was good that Bailey's wasn't busy, what with everyone traveling and prepping for Thanksgiving, because she was in a weird mood.

She wasn't sure what she was trying to do by looking at apartments for rent. She didn't want that.

Her sister was right.

She should dream big. An inn had been her dream before Emily was born. It was time she embraced it again.

Putting away her phone, she pulled out the notebook she'd stashed under the bar. She still worried she was letting her impetuous heart make a terrible decision because it sounded exciting, but that worry didn't have any foundation, so she let the fear drift away as quickly as it puffed to life. The more she planned, the more lists she wrote, the more confident she got that this could actually work.

She just needed to find the right place.

It's in Wiarton, and still on the market.

When the door chimed, she shoved her notebook under the bar and straightened up with a welcoming smile on her face.

Speaking of terrible decisions, this one was wearing four-hundred-dollar jeans and a smooth smile.

"David," she said as she leaned back. "You're fifteen hours early, and in the wrong place."

Her ex shrugged. "We decided to drive up tonight instead of tomorrow morning."

"We?" She exaggerated her curious glance at the empty space on either side of him. "You seem very much alone at the moment."

"Don't be like that."

"Okay, I'll ask straight-up. Where's your girlfriend? If you're here, I might as well meet her before she meets Emily."

He just shrugged again, because he was an asshole like that, and she forced herself to take a deep breath. "Why are you here tonight? Do you want a drink?"

He shook his head. "She's waiting in the car."

She. Did he even hear himself? "That's…weird."

"We had a long drive and I knew this stop wouldn't take long."

"Gotcha. And do I get to know her name before tomorrow?"

A ruddy stain darkened his cheekbones. "Sable."

That's not a real name. Good lord, her conscience was catty. "Tell Sable I look forward to meeting her."

"I will." He hesitated again. "Do you think, since we're here early, we could take Emily for a few hours tomorrow? We'd stay close."

Her heart lurched in her chest, but then she nodded, knowing there was only one answer. "Uh…yes." Except, no no no no. Not before she met *Sable*. And also, Emily needed time to warm up to both of them.

It had been months since she'd seen David, although Natasha did her best to keep him present in her daughter's mind. She had a couple of pictures of him on her phone and Emily liked to look at them—asked often enough for Tasha to keep trying to build a bond where one clearly didn't exist.

And she'd try again tomorrow, because her daughter deserved a relationship with her father. "Or maybe, since we're eating early, you could have the time after dessert until bedtime?"

"Which is eight o'clock."

She nodded, relieved he remembered this time. "That's right."

"Thanks." He gave her a tight smile, then left.

Her hands shook as she wiped down the bar. It was only a few hours, and probably just to impress a woman. *Don't use my baby like that,* she wanted to scream. But for better or worse, Emily was his baby, too. Regardless of his reasons, as long as he was a responsible grown-up and didn't hurt her, Natasha couldn't say no to visitation.

Instead of reaching for her notebook again, she thought

about grabbing a bottle of rye. Then she thought better of both of those options and grabbed her phone.

Natasha: Happy early Thanksgiving.
Matt: Same to you.
Natasha: Are you working tomorrow?
Matt: No. Family dinner, but I can get out of it. There are a million of us, nobody will miss me.
Natasha: We're eating a late lunch. Mid-afternoon. And Emily's dad is taking her after that for the evening.
Matt: Where do you want me to meet you, and what time?

Just like that. She didn't even need to ask him. She sagged against the bar in relief.

Natasha: I hadn't thought that far ahead.
Matt: I've got a terrible idea.
Natasha: Don't say it. If you say it, I'll probably say yes.
Matt: In that case, how about I find a private place in the country for us to meet up?

Private. God, yes.

She squeezed her eyes shut and pressed her phone to her chest, barely able to contain the ridiculous glee rioting through her body.

It really was a terrible idea.

And she couldn't wait.

Natasha: Three-thirty. You pick the place and I'll be there.

The next day, David and Sable showed up right on time.

They brought wine, and Sable—who was exactly as young as Natasha expected—brought Emily a stuffed bear. But she seemed nice enough, and got right down at Em's level to say a quiet, tentative hello. David was awkward with Meredith and Dan, who barely managed to contain their disdain when it was only adults in the room.

By previous agreement, none of them told David about the upcoming move. She felt a flash of guilt about that, but it went away when he talked about working ninety-hour weeks now that he was trying to make partner. It wasn't her job to bend her life around his. And he'd opted out of hers as soon as she'd told him she was pregnant.

Mer outdid herself with the feast, and the kids were mercifully on their best behaviour—especially Emily, who could have acted out. But after her initial quietness, she was curious about Sable in a sweet way, and David's girlfriend answered every single question the three-year-old threw at her. When the topic of going to the park with her dad came up, Emily nodded enthusiastically, blissfully unaware of any tension Natasha felt.

It didn't make the ache in her chest go away at all, but it made it more manageable.

Still, Tasha let out a sigh of relief when they cleared the dessert plates from the table.

There was a bit more small talk, but it didn't take long for Sable to poke David, and David to clear his throat. "We should get going, then. We'll bring her back around eight?"

Natasha nodded. "Text me if you're going to be earlier than that, though, because I'm going out for a few hours."

She ignored the question in David's eyes. It was none of his business.

She knelt next to Emily so she could zip up her daughter's fall jacket. "You have a great time, okay?"

"Okay." Emily wrapped her arms around Tasha's neck and squeezed. "Love you, Mommy."

"Love you too, baby. So much." She followed them outside and carefully watched as David buckled their daughter into a brand-new carseat.

As soon as they were gone, she dashed downstairs. She checked her hair, fixed her makeup, and changed her top three times before putting on the same fitted flannel shirt she'd worn earlier.

Meredith gave her a knowing wink on the way out the door, and her cheeks heated up.

———

MATT WENT BACK and forth on whether or not to tell Dani and Jake he'd be skipping the big Foster-Minelli-Howard dinner at their place. He ended up going over there mid-day.

Dani hollered for him to let himself in when he knocked, and he found her in the kitchen, prepping the turkey to go in the oven.

"Where's my brother?" Matt asked as he snagged a carrot slice from the cutting board.

She waved her chef's knife at him. "What are you doing here so early?"

"Answering a question with a question, interesting tactic."

She rolled her eyes. "He's in the backyard with Calvin, trying to teach him how to play soccer."

"Seriously?" The baby was eleven months old.

"Dead serious. You should go and help. Or stay here and help. Do you want to roll dough for the apple pie?"

"Uh..." He stuck his tongue in his cheek. "Yeah, I'll help here first."

She gave him a curious look as she handed him the rolling

pin, then fetched a chilled ball of dough from the fridge. "What's going on?"

"I actually came by to say that I wouldn't be staying for dinner."

"Oh." Her eyebrows jogged north, then she shrugged. "Okay."

"You aren't interested in knowing why?"

She made a confused frown. "Do you want me to know why?"

"I don't know." He huffed out a breath as she laughed at him and pointed to the pie dish on the island. "Hey, I didn't come here to be mocked."

"Sure you did. Now make me an apple pie, kiddo."

"I'm older than you."

"Not in spirit. Roll. And tell me where you're going."

"To see a woman."

She groaned. "Matt, seriously? That couldn't wait until later? I thought it was a work thing. Something interesting."

"Hey!"

That got him a snort. "Your dating life isn't interesting in the least. It's predictable and dirty and not really something I want to spend any time thinking about."

"Whoa." His tone was sharper than he meant, and Dani heard it.

She held up her hand. "Sorry. That was too much."

"Little bit." He dragged in a deep breath. "This woman is different."

"Yeah?" She searched his face, then her expression softened into a smile. "Good. It's about time you meet someone who's good for you."

"There was nothing wrong with anyone else I dated."

"Dating is a generous term for what you usually do."

Now it was his turn to groan. "Fair point, but this

woman…" He thought of Natasha. Of Emily, and cooking classes, and last week at the bar. Of what he wanted to do today. "This really is different. I'm taking things slow. This will be the fourth time I've seen her, and I'm really looking forward to it."

Dani nodded. "That's great, Matt. Truly."

"She's a single mom."

His sister-in-law didn't blink. "Cool."

It was an opening to a bigger, messier conversation, but now that he was standing here, he realized it wasn't his opening to take. Not yet.

He focused on finishing the pie crust, then slid it over to her. "Tell my brother for me, okay?"

She frowned. "You sure you don't want to go out back?"

"Nah," he found himself saying. "I've gotta get going."

He headed back to his place and got ready, then texted Natasha instructions on where to meet him.

When she arrived at the rural community centre ten minutes outside town, he was sitting on the tailgate of his truck. He hopped down as she parked her Jeep, eager to see her and give her a hug. Her texts the night before had spurred him to find just the right place to escape from her worry for a bit. He'd reached out to a couple of Army guys who lived in the area and asked for their best tips for a private, hidden date spot anywhere near Port Elgin.

This was a total win. The weather had been good to him, too. It was a gorgeous afternoon, sunny and bright. They could spend hours exploring the wild apple orchard behind the centre, and they'd probably have it all to themselves.

Like him, Natasha was dressed for the outdoors. Jeans that hugged her thighs, hiking boots on her feet, and a warm looking flannel shirt wrapped around her curves.

But the best part was the smile she gave him as they met

beside her car. Like he was all she could see, all she wanted to see, and everything she needed right in this moment.

God damn, but that was a good feeling. "Hi," he said, grinning back at her. "I found us a place to explore."

"Amazing."

"We're all alone," he added.

"Even better." She laughed and stepped closer, reaching for him. The hug they shared was warm and long, getting tighter as they fit their bodies together. And if he hadn't felt her little exhale at the end, a little hint of frustration, he might have tried to kiss her, too.

But they had the whole afternoon for that.

———

NATASHA HADN'T REALIZED how much she'd needed that hug until Matt wrapped his arms around her and squeezed tight. It had been quite the day so far, and she'd had to keep so many feelings in close check in front of David and Sable.

Matt turned them toward his truck, where he grabbed a Thermos and a blanket from the bed before closing the tailgate. He gestured around the back of the building. "Apple theme. I brought hot cider, and there's a secret orchard here, apparently. A bit of a walk back."

A blanket.

An apple orchard.

Cider in a single Thermos.

Matt Foster was slick. And the way he grinned at her made her feel way too good inside.

"Does that sound good?"

She found herself close to giggling. Yes, yes it sounded amazing. She gave him a warm-cheeked smile. "Sure."

They fell into step together, walking side-by-side, hands

almost brushing. On the other side of the community centre stood an overgrown garden, and on the other side of that, the twisted branches of fruit trees called to them.

The orchard had a well-worn path through it, although the trees got wilder the further back they went. All were heavy with small fruit.

Matt reached up and snagged one and held it out. "Want to try?"

Tasha took it, well aware of the little sizzle of energy that jolted up her arm as their fingers touched. "I think it's probably too tart. Wild apples usually are."

He reached for the apple. "I'll eat it."

She jerked her hand back. "I didn't say I wouldn't eat it."

He stepped closer, a teasing smile lighting up his eyes. "Take a bite, then."

"I will." She brought the apple to her lips, then paused. "Although it might be better to save this to make crabapple jelly."

Laughing, Matt leaned in. "That particular one?"

"Yes," Natasha whispered, playing along. "So I can't eat it. Unfortunately. I was really looking forward to trying it."

"I can pick you another." His eyes sparkled in the sun. Dark brown with warm hazel flecks.

"I can pick my own," she murmured. Twisting, she pulled an apple from the trees and passed it to him. Another glancing touch, another jolt of awareness. "Here," she said. "Try it. It's tasty."

He put it to his mouth, then stopped. "You didn't try yours."

She grinned and started walking again. "Didn't I? Hmm."

Out of the corner of her eye, she watched him take a big bite, his cheeks puckering as the sourness hit his tongue. Laughter shook her body as he tried not to react further.

"Tasty indeed," he finally said, bumping his arm against hers.

She turned her hand around and laced their fingers together. Another baby step, like inviting him to spend the afternoon with her.

"So you know how to make crabapple jelly?"

"Sure." She knew how to find and follow and adjust recipes, anyway.

"What other secret talents do you have?"

She laughed. "Making jam isn't really a secret talent."

"It impresses the heck out of me."

"Hopefully you aren't the only one." It slipped out, but the idea of an inn or a bed and breakfast had been occupying so much of her spare thoughts recently, she wasn't surprised.

She felt him look at her curiously. "Yeah?"

"It's a thing I'm thinking about doing. I don't know."

"A cooking thing? You said you might like to teach those cooking classes."

"Did I say it like that?" She thought back over their conversations. So much had happened since they met. "Yeah, I guess that's part of it. But it seems out of reach right now."

"One thing at a time?"

"Yeah." She kicked at a fallen apple. "I need to figure out where Emily and I are going to go, what's actually do-able, before letting my dreams run wild."

"Smart to be practical, but dreams are hard to contain." He squeezed her hand.

She squeezed back. "True story."

"Can I ask what they would be if you let them run wild? Is that a good thing to talk about?"

"It's a great thing to talk about." She breathed in deeply and stopped in the middle of the orchard. "That one day I'd have an inn of my own, something boutiquey in the country.

Maybe partner with a local spa to offer services, and have amazing food, but also hands-on stuff, like the rotating cooking classes. I was really stunned when the community cooking classes schedule came out, because it was so closely aligned with what I'd imagined." She lifted one shoulder and gave him a small, rueful smile. "Good to experience it as a customer, I guess."

"But it's not what you really want."

She turned and looked at him. "No."

"An inn, eh?"

"Yeah."

"That sounds really cool."

She took a deep breath. "I hope so. I've been playing around with ways to tiptoe in that direction, get back into hospitality and tourism." She shrugged. "But again, I don't want to get stuck on the outside looking in."

"There's nothing wrong with wanting more."

She worried the inside of her cheek, suddenly nervous that she'd shared too much, showed him too much. "Shall we keep going?"

It wasn't the most subtle of conversation changes, but she wanted to know what he had planned for the blanket and the Thermos of cider.

They kept walking until they reached a clearing. Matt pointed to a soft, grassy spot. "We can sit over there." He stretched out the blanket, then held out the Thermos.

She took a sip of the hot, sweet cider. "God, I think it's been years since I've had cider. It's so good."

"Yeah?"

She groaned, and his eyes sparkled as he watched her.

"I like the sounds you make. Who knew cider was such a good move?"

She shook her head. "I don't believe for a second that you

haven't done this cozy-cuddle-in-an-orchard routine before. You're an irrepressible flirt."

"Nah. We're just talking about dreams and crabapple jelly and drinking some cider. We could start an orchard-visiting club." He reached his hand out. "Join me on this blanket and let's discuss the founding terms."

She laughed despite herself and slid her fingers over his. Warmth sizzled between them as she dropped to her knees, then sideways. "An orchard-visiting club?"

"You're right, that's too seasonally specific. We can broaden the scope. Maybe in the winter we could meet at a pub."

"That sounds suspiciously like a date." A perfect, no-pressure kind of date.

"Mmm. I'm sure it's just a coincidence." He grinned at her. "Although since you put cuddling on the table…"

She mock-gasped. "Did I do that?"

"I think you did."

"Huh. Interesting." She took another sip of cider, then handed it to him.

He drank a bit before leaning in to brush his lips against the tip of her nose. "How was your Thanksgiving?"

"Complicated."

"Do you want to talk about it?"

She didn't know. "Maybe. Maybe not."

He just smiled and handed her the Thermos again.

She sipped the cider and watched him watching her. When he smiled, she held it out to him. "Want more?"

The double meaning bounced in the air between them.

He smiled and reached for the Thermos. "Always."

Wasn't that the rub right there?

After he took a big drink, he put the lid back on the cider and set it aside. "I know we need—I need—to be careful here. This isn't a casual hook-up." He gave her a meaningful look.

They both knew what that was. That was their wheelhouse. Easy, fun, hot sex without any strings, and right now, she wanted that. With Matt. Under Matt. On top of Matt.

From the way he was looking at her, he wanted it too. The blanket practically promised something dirty.

And for the first time since her daughter was born, she found herself longing for the carefree lifestyle she'd given up. Just a little. Just for an afternoon.

A roll in the grass with a hot young paramedic.

"A part of me wishes that it were," she admitted, wanting to give him that honesty if she couldn't give him her body just yet.

"Yeah?"

"It would be easier."

"Only easier if it's possible. And since it's not…"

She smiled. "Right."

"So we're going to do this the old-fashioned way, and I'm going to come courting as often as it takes until you're ready to let me sneak into the parlour."

She laughed. "Courting. Is that even a thing?"

"It's the only option in front of us." His eyes glittered as he stretched out and propped his head on his hand.

"Returning to be friendly strangers would be another option," she whispered. It hurt to even say it.

He shrugged. "That might get awkward when we bump into each other and you blush."

"That won't happen."

"It already has, and from across the street. When we actually collide in a grocery store or at a garden centre, and my hands fall on your hips to keep you steady…"

Now she was thinking about his hands on her hips, and it was hard to not squirm. It was hard not to stretch out on the blanket and tug him on top of her.

As if he could read her thoughts, his gaze burned into hers. "No one will believe we're strangers."

Maybe she didn't have a choice in the matter. The universe clearly kept putting him in her path.

"Zero drama. That's my middle name," he said as he looked her in the eye. "I promise."

Instead of responding, she looked up at the sky. It was a gorgeous day. Cool breeze, warm sun. A few more weeks and it would be too cold to lie outside on a blanket.

"I know," she said, her voice sounding funny to her own ear. "You've been great."

"There's something here." He quietly tapped his chest, then reached for her, his fingertips grazing her shirt above her breasts. "Between us. I didn't see it coming, but now that I've found you, I don't want to shy away from whatever this is."

Now that I've found you.

It was hard to ignore the intensity in those words. And yet he was accepting her rules, making it clear he was willing to wait until she was there, too. It was everything she could possibly want.

"Full disclosure—I'm terrified by all the options here." She took a deep breath, trying to unscramble her thoughts and tame her rioting heart. "I don't want something casual. But dating for real? That would mean the whole meet-your-family thing at some point, which would include..."

"Jake, who you've already met." He gave her a faint smile, and his eyes stayed warm. "But honestly, I don't care. We can talk more about that if you want, but it's just...nothing to me. Is it a big deal to you?"

She sighed and pushed herself into the blanket, stretching her legs out as long as she could make them. "*It* isn't a big deal. Obviously, we both have histories with people. I've kissed a lot of frogs in my life, etcetera. But the last time I saw

Jake, and then the last time I spoke to him…both of those were not me at my finest hour." She screwed up her face. "Honestly, I'm embarrassed by how I acted then. But I refuse to be shamed at the same time. It's a fine balance to walk."

"Hey, I get that." He crawled his fingers across the blanket between them, tapping them against the fabric like a tiny, invading army. "Nobody will shame you. I personally guarantee it."

"Because you'll threaten to kick their asses if they do?"

He hesitated before giving her a charming grin. "Yes."

"Just like that, you're on my side?"

"Are there sides to this? I don't see it like that." He brought his fingers up to hover over her lips before she could protest again. He didn't cut her off, just stilled her words for a beat.

She smiled against his touch. "Maybe you would if you knew more about how messy it was."

He curled his hands, brushing his knuckles over her cheek. "Maybe you should tell me, then, so I can show you how much I really don't care about the details."

Her head swam as he slid closer, as his mouth found hers in an almost kiss.

"I want to know more about you," he said gruffly against her lips. "I want to know everything. Your dreams. Your fears. How to make crabapple jelly."

"Can I start with the jelly?"

He smiled and kissed the corner of her mouth.

She groaned and twisted her head so their lips brushed.

"I like that," he whispered.

"Me too." She closed her eyes and rolled onto her back. His hands stayed on her skin, and she sank into their warmth. "There was a time when I was foolish and stupid, and thought your brother might be the right guy for me. Stable, kind, reliable."

To her surprise, Matt laughed. Gently, very gently, but he was still laughing.

She pulled her head back and looked at him. "What?"

He smiled at her. "That's funny, because I swear, I have always known that about my brother, but I always thought it made him a buzzkill. I never in a million years thought it would be a reason to be jealous of him."

"Jealous?"

His smile didn't waver, telling her he wasn't really bothered by it. "I'm just not that kind of guy. Or I never have been in the past."

She shook her head. "Oh, I'm not looking for any kind of white picket fence anymore, trust me. But after everything that happened, I wasn't looking for any kind of guy. Then you walked into my life and declared you wanted to be my friend."

"Sorry for messing up that plan." His gaze grew serious. "Am I the first guy you've dated since Emily?"

"Yeah. Not that we're dating."

He didn't miss a beat. "Right. The first guy you've joined an orchard club with."

"The very first."

"And if we did keep meeting like this, for discussions of crabapple jelly and dreams, would you want it to be secret?"

God. That was the question, wasn't it?

Matt propped himself up on his arm and gazed down at her. "Can I be honest?"

Could she handle it? "Sure."

"I don't want to keep you a secret. If we're friends, if we're more than friends…whatever we end up as, I want to tell my brother at some point. I honestly thought about telling Jake about you this morning." Her eyes went wide, and he winced. "I went to their house to apologize for skipping Thanksgiving, and I ended up just talking to Dani instead."

"About me?"

"About a woman I'm interested in."

She couldn't breathe. "What did you tell her?"

"I told her this woman is different. That I'm different when I'm with her, and I really like her. I like her daughter, and I like spending time with her. I mean, I think I said all of that. I was pretty nervous the whole conversation, because I realized as I was telling her that little bit that I really needed to talk to you first."

"Oh."

"Yeah."

"I don't know what to say." That was the whole truth. She was speechless.

He caught her hand and twisted their fingers together. She stared at that point of connection, knowing he was looking at her face, and unable to meet his gaze.

"The thing is," she whispered, "I'm interested in you, too. But I don't know where this is going to end up. So until I do, I want it to stay between us. Not a secret, exactly. I don't ever want to be anyone's dirty little secret ever again. Just…"

"This is precious," he said, his voice rough. "I get it, Tasha. I'll protect you."

Him using her nickname for the first time pushed on something soft and achingly sweet inside her.

"You haven't called me that before," she whispered.

"I didn't know if you liked it."

"I do…" She leaned in, needing his warmth. Needing some reassurance, too. "It's actually my name, most of the time. It's what…men call me. Everyone, really, but Tasha is my flirty, fun identity, I guess. And something made me give you my whole name when we met."

"I like flirty and fun," he murmured. "Look at me."

She lifted her gaze to his face.

"I don't care who else called you that. I think of you as Natasha Kingsley, mother of Emily, age three-years-old and fan of all things pink. But when you're this close to me, and I can catch the faintest hint of the scent of your skin…I think of you differently. My brain short-circuits and all I can think is…" He leaned in, close enough for their lips to almost brush. "Tasha…I want to kiss you so much it hurts."

She tumbled back, and he followed, pressing against her as she stretched beneath him. Like their first kiss, this went from zero-to-sixty in a heartbeat. Parting her lips, she welcomed his questing tongue. He kissed her like a week had been too damn long, like he knew it would hurt to go another stretch of time before they could do this again.

He kissed her like her kisses mattered.

Like he needed her.

Her head spun with that thought. How could that be? Nobody needed her, except Emily.

He bit her lower lip and she arched beneath him.

"Can I touch you?" he asked, running his fingers over the bare skin at her waist.

She nodded and he slid his hand up her shirt, dragging goosebumps over her ribcage before covering her bra with his fingers. His hand was so big he cupped her entire breast, his fingertips grazing the bare skin on her chest.

And then he squeezed.

Oh, yes.

She tore another kiss from his mouth, then threw her head back. He dragged his lips down her throat and buried his face in her neck as he cupped and caressed her curves.

She wanted to touch him, too. It wasn't really warm

enough to take their shirts off, but they were both wearing buttoned-down shirts over tees.

"Take your shirt off," she whispered.

He didn't hesitate. Off it came, the blue Oxford fluttering to the blanket beside her. She ran her hands over the hair dusting his forearms, then up onto his flexing biceps.

He was built like a Roman god, all sculpted muscle, tensed and ready for action.

"Can I touch *you*?"

He grinned down at her. "Please do."

He had goosebumps on his arms now, probably more because of the cool autumn breeze than anything to do with her. She rubbed her hands back and forth over his skin, then pushed gently at his chest. "On your back, mister."

He stretched out and she leaned over him, brushing her lips against his. Whisper kisses, smiling kisses, and then when he lifted his head a bit, deeper kisses. The whole time she touched him, stroking her fingertips over his chest and then down his solid, tight midsection.

He shuddered when she finally tucked her hand under his shirt. His muscles clenched into tight ridges and she blindly explored him. Fur down the middle of his belly, a narrow line that made her thighs quiver.

She forced her hand up, not down, but it didn't take long for her fingertips to find their way back to that treasure trail. Matt groaned in her mouth when she touched his belt buckle.

His hand closed over hers, and she lifted her head.

It was hard to re-focus her eyes on his face. She was breathing hard, too. Giving him a wobbly smile, she tugged her hand back. "I guess that's, uh, not in the spirit of old-fashioned courting."

"Probably not," he rasped, rolling onto his side and

tugging her close again. "But we'll revise the terms of that as we go."

As we go. Three words had never sounded so good to her.

She gave him a happy, dorky smile and he caught her fingers and brought them to his mouth.

"That felt really good," he murmured. His eyes hooded as he looked at her, and slowly, he dropped their hands between their bodies. His knuckles rubbed against her stomach. Back and forth, back and forth, and slowly her shirt pulled up.

They both sucked in a breath when the backs of his fingers grazed her bare skin.

"And you feel good, too." He licked his lips. She was transfixed by the look on his face. Hot, bright, intense. "We're going to take this slow," he said. "But I'm going to get carried away, too, so we're going to both have to stop the other. Just know if I stop you, it's not because I don't want what you're doing."

He rocked his hips against her hand, and she felt the hard press of a thick erection.

"Right," she breathed. "Yeah."

"Come here," he urged, and she pressed against him. More kissing. The barest of touches. And just before they broke apart, his fingertips nudged their way under the waistband of her jeans.

She was dizzy and turned on like crazy when he laughed and rolled onto his back.

This time, she stretched out beside him and kept her hands to herself.

Never in her life had she been this horny. It felt really weird that they weren't going to do anything more about that.

And strangely, wonderfully good.

He carefully got to his feet, then hauled her up before kissing her one more time. "Do you want to pick some apples?"

No, she wanted to lie back down and let his hand get further down her pants this time. "Yeah, we should do that. That's exactly what we should do."

He bumped against her hip, sending flames of need shooting through her.

Two could play that game. She leaned over, taking her time gathering up the blanket and the Thermos.

His eyes were on her ass the whole time.

Slowly, she straightened up and handed him the blanket. "Okay. Let's go pick some fruit."

CHAPTER THIRTEEN

THE NEXT DAY and a half flew by in a blur of unexpected over-time work and exhausted sleep for Matt. When he could, he stole a minute or two to text Natasha, but by Wednesday morning, he was ready to see her again. When he finished his run, he texted her.

Matt: What are you and Emily doing today? I've got parade tonight in Wiarton, I could head down early, swing through Port Elgin.
Natasha: Because it's on the way.

He grinned. It wasn't. It was another forty-five minutes south, but an hour and a half round trip seemed like a perfectly reasonable price to pay to see two of his favorite happy faces.

Matt: It's a nice day for a drive.
Natasha: We're free all afternoon. Need to pick up my niece and nephew from school at half-past three.
Matt: Can I buy you coffee?

**Natasha: Sure. Or I have coffee…do you want to
come here?**

She texted him her address.

He stopped at the bakery before leaving town and picked
up a dozen assorted sweets, making sure there were two
cookies with bright pink icing on them for Emily.

It was too cold to drive with his window down as he
headed south. He wasn't ready for winter again. It would be a
long, cold slog until spring.

When he got to Port Elgin, he followed his GPS to the
address Natasha gave him to a sprawling ranch close to the
park. When he found it, both Natasha and Emily were out
front, dressed for the cold weather but otherwise undeterred
from enjoying the sunshine as Emily chased a hockey puck
around the driveway with a mini stick.

He parked on the street, then grabbed the box of cookies
and hopped out of his truck. Natasha watched him, her gaze
unwavering, as he waved and strode along the sidewalk. That
warm expression, that pleased smile—he'd been right. It was
worth every second of the drive.

Emily met him at the foot of the laneway. "Matt!"

"Miss Monkey," he said solemnly. "Nice stick."

She waved it in the air. "It's pink."

"Of course it is."

"What are those?" She pointed to the bakery box.

"Treats to have with coffee."

"I don't like coffee," she giggled.

"But you like treats," he countered, winking at her mom
who had come up behind her.

"I *love* treats," Emily said solemnly.

"Grab your puck," Natasha said, pointing to it at the top of the drive. "Then we can go inside and see what Matt has brought you."

They followed Emily as she sprinted to the house with a happy yell. Natasha kept pace with him, walking side-by-side, and even through their jackets, Matt was aware of her shoulder brushing against his arm. She was wearing the same boots she'd worn to the orchard, without a heel, which brought her forehead exactly to kissing height.

He liked how tall she was.

She glanced sideways at him. "Hey."

"Nice to see you."

"You keep saying that, I'm going to believe it."

"Good."

Inside was a bright, comfortable family room and eat-in kitchen combination, with a table almost as big as the one at Jake's house.

"Nice place," he said, setting the cookies on the table.

"I'll tell my sister," Natasha said with a laugh. "But we like it—and we'll miss it."

"Any progress on finding…" He glanced at Emily, who'd sank to her knees in front of a basket of stuffed animals.

Natasha shook her head and lowered her voice. "She doesn't know yet. One thing at a time."

"Sorry."

"It's fine. Coffee?"

He followed her into the kitchen space and stood mostly in the way, taking up a lot of room, but not wanting to be too far from her.

It was weird to just want so intently to share space with someone.

She made the coffee like a barista, in a French press with carefully measured grounds and boiling water. "How do you take it?"

"Milk and sugar."

"Steamed milk or cold?"

"Fancy options. I'll do steamed, I guess." That made him think about the dreams she had for the future. Fancy food and drink, quality service. "Where did your love of all things elegant come from?"

She lifted one shoulder as she poured milk into a small pot. "I'm not sure. I remember in high school reading about gourmet food and thinking, *That's cool. I want to know more about that.*"

"What's your favourite?"

"Food?" She cocked her head to one side, thinking on that. She didn't answer until she'd steamed the milk and poured it with the espresso into two mugs. "Anything French, really. I went to Paris during my first year of school, my only trip overseas, and it was just...I fell in love. More with the desserts than anything else, but the food, too. Cream sauces, perfect vegetables—butter makes everything amazing, of course."

"I've never been overseas," he blurted out. His brothers all had. He'd been too busy partying.

"Where would you go? If you wanted to, I mean?"

"Paris sounds good." He rubbed his jaw. "Australia sounds amazing. South Africa, Hong Kong. Sean ran a race in Peru once, and he raved about it. I always thought I'd have time to travel with him later on."

Natasha searched his face. "You can't now?"

Matt blinked at her. "Oh."

"Oh, what?"

"You don't know about..." He took a deep breath. He'd just assumed she knew, but there hadn't been that much media coverage—Sean being a total asshole and refusing interviews had helped with that. "Ah. My brother—Sean, the youngest—

was injured in Iraq earlier this year. He's fine. Now. The spring was a bit rocky."

Her mouth dropped open. "Matt…"

"He's really fine." He swallowed hard. "Shall we dig into the cookies?"

"Yeah…" She didn't move though. "That must have been upsetting."

He reached for her and pulled her into a hug. "Thank you," he murmured. "For being sweet."

She squeezed her arms around him. It took her a minute to pull away, and part of him knew he should give her a bit more information. But he didn't want to talk about the spring. He didn't want to talk about any of the things that were ugly and upsetting in his life, not when there were pink cookies on the table.

As soon as Emily saw them, she sat at the head, right in front of the bakery box. Natasha gave her an indulgent smile and went all the way around, sitting on the far side. Matt took the seat directly across from her and then helped Emily open the treats.

"Cookies!" she squealed. "Mommy, they're pink."

Natasha leaned in to take a look, and smiled. "And some of them are French," she said as she picked up a purple macaron. "Delicious."

He grinned. "A lucky coincidence, but let's pretend I knew you liked those."

"Where did these come from?"

"A bakery in Pine Harbour." He pushed through the awkward beat there. "I picked the ones for Emily, and asked for assorted others."

"The pink ones are for me?" The three-year-old beamed at him, and he gave her his full attention.

"Yep. Both of them, but you should save one for tomorrow."

"Okay."

Matt took a sip of his coffee and groaned in appreciation. "So good."

Emily nudged the box of treats towards him. "Cookie?"

He took a peanut butter one and devoured it in three big, nervous bites. "Thanks," he said after washing it down with more coffee.

Natasha watched him, and he looked right back. He had a million questions for her, and he didn't know where to start. Wasn't sure what was off-limits, if anything, and what might be awkward.

Emily had the conversation covered, though, at least as long as she had a cookie to eat. "Matt," she said slowly as she licked a sliver of pink icing off the edge of one flower petal. "Where do you live?"

"In an apartment in Pine Harbour."

"Apartment." She repeated it slowly.

"Part of a house."

"I live in part of a house."

"Hey, that's something we have in common."

"Okay."

Natasha smothered a giggle, and he remembered she'd said that was Emily's go-to response lately.

He fingered the bakery box, and Emily gave him a cross look. "Just one cookie."

"For you. You're little," he teased, but that was a mistake because the cross look intensified to a serious scowl. "Okay, I'll save one for tomorrow, too."

"Are you coming here tomorrow?"

A pang zapped through his chest. "I have to work tomorrow. But I'll see you next week at our cooking class," he promised.

She leaned in. "For colouring?"

"You bet."

Natasha made them each a second cup of coffee, and Emily went to play. He leaned across the table and rubbed his fingertips against the edge of her hand. It was the most intimate contact they could have today, and from the way her gaze softened, he knew she felt it as keenly as he did. "I'll see you next week, too."

Two promises he meant with all his heart.

But he'd need to break them, because at the end of the week it started snowing, and didn't stop. His overnight shift ran four hours overtime, well into Monday morning. The first bite of winter had caused two bad car accidents and he wound up stuck with a long off-load delay at the hospital.

Between the long shift, lack of sleep, and the crappy road conditions, he knew it wouldn't be safe to drive to Port Elgin for the cooking class. He swore under his breath and pulled out his phone.

Matt: My shift went into overtime and I haven't grabbed any sleep yet. Won't be able to make it today.

Natasha: No worries. We want you safe and rested.

Matt: I wanted to see you. Both of you.

Natasha: I understand, really. Miss you, though.

Matt: Same. Miss kissing you.

Natasha: We wouldn't have done that today.

Matt: True, but I'd have looked at your mouth and you'd have felt it like a real kiss.

Natasha: So cocky.

Matt: Tell me I'm lying.

Natasha: Not even a little bit. It would feel so good.

Matt: Now I miss you even more.
Natasha: I know. It's my superpower. Go get some
sleep and dream of kissing me.

He'd dream of more than that. And when he woke up, he'd be texting her again, because they needed to see each other sometime this week.

He needed to see her. Hold her.

Kiss her and breathe her in.

Tucking away his phone, he grabbed his bag and headed outside, the cold nip of early morning bracing. Another week and he'd need a heavier coat. Summer was gone and winter was fast approaching.

The brief, beautiful autumn hadn't been nearly long enough.

———

THINGS OFTEN HAPPENED IN THREES, Tasha believed. After her text messages with Matt, she got an email from David, asking in the most polite way—full credit to Sable, Tasha decided—if they could come up on the weekend for another visit with Emily.

She took a deep breath and replied in an equally polite way that yes, of course that would work, and Emily would be thrilled.

So when her phone rang at the end of cooking class, she knew before glancing at the screen that this was the third thing to discombobulate her world today.

She was not wrong.

The number on the screen was that of the real estate agent in Wiarton. Emily was helping move the chairs in the sunroom at the back of the restaurant, and Mrs. Cargill waved

Tasha toward the front doors. "Take the call, I'll keep an eye on her."

"Thanks," she murmured before tapping the green icon to accept the call. "Hello?"

He introduced himself again, then dove right into it. "The house you looked at has dropped in price. I thought you might like to know, in case that changes your budget at all. There may be other offers coming in because of the reduction."

Her heart skipped a beat. "How much of a drop?"

He told her and she fisted her hand in the air as she did a happy dance.

"Thanks for letting me know. I'll give it some thought." Her voice sounded so reasonable. Nothing like the riot of feeling in her chest.

She needed to talk to her sister.

Did she want to put in an offer? Could they still go in with a low-ball starting point if she was flexible on everything else? And why was her heart filled with excitement at what should be a terrifying, nauseating prospect?

She fired off a quick SOS text to Meredith, then went back to collect Emily from Mrs. Cargill's careful watch.

"Your friend didn't come today," the older woman said. "Matt."

"He had to work," Natasha said.

"I wanted to ask if he was related to Dean Foster." Mrs. Cargill's eyes twinkled. "Maybe try to wrangle myself an invitation to the wedding, whenever they get around to setting a date."

"Uh…" Natasha laughed, not following. "Pardon?"

"His brother, dear. He's engaged to Liana Hansen. The country music singer. But they seem to be one of those modern couples, in no rush to actually tie the knot."

"Oh." It was weird that other people knew more about

Matt's family than she did, but she'd blocked all things Foster out of her peripheral radar four years ago. Huh. "Well, I won't be going to the wedding either, so there you go. We can miss it together."

By the time they got home, Meredith was waiting for them. "I took a personal afternoon," she said. "Shall we do a girls' trip up to Wiarton just to look at it again?"

"Look at what?" Emily jumped up and down.

Natasha lifted her daughter up and kissed her cheek. It was too soon to tell her about moving, wasn't it? She might not understand the concept anyway. "A house Mommy and Auntie Mer saw on the internet. We can stop and get hot chocolate on the way, too. Sound like a plan?"

"Yay!"

They called the realtor from the car. He met them at the house for another walkthrough. Emily danced from room to room with wonder in her eyes, and didn't ask why they'd come to see an empty house.

Natasha tried hard not to cry. This was all happening too fast.

"Go for it," her sister whispered. "Step one in the Big Dream Plan. We can co-sign the mortgage if need to be."

So with Meredith squeezing her hand so hard it hurt, Natasha agreed to put in an offer with as few conditions as possible.

"I need a home inspection," she said, her voice shaking. "But everything else can be waived. Oh God, did I really just say that?"

The realtor chuckled. "Be sure."

"I'm sure." She nodded. "Let's do this."

"Do what, Mommy?" Emily launched herself into Natasha's arms.

There was a long to-do list before Tasha would feel right

answering that question. Maybe it was to protect her own heart more than Emily's, but she didn't want to get her daughter's hopes up too soon.

First she had a bunch of hurdles to clear with the bank, and who knew what the home inspection might find.

Then she needed to figure out what she was going to do for a job, and childcare.

Then she could tell Emily they were moving to a beautiful old house they would make all their own.

One thing at a time.

———

MATT SLEPT UNTIL DINNER TIME, then woke up, texted Tasha, and got himself ready for work.

She didn't reply until he was already at the station, getting ready for his shift.

Natasha: Sorry, kind of an insane day here. I bought a house.
Matt: Wow, congratulations! Where?

She sent back a big, grinning emoticon.

Natasha: That first one I saw in Wiarton.

He pumped his fist in the air.

Matt: That's fantastic!
Natasha: But stressful. They want to close immediately, so I have a lot of work to do in the next two weeks. Ahhh!
Matt: You'll get it done.

Natasha: *deep breaths*
Matt: Let me know how I can help.
Natasha: Thanks.

She didn't text again over the course of his shift, and when he crawled into bed the next morning, he fired off a quick message so she'd know he was thinking of her.

When he woke up mid-afternoon, she hadn't replied yet.

He had another shift that night, but that was it for the week. The next day, Wednesday, was a parade night, but he could probably escape the armouries at ten, which would get him to Bailey's by eleven at the latest.

At least one hour in Tasha's shift for him to sit at the end of her bar and tell her she was pretty.

Matt: Hey, how would you feel if I showed up at the bar tomorrow night? Late, after my parade night with the army.

It took her ages to respond, but when she did, she made him smile.

Natasha: How would I feel? All nervous and excited inside. Like, will we get a chance to make out in the alley? Is it too cold for that? Will you be wearing a coat big enough for me to climb inside? How can I make sure that it's dead so we can flirt over whiskey again?

As he was reading that, his dick getting a little thick at the idea of her wanting to make out again, another message popped up.

Natasha: Was that too much?

Matt: It's perfect. And I'll wear an extra big coat.
Natasha: The weird things I get excited about.
Matt: Speaking of excited, I can't wait to hear more
about this house of yours.

His phone rang.

"Is this a bad time?" she asked breathlessly.

"Not at all."

"I'm just driving to work, so I've only got five minutes, but this way I can talk on hands-free while I drive."

He needed to be at work in twenty minutes himself. He dropped onto his couch and put his feet up. "Sounds perfect. So—the house. I want to hear everything."

"I told my sister it's like step one in the Big Dream Plan. Part rental property, part bed and breakfast, it gives me some different options if one route doesn't work out." She described a big, turn of the century house that had been badly broken up into three units, none of them quite big enough to rent out to maximum profit at the moment. "But I bet there are hipsters in the city who would love to rent the studios for a weekend in the country, if it's packaged properly," she said with all the confidence in the world.

And he bet she was right.

"So it'll be a lot of renovation, which I'll have to do myself, and a crazy amount of hustle to get it done fast enough so I can be making money by the spring," she added, laughing. Less confident now, more shaky, but still excited. "Was it just last week that I was telling you about this as a wild dream type of thing?"

"You're going to run with this," he said. He could picture it, exactly as she'd described. "You know exactly what you want, and now you're going to make it happen. It's going to be incredible."

"I hope so. Okay, I'm at work, so I need to go. I'll...see you tomorrow night?"

"Absolutely."

She exhaled in his ear, a soft, warm rush of air that warmed him from the inside out. "I can't wait."

———

AFTER THE TEXTING the day before, Matt was pumped as he drove to Port Elgin late on Wednesday night. He liked whatever this was that he was doing with Natasha.

He liked her. A lot.

And when her face lit up as he walked into the bar, something solid and warm shifted inside him.

"You kicked everyone out just for me?" He gestured at the empty bar.

She pointed to the back corner. "One group still there."

"How late are you open tonight?"

"Another forty-five minutes." She smiled as she wiped down the bar. "And then I close up on my own tonight, because the kitchen's already shut tight."

Hot fucking damn. "Can I help stack chairs?"

"You sure can." She winked at him. "I offer the best dates. Vomiting customers, manual labour..."

"Bring it on." He shrugged out of his coat and sat at the bar. "You also make amazing lattes and mixed drinks, too."

She laughed. "What do you want tonight?"

"Just a Coke is fine."

She set a bowl of pretzels in front of him too, and he checked his messages while she headed to the back to check on her last customers.

Her hair was braided tonight, a loose plait that ran down her back, revealing more skin than he'd seen before. He found himself transfixed by the curve of her neck and the play of her muscles just above the neckline of her shirt.

Tonight, he wanted to kiss her there.

One day he would kiss her everywhere.

"They're just finishing up," she said when she came back.

"Cool. Busy night before this?"

"Not too bad. Which was good, because I have a million lists to make." She pulled out a notebook from a hidden shelf under the bar. "Planning, packing, budgeting…it's insane. Total whirlwind. And I had to give my notice here tonight, too, which was bittersweet, although Malcolm wants me to stay on until Meredith leaves and I lose my nighttime childcare. I'll work weekends, at least, and drive back and forth. It'll give me time to find something in Wiarton."

"You like bartending."

She nodded, looking around the space. "Yeah. I do. I think I can give myself three months to focus on the house and try and get the studio apartments ready for rental, but then I'll need to find a new job, and the reality of childcare costs mean that'll have to be a daytime position…so like, waitressing?" She made a face. "Which is way less fun. Reality. Blargh. What a buzzkill."

He laughed. "Well, here's hoping you find something not buzzkill-y, and the rental units really take off."

She lifted one shoulder in a small shrug. "I do need to stay realistic, too. This is a big opportunity, but it's also a big risk. That's something I would have been all over when I was younger, but now…"

You're still young, he wanted to tell her. Young, gorgeous, perfect. But he knew what she meant. She'd lived a lot in the last few years, and he knew a little about losing the innocence of youth in a hurry. She knew a lot more.

"Tell me more about young, adventurous Natasha."

She tossed her head back and groaned. "The player girl? She was wild."

He'd had a taste of that wild. He knew it was still inside her. "What did she want her future to look like?"

That got him an amused look in response. "Not quite this. But she didn't know how good it would feel to have a toddler's arms wrapped around her neck, either, so… the dream shifted a bit to accommodate that. For a long time, I didn't think the dream was in reach at all, and now I'm making crazy lists."

The party in the back corner approached the bar, and she broke away to settle up. Then she followed them to the door, holding it open until the last customer was through. After she swung it shut, she tossed the deadbolt with a happy sigh.

"So," she said, approaching him on his side of the bar. "We are all alone."

"Good." He pulled her into the open V of his legs and kissed her. As soon as their mouths connected, a rush of relief pulsed through him. Yeah, he'd missed this.

"What are we doing?" she whispered breathlessly after he'd had a thorough taste of her.

"Making out. Maybe I didn't give you a good enough demonstration."

She laughed. "Yes, please show me again."

He did. But he knew what she'd meant.

This was quickly becoming something regular. He was making time for her twice a week, easy, and half the time she was off-limits, physically. Not that he minded sharing his time with her with Emily.

He wanted to see them both, get to know them both.

He was tumbling hard for a woman he'd only kissed a few times.

She was right to ask what they were doing, and he was a coward for avoiding the conversation by kissing her instead.

"So…," he said slowly as he rubbed his hands over her body. "What are we doing? You are being a very good friend to me."

"In this time of need?" She said it lightly, because she had no idea.

She'd shared a lot about her life and her dreams. Her fears. Maybe it was time for him to do some sharing of his own.

"Yeah." He chased her mouth again, and she kissed him. Her hands traced the muscles in his neck, her touch light enough to make him shiver, and then she tangled her hands in his hair.

"What do you need?" She whispered the question against the corner of his mouth.

"You. As a friend." He didn't have many of those, and none anything like Tasha. She made him want to open up about all sorts of things he couldn't even name.

"Friend with benefits?"

He hadn't meant it like that, and if he had, it would be more *friend with responsibilities*, he wanted to say. But maybe his head was in a different place than hers. Maybe it was too soon to dive deep into the mess of his complicated feelings. "Yeah," he rasped. "I guess. No pressure."

She went still in his arms. "No pressure is good, but I don't like the idea of you having other friends with benefits, for the record."

He burned at the thought of another man getting under her skin. "Deal. I'm all yours, and only yours, for however long I can be of service."

"That's really important to me. David…was flexible with the truth—and fidelity. I promise you can't hurt me with the truth, but you can harm me with lies. Even lies of omission."

Her eyes glittered as she said the last sentence, and Matt wanted to pound her ex into the ground.

He held up his fist between them, his pinky finger extended. "I promise to be straight with you. You know I'm attracted to you, but while I really want to get you into bed, I can take my time with that. There's no-one else, and there won't be anyone else. I don't want to hurt you."

She let out a watery laugh. "For some really weird reason, I believe you."

"You can trust me. We're on the same page. I like having you in my arms, but I like coffee and cookies with Emily, too. I'm never going to be mistaken for Mr. Right, but I'm not playing here, either."

She stared at him in disbelief. "You're kidding, right? You're exactly Mr. Right, at least on the surface."

"I'm generally understood to be a shameless flirt and have historically been a bad bet for more than a single night, although I'm more than happy to break that tradition for you."

She gripped his hair and tugged gently, looking him right in the eye. "That's the weirdest pitch for dating someone I've ever heard. 'Give me a chance, I'm terrible.'"

"You should, and I am."

"I could match you, I'm sure. I'm *so* not the girl you bring home to impress your parents."

"Yeah, that's not a concern for me. I make my own decisions."

"Again with the right words."

"It's the truth. I know we've been over this ground before, but it can't be said enough. I really like you."

"I like you, too." She smiled. "So…something simple. No strings."

"Simple is my middle name."

"Did you recently have a name change?"

He tugged her and kissed her gently after laughing against her mouth. "Yes."

"I like it."

"Yeah? Good."

He embraced her again, a searing kiss this time that made him want to do inappropriate things to her. Setting his hands on her hips, he lifted her up and sat her on the edge of the bar. She spread her legs and made room for him.

"Is this okay?"

"He asks after doing it." She grinned. He liked how she bounced back to happy, no matter how worried or distracted she might get. "Yes, this is fine."

"Fine?" He squeezed her knees and tugged her right to the edge. If he stood on the ledge, she was at exactly the right height for him to rock his pelvis up against her body. "I can give you a lot more than fine."

"Yeah?" Her eyes blazed at him. "Show me."

He dragged his knuckles up her thighs, over the hard press of her muscles against her jeans, and onto her hips. Her eyelids drifted low and heavy as he squeezed there, his thumbs brushing her belly, then higher.

Under the t-shirt.

Bare skin.

Sure hands.

"Matt," she breathed.

"You're so beautiful." He cupped her breast, squeezing and toying with her flesh the way she'd liked in the orchard. "So sexy. I can't get enough of you."

"Soon I'll have a place all to myself."

"Don't think I haven't thought about that. I want you to sneak me in and out of your bedroom. Your living room. Hell, I'm happy to make out with you just inside the entranceway."

"I want to do a lot more than make out," she whispered, and he ground his cock against the apex of her thighs.

Hell yeah. "Tell me what you want."

"I want to feel your skin against mine." She ran her fingers over the tendons in his neck. "Feel your weight on top of me."

Jesus. Yes. "Soon, baby."

"I needed this tonight."

"Me too." He stole a kiss, sucking on her tongue, her lips, the corner of her mouth. Worth the drive for this kiss, this conversation, another step forward into the unknown territory of a complicated, adult relationship.

He kissed her hard enough to push away the remaining weirdness about her history, his track record, and any problems that might stand in their way.

Right now, there was only this. Two bodies and zero space in between.

"I want to get you off," he murmured, and she stiffened. "Not here, I know."

She tipped her head back and rocked her hips against him.

So tempting. He gave in and ground against her, showing her just how much he wanted every inch of her.

But when she pulled back, he dropped his head to her shoulder and counted to ten.

She dragged in a deep breath. "Soon. I'm moving in two weeks."

He nodded.

"Holy crap," she said breathlessly. "I'm moving in two weeks. It doesn't feel real."

"I can help. I'm pretty strong."

"Oh, I wasn't—" She cut herself off. "That wasn't why I said it."

He held her gaze. "Friends, remember? Friends help on moving day. That's a rule."

But it probably wasn't one she'd had a lot of benefit from over the years. He knew she wouldn't want to rely on him in any way, because she'd been burnt, over and over again—and at least once by his own flesh and blood.

"I want to help," he gently added. "Tell me where to be when, and what to bring."

CHAPTER FOURTEEN

EVEN BEFORE MOVING DAY ARRIVED, Matt made good on his word that he wanted to help. Two days later, he met Natasha and Emily for lunch when she had back-to-back appointments with the bank and the lawyer. It was an unseasonably warm day so he took Emily to the park so Tasha could focus.

After she finished her meetings, she went to find them at the park.

Emily was running around the climbers and Matt was chasing her, letting her stay just ahead of him as she giggled with glee. Just as he closed in to "catch" her, she leapt onto the first rung of the climber and screamed that she was safe.

Tasha slowed her approach and watched them repeat the game again, and this time, when Emily leapt onto the climber, she kept going up the vertical ladder, all the way to the top. Her mom instincts freaked out, but Matt was watching closely—and worrying, too, from the sounds of it.

"You're seriously going to give me a heart attack, Miss Monkey," he said as Emily laughed hysterically and scampered faster across the horizontal bars. Beneath the climber, he spotted her the entire way, and when she carefully wiggled between the bars and dropped into his arms, he gave her a tight squeeze before setting her down.

He squatted down to her level, and Natasha's heart just about exploded with happiness.

"That was a fun game," he said. "Thank you for teaching it to me."

"My Daddy taught me," she said, and Tasha's heart careened wildly in a different direction. "He's coming to visit tomorrow."

Maybe, Natasha thought. She pulled out her phone and took a picture of Emily climbing. She sent it to David.

Natasha: She's looking forward to your visit tomorrow.

She shoved her phone away and went to join them, trying hard not to worry when so much was going right for them all.

It took David ages to reply. Not until after they got home and Matt had headed back to Pine Harbour did he send a message back.

David: So are we.

Tasha exhaled roughly. Great, she thought. But it wasn't great that she'd worried for a while. Or at all. Or had three years of history behind her to justify that worry.

It occurred to her while she was at work that night that if Emily was talking to Matt freely about David, it would probably be true the other way around as well. And she'd made a point to her ex about knowing Sable's name before she spent time with Emily, so she should probably reciprocate the information sharing.

But what would she say about Matt? She had a friend Emily was getting to know?

Yes, that's exactly what you say.

Why was it so hard? She didn't know what she was balking at, but she didn't text David in the end.

She waited until they arrived the next day, and while Sable —still nice, still annoyingly young—was helping Emily into her coat and gloves, Natasha pointed outside. "Can I talk to you for a minute?"

David stepped onto the front porch with her, and she took a deep breath. "First of all, I'm really glad that you guys are coming up to see Emily."

He rubbed his hands together. "Good. I know this is a change in, uh, how we were doing things…"

"Yeah. We should talk about that sometime." Wow, her voice sounded so distant to her own ear. This was a man she'd once been intimate with on every level, thought she might even love, and now it was like she'd never truly known him at all.

And maybe she hadn't, because she couldn't read him right now. Hadn't been able to ever since he'd started expressing more of an interest in parenting.

She'd gotten so used to parenting entirely on her own, but now here he was, on her sister's porch, and she needed to open up to him.

It was terrifying.

"I'm moving," she blurted out. "Not far." Was forty-five minutes north not far? "To Wiarton. It's closer to your family cottage, actually."

"Oh." He frowned. "So…not closer to the city?"

"I have a limited budget." And big plans. Those two did not mesh anywhere near the city.

"I understand."

"Good."

"Was there anything else?"

"Emily might mention a guy. Matt. He's a friend of mine. We met in cooking class. He decorated cupcakes with Em."

David smirked, and that was the end of her goodwill toward him for the day. Sure, if he wanted to judge where she met a man, that was his prerogative, but she'd shared everything she needed to and now had a clear conscience.

"That's it," she said brightly. "Have a great day. Text me if you need anything, I'll just be packing."

———

WHEN ALL YOUR earthly possessions fit in eight boxes, plus two beds, three dressers, and a few garbage bags of precious pink toys, it didn't take long to get ready on moving day. Tasha was up at six and had her bed dismantled before seven, when Matt showed up.

He brought coffee and donuts, and barely had a chance to hand them over before Emily flew into his arms.

"Hi, Miss Monkey," he said, giving her a soft smile.

"Hi, Matt. I get a new bedroom today," she told him, pressing her hands on either side of his face to hold his attention.

"I know," he said. His eyes were bright with amusement. "Can I help you carry your bed into your new room?"

"I can't carry it. I'll be the boss, though."

"That sounds fair." He cleared his throat. "Hey, can you introduce me to your aunt and uncle?"

Emily twisted in his arms and pointed to Meredith and Dan. "This is Auntie Mer and this is Uncle Dan. They're moving far away."

Tasha groaned and pressed her hand to her chest. "The ruthless honesty of children, eh?"

Meredith brushed a knuckle beneath her eye.

"Sorry," Matt said, holding out his arm and giving Mer his most charming smile. "But I brought you donuts."

She laughed and took the box from him. "Apology accepted. Nice to meet you for real this time."

Matt winked at her and then offered his hand to Dan. "I may have flirted with your wife from a distance a while back. It was all a ruse to impress Natasha, I promise."

Dan chuckled. "I appreciate the honesty. And the use of your truck today."

"Wouldn't miss moving day for the world." Matt finally turned his attention to Tasha, and even though they were surrounded by people, the room felt suddenly hot and the way he was looking at her purely indecent.

"I'll be sure to order beer and pizza later," she said softly. "Or something."

His eyebrows twitched just enough to make it clear he'd be up for *something*.

"Donuts, eh?" She spun on her heel and opened the box Meredith had set on the table. "Yum."

Everyone else gathered around, and once she'd snagged an apple fritter, she moved out of the way.

Matt followed. His hand landed on her hip briefly, just long enough to give a reassuring squeeze, then he crossed his arms over his chest. "Okay, so what's the plan today?"

She swiped a bit of icing off her apple fritter. "Well, first we put all my stuff in as many vehicles as it takes…and then we unload it all into a big, old, empty house that I'm going to start demolishing tomorrow."

He choked on a laugh. "Excellent."

"I'm terrified," she whispered. "I know you already know that, but…"

"Hey, you aren't alone today." He lowered his voice. "And you don't need to be alone tonight, either."

Her cheeks heated up and she shoved a bite of donut into her mouth to keep from babbling about how much she liked that offer. Liked it, couldn't take him up on it, and was already thinking about when she could.

They loaded up Matt's truck, and her Jeep. Dan and Meredith ended up only having to put Emily's toys in their van, which left lots of room for the kids, Emily riding along with her cousins so she could guard her toys. And off they went in a caravan of three vehicles.

Once they were on the highway, her phone rang, and she told the hands-free device to answer the call.

"Now that we're all alone," Matt said over his own speakerphone. "I thought I'd be more specific about my earlier offer."

Tasha glanced in her rearview mirror. She could just barely make him out behind the sun-glare on his windscreen. "I liked the idea of you hanging around after we finish unloading. I don't have that much stuff." She smiled. "But my sister and brother-in-law know that. They'll probably leave after lunch."

"They have their own packing to do, right?" Matt was so smooth, so slick, he followed the narrative she needed.

"Yeah. It would be a great help if we could send them off pretty quickly."

"I can definitely help with that." He made a warm, welcoming sound, like a cross between a sigh and hum. "But seriously, I'll stay all night if you want. On the couch."

"I don't have a couch."

"Right. I knew that. Didn't load one into the back of my truck."

Her pulse jumped a gear. She had a big bed. And once upon a time, she'd have happily pulled anyone into it.

A part of her really missed that easy sexuality. She wanted to get back there, but she just wasn't quite there yet. "Company into the evening is good," she whispered. "But I think tonight, overnight, it should just be me and Emily." For the first time since Emily had been born, it would just be the two of them in their very own house. It was a big milestone. She wanted to forever remember this night, and tomorrow morning, as her and Emily's. Just the two of them. There was something sacred and special about that.

And her first night with Matt was worthy of its own time and space, too. They'd have that soon enough.

"Then I'll stay and help unpack as long as you need me to, and then we can have a celebratory nightcap before a good night kiss."

She sighed happily. "That sounds amazing."

"Damn straight. Now drive safe. I'm right behind you."

When they arrived, the realtor was waiting out front to give her the keys. She parked in the drive, right close to the house so someone could pull in behind her, then hopped out.

Matt parked on the street, leaving the space in the drive for Meredith's minivan. She waved to the realtor, then went to the van to get Emily first.

"Ready?" she asked her daughter.

Emily craned her head to the side and gasped. "Oh, *this* house! Mommy, I love it!"

Yeah, they were both ready for this.

Each step she took up the walk toward the front door felt huge, momentous—and filled with emotion. By the time she was standing in front of the realtor, her eyes were wet and she tried to make an excuse.

"Congratulations," he said. "And it's okay to cry."

"I don't want to," she whispered. "I'm happy."

"That's a legitimate reason to cry, I'm afraid to break it to you." He handed over the keys. "Here you go. Welcome home."

Her hands shook as she unlocked the door. Emily helped her push it open, then they stepped together into their first house as a family of two.

Behind her, everyone else filed in. Heavy footsteps, little footsteps, and a flurry of excited noises.

She wasn't really absorbing any of it.

The house was empty, exactly as it had been when she'd looked at it before. But today, even though it was cold and grey out, a typically gross early November day, it glowed for her.

All she could see was the potential.

And when she turned around, she saw the same enthusiasm for it reflected in the faces of Meredith and Dan. She held her breath as she glanced past them to Matt, who was standing in the doorway.

His eyes were cast upward, checking out the ceiling. But when her gaze settled on him, he immediately gave her his attention.

And he beamed.

"Wow," he said. "It's even better than you described. What amazing bones."

"Exactly." Her voice came out all whispery and weak, and she tried again. "I mean, right? I'm…" She shook her head. Damn it. She was totally going to cry, and this was *not* a crying situation. "I'm so glad everyone likes it."

She whirled around and walked briskly through the front room to the kitchen in the back corner. Definitely the ugliest room in the house, she was looking forward to taking a sledgehammer to the ancient cupboards and the awful bulkheads that ruined the lines of the twelve-foot ceilings.

"Hey."

Natasha waved her hand at the sound of her sister's voice. "Hi."

"Overwhelming, eh?"

"Little bit."

"The guys took the kids into the backyard." Meredith came closer, and when Natasha turned around, she saw her sister was holding a gift bag. "Here. Happy New Home Day."

"What is this?" And how had she missed her sister carrying it inside?

"A little housewarming present."

Natasha took the bag and pulled out the tissue paper on top. Inside were three things. A brand-new kettle, shiny and red, a box of instant oatmeal, and a tin of English Breakfast tea.

"Oh, Mer…"

"There are going to be times when you need tea," her sister said. "Like now, for example."

"I need to unpack the mugs first."

"Yeah."

She set down the bag and gave her sister a tight squeeze. "I'm going to miss you."

"Me too. But you're also going to have an amazing adventure here. And whenever you need me, you pick up the phone and we'll make tea together from a distance."

The side door slammed open, and Emily came sprinting in. "Mommy, can I have a swing?"

"Uh…yes. Of course. We'll keep our eyes out for a good deal on one, okay?"

Matt appeared in the door behind her. "That's my fault. I said to Dan that the big oak tree would be perfect for a tire swing, and…"

"Little ears." She nodded and smiled. "Story of my life."

She made a mental note to search online for a used tire.

"Should we start bringing stuff in?" Meredith asked.

"First I want to do a quick scrub down of Emily's room."

"I can help with that," her sister said. "I'll grab the box of cleaning supplies from your car."

Emily raced away right behind her aunt, heading upstairs to see her room.

Which left Tasha alone with Matt, who took a quick look around before he pulled her close.

"You haven't had enough kisses today," he whispered. He tugged on her braids, tipping her face up so he could lean in and remedy that.

She gave herself to him willingly. They didn't have a lot of time and he wasn't wrong—it was the worst kind of torture to be this close and not be able to touch him, taste him, hold him.

"More kisses tonight," he promised.

Yes, yes, yes.

That was exactly what she needed. Matt was exactly what she needed.

———

ONCE EMILY'S room was scrubbed down, Matt carried in the pieces of her bed. It was pink, of course, and impossibly small.

"Is it just me, or is her bed half the size of a regular bed?" he asked Natasha after they set it up.

She grinned. "It's called a toddler bed. That's her crib mattress."

"Right. I could have figured that out myself."

"You're cute when you don't know things, though. You get this little frown line between your eyes, like you're really surprised that something is outside your grasp."

He could feel that little frown line deepening. "I do not."

She nodded her head happily. "You do. And it's cute."

Before he could respond, Emily's cousins came parading in

with the bags of toys, with the three-year-old bossily telling them to wait for her to open them.

"Guys, we're not ready for those just yet," Natasha said, but it was too late. Dolls and stuffed animals exploded in all directions.

She waved her hand at the bare mini-mattress. "Fine, let's let them play while we get the other furniture up here. And if you want, I'll give you the rest of the tour."

The house was big, but it was divided into three separate apartments. The front half of the house, both stories, would be their personal space. Two bedrooms upstairs, one already claimed by Emily, the other for Natasha. In between was a bathroom with a big clawfoot tub that had seen better days.

From the rear of the house there were separate entrances to two studio apartments that both needed a lot of work to be functional again. He stole another kiss in the second one.

"We should get back," she whispered against his mouth.

"Definitely."

They kissed again instead, and by the time they got to his truck to grab her bed frame, her cheeks were pink and her lips were swollen.

Meredith gave him an approving look when they passed each other on the walk.

After they set up her bed in the cozy front bedroom, Natasha left him and Dan to carry up the dressers while she ordered pizza for lunch.

The day flew by in unpacking and scrubbing and cleaning, and by the time the afternoon light was fading, Meredith's family was piling into their van. Matt headed back inside to give Emily and Natasha a few minutes to say goodbye in private.

There wasn't really enough pizza left over for dinner, so

when they came back inside, he offered to take them to dinner. "My treat," he said, "to celebrate a really big day."

"It should be my treat," Natasha insisted. "By way of thanks."

"Sure. But I've been angling for a dinner date with the two of you for months now."

"We had lunch last week," she protested. "And it hasn't been *months*."

Seven long weeks. "Feels like it," he said gently. "From the minute I met you—and you," he added, looking at Emily, who'd twisted herself around her mother's legs, "I knew I wanted to spend a lot of time with you both."

"With me?" Emily beamed at him.

"Yep." It hit him squarely in the chest just how seriously he meant that. "Now, how about dinner?"

They went in Natasha's Jeep, because Emily's car seat was already installed in the back. He rode shotgun and gave directions to the pub the Army guys often hit up after training on Wednesday nights.

It had been a while, and he didn't recognize anyone there, which was good. They grabbed a table, Emily claiming the chair between her mom and Matt.

They ordered burgers all around, with Emily's coming in the form of two mini sliders. Natasha gave her a small dollop of ketchup on the side of her French fries and made her promise to actually eat her fries, and not just the sauce.

Emily carefully triple-dipped her fries, then took a bite every time her mom gave her a look. "I'm eating them *slowly*," she said.

Natasha made a disbelieving noise.

"I bet I can eat a fry even slower than you," Matt said, picking one up off his plate. No ketchup for him, just salt and vinegar. He took the tiniest nibble.

Emily giggled and matched him.

He did it again, and she repeated it, all the way down the fry.

"Fine, you got me. You can eat a fry just as slow as me." He exaggerated a sigh. "But can you eat one *faster* than me? Should we race?"

"Okay." Emily picked one up. "One-two-three-go."

"That's cheating," Matt protested, gobbling his fry down.

She giggled and grabbed another one. "One-two-three—"

"Go!"

They kept that up until both of their plates were clean and Emily was curled up in her mom's lap.

Matt leaned back in his chair. "So, I met your sister and survived to tell the tale."

"Dan's the one you need to watch out for." Tasha glanced at Emily, and Matt guessed at the unspoken next sentence. Her brother-in-law didn't like the ex.

Good. Matt imagined there was a lot not to like about the guy. Although since the ex was Emily's dad, that probably wasn't the healthiest attitude.

Would Matt get a chance to meet him? How would that go?

Not fucking well. He should work on that attitude more just in case. He grinned. "I like Dan. And your sister. They seem genuinely nice."

"They really are." She lowered her voice. "We weren't that close in the past—they married young, and have a delightfully square life, so they had lots of concern about my lifestyle that I read as judgement. But as soon as I found out I was pregnant, they didn't hesitate to take me in. Not just that, they were happy to have me." She ran her hand over Emily's curls. "Have both of us. They're so close to Emily now. It's going to be a hard transition. Isn't it, baby?"

Emily gave her a sleepy smile and yawned.

By the time they got back to the house, Emily's eyes were drifting shut. "I want a story," she protested as Natasha handed Matt the keys so he could unlock the front door.

"Sure thing."

The stairs were immediately inside, so Matt got out of the way and Natasha started to climb.

"I want Matt, too," Emily whispered.

His heart squeezed. Natasha glanced at him, and he gestured that he would follow.

She hit the light at the top of the stairs and quietly stepped into Emily's room. They'd transformed it this afternoon. The rest of the house was empty, echo-y, and waiting for Natasha to pour her personality into the rooms, but this space was cozy and perfect.

Dark curtains covered the unfamiliar window. A low, wide dresser was covered in toys, a rug warmed up the floor, and her wee toddler bed had pink princess bedding ready for her to curl up in.

Even though she was nearly asleep, her eyes still popped open when her head touched the pillow. "Story," was the stern reminder.

"Please," her mother said before picking a short book off the shelf.

"Please," Emily whispered, her eyes drifting shut again.

By the time the book was done, she was out like a light.

Matt led the way back downstairs.

"It's weird how empty this place is," Natasha said once they were on the main level. "Do you want a drink?"

He grinned. "Sure."

"As you know, we're working on limited resources here," she said as he followed her into the kitchen. She opened the only occupied cupboard that held her handful of dishes, plus some paper plates and plastic cutlery. And behind those, a bag of…pink cups.

"Emily picked these out?" He closed the gap between them and grabbed the bag.

She twisted in his arms. "Yes."

"Cute." But he wasn't looking at the cups anymore. He was looking at her. "Really cute."

"You're distracting me from getting us drinks."

"Right. What did you want?"

She lifted her chin, her eyes bright, and her lips parted. *You.* She didn't actually say it, but she didn't need to.

They came together. Neither of them made the first move, but suddenly they were kissing. Soft, endless tastes that made his head spin and his balls pull tight. He braced his hand against the cupboards and arched over her. Deeper, hotter, until they were both panting.

He'd made some crazy promises to take things slow. Then he'd blown that out of the water two weeks ago, although he'd been good since.

"You are irresistible," he finally said, tugging on one of her braids.

Her eyes flashed dark and glittery as she smiled up at him. "A girl likes to hear that."

"Should we have that drink?"

She nodded. And she didn't move.

He chuckled and kissed her cheek before reaching into the cupboard again and grabbing two glasses.

"I have beer," she said. "Or rye."

He made a face.

"I have ginger ale too, if you want a mix."

"I drank it on ice when you served it to me last time."

She winked. "And you hated every sip. A bartender knows."

He groaned. "Damn it. I was trying to impress you."

"You impress me by having French fry races with my daughter. I don't care what you drink."

"Then a beer sounds great."

She grabbed him a bottle from the ancient fridge, and he twisted off the cap while she poured herself a shot of rye, neat.

He held out the bottle. "To your first night in your new home."

She smiled and clinked her glass against the bottleneck.

They drank together in companionable silence, exchanging warm, curious looks. Sizing each other up, maybe, although they'd already shared so much.

He knew Natasha better than any woman he'd ever been with—and there was still so much more to know.

When she shifted closer, bumping against him, he snagged the elastic holding in one of her braids and tugged it loose, then the other. She shook out her hair for him and leaned back against the counter.

He remembered something he'd wanted to ask her. "Hey, when you said your sister and brother-in-law judged you in the past…"

She held up her hand. "Well they didn't. I just thought they did. Perception is a funny thing like that."

"Got it."

"It's important to me that I don't cast them in a bad light."

"Of course." He tipped his head to the side and looked at her carefully. "But I want you to know that everything you share…I like all of it. I find you endlessly fascinating and interesting. I want to hear more about your nomadic life and your adventures."

"Nomadic. I like that description."

"Is it accurate? That's what it sounds like to me."

"Yeah. For years, I left most of my stuff at my parents'

place, and had a bag or two in the back of my Jeep. I've put so many kilometres on that thing—I had the engine replaced just before I found out I was pregnant with Emily. It was like having a whole new car again."

"Where did you go?"

"Up north to Elliot Lake and the Sault. South to Toronto. Wherever the wind would take me."

"For work?"

She made a face. "For David, more often than not."

"Ah. And that fuelled some of the tension with your sister?"

"They never liked him. Never understood…"

"What you saw in him?"

She nodded. "Yep, pretty much. David is…slick. Now I see that, but before…he had a certain appeal right up until the moment he very much didn't. In hindsight, he was a mess. I didn't see it when we were together, because he wore a good mask. But as soon as I found out I was pregnant, suddenly it was like I could see him for who he really was." She shook her head. "And I think there are reasons there, you know? Why he copes with life in such dysfunctional ways." She gave him a bright smile, a little bit forced. "Anyway, none of this is about him. That's just why I have some trust issues, and why my sister and brother-in-law are so protective. But you're nothing like him. You're more like me, I think. Wary but pragmatic."

Matt wasn't sure he was quite worthy of that assessment. But Jesus Christ, he didn't want to be anything like her ex, either. He made a private vow that he wouldn't let his own struggles impact her. He wouldn't wallow in them, wouldn't let them consume this wonderful friendship he'd discovered.

"Pragmatic," he said slowly. "Yeah, that's the goal. Hey…" He took a deep breath. "Since you live closer now, and I'm going to be obnoxious in my regular visits, how would you feel about me telling Jake about our friendship?"

She looked at him, not blinking, for agonizingly long seconds. Then she nodded. "I guess it's time."

"You sure? Because—"

She cut him off with her mouth, both of their drinks clumsily landing on the counter beside him. She tasted like whiskey and fire and sweet, victorious pride.

They kissed until they were both breathless, and then she hugged him.

Simple, long, hard.

"I'm sure," she whispered in his ear.

He wanted to pick her up and carry her upstairs, but tonight was her night to celebrate her independence. Her motherhood and her dreams.

"I should go," he whispered back.

"You'll be back soon?" She looked up at him, her face soft and shining and beautiful.

Damn fucking straight.

"Wild horses couldn't keep me away." He leaned in and tasted her pride one more time. "I'm so impressed, Tasha. With this house, and your fierce mama bear routine, and all of your dreams. Every bit of you impresses me, and I want more."

He just hoped that he could live up to being what she deserved.

CHAPTER FIFTEEN

MATT DROVE ALL the way home in silence, then went to bed without turning on the TV. He woke up before the ass-crack of dawn, driven out of bed by enthusiasm rather than anxiety for once, which was a nice change of pace. But even so, it was too early to politely drop by to have the long-overdue conversation with his brother.

That almost didn't stop him, because he was riding so high on the night before—even with only a few hours sleep.

Who needed rest? Overrated in the face of something as special as a friends-with-responsibilities relationship with the sexiest, sweetest woman in the entire county.

Instead of waking Jake up, he drove out to the Search and Rescue team's training facility to burn off some steam first. A run didn't feel like it would be enough. He needed to burn.

He flashed his EMS badge at the gate to the provincial park, then carefully crawled at the indicated speed limit until he got to the clearing with the lodge and the climbing and rappelling tower.

He had the space all to himself, which suited him just fine.

He parked beside the tower, then grabbed some rope from

the shed around back. It was cold, so he left his coat on at first, but once he got going, he shucked it off and let the movement keep him warm instead.

The exercise, and his burning thoughts.

He didn't want to become Natasha's dirty secret—or vice versa. She hadn't made him feel like that, at all, but there was an unexpected pride bursting forth from within him.

Inside the four walls of her house, everything felt right. Perfect. He could live for more nights like last night, and not just because of her. Hell, he'd already fallen head over heels for her kid. Watching her put Emily to bed last night, he'd thought, *why didn't I meet them three years ago? Why couldn't it have been me that made this amazing little girl?* But that wasn't the right time.

She'd have hated him then.

Or loved him for a single night before seeing him for all that he wasn't. Whatever, he didn't want to dwell on what could have been.

But right now, they were at a crossroads.

She wanted to date him. But he got the strong feeling that she saw her future as just her and her daughter.

He could take that as rejection, that there was no future between them. This was all he got, which would painfully be everything he hadn't known he wanted, and still not enough at the same time.

He landed heavily on the platform at the top and sucked in a painful breath. It would be a fucking cruel twist for the universe to show him all he'd been missing this whole time, then take it away in the next breath.

Except he didn't think the universe would be that hard on Natasha. Him, maybe. He deserved to be taken down a peg or two. But her? She'd been through enough.

No, the universe had put him in her path for a reason.

Now he just needed to figure out how to show her that.

"What are you doing here?"

He looked over the edge of the railing and saw Tom Minelli standing in the clearing below the tower. "I could ask you the same thing."

"You talked your way past the gate staff, and they called me to find out if there was training happening this morning that I'd forgotten to put on the schedule."

"Sorry about that."

"It's fine. I was heading out here this morning anyway. What's going on?"

"Nothing. Just felt like climbing."

"Without a spotter?"

"I'm in one piece."

Tom laughed. "It's my job to point out that's not safe."

"Yeah, well I had a lot on my mind, and breaking down my brother's door at six in the morning seemed like a bad idea."

"Excuse me?"

He'd meant to mutter that under his breath, but it had clearly carried. "It's a long story."

Tom held up a Thermos. "I've got coffee. Or we could go hit Mac's if you're hungry."

Matt wrapped the rope around his arm and tested his hold. "No."

"You coming down?"

"Yeah." He swung his leg out, then grabbed the rope with his other hand, confidently descending. "See?" he said once he was on the ground. "Undamaged."

"Don't let anyone else on the team see you do that."

"Sure thing, Dad."

"I rescind the offer to share my coffee." Tom led the way over to the training lodge, opening the door. "It's also fucking cold out, you idiot."

"I've got gloves on. It's good practice."

Tom just shook his head. "Come on in. Sean's on his way, too, so if he's the brother you're pissed at, this could get awkward."

"I'm not pissed off at anyone."

Tom ignored that and crossed to the kitchenette.

Matt hung his head. Fuck. He hated it when Tom went all Zen and philosophical.

He should leave.

He didn't.

When his friend returned, holding a steaming mug of coffee in one hand, and a couple of creamers in the other, he took them and doctored his coffee.

"So that's a no to telling me what's going on?"

"That's a fuck right off with your nosy questions."

"Nice language."

Matt closed his eyes. "I've met a woman. And don't say that I meet women every day, because that stopped a long time ago. This woman...I met her months ago, man. *Months*. And I haven't been able to get her off my mind since. She's perfect."

"That's the worst problem to have," Tom said mockingly. "My fucking condolences, you selfish prick."

"Don't get me wrong, I know I'm lucky. It's just that today, this morning, I'm realizing I may want more than she can give me right now."

Tom laughed. It was gentle at first, almost kind, but then it grew. "Well, you can't win 'em all."

Matt frowned, not liking his friend's easy dismissal.

"We all make questionable choices from time to time, and they don't always pay off. For example..." Tom said. "I slept with Chloe."

Wait, what? Maybe Tom wasn't doling out wisdom about Matt's situation. "Chloe who?"

Tom scowled at him. "Davis."

Matt choked on his coffee. Jesus. Apparently they both had woman troubles. "Get out."

"What? You don't think I'm her type?"

"I know you're not her fucking type. She's so far out of your league it's not funny." The Pine Harbour librarian was smoking hot. Curvy, pierced, tattooed, sassy... and she'd turned Matt down the two times he'd tried to hook up with her, ages ago. He knew she had impossibly high standards, and there was no way in hell his straight-laced buddy could ever meet them. Plus he liked the change in subject. "So it didn't go well?"

Tom's scowl deepened. "She came to me, for the record. And it went better than well, not that it's any of your business."

"What do you mean, she came to you?"

"She showed up at my place the other night..."

"Are you blushing?"

"It went very well, thank you very much."

Matt laughed. "For you, maybe. But if she didn't want a repeat, it wasn't that great for her."

"You never want a repeat with anyone, but you've never seemed disappointed."

The irony wasn't lost on him. "I didn't know what great was, it turned out. Now I want—" He choked on the next words. *A lifetime of repeats* was what he'd been about to say. And they hadn't even gotten all the way naked yet.

Cart *way* before the horse.

"You're serious about this woman?"

"Very."

"Who is she?"

He rubbed his jaw. "Her name's Natasha. We met when I was in Port Elgin for a training course, and there was something about her from the first moment I laid eyes on her." He chuckled. "Although I met her daughter first."

You could have heard a pin drop in the lodge if anyone were to drop one. But nobody would, because Tom was his only audience, and he knew without looking at his buddy that he'd died of shock.

"She's got a three-year-old. Emily. Really cute." He kept going. *In for a penny…* "Oh, and a few years ago she had a short fling with Jake."

Really not a big deal when he said it out loud. Totally—

"Your Natasha is Jake's *Tasha*?"

"She's not Jake's anything." *She's mine.* Another fact not completely yet in evidence. "And watch what you say next." Matt shoved to his feet and balled his hands into fists. He didn't care if Tom was his friend, nobody talked about Natasha in anything but the most glowing of terms.

Tom gave him a hard look, but didn't get out of his chair. "Why have you kept this a secret?"

He hadn't meant to.

"Does she know who you are?"

He reared back. "Yes. Fuck you, of course she does."

Tom looked at him, long and hard. "And that's why you were thinking of breaking down Jake's door at dawn?"

Before the conversation could go further, a truck pulled up outside, the engine noise interrupting them.

Tom waved his hand toward the door. "That's either Sean or Owen—he's helping with the new training plan, too. You're welcome to stick around if you'd like. I can dole out more exceptional relationship advice."

Matt snorted. "Since when are you a relationship expert?"

"I'm an observational scientist. And I'm not a monk. Just because I keep my liaisons discreet doesn't mean they don't happen."

"I'm pretty sure they don't happen because nobody calls them liaisons."

Tom shrugged. Mr. Fucking Casual.

"Nah, I'm gonna get out of here. I need to go find Jake and tell him so this can stop being a thing hanging over my head."

Of course Sean had to walk in as he said that, and Owen was right behind him.

Matt waved at Tom. "I'll see you later."

His brother gave him a confused look, but accepted his fist bump on the way past.

Owen, however, followed him outside.

"Hey," his friend said. Or maybe Owen was being his boss right now. They hadn't talked again since Owen brought up his concerns in his office, but Matt had felt observed at work.

He took a deep breath. "Hey."

"Is everything okay? I heard the tail end of that. Something hanging over your head?"

Matt turned in a slow circle. "You know what? This peninsula is too damn small. I have too many damn brothers and I can't even come out here to have a punishing workout without tripping over my boss."

"I'm not your boss right now. I'm just a fellow guy on the Search and Rescue team who's worried about his friend."

"You want to know what I was telling Tom? About a woman I'm interested in. That's it. I don't see whatever it is that you think you see about me, man."

"Why'd you need a punishing workout this morning?" Owen glared at him. Well, the guy had a heavy, hooded gaze at the best of times, but it felt like a glare. It felt piercing and judging.

"I'm a fit guy. I go for a hard run almost every single day."

"I was your partner for a year. You don't like running."

"Didn't. Now do. People change."

"People self-medicate with endorphins, too."

"And what the hell would I be self-medicating about?"

"I was there, remember?"

No. Matt had no idea what Owen was talking about. And he didn't really want to find out, either. He threw his hands in the air. "Not now, okay? I'm in the middle of something important. I gotta go. See ya."

He turned, giving his boss—and his friend—his back. He didn't need to be derailed this morning. Maybe Owen didn't see that, but that wasn't Matt's problem.

His blood was pumping as he pulled away in his truck. He was still a bit worked up when he parked in front of Jake and Dani's house, so he pulled out his phone.

Natasha answered on the first ring. "Good morning."

God, he loved that warm, happy bounce in her voice. It immediately soothed him. "Same to you."

"We're just making oatmeal," she said.

"Sounds like fun. How was your first night in the new house?"

"We both slept in a little, so pretty good." Her voice drifted away from the phone as she told Emily to sit with her oatmeal, then she was back. "What's up?"

"I'm sitting outside Jake's house."

"Oh." Then she laughed, a little, worried sound that made him second-guess everything. "Sorry, that's all I've got right now. Oh. But..." She exhaled. "Okay. Sure. Brave new world, big new adventure, let's rip bandaids off, too. Let me know how it goes."

"I will." He gripped his phone tighter. "And Natasha?"

"Yeah?"

"I miss you." It was his secret just how much that meant. Wanting more was a uniquely Natasha-related effect.

"That is...an excellent follow-up." This time, her laugh

didn't sound worried. "I should get back to the oatmeal princess."

"Sounds good. Say hi to Emily for me, okay?"

"Will do."

"Later."

Since it was still early, he didn't hop out of his truck and go right to the front door. He called his brother next.

"Why are you sitting in my driveway?" Jake said when he answered.

"Good morning to you, too."

"I was just about to come outside."

"It's cold out here."

"Then come in, but be quiet. Dani and Cal are sleeping in, we had a rough night. Teething."

Matt took a deep breath and hung up the phone.

His brother swung the door open as he approached, and after he kicked off his boots, they headed into the kitchen.

Jake filled the coffeemaker with water. "What brings you in this direction so early?"

"I wanted to talk to you about something. About someone, actually. Someone important to me." He gestured to the appliance. "But coffee first."

Jake measured out the grounds, then got it started. "Are you hungry? I might put some toast and bacon on."

"Sure." It wasn't that he was delaying the conversation. Just...creating a normal framework for it to happen within.

And he didn't put it off that long. As soon as Jake set a cup of coffee in front of him, he dove right into the heart of it.

"In September, I met a woman. A single mom, and her daughter, at a cooking class of all places. We hit it off and we've been very slowly exploring a friendship ever since." He swallowed hard. "You know her."

"I do?" Jake took a sip of his own coffee.

Matt waited until his brother didn't have scalding liquid in his mouth before he explained further. "Natasha Kingsley."

Jake's eyes flared wide, and after taking another deliberate sip of coffee—slowly—he leaned back against the counter. "Wow."

"Is that all you have to say?"

"No." Jake pulled a face. "It's a small peninsula, I guess."

"Yeah."

The facial contortions continued as his brother tried to pick his next words carefully. "Where is she now? I haven't seen or heard from her in years."

"She was in Port Elgin. She just bought a house in Wiarton. Moved in yesterday, as a matter of fact."

"Sounds like you're more than friends."

"We're something. It's a friendship I'm hoping may turn into something serious."

Jake's face tightened up. "Be careful."

Matt's first instinct was to slam his cup down and tell his brother to shut his mouth. Instead, he set the cup down gently before saying it in a slightly nicer way. "Don't go there."

"Matt, you don't understand. Tasha's needy."

"No, *you* don't understand." God, he got mad over this easily. Did other men feel protective as fuck like this, with a hair-trigger? He also didn't want to hear her name coming out of his brother's mouth. Not like that.

Jake didn't seem to notice the rage rising. "She's looking for a father for her daughter."

"No, she really isn't."

"Yeah. Don't you remember—"

"She hasn't dated since Emily was born," Matt burst out, cutting off whatever bullshit Jake was going to spew about the past. "I had to convince her I was worth a shot. Convince her my family wouldn't be a problem, because the past is the past. That's what I promised her. Don't make me a fucking liar."

"Emily?"

"Her daughter. I know you probably haven't thought of her again, but Natasha has this whole amazing life. Emily's three. And adorable."

"Okay. Look, I only want what's best for you, but maybe you don't know everything that went down with Tasha."

"*Natasha* is what's best for me. And if you call her Tasha again, I'll break your fucking face."

Jake gave him a wary look. "I hear you. I don't mean anything by it."

"You do. When you say that, what you're saying is, you don't value her as anything beyond what she once was to you. But that was nothing. It was a single night, and some residual stuff around that, but we all know you were always meant for Dani. And Natasha didn't want you, not really. You were just a good guy when her ex was being an asshole. Right personality type, right time, but very much the wrong guy."

Jake's mouth fell open, but he recovered quickly. "She told you all that?"

"She's told me enough. I've figured some of this out on my own, too. I'm not stupid."

"No. Right, of course not."

"I've had a lot of experience being the wrong guy at the right time, you know. I know exactly how nothing that combination is. Physical comfort that works in the moment but needs to be washed off as soon as humanly possible. Which is kind of fucked up when really, it's just another form of friendship."

This time Jake winced. "You're right."

"You're God damned right I'm right. And now I've got something different. Now I know what real friendship is, the deep, lasting kind, and I want more with her, but I need to be able to promise her you aren't an issue here."

"I'm not." Jake leaned in and looked him straight in the eye. "I'm really not.

"Good."

His brother laughed. "So, Natasha, eh?"

"Yeah. She's amazing, you know that?"

Jake nodded. "I guess I do. She was a good friend to me."

Matt pumped his fist. "Yes. There you go. Give me something else. Remember her as something else."

Jake nodded. "She's brave."

"Hell yes."

"And a hard worker."

"Yeah. She is." He dragged in a breath. "I'm going to convince her that this family is worth getting to know, and I want to trust you're going to be a good brother when I finally get her to come out to dinner."

"I can do better than that." Jake sighed. "I should talk to her. I mean, I should apologize. I didn't handle the conversations around her pregnancy as well as I could have."

"One thing at a time." The last thing Matt needed right now was for Jake to go surging in as some kind of misguided saviour. "If there comes an opportunity to make that right, take it. But don't go inserting yourself into her life."

"Understood. Really, that's...I get it."

Footsteps on the stairs cut them off, and a moment later, Dani appeared in the doorway holding a red-cheeked and cranky little Calvin. "What's up?" she asked, passing the toddler to her husband. "And is the toast burning?"

Matt and Jake turned as one to the toaster oven, and the four scorched squares inside that used to be bread. "Shit," Jake said. "Yeah, I'll make more."

Dani poured herself a coffee, then took Calvin back and set

him on the counter. "Do you want a banana?" She held up the fruit and touched her fingertips to her mouth. "Are you hungry?"

Cal burst into tears.

"Okay, today's not the day to practice baby sign language, got it." She groaned and picked him back up again, rocking him on her hip as she drank her coffee.

Matt thought for a minute that her sleep deprivation might prevent her from asking again why he was there, but he wasn't that lucky. When her cup was empty, she handed it to Jake to refill while she pinned her gaze on Matt. "So why are you here?"

Before he could answer, Jake handed his wife a fresh cup of coffee and the answer all in one fell swoop. "He's been dating Tasha—Natasha—Kinglsey."

Dani's eyes bugged out, for just a second, but then where Jake had gone all serious, her face went soft. "Really? For how long?"

Matt shifted in his chair. "Since mid-September."

"So ditching Thanksgiving…"

"That was to spend the afternoon with her."

"Oh, Matt." She squeezed Cal and rubbed her cheek against her son's hair. "That's great."

He felt his cheeks heating up. "Yeah. It really is."

"So…" She searched his face. So many questions. He understood, but it still made him squirm a bit. "She has a kid, right?"

"A daughter. Emily. We met first and bonded over cupcakes."

Jake inserted the detail about the cooking class, and Matt suffered through a little laugh on Dani's part. But she seemed genuinely happy for him.

"You're dating a single mom." Dani grinned. "If this

weren't a sensitive topic for other reasons, I'd have a lot of fun with that."

"It's not that sensitive," Jake growled.

Matt took a deep breath. "Yeah, I think it's better to just make it as chill as possible. One day, I'm going to bring her to a family dinner, and I want it to be completely normal."

"Did she have a family dinner for Thanksgiving?"

"Yeah. Her family. They ate at lunch, then we met up afterward when her daughter spent some time with, uh, her ex." He was probably telling them more information than was necessary—more information than was his to share. "Anyway, don't feel bad for her. That's not what this is about. She doesn't need me. Very much the opposite. I want every bit of her, and she's wary and reluctant. So I need you both to know that, and know how important she is to me. Got it?"

"Crystal clear," Dani said softly. "We'd love to see her again and get to know Emily."

Jake choked on his coffee.

Dani gave him a pointed look. "You sure it's not a sensitive topic, husband-of-mine?" She turned back to Matt. "We would *love* to meet them both, and any time. Soon, later, whenever. We'll work on our reactions, too."

Matt got up, put his mug in the sink, then gave her a hug, carefully including grumpy Cal in it. "Thanks. You remain my favourite member of this family."

She squeezed him back with her free arm. "Thanks for telling us."

When he got home, he threw in a load of laundry, then grabbed his phone.

Natasha answered on the second ring. "Hello, stranger."

"I just got home."

"Ah." She waited a beat. "How was it?"

"It went well. I should have led with that." It went well eventually, which was what mattered.

She took a deep breath. "Okay."

"Is it okay?"

"Yeah. I'm glad you told him. I'd built it up into a big thing in my head, and I'm glad you took the lead there."

"I'm happy to take the lead wherever you want me to."

She laughed. "Nice segue."

"I mean it. House painting, cheesecake baking, recreational bondage. I do bossy really well."

He loved the sound of her giggle. "Noted. We can explore all of that."

"Yeah?" He rolled his lower lip between his teeth. "I can't wait." His phone vibrated. He pulled it away from his ear and groaned. "Hey, so…my brothers are texting me en masse to razz me about having a girl I like-like. This is a first in thirty years so I'm going to have to go and take some abuse."

She laughed gently in his ear. "Okay. Have fun with that."

"I won't. Ah, maybe I will. I do like-like you after all."

"I like-like you too."

He had the goofiest grin on his face as he ended the call and slid into his text messages.

Dean: You told Jake first?

Sean: Seriously, WTF? I just saw you this morning. No heads up for your favourite brother?

Dean: You are not the favourite.

Sean: By all objective measures I am.

Jake: Guys, I told you that in confidence and now I'm putting Calvin down for a nap. Can we do this later?

Dean: Oh, we're going to be doing this for days, don't worry, you're not missing anything. Matt has a girl-friend? This is gold material.

Matt: I can see you all, you know. You're ridiculous.
Sean: Whenever you want to talk, I'm here for you.
Matt: Thanks. I can feel the love.
Sean: Do you want to come over now?
Matt: Not a chance in hell. I have to rack out. Later.

He was still grinning, though. They were jerks, but they were his jerks.

CHAPTER SIXTEEN

AFTER BREAKFAST, Natasha and Emily got to work.

For Emily, this meant carefully packing which stuffed animals to take over to the apartments while Mommy worked. For Natasha, it meant packing all the garbage bags and household cleaners she could carry at once.

She scrubbed the floors and stripped the walls of remnant wallpaper. Emily helped by spritzing water on the walls. It felt good, like any other Mommy-and-Millie day, until the late afternoon.

Right on schedule, Emily curled up beside her, clutching a teddy bear, a frown pulling her little eyebrows together. "I miss Nollie."

Of course she did. This was the time they should go and pick her cousins up from school.

"We're going to go to see her day after tomorrow," she said reassuringly. She was doing a couple of evening shifts at Bailey's a week up until Meredith left, to line the coffers a little more and to give the girls extra time together before they lived on opposite sides of the province. "Do you want to call her in a little bit?"

"Mm-hmm. And a cuddle now."

"Of course."

They were sitting on a blanket on the floor in the living room, their picnic snack stretched out in front of them. Crackers and cheese and juice boxes.

Emily crawled into Tasha's lap and closed her eyes.

"You have been such a good help today," Tasha said as she stroked her daughter's hair and cheeks. Endlessly soft, effortlessly perfect.

Emily didn't answer, just snuggled deeper. Because she'd always worked nights, Emily had always slept on her own, but suddenly Tasha felt like she'd missed a chance the night before. "Hey, do you want to have a sleepover in Mommy's bed tonight?"

Emily laughed. "No."

Oh, fine then. Tasha grinned. "No?"

"I like my bed."

"And do you like it here?"

"Mm-hmm."

Relief swelled in Tasha's chest. "That's what I was hoping to hear," she whispered, too overwhelmed to speak any louder.

"Mommy?"

"Yeah, baby?"

"Do you want a sleepover in my bed?"

She laughed out loud. "No, but thank you."

That new house joy lasted for three more days. Then she got an email from David.

Since she wanted everything in writing, it said, he was officially asking for a full weekend with Emily over Christmas. She fired back a quick reply—yes, of course he could have time with her. Could they maybe do a single overnight visit before the holidays as a test run?

He took his sweet time replying, but finally said he wasn't sure his calendar would allow it, but he'd come up for another day trip at the very least.

Sweet mother of mercy.

She exhaled slowly, then picked up her phone.

He answered right away. "I thought you wanted a paper trail of all our communication."

Sure, she had said that. But then they'd had what she thought was a decently productive conversation where she shared the changes in her life, so… "We can follow up with email summaries of this call," she said more smoothly than she felt. "But it's easier to just hash this out over the phone."

"That's been my point all along."

She rolled her eyes. "Okay. Good. How about if I bring Emily to Toronto for a night? I have friends I can catch up with, and then you won't be out any travel time. And I'll also be close by if she needs me."

"She won't."

How would you know? "Just as a backup option, of course."

"Don't you need to work?"

She winced. Right, that minor detail. "Well," she carefully said. "I've cut back my hours at the bar since we've moved."

David didn't say anything. He was silent long enough that she thought he might actually hang up on her, but then he cleared his throat. "Is that wise?"

It wasn't any of his business, she wanted to point out. "I have a plan. It's fine."

"I looked up Wiarton." She could just imagine him Googling small-town Ontario with disdain. "It's quite a bit further from the city. One could make an argument that's a passive aggressive move on your part."

"Not really. Straight shot up the highway, no need to turn left now."

"Don't make light of this. You moved my daughter further away from me."

"I already told you, it was for economic reasons. Real estate is much more affordable up here."

"Real estate. You bought a house?"

Oops. Maybe she'd left that minor detail out. Then again, maybe it was none of his God damned business.

"I did."

"And you cut back your hours?"

To almost nothing, but he didn't need to know that, and it was time to point out the unspoken truth now. "That is none of your concern." *I have a plan. A Big Dream Plan. It's going to be awesome.* "Anyway, please think about a single night visit first."

They ended the call on that standoffish note, which didn't feel great.

When she arrived at Meredith's house in Port Elgin the next night, she told her sister about the conversation.

"Has he gotten back to you yet?"

"Nope. And I emailed after the conversation, too. No response."

Meredith shook her head. "So frustrating."

"Yep."

"And how's your sexy paramedic?"

"Matt's good. He wants to help me paint." She took a deep breath. "And he told Jake we're friends. Apparently, it went well."

Her sister beamed.

"Say it."

"I told you so."

Natasha laughed. "You did. But you get why it stressed me out, right?"

"Yeah, of course." Meredith glanced at the clock. "Okay, you should get going to work."

"Thanks for watching Emily tonight."

"Thanks for taking my kids to school tomorrow." Meredith was winding down her job and packing up their house. Three more weeks, and they'd move to Ottawa—just in time for Christmas. Until then, Natasha was going to work at Bailey's a couple days a week and crash on Meredith's couch, but they were slowly disentangling their co-dependent lives.

It was harder than she'd thought it would be, and she'd thought it would be brutal.

It was nice to go to the bar, though, and do something she was effortlessly good at for a few hours.

When she got back to her sister's place after midnight, Meredith was still up. They had a cup of herbal tea together, then Tasha got out her computer. She hadn't set up internet at her house yet, so she took this opportunity to do some banking and emailing that was easier on the computer than on her phone.

Then she went to social media and did something she hadn't done in months—she lurked on David's profile to see what he'd been up to. Apparently, he'd been up to all sorts of everything with Sable.

Meredith craned her neck over to look at the screen. "Are you creeping on David's girlfriend's Facebook?"

"I'm checking out the supposed grown-ups who will be responsible for my daughter for two whole days over Christmas. And technically it's his profile, not hers, although it's hard to tell."

Meredith snorted.

"Do you realize she always takes exactly the same picture of herself? Like, what's wrong with the right side of her face? We've seen it in person, it's perfectly acceptable."

"Creeper," Meredith said in a sing-song voice.

"It's a reasonable question."

"It's none of your business."

"Right." Tasha poked through a few more pictures, but really, there wasn't anything to learn there. She sighed and closed her laptop. "It's going to be fine, right?"

"Yes."

"I'm totally going to freak out as soon as she leaves."

"Yes."

She sighed again. "Why is being a mom so hard?"

———

TWO DAYS LATER, they were back in Wiarton, in their big empty house that needed so much work it made Tasha nervous and excited at the same time.

It also made her want to curl into a ball in a blanket fort, but that wasn't possible. For one thing, she didn't have enough blankets to build a proper fort. For another, she didn't have time for that kind of thing.

One day, they'd have a Mommy-and-Emily blanket fort staycation and it would be glorious.

On Thursday, she threw herself into gutting the studio apartments. During the day, she did the stuff that Emily could be around. And once her daughter was in bed, she carried a baby monitor with her and did the more dangerous demolition on her own.

By late Friday night, she had two pretty much empty spaces.

They needed a hell of a lot of work still. New paint, new trim, new floors.

She'd been watching the flyers like a hawk. She'd set herself a strict budget for each apartment and she was going to come in under it, no matter what. So she needed to get the best price possible on the big-ticket items, like flooring and new cabinets for the kitchenettes.

The bathrooms terrified her, though. They would be expensive no matter how she cut it, and the more she learned about tiling and shower drainage, the less she wanted to tackle that herself.

One thing at a time.

Once she was back on her side of the house, she dragged her weary bones upstairs and ran the bath. Bubbles and a good long soak would help.

Which reminded her, she needed to text Matt again.

He'd sent her texts all week. Playful ones, sweet ones, even a couple of innocently dirty ones that made her blush. He had a way of reading her mood from a distance and no matter which tack he took, it worked to make her smile.

Which didn't mean she didn't worry, too.

Every time her heart soared, she told herself to keep a lid on her feelings for him. That it was still, essentially, nothing. A friendship with some flirtation that could be yanked away from her at any moment.

It didn't feel like nothing, though.

It felt big and round and happy.

So she grabbed her phone. Her heart pounding, she took a cute, nervous, hopefully adorable selfie of her face. Then she got into the tub and held her arm further away, angling it above her so she caught a good slice of cleavage and bare leg bursting out from the floating bubbles, reaching for the far side of the tub.

It was magical what perspective could do. Her leg looked long and sexy and really, this was how all photos of her legs should be taken.

She messed around with an app to filter the photos just right, then texted them to Matt.

Natasha: End of a long day. Taking a bath and thinking of you.

She was blushing after she hit send, and she closed her eyes. Would he like it? Would he text back and ask her for more?

The phone rang in her hand and she blindly answered it. "Did you like my picture?"

"What picture?" David asked.

Natasha shrieked and her leg slipped off the edge of the tub. Into the water she slid, her phone thankfully tumbling the opposite way.

When she hauled herself out of the water and looked over the edge, her phone was lying on the towel, and David's name and number were on the screen.

Crap.

"Sorry," she called out, quickly drying her hands before she picked up the phone. She carefully leaned out of the tub, not wanting to risk dropping it again. "Okay, hey. Hi. What's up?"

"You didn't send me a picture."

"No, I didn't."

"You said—"

"You must have misheard me. I think I said something like, 'This is a surprise'." She winced. That sounded ridiculous. But he bought it.

Sort of. He sighed in her ear. "I cleared my schedule. I can drive up tomorrow and pick Emily up. I thought we might take her to the family cottage in Collingwood, because that's where we'll be for Christmas. Familiar space and all that."

"Tomorrow."

"We'd arrive around lunch."

She cast a wild-eyed look around her falling down bath-room, with the chipped tile and the peeling paint. No, there was no way David could come here tomorrow. "How about I meet you in Collingwood? I need to drive into Owen Sound to get paint anyway, and it's halfway there." Sort of. Crap. There went an entire morning of driving.

"Is everything okay?" He sounded suspicious, and for good reason.

She was acting like a loon. "Totally fine."

He hesitated before continuing. "Do you remember where the cottage is?"

"Yep."

"I can send you a map."

"I'm good."

"Because—"

"I have to go. We'll see you tomorrow." She ended the call and sagged, letting her phone tumble back to the towel on the floor and resting her cheek against the curved edge of the tub.

From the floor, she heard her phone vibrate.

Maybe it was Matt texting back. Maybe it was David sending her detailed instructions on how to get to a cottage she'd been to half a dozen times.

She didn't care. She slowly sank into the hot, soapy water and closed her eyes. Her baby was going to spend the next night away from her.

Sure, she'd left Emily with Meredith hundreds of times, but never all the way overnight. In three years, Natasha had always been there when Emily woke up—in the middle of the night, in the early morning.

And now she was going to have to trust David and Sable, the annoyingly nice selfie queen, to be there instead.

———

MATT WAS WORKING his last shift for the week, and feeling the drag of four shifts in a row. Tasha's photo made his night, though, and saved him from barking at the new ride-a-long student, Marco, who wasn't nearly as competent as the last one. He'd already snarled twice, and now he was painfully aware that he wasn't being a great instructor on this night shift.

The text from Natasha had been just what he needed. A little rush, a little zing. A big zing, actually.

It took him a while to respond properly, because they'd been stuck in an off-load delay and he didn't have any privacy. Now they were back at the station, and Will took the kid into the break room, so Matt stayed in the ambulance bay and dug out his phone.

> **Matt: I keep looking at this. It made my night.**
> **Natasha: Now I'm all squeaky clean and curled up in bed.**
> **Matt: I like that too. Lucky bed.**

She'd started the flirting, but he didn't want to be too forward. He changed the subject to something more…courting.

> **Matt: Maybe I can visit this weekend? I'm not working.**
> **Natasha: I'd love that. Emily's going for her first overnight with David, though, so fair warning, I might be kind of mopey.**
> **Matt: In that case, I should bring dinner and wine.**
> **Natasha: That would be amazing. The Kingsley kitchen**

**has a limited menu right now, mostly just instant
oatmeal and crackers and cheese.**
**Natasha: Oh, and I'll be painting in the afternoon, so
there will be fumes.**
Natasha: I'm really selling this date.
Matt: I promise I can't wait. See you tomorrow.

The radio squawked with a new call-out, in support of a midwife at a home birth. The labour was progressing quickly, and her backup midwife might not arrive in time. Even as Matt was listening to the dispatch, Will and the now-more-than-ever-nervous Marco were hustling onto the ambulance.

Out into the night they went. It took twelve minutes to arrive at the farm just off highway 6. The wide-eyed father-to-be answered the door, inviting them into a quiet kitchen.

"Exciting night, eh?" Matt asked, snapping on a pair of blue gloves. "Where are they?"

"Through here."

He followed the dad to the living room, where the labouring mom was on her side on the floor. He didn't recognize the midwife kneeling beside her, but he knew his sister-in-law, Jenna, was the second one on her way here.

"Hey," he said. "Matt Foster. We're here if you need us, but we'll stay out of your way if you don't."

"Thanks," the dark-haired woman said, flashing him a quick smile. "I'm Kerry. This is Teresa. She's fully dilated and baby is descending quickly. She's doing her best not to push, but some of the contractions are moving the baby along without her." She leaned forward and listened to the woman's belly. "They're both doing just fine, so I don't want to ask her to wait any longer."

Protocol and best practice dictated there be a medical professional caring for both the mother and the baby once delivery took place. Matt had only attended one other home birth, so he was more than happy to be bossed around here. "Sounds good."

"Teresa, this is Matt, he's going to hang out with us while you bring your baby into the world, how does that sound?"

"Intense," the mom-to-be groaned, and Matt chuckled.

"It's even more intense because we've got a wide-eyed student along with us tonight," he said as gently as possible.

The mom laughed weakly, and it turned into a groan as her next contraction took hold. Her husband knelt behind her and she pressed herself back, then sagged at the end of the contraction.

"It's burning," she groaned, her face contorted.

Kerry shifted to between the birthing woman's legs and nodded. "Baby's crowning. Okay, Matt, we're doing this. You're going to observe for vitals once we deliver baby onto mom's chest. There's a stack of receiving blankets there."

He knelt down and waited through two more contractions as Teresa bore down and Kerry gave her instructions. Slow, good, easy, breathe.

Then with a gasp, Kerry had a wet, squirming bundle in her hands, and before the baby was even set on his mother's chest, he was crying.

"It's a boy," the brand new father said, looking over his wife's shoulder.

"And he's got a healthy set of lungs on him." Matt covered the baby with a receiving blanket, cocooning him against the warmth of his mother's bare chest. He quickly took a listen to the baby's heart rate. Well over a hundred beats per minute, nice and healthy. The pale blue tinge to his skin was fading fast, and then gone as he yelled lustily. *Angry little alien*, Matt thought with a grin.

He looked at Kerry, who was cleaning up and replacing the

oversized blue disposable pads under the new mom. "Are we clamping the cord?"

She glanced at her watch. "Sixty more seconds."

From the kitchen, they heard the front door open and close.

"Hello," called Jenna.

"In here." Matt glanced up as his sister-in-law walked in. "Surprise."

She winked at him and turned her attention to her partner. "Sorry I missed the excitement, Teresa, but I see you were in good hands."

He gave her a quick report, then she took over, clamping the cord before the new dad did the cutting honours.

Matt retreated to the kitchen, where he found Will and Marco. Will handed him the computer to document what he did, then they quietly headed into the night.

"That was wild," Marco said, shifting restlessly in the jump seat. "I know Will said we didn't need to take her to the hospital, but…"

Matt snapped his head up. "But, what?"

"I mean…" Marco's words faded. "Nothing."

"Nah, spit it out."

Will cleared his throat in a warning that Matt knew he should heed. There was just something about this kid that rubbed him the wrong way. Too cocky, maybe.

Matt let out a slow breath. "What's your question?"

Marco, to his credit, lifted his gaze and looked Matt right in the eye. "Doesn't that baby need to be in the hospital for a day or two?"

"Nope. You know the elements of an APGAR score, right?"

Marco searched his memory and came up with most of the points. Matt added the one about heart rate, then explained how that was an important immediate metric. "The midwives will stay for a few hours, make sure baby nurses well, then tuck everyone in for some much-needed rest."

"Do you know all of this because you're related to the hot one?"

Jesus fucking Christ. "Excuse me?"

"What? We're all guys here."

"We're all *professionals* here," Matt snapped. "And so are both of those midwives."

"Okay," Will said from the driver's seat. "Changing the subject because Matt is right, but it's also been a long evening… Marco, what are some other situations where we might be called in to a delivery?"

The student sputtered, then spit out a couple of other scenarios.

"Yeah," Will said. "One of my first ride-a-longs was a spontaneous delivery in a car on the side of the road. Compared to that, a home birth with two midwives is pretty well managed."

"I guess. But when my girlfriend wants to have babies, I'd rather we do it in a hospital."

Spoken like almost every other medical professional Matt had ever known.

He'd never given it any thought himself. For one thing, he'd never thought about having kids. And if he had gone there in his head, it wouldn't have been his body, so he'd probably have said whatever his partner wanted.

Now he found himself wanting to know Natasha's birth story with Emily.

That surprising little thought carried him the rest of the way through his shift and all the way to bed, where he racked out hard.

When he woke up at dawn, there was a text message waiting for him from Owen.

Owen: Give me a call when you've got some time to chat. Asking as a friend.

A meddlesome friend.

Matt was off work for a couple of days. Whatever it was, it could wait. He didn't feel like being jacked up for telling someone off for being a bonehead.

CHAPTER SEVENTEEN

EMILY WAS happy to pack a bag and go and see her Daddy, which made the drive to Collingwood easier—although the lonely drive back was still difficult for Natasha.

She stopped in Owen Sound and picked up paint on sale. Then she went to the liquor store and bought a decent bottle of wine and a small bottle of gin. At the grocery store she picked up pancake mix and maple syrup, as well as limes and tonic water.

Everything she needed to seduce the pants off Matt and then feed him in the morning.

She got home by the early afternoon, fully prepared to spend the next few hours painting by her lonesome, but when she pulled onto her street, she saw a familiar pickup truck parked outside her house.

Matt was waiting on the front step, bundled up in a winter coat.

She didn't grab her groceries, or the paint, or even say anything to him. She just launched herself into his arms.

"Hey," he whispered into her hair. "What's this all about?"

"Big feelings," she finally said, dragging in a breath. "Hi."

"Ah." He hugged her tighter. "Hi. And I'm sorry."

"Emily was totally fine being dropped off. It's a good thing. In theory. In reality, I'm a nervous wreck. And kind of grumpy."

"Is this the first time he's ever had her overnight?"

She nodded. "I know, that's insane, but he's never been interested before."

Matt shook his head. "I'm sorry. Well, I'm here to help you paint. I'll go out and grab dinner for us later."

"I bought pancake stuff. I mean, I got it for breakfast tomorrow, but we could have them for dinner."

He grinned down at her. "Emily's away, so I can stick around for pancakes in the morning?"

"I was hoping you might."

He cupped her cheek and pressed his lips against hers. "Yeah," he rumbled. "I'm here until she gets back tomorrow. Or whenever you kick me out."

She kissed him back, hungry for his warmth and softness and strength. Especially for that strength, because she was perilously close to crying over Emily and David and life.

"We could continue this inside…"

"Right." She took a deep breath. "Oh, groceries."

He helped her carry everything in, then shrugged out of his coat. Under it, he was wearing a buttoned-down plaid shirt, which he quickly took off as well, leaving himself in a snug white t-shirt that looked pristine and definitely not painting appropriate.

Of course, if he took that off as well, they'd never get to the painting. And she was still worked up over Emily being away, which wasn't fair to Matt. When they got to that, she wanted to give him her full attention.

"Pretty nice shirt to paint in," she murmured.

"Pretty nice woman to invite me over for painting foreplay. I had to dress appropriately."

She laughed despite herself. "Painting foreplay?"

"Oh yeah. Remember when you asked me about my A-game? This move is currently theoretical, but I'm looking forward to putting it into action." He gave her a careful look. "Do you want to hear my hypothesis?"

"As a fellow player, I really should know about this. For science."

He grinned. "Flirting science."

"Tell me, sexy professor. What is your hypothesis?"

"I think that there's something deeply rewarding about repairing, building, restoring. Moving you into this place last weekend—that was special. Helping you paint, helping you build…whatever you need. I want to do that, too."

Wow. That wasn't what she'd expected him to say. She bit her lower lip and gave him a small smile.

"And then I want to take you to bed, and work out the frustration we'll surely build up in the close proximity while we're working together."

That was more like what she'd expected. She nodded. "That's a pretty solid hypothesis."

"Shall we move into the research trial part of the study?"

She laughed again and swayed against him. "Definitely."

His hands tightened on her hips, pulling her into his rock hard body. "Unless you want to cut straight to the more direct method of stress relief."

That was very tempting. But she had some restless energy to burn off in a productive way first. "Honestly, first I want to paint a bit and be grumpy."

"That sounds like so much fun," he deadpanned.

"Right?" She blinked innocently.

"Fine. Put me to work. What are we painting first?"

Her goal had been to get a coat of primer on one of the apartments, but it turned out Matt knew more than a little about painting, and in two hours, they'd done both apartments. He was quick and confident in his movements, and had a system down pat.

After they moved all the supplies back to her side of the house, he asked if she wanted to keep painting in there. "Might as well get as much work done as we can, right?"

"You don't mind?"

"Not at all. Do you want to break for dinner first?"

They decided it would be easier to go out—and eat on a real table—so they went to the pub for hamburgers, and while they ate, she thought about what she wanted to tackle next.

David had accepted that she'd drive Emily one direction, but he might get suspicious if she refused to have him come to her place again. "I think I want to paint the entranceway tonight," she said slowly. "Get that looking somewhat decent."

"We'll make it shine." Matt grinned. He didn't ask her why, and she didn't confess her worry about looking bad in her ex's eyes. That seemed like an unnecessary downer on an unexpectedly lovely afternoon.

After she texted David for an update, and Emily called to say goodnight, they got back to work. They zipped through applying the primer, and after a quick drink break—where Tasha learned that Matt liked wine a lot more than he liked rye—they returned to put the first coat of colour on the walls.

"You have a lot of experience with painting," she said, watching him effortlessly roll the longest wall in smooth strokes.

As soon as she said it, she regretted it, because the experience probably came from helping Jake and his construction business.

Matt finished his roll down the wall, then gave her a slow, careful look. "Yep."

She sighed. It was a stupid thing to worry about. "With Jake?"

"Yep."

"I shouldn't still feel awkward about that, should I?"

He shrugged. "I don't know how much *should* applies to feelings. They are what they are."

Heat bloomed in her chest. "That's probably true."

"Do you want to talk about him?"

She wrinkled her nose. "No."

"Do you mind if I talk about him?" Like it was no big deal.

And the way he asked it, maybe it wasn't. "Sure."

He went back to rolling the wall as he talked. "My brother is an idiot."

"That's a great start to the sharing," she murmured under her breath as she picked up the putty knife to fill in the nicks and screw holes in the wall.

"He was born a grown-up. When I was younger, I thought both Jake and Dean were like that, but in the last couple of years, Dean's chafed at the responsibilities of being the oldest. But Jake...he loves that shit. He loves being a dad, and a husband, and a business owner. And it's all so wholesome. Which makes him an idiot, in some respects, because he doesn't value any other framework for happiness. So, he would have never been a good fit for you, regardless of external influences."

"That's...very logical."

"Since he's my brother, the clearer we all are that your history was an always-doomed, never-a-big-deal thing, the better. He was never going to be the guy for you. Me, on the other hand..."

She grinned. "Yes, you."

"I think I'm a very good fit for you."

She agreed wholeheartedly. "We do seem to have quite the connection."

Tasha gave up her attempts to patch. She sat down on the step stool and looked over at Matt. It was easy to miss that he was more than a pretty face, because he was so extraordinarily good-looking. And yet behind the perfect face and the remarkable height and the tightest, sexiest rear-end she'd ever seen was a sharp mind with a keen insight into the world around him.

"What do you think of me?" she said abruptly.

He glanced at her over his shoulder. "I think you're incredible."

Damn, Skippy. "That's not what I mean," she whispered, but her body was already heating up.

He put more paint on his roller. "What do you mean?"

"You're spot-on with your assessment of your brother and why he wouldn't have been a good fit for me. I bet you've got assessments of everyone you know."

"Sure, I guess."

"So what's your assessment of me?"

"You're different. I don't think about you like that." But he rolled a little faster. She watched the muscles in his arms flex and roll as he covered her hallway in an even coat of paint.

How do you think about me?

She picked up the sandpaper and went back over the far wall.

The next thing she knew, Matt was behind her with the paint brush. "Time to cut in this wall," he said softly.

"I can do that." She reached for the brush, and he handed it over, but he didn't pull his hand back. He let her cover his fingers with her own, wrap her hand around his, and pull him close.

She pushed up on her toes and pressed her mouth against his, kissing him softly at first, then harder.

"You're different," he said roughly when they broke apart. "I have all sorts of complicated thoughts about you, and I'll share them if you really want to know. But most of them circle around the notion of wanting more of you, more of this, more of Emily. More than maybe you can give."

"I'm getting there." She kissed his jaw. They could get there right now, right here on the floor of the hallway surrounded by wet paint.

"I mean it when I say want to take you to bed tonight, Tasha. I want to show you how I feel, what I think, in the best way I know how. I've been thinking about this for a long time now, and what it means."

She blinked up at him, surprised at the rough tenderness in his voice, even after all they'd said and done. Of course she'd been thinking it too, but hearing Matt say it—and like that. *I want to take you to bed.*

It was almost old-fashioned. Definitely sweet.

I want to make love to you. He didn't need to say it for her to know that's what he meant.

"I could take you here," he said with a laugh. "Don't get me wrong, I'm down for whatever. But I'm not in a hurry, because we have all night. And I want to take you *to bed*, to stretch you out and have you make all sorts of noise."

Sweet in a dirty kind of way. She wobbled her head in a distracted nod. "I want that very much, too."

"So let's finish painting this hall," he said with a growl. "You cut this in, I'll roll it, and then you can warm up the shower while I put a quick second coat on everywhere."

"Let's do that together," she whispered. *Let's do it all together. I've never had anything like this before, and I don't want to miss a single second of it.*

"Deal."

Except it wasn't easy. With the promise of taking their relationship to the next level—the naked bodies, blissful orgasms, emotional connection level—she was having trouble concentrating on getting their work done.

Luckily Matt was a consummate professional. And before she knew it, he was almost done, so she started to gather everything they'd need for the world's fastest clean-up.

"There. Done." He was grinning as he turned toward her. "I could use a—"

She held out the plastic grocery bag she'd already grabbed for the roller. "Here."

There was no way that wrapping up a paint roller should be sexy, but Matt made it work. From the snap of his wrist as he puffed out the bag to the obscene way he smoothed his hand down the suddenly phallic length of the roller, Tasha could hardly stand how good he looked tidying up.

And he knew it.

His grin got more wicked, ever bolder, as he carefully set the roller in the middle of the drop cloth, and knelt beside the paint tray.

"Do you want to open the can for me?"

Was that a euphemism for take off her shirt? Because yes she did.

"Tasha?" The flash of white teeth as he laughed with her was just the icing on the perfect sexy boyfriend cake. "I'm serious. We need to put the paint away."

"Yep." She grabbed the can and set it between them on the drop cloth. "I'm with you."

"Am I distracting you somehow?"

"You know you are." She popped the lid of the can and took a deep breath. "And I'm enjoying it, I promise."

"I've never seduced a woman while painting before."

"I think technically you seduced me ages ago. This is just the…culmination of a lot of foreplay."

Matt dragged his lower lip between his teeth as the last of the leftover paint rolled slowly out of the tray and back into the can. "I want you to know, this wasn't exactly my plan when I came over. I really did want to cheer you up and help you paint."

"Mmm." She waited until he'd tapped the lid back onto the can and everything was neatly stowed away before she began unbuttoning her shirt. "And how many condoms did you bring with you?"

"The standard three-strip that I've been carrying around with me since Thanksgiving." He reached for the loose flap of her work shirt, but she dodged out of the way. He gave her an easy grin. Oh, those sexy smiles. They melted her every time, even when he was being cheeky. "I didn't want to be presumptuous."

She took another step away from him as her shirt fluttered to the floor.

It felt good to have his gaze on her. Hot, heavy inspection of her simple bra, her bare flesh. She reached for the button on her jeans. "It's a good thing I bought a big pack the other day, then."

His gaze jerked from where her fingers were teasing up to her face. "You did?"

"Yeah."

"Tasha…"

She started moving again, walking backwards, until she bumped into the stairs. "I have a confession to make," she whispered. "I can't really warm up the shower. It's a shoddily rigged-up temporary thing over a bathtub that I think might be a hundred years old."

"I've never had a better invitation than that," Matt growled as he closed the gap between them.

"It could fall down on us if we're not careful."

"Careful is my middle name."

"You have a lot of middle names," she breathed as he cupped her cheek.

"As many as it takes to promise you I'm whatever you need me to be."

She wasn't sure she wanted him to be careful tonight. But instead of saying that, she kissed him.

His hands covered her body. Big, wide, hot. He touched her all over, and then under, nudging her jeans down her hips until he had her ass in his palms.

When he lifted her up, she gasped and flung her arms around his neck.

"Hang on," he growled as he wiggled her out of her pants, one arm holding her up the whole time.

As soon as her legs were bare, she squeezed them tight around his waist and buried her face in his neck. Her heart pounded a mile a minute as he climbed the stairs, carrying her toward the barely functional shower set-up and her empty bedroom after that.

There was nothing impressive about her house right now. Little impressive about her, really. She clung to him as doubt tried to invade this moment. Whispered thoughts of not being worthy, not being enough.

She pushed them away and kissed his skin instead of giving in to worry. He tasted warm and masculine, faint remnants of an earlier shower still clinging to his skin.

They could make this quick. Just a rinse off, then they could crawl under her covers and get to the good stuff.

But Matt wouldn't be rushed. When he set her down in the bathroom, and she started the shower, he took his time stripping off his clothes, then peeling her out of her underwear.

"You're so gorgeous," he murmured as he traced his fingertips down her arms, then up the middle of her torso. He grazed her breasts, her collarbone, then back to her face. By the time he'd finished kissing her, the bathroom was nice and steamy after all.

"See? We warmed up the shower together."

"I don't think I've had a shower as long as that kiss in the entire time we've been here," she admitted. "And never with the door closed. I didn't know it could get all warm and cozy like this."

"We had one of these tubs growing up. My dad didn't bother to renovate the bathroom until after his hooligan sons all moved out."

"It's more about not wanting to leave Emily alone," she admitted, which was the least sexy thing to say in this particular moment.

Matt just laughed and leaned in to kiss her again. "We don't have that particular problem right now, so that door can stay closed and we can be steamy together for as long as you want."

Carefully, they climbed into the tub, taking turns standing under the spray. Once they were both wet, Matt reached for her body wash and squeezed a good dollop into his hand.

"Turn around," he said, tugging her close.

She pivoted slowly, rubbing her hip and then bottom against him, but he didn't take the hint. He took his role as back washer seriously, soaping her up everywhere before shifting her back under the water so she could rinse off.

He used her soap on himself, too, which she liked. She wanted to watch him take himself in hand later. Her brain flashed sharp, hot ideas. *Show me what you like*, she'd whisper. And he'd show her, because he'd give her anything she wanted.

He filled his hands again with soap, and gently smoothed his palms over and around her breasts, against her nipples, until her flesh was heavy and hot and so ready to be dried off.

"Lower," she breathed.

He trailed his fingers over her belly.

Over her mound, just grazing her clit. She rocked into his touch, helping him wash her and turn her on and drive her crazy.

"Show me," he murmured, and the echo of her own thought—how right it was, how right *he* was—ratcheted up her arousal.

"Slow," she told him. "Mmm, yeah. Long, slow, hard. You can squeeze me there."

He cupped her entire sex and tightened his grip, kissing her at the same time.

Her head started to spin in the best way. "Bed," she gasped.

Somehow he figured out how to turn off the water while still licking his way through all of her erogenous zones, and then it was her turn to blindly grab two towels.

Drying each other off was another excuse to get tangled up and practice more show and tell with what each other liked. She stroked his chest, the hard planes of his abdomen, and then wrapped her hand around his cock the way he had in the shower.

That first feel of him, heavy and pulsing against her palm, was electric.

She breathed his name. "Matt…"

The next breath was a gasp as he flattened them both against the bathroom door, his thigh insistent between her legs. "Bed," he growled.

Right, she'd already said that, too. They were both reduced to single syllables of need. Names, nouns, pleas.

More, yes, there. Hard. No, slow, yes—again and again,

because there were a lot of whispered confirmations back and forth.

Lick.

"Oh," she sighed as he traced his tongue down her neck and over her collarbone. "Definitely bed."

They both went for the door at the same time, which made her laugh and him growl again. He stepped back and gestured for her to lead the way, which meant she could feel his gaze on her back, on the bare curve of her skin, her ass, as she led him to her bed.

A man, in her bed, for the first time in years.

But she'd wanted this for weeks, and the heat between them had zoomed straight to combustible in the shower.

This was going to be good.

"Hey," he murmured as he caught her around the waist just shy of her bed. He sucked in a breath as their naked bodies collided, his muscles hard against her softer, rounder parts. "God, it's hard to think when you're against me like this."

She twisted in his arms, and this felt even more incendiary. Her nipples brushed his chest, and heat slicked between her legs.

Every part of her was eager, wet, greedy.

"Let's not think, then," she said in a rush as their lips connected.

"Deal." He lifted her up and onto the bed.

Her legs fell open and he crawled on top of her, resuming the licking that had driven her to distraction against the bathroom door. His breath brushed the top of her chest and over her breasts, his tongue circling her nipples one at a time before sucking the left peak into his mouth. His hand found the right, following the same principles she'd whispered to him in the shower. Slow, hard.

She arched into his firm touch, into the perfect tug of his

mouth against her skin.

They needed a condom and they needed it now.

"I want to taste you," he growled as she shoved him toward the bedside table.

"Later."

He laughed and rolled protection over his cock. She reached for that beautiful length and tugged him back between her legs.

"I need you," she said softly as she rubbed the crown against her clit, then lower, easing him into her slickness.

He braced his hands on either side of her and used his entire body to push them together, filling her with three careful, increasingly deep thrusts. On the last one, as her body made way for the last bit of him and he stretched her from the inside out, he caught her gaze and groaned.

They held a shared, raw connection as he throbbed inside her.

This was so much more than just having sex again for the first time in ages.

This was so much more, period.

"I need you, too." His voice was thick, the words heavy, and she reached for him. He lowered onto her as he started to move. Fluid, skilled, but with an edge that echoed the raw expression she'd seen in his face.

Like he barely had a hold on his control here.

She wanted to make him lose that last bit of it. She wanted to feel all his emotions, all of his need tonight.

Hooking her arms around his body, she moved with him. Rose to meet each thrust, squeezed around him as he pulled away. She listened to each of his groans and growls and doubled down on all the things that ripped those beautiful noises from his body.

But she wasn't the only one with an agenda for pushing the

limit. He used his hands and mouth to do the exact same back to her, and before long she was losing her ability to track what he liked and wanted.

He'd reduced her to the circling, curling, climbing desire deep inside her, a primal sensation of ascension that felt nothing like the functional orgasms she could give herself.

She burst apart as he closed his mouth once again over her breast and pulled her nipple hard against his fluttering tongue.

Oh, that tongue.

Those hands.

She wrapped herself hard around his body as her climax ripped through her body. With a few shuddering, broken thrusts, he followed her into his own orgasm, and then he collapsed hard on top of her.

"Fuck," she finally whispered.

"Yep. We did—and how," he said in a strained voice, holding back a laugh.

She pressed her face against his sweaty shoulder. "Oh, God."

"Mmm." He lifted off just enough to grab the condom, then rolled away.

She followed and licked his back, giggling the whole time. "That was…perfect. And not even perfectly imperfect. I mean, that was—"

He rolled her onto her back and settled on top of her, heavy and thick and…actually perfect. "I know what you mean," he murmured as he traced her jaw with his fingertips. "I think I'm actually speechless."

"We've already said some nice things," she whispered.

"Maybe we should try not talking again."

"Again?"

He grinned.

Even perfect had an upgrade option with Matt. Yes, again.

CHAPTER EIGHTEEN

MATT WOKE Natasha up the next morning with an erection, an orgasm, and then pancakes.

It was glorious.

Then he let her put him to work again.

They painted both studio apartments. The trim and baseboards still needed to be replaced, and the bathrooms gutted, but at first blush, the apartments looked halfway decent now.

She double-checked her measurements for the baseboards, then grabbed her power drill and put the last few cover plates on the electrical outlets.

"I like watching you work with tools," Matt said as he handed her the last screw.

She buzzed the drill at him. "Yeah?"

"You're fascinating to me."

"I like whiskey, cookies, and power tools, Matt. I'm a complicated girl."

"Competent girl, too," he murmured, leaning in for a kiss.

"With very competent help." She sucked on his lower lip. "How can I thank you?" She meant it in a dirty way, but Matt's next kiss was soft and gentle.

"Let me come back," he murmured. "Let me get my hands dirty and be helpful. It feels good." His eyes lit up. "And you feel good, too."

"I'll feel even better in the shower."

They tumbled naked into her bed after the shower, and somewhere between orgasms, she lost track of time. So when her phone vibrated late in the afternoon with a text message from Sable, saying they were fifteen minutes away, she was not prepared.

"Oh my God," she whispered, leaping into the air.

"What?"

"They're dropping Emily off in fifteen minutes. How much does my hair look like I just had amazing sex?"

"Yeah, total give away." He grinned at her as he pulled on his pants. "It's fine. Ponytail that delightful mane, give me a kiss goodbye, and don't worry about what they think. Where's my shirt?"

She couldn't find his t-shirt, so she tossed him his buttoned-down, then chased it to give him the world's fastest kiss before she darted into the bathroom to find a hair elastic.

When she was done de-sexing her hair and face—god, that flush was both amazing and borderline obscene—she found him downstairs, shoving his feet into his boots.

"You could stay," she said weakly. It was dinner time, and then Emily would be off to bed.

He shook his head. "This isn't how I want to meet Emily's dad. And I don't want to make this more stressful than it needs to be for you." He cupped her face and gave her one last kiss. The hundredth, maybe, over the last twenty-four hours.

And definitely the sweetest.

"I'll see you soon," she said. She meant it. "Drive safely, and text me when you get home."

"Give Emily a secret kiss for me."

"Will do."

She sagged against the door after he left and waited for the next emotional wave with Emily's arrival.

It didn't take long. Less than a minute after Matt's heavy, rumbling truck engine sounds disappeared, the quiet purr of David's import SUV signalled their arrival in her driveway.

She took a quick glance around the entranceway. It looked old, but the bright orange paint was gorgeous. Her house was going to be stunning when she was done with it. She had every reason to be proud, so she squared her shoulders and opened the door.

David wasn't getting further than the entrance, anyway. Her house, her rules. He could say goodbye to Emily right here.

Her chest seized tight as her ex got out of the car. Sable didn't, but she waved from behind the passenger side window.

Tasha waved back as David opened the back door, and then Emily was sliding past his legs and racing toward her.

She dropped to her knees and let her tiny cannonball power right into her.

"Mommy!" Emily cried as Natasha buried her face in her daughter's hair.

"Missed you, baby."

"Me too."

"Did you have fun?"

"Yes. We set up a Christmas tree!"

God, that hurt. Tasha pasted on a smile and glanced up at David, handsome and urban and so supremely good at faking interest in everything—from her to Christmas and, God forbid, maybe even their daughter. "A tree, eh? Fun!"

David shrugged. "My parents have an artificial one in the

storage space. Sable thought it would be a good way to explain that we'll go back there over the holidays."

Ah. Tasha breathed again and flashed a quick smile toward the car. Good. Sable had the right idea, and it wasn't just David playing at being Daddy Awesome.

"That's smart." She stood up and turned Emily around. "Say goodbye, baby. You'll see your dad in just a couple of weeks, right?"

Emily gave David's legs a tight squeeze, then disappeared inside and upstairs.

David handed over her bag. A favourite stuffie hung loosely out of the open zipper, and Tasha white-knuckled the doll and the backpack.

"So that was good?" she asked brightly.

"We think so."

Good lord, learn to think for yourself. "Great. Okay, well, I'll see you at Christmas. You'll email an exact date and time? We're not picky. Meredith is heading to Ottawa before the holidays, so it'll just be the two of us." In fact, she probably wouldn't decorate for the holidays. Maybe it was good that Emily would get that at her dad's. "Are you thinking of coming up for Christmas Eve? I…" She took a deep breath. "I wouldn't want to make this an annual thing, but if you wanted to have her for Christmas Eve and Christmas Day this year, I wouldn't mind. And next year we could split the days?"

"Sure." He frowned, like there must be a catch.

"You've got the tree set up," she said softly. "And I'm not going to have one this year."

He gave her an uncomfortable look. "Did you want…to join us?"

Ha. No. She laughed out loud. "I'm fine. Really. No. Thanks." She cut herself off. "But I appreciate the invitation."

"Since you invited us for Thanksgiving…"

She'd only invited him, but sure, whatever. Inclusivity. "I'll have other plans for the time that you have Emily." She hoped Matt could get away. Now that she'd re-ignited her long-dormant libido, she already missed him.

David glanced past her. "How's the house?"

"Great."

"Emily says you don't have much furniture."

"Not yet. We're going shopping this week."

"She has— Does she have everything she needs?"

Tasha tried and failed not to scowl. "Yes."

He nodded. "Good."

"Okay, bye."

He reached out and stopped her from closing the door. "Wait."

"What?"

"Are you okay?"

The question took her by such surprise that she burst out laughing. He looked genuinely confused by her reaction, which only made her laugh more. "Yeah," she finally said with a sigh. "I'm…fine. Truly. I just… This is kind of stressful for me. I'm not sure what to expect, and we haven't talked a lot, so…"

He nodded. "Got it. Well, we really did have a good night with her."

"Good."

They exchanged slightly-less-awkward nods, and she added a genuinely pleasant, "See you at Christmas," before closing the door.

Upstairs, she found Emily checking to make sure her pink room was exactly as she left it.

"Are you hungry, baby?"

"A little," Emily said, hugging her dolls.

They ate quickly, then Emily just wanted to go back

upstairs. They read a few stories, but Emily kept interrupting to put her dolls to bed, and finally Tasha took the hint.

"I think it's bedtime for you, too. Let's go brush your teeth."

Once Emily was asleep, Tasha thought about dragging herself to the apartments to do some work, but the call of her own bed was too strong. She plodded down the hall and turned on her light.

Her eyes immediately tracked to a flash of white just under her bed.

Matt's t-shirt.

She picked it up and brought it to her face, breathing in the scent of him. She took off her clothes and slid the shirt over her body.

She grabbed her phone and crawled into bed, happy for an early bedtime herself, just as Matt texted her.

Matt: Made it safe and sound. Stopped to do some grocery shopping on the way.
Natasha: I just found your shirt. I put it on to sleep in.
Matt: Excellent call.
Natasha: Glad you got home safely. And thank you for keeping me company yesterday and last night.
Matt: Always. When are we painting next?

Her heart slammed against her ribcage. *She* was painting again tomorrow. Just her, because as nice as the help was, she couldn't ask him to help her that much.

Natasha: Maybe we can do something more fun next time. On your next day off?
Matt: Definitely. But painting is fun, so if you want me to come over at night...

Oh, she wanted him to come over at night, all right. But was that too much, too soon? The last thing she wanted was to cling to him and cross a line into taking advantage of his kindness. She took a deep breath and sent him a smiling emoticon instead of a real response.

Taking things slow was a new kind of dangerous. She dreamt of him all night, and when she woke up, restlessness jangled at her nerves.

She channeled it into her house.

Instead of art, she plastered the walls with lists for the Big Dream Plan, drawings, and clippings. She wrote and re-wrote the to-do lists, trying hard to stick to a logical sequence of events. First the bones of the apartments had to be made amazing. Then she could furnish them. But the rational side of her brain couldn't stop her heart from imagining what they'd look like when she was finished—or her fingers from searching the used buy-and-sell sites for deals.

And that was how she ended up buying a couch a few days later.

It started with a crazy deal on some hairpin coffee table legs. They were free, as long as they were picked up immediately. The person who was looking to get rid of their stuff was moving the next day. Everything had to go. So Tasha buckled Emily into her seat and off they went.

When they arrived, it was just in time to witness a disagreement over a red velvet sofa from the safety of her car. Tasha was only there for the metal coffee table legs, which presumably the moving owners had always intended to do something with, but never quite got there. Her win.

But this other person was haggling over a couch.

"The price is firm," the owner said, frustrated enough that Tasha heard it from the curb and through her open window.

The other guy left.

She hopped out of her Jeep. "Hey," she said, holding up her hand. "I'm here for the coffee table legs. But how much do you want for the sofa?"

"Two hundred bucks."

It was fair, but it was more than she had in her purse. She opened her wallet and pulled out all her cash. "I have a hundred and sixty. I could go and get more."

He shook his head. "That's fine. I just want it gone."

And this was why she always carried bungee cords and rope in her trunk.

He helped her get it up on top of her car and battened down. She grabbed the coffee table legs she'd come for, as well as an ornate birdcage and an oversized clock, and told the man he'd made her week.

Then she had the very real dilemma of how to get the couch off her car and into her house when they arrived back. Technically she did have multiple options. She could call Meredith, or post on the buy-and-sell boards for two burly guys.

But she only needed one guy, really, and she was pretty sure he'd be happy to help. *Ask him. Don't be afraid.* She had to psych herself up for it before she texted him a picture of the top of her car.

Natasha: Any chance you want to come over and make out on my new couch?

He called her back immediately. "You got a couch."

"I did."

"I like couches. I can be there in an hour."

He made it in forty-five minutes, and he brought food with him. Sandwich fixings, nothing fancy, but Emily was happy to see him and very proud to help him assemble sandwiches for dinner after they got the couch into place facing the wall of Big Ideas.

As they "cooked", Natasha set up their picnic blanket with water bottles, napkins, and a bowl of pretzels.

At some point, she'd like to take Matt on a real date. Dress-up clothes, fine china. Even just a table would be an improvement.

Maybe they should have gone to the pub, not that she could afford to eat out regularly.

She went back into the kitchen just in time to see Emily grab her phone off the table.

"Whatcha doing, baby?" Emily had discovered games and apps, which was useful sometimes, but also dangerous.

Tonight, though, she wanted music. "Mommy, play the Havana song." It was her favourite lately. It made their hips wiggle, Emily liked to say.

They didn't usually have an audience for that, though.

Natasha put it on, tapping the mini Bluetooth speaker on the shelf so the sound filled the kitchen.

Emily twirled around for Matt. "I'm a dance-y-pantsy."

He laughed. "So you are."

"I like dancing. So does Mommy."

Natasha's face heated up as Matt caught her eye. "I know."

He'd already seen how much she liked to dance when he caught her dancing to the same song at the bar.

"I need Polly!" Emily sprinted from the room.

Matt gave Tasha a dirty grin and closed the gap between them.

Her breath froze in her chest as he set his hands on her hips, moving her to the music. "I like to dance, too," he murmured, his breath warm and intoxicating.

Instantly, she felt herself go all hot and limber. A roll of the hip under his touch, a step of her foot, and they were dancing, their bodies in contact from chest to thigh.

He moved like liquid grace, effortlessly turning a grind in her kitchen into something hotter than any club night she'd ever had. When the trumpet solo started, he spun her around, tugging her ass against his pelvis.

But the bounce of little feet bounding down the stairs ended that before it really got a chance to begin, and Tasha buried herself in the fridge, looking for something—anything—to cool her face down.

Emily danced with Polly twice, then they sat down in the no-longer-bare living room and ate their sandwiches. When they finished, Matt hung around for Emily's bedtime, but then he said an early goodnight.

"I have to go," he grumbled into her hair. "I have a day shift tomorrow."

She ignored the tug of frustrated desire deep inside her. "Of course."

"I'll be back soon."

"I have no doubt. Who could resist basic sandwiches and interrupted kitchen dancing?"

"Not me," he whispered, hauling her against him again. "Not me."

———

MATT SLEPT LIKE SHIT, but that wasn't anything new. He'd wished he could have slept with Natasha, because that single night with her had been the best sleep he'd had in six months, but he wasn't going to ask for that while Emily was in the house.

So he pounded out a run at dawn, then got to the station early. The shift started just fine. They headed up to Tobermory at the tip of the peninsula to cover that area while another bus did a long transport to Toronto.

All good.

Right up until it wasn't.

They got a call about a woman with breathing difficulties. No history of asthma, but a recent respiratory infection, and the call was being placed by the patient's daughter, who had come for a visit and found her mother struggling.

Lights on, siren on, and they got to the house, a bungalow on the edge of town, really quickly. The last report was that the patient was still talking, but just in case that changed, they put the bags on the gurney and rolled it inside.

The woman was in her late fifties, maybe early sixties, and had two younger women with her. Mother and daughters, probably.

They introduced themselves, one of the daughters talking over the other. Matt took the history while Will did the vitals.

The quieter daughter handed over a nebulizer. "We got this thing at the hospital two days ago, but her colour is still not good, and she sounds terrible."

"Okay, we can help you use this." Will showed them how, having to interrupt the talkative daughter a few times to get the instruction clear. But even after administering the drugs, he didn't like the numbers. "Sat's not coming up, let's give her some oxygen," he said to Matt.

They hooked her up with a nasal cannula, then Will stepped aside to call in to dispatch and find out which Emerg could take her.

Matt crouched down in front of the patient. "Do you have a bag to bring with you? A pair of pyjamas, your health card, some toiletries?"

"I...don't need to go...to the hospital." She inhaled

painfully through her nose. Even the extra hit of oxygen wasn't helping her colour.

"And you said you haven't ever had asthma before?" He glanced at her daughters as she shook her head.

The chatty one agreed with her, but Matt noticed the other daughter bit her lip.

"Any history of colds getting into her chest, trouble breathing?"

Shrugs. He didn't know what the weird dynamic was here, but it was possible they didn't have time to sort that out.

He turned back to the patient. "Okay, so right now it might feel like you're just having a bit of trouble breathing. And maybe that's been going on for a few days, so it feels like a temporary normal. But this increased difficulty is actually pretty dangerous."

Fred Carleton flashed through his mind, and his chest tightened up.

"Really dangerous," he amended. "Honestly, it's a no-brainer. You need to be admitted for the night, get proper care."

That wasn't the right thing to say. Her face tightened up. "They didn't do anything for my flu, did they?"

He took a deep breath. "Right. I hear that was frustrating. Hopefully this will be different."

"Hopefully." The bossy daughter snorted, and Matt wondered how much she was contributing to her mother's negative thoughts about the hospital.

"No," her mother wheezed.

"Just help her with the medication," the daughter said. "It's not getting in her lungs."

Yeah, because her lungs weren't working. What the fuck did she think they could do with their gear? They weren't a walking hospital, and she could stop breathing at any moment. Heat crawled up his neck. "Honestly, I don't want her life or your blame on my hands."

As soon as it was out of his mouth, he knew he'd gone too far.

Over the patient's head, he saw Will give him a sharp look.

God. Fucking. Damn. It.

He forced a smile onto his face and shoved down the intense and unexpected panic in his chest. *Not now. This isn't about you.* "Let me re-phrase," he heard himself say. He heard the tremor in his voice, too. "Is there anything I can do that will make that transfer easier?"

The woman started to shake her head, but before she could answer, she started coughing again. Shallow, weak, unproductive. Her lips turned blue, and Matt didn't need to take another pulse-ox to know it was too low.

Will stepped in, gesturing for Matt to ready the stretcher. "There are risks to staying home," his partner said. "We want to make sure you're clear on that, and we want to help you get more treatment at the hospital than you did last time. How does that sound?"

It sounded fucking professional, unlike the bullshit he'd spit out a minute earlier.

Quietly, one of the daughters crouched down next to her mother and whispered something.

The woman closed her eyes.

Maybe she didn't want to think about the risks. Or maybe she was tired of them. Who knew what else was going on in her life, her head. Matt had lost sight of those possibilities— and a myriad of other unseen factors he usually understood.

He glanced at Will, who shrugged. Yeah, they weren't going anywhere, but they couldn't force her to transfer to the hospital, either.

And if they were lucky, she wouldn't die today.

Another flash of Fred through his mind, another tight pinch in his chest.

Finally, she consented to transport, and they headed off, with the daughters following behind in their own vehicle. Will gave him the keys, the message clear. Matt had failed on patient communication today, and there'd be some follow up on that sooner than later.

He white-knuckled the wheel the entire way to the hospital.

This time, Owen wouldn't be sending him a text message as a friend. And Matt knew that he'd probably burned his chances to have that conversation off the record.

"I was there, remember?"

Yeah. Now he remembered. Every joke, every casual aside. An endless parade of opportunities missed where he could have been more of a professional and less cocky, and maybe saved Fred Carleton's life.

But that guilt had been shoved aside because the days that had followed had yawned wide with their own horror. Fear about Sean's injuries, confusion about his recovery. And then when he was flown home, the agonizingly slow recovery. Anger. Frustration.

It had consumed his family.

And in the midst of all of that, Matt had forgotten about Fred—and that made him doubly an asshole all over again.

CHAPTER NINETEEN

AFTER THEY HANDED over the asthma patient to the Emerg staff, Will did the post-call paperwork and Matt texted Owen, giving him a heads-up he had an incident on a call that he needed to report. His boss wasn't working today, but apparently that wasn't going to postpone a discussion about what just happened, because he texted back a terse, short message.

Owen: Understood. Meet you at the station.

They went on air again, but after an hour of no calls, dispatch returned them to the station. When they got back, Owen's truck was in the parking lot.

Matt guessed his shift was done a bit early.

Will clapped him on the shoulder before disappearing, a tight squeeze that said a lot. He knew he'd earned a lot of goodwill with both men over the years, but he'd burned some of it up over the last little while, too.

Fuck.

He knocked on the supervisor's door and nudged it open after a growled instruction from the other side.

"Hey," he said with a sigh.

Owen didn't say anything back, but gestured for Matt to first close the door, then sit down.

"So…" Matt took a deep breath. "I snapped at a patient today."

His boss just looked at him.

"It was inappropriate, and in hindsight, I can see how I ignored some warning signs in my behaviour that led to it."

That got a nod, but still no words.

Fuck.

He dragged in another deep breath. His chest was tight, and the constriction was growing. "What else do you want me to say? I know I crossed a line. It won't happen again."

"How did it happen this time?"

Matt shook his head. "I was worried, and frustrated. I lost track of the boundaries a bit."

"So you're just going to be better in the future? That's your solution?" Owen shook his head. "This is going to happen again, unfortunately. Because it's not about you saying the wrong thing."

"Then what the hell do you think it's about?" It was a stupid question to ask. Matt knew the answer. *Fred Carleton.* The name bounced around in his head like a bullet. It thudded against the inside of his skull, back and forth, until it landed heavily in the middle of his mind and sat there, ready to explode at any second.

Owen just looked at him.

Matt shifted uncomfortably. "I know you've tried to talk to me before."

"You didn't want to hear it then, and you don't look like you want to hear it now."

"I don't."

"I'm worried that you're depressed."

Matt jerked back in his chair. "What?" He'd expected PTSD or an operational stress injury concern. "I'm not depressed. I'm fine. Maybe just burned out. It's been a complicated year."

"You aren't fine. You acted unprofessionally and this isn't the first time I've wondered if something was going on with you."

Damn it. "Then write me up."

Owen cocked his jaw to the side and scowled. "You'd rather I make this a disciplinary matter than talk about your feelings?"

Was he really that defensive? Fuck, Matt didn't like that, either. He crossed his arms over his chest and shrugged. "No."

"You need to take a break. You're stretching yourself to the limit."

"It doesn't feel like I am. Honestly."

"Well, your behaviour has indicated otherwise. I want you to take a week off, see how that treats you."

Matt stared at his boss. An entire week? His chest was now tight enough to make him actually worried. He pressed his hand to his sternum. "That's not necessary."

Owen gave him a tight, intense look. "Why do you not want time off?"

"I like to work."

"Like to stay busy? Like to be needed?"

He swallowed hard. "Yeah. There's nothing wrong with that."

"Maybe not. But if you can't handle downtime—"

"I can." He'd find a way. Help Natasha with her renovations.

"I think you're already trying to fill your time in your head."

This time, Matt's curse was out loud.

And Owen laughed at him. Gently, but still. "See?"

"No, I don't."

"We are the worst fucking patients, I swear to God," Owen muttered. He leaned to the side and picked something up. A thick paperback book. He handed it over. "I want you to take a week off and read this."

The title was fitting. *I Don't Want to Talk About It*. Yeah, Matt didn't. Especially not if it was a book about male depression, as the subtitle promised.

"Read this. It's hard, but good. You're going to see yourself in the pages and it's going to hurt."

"Your pep talks suck ass."

"I'm still new in this supervisor gig, cut me some slack." Owen gave him a serious look. "I also want you to talk to Sean and tell him about the day Fred died. I think that day rocked you more than you've ever let on, and I'm sorry for not saying something sooner."

Jesus. "You have nothing to be sorry about." It came out in a broken whisper. "I'm…fine." Really, he was. "I can see how I've been dealing with that kind of clumsily. Sure. But I don't need to burden my brother with anything. He's back on his feet and things are going well for him. And I've met someone, and it's getting serious."

Owen held up his hand. "Your personal life is none of my business, but you are not fine, Matt. You snapped at a *patient*. You may have some good stuff going on, but do not use it as a band-aid to cover up a festering wound."

Matt's stomach rolled over. Natasha was not a bandage.

He didn't have a festering wound.

He held up the book. "I'll take a couple of days and read this. But don't make this a bigger deal than it is. Okay?"

Owen gave him a wary look. "Keep in touch. I want daily texts."

"Sure thing, Mom."

"And get some sleep."

Sleep was not what he needed.

———

NATASHA WAS WORKING on her numbers, trying to figure out how to make the studio apartment kitchenettes look slick and modern and hipster and fun, all on a nothing budget.

There wasn't really any way for that to happen, so the next step was that she needed to find a job. She had a few more weekend shifts at Bailey's, but it was time to find something more local.

Which meant looking into pre-school for Emily.

She grabbed a red marker and stomped to the to-do list part of her planning wall. They wouldn't get done unless she literally scrawled them on the task sheet.

Find a job - fifteen hours a week
Find pre-school or part-time daycare for Emily

HMM. Now that she was looking at them written down, they weren't that upsetting. Em might like to have friends to play with, especially now that she was having to say goodbye to her beloved cousins.

She took a deep, restorative breath. Okay. This was going to be just fine.

As a smile settled on her face, she heard a knock at the door. She did a cursory check to see that the entranceway looked tidy before opening it, but it wasn't a new neighbour.

Matt was standing on her front step.

"Hi," she said softly. "I thought you were working today."

He nodded and stepped inside, glancing past her and moving right into her space at the same time.

"Em's upstairs," she whispered.

He pulled her into his arms. The kiss was hot and demanding, almost ruthless, and it took her breath away. With a little whimper, she fisted her hand in the front of his jacket and tugged him backwards, away from the bottom of the stairs and into the living room and onto the couch.

She'd missed him too, but they needed some privacy.

She didn't buy the sofa so they'd have a place to make out, or least she hadn't thought that was why, but now that he was pressing her back against the pillows, it seemed right.

And very, very wrong. "Shh," she reminded him.

"Right." He glanced up, cocking his ear toward the top floor. "I hear a tea party."

"She's playing."

"We should play, too. That's an excellent idea," he whispered as he brushed his lips against hers. "Doctor, for example. I'll be the patient, you can be the very thorough GP. Or we can play naughty schoolboy and the stern principal with the secret sweet side."

What had gotten into him?

Not that she was complaining.

"What if I want to be the naughty school girl?" she asked breathlessly, which was exactly the wrong thing to say when she should be putting distance between them, but this was a whole new side to Matt, and she liked it.

"I'm game for that. Detention every night." His lips bruised hers roughly as he kissed her again.

She really did want to play with him. She closed her eyes and squeezed her hands around his biceps, big and solid as he braced himself over her. "Stay for dinner," she said without looking at him. "And once Emily's asleep…"

"Yes." He pressed his mouth against hers. "Yes, yes, whatever you want to do, yes."

"Maybe you can stay over if you leave early enough. If you want."

He grabbed her ankle and stretched her leg into the air, teasing the sole of her foot with his fingers. A shiver raced down her calf and up her thigh as he gave her a hot, focused look. "What do you want?"

"I want you to stay," she whispered.

He dropped her leg and fell on top of her, his kiss ravenous. He kissed her until there was no more room in her head for anything but hungry, helpless wanting.

Which would have to wait until bedtime.

"Matt." She pushed against his chest and he hauled himself upright. His chest was heaving and his eyes were a little wild.

"Sorry."

She shook her head. "No, it's…we both wanted that." She crawled onto her knees and kissed the corner of his mouth sweetly. "Maybe we both needed that, eh?"

"Yeah."

"Is everything okay?"

He scrubbed a hand over his face. "I had a rough shift. I'm okay. Got done early, and wanted to see you, that's all."

"Well, we have the finest sandwiches to offer for dinner—again—and I even have beer if you're interested."

He shook his head. "Not tonight. But a sandwich sounds amazing. And I want to be put to work if there's stuff to be done. Can I paint? Build something?"

"I was planning kitchenettes for the studios when you arrived." She picked up the notebook from where she'd discarded it. "We could grab Emily and go around back to do some measurements."

He gave her a happy, contented nod. "That would be fun." Lifting his voice, he called out. "Miss Monkey, I've come to see you!"

Emily flew down the stairs, tiny footsteps thumping quickly in his direction. "Matt!"

"I'm going to help your mom measure stuff. Want to come with?"

She slid her hand into his and tugged him toward the back door that separated their part of the house from the apartments. "Come on!"

Natasha grabbed her measuring tape, notebook, and pencil, and followed along.

It turned out, as a serial apartment renter who didn't like to cook as much as she did, Matt had more perspective on what people's minimum requirements for a kitchen space was. "You don't really need a ton of cabinetry," he said as she showed him her sketches. "If someone is staying here for a weekend while they explore the peninsula, how much cooking are they going to do? And really, how much cooking do you want them to do? Look at you and your minimal use of your kitchen right now. You're surviving just fine, and you *like* to cook. I bet most people want a kettle, a single hot plate, and counter space to prep ready-bought food."

She tapped her pen against her chin as she thought through what he was suggesting. "So…more like a counter-height table or an island? Butcher block on legs?"

"Yeah. If you do it as butcher block, it would look like a kitchen space, but function as a table, too."

"With stools…" She scribbled that down on her notebook.

"I like it."

"I do, too." She grinned. "Hey, this is good! You've just saved me some money."

Which she could spend on the bathrooms, upgrading the tile in there. Everyone liked a fancy bathroom on these short-term rental sites. Made for nice pictures.

The discussion of what she wanted to do with the apartments continued as they made dinner together, with Emily standing on a chair between them. Natasha didn't miss that she asked for lettuce on her sandwich after watching Matt put some on his—although the hero worship didn't extend to tomato slices, which she wrinkled her nose at.

More for the grown-ups.

"My Daddy doesn't like tomatoes," Emily said.

Or not.

Matt nodded. "Neither does my best friend, Tom."

"My best friend is Nollie."

"And what does Nollie like?"

"Cheese."

He picked an extra piece off the plate and took a bite as he winked at her. "Me, too."

Natasha could watch the two of them talk for ages. The mix of patience and genuine interest Matt had in her daughter felt like a rare treasure.

The two of them traded bits of information back and forth as they ate, which gave Tasha time to let her imagination wander about the rental units. Tomorrow, she was going to source butcher block countertops. She knew she could order them from a big box store for a reasonable price, but she'd like to find a local contractor if possible.

After dinner, Natasha gave Emily a quick bath while Matt tidied up the kitchen. It was a slice of domesticity she'd never had before, and once again, Natasha said a silent prayer of thanks that she could now tuck her daughter into bed every night.

When Em was out of the tub, Matt came upstairs for stories and what felt like endless extra questions from the three-year-old bedtime star, who didn't want their visit cut short in any way.

Finally her daughter's eyes drifted shut and they were alone again.

Matt looked exhausted, so instead of going back downstairs for a drink, she took his hand and led him to her bed. "How tired are you?"

"If you want to take advantage of me, I'm game."

"Actually, I was thinking of taking care of you tonight."

He laughed. "That's going to definitely go both ways, but be my guest."

He watched through hooded eyes as she stripped him down. Under his jeans she found bright red briefs. "A little bit of colour for a gloomy winter night?"

"I bought them for Christmas, but after my shift I was like, fuck it, a bonus night to see you is better than any holiday."

"Aww," she whispered as she crawled up his body, her fingers lingering over the thick bulge beneath the tight cotton. "I love my present, thank you."

Under her inspection, his cock flexed, tenting the fabric.

"I want your hands on me," he said, his voice husky and low. "Or your body against me. I want to feel you and touch you and hold you. I want *this*, and I want it with you. Get naked."

Her hands shook as she took off her shirt. She could feel his gaze on her breasts. He'd touched her before. Felt the weight of her flesh, the response of her skin. But today felt different, like he was really seeing her without the heady rush of it being their first time.

"We have to be quiet," she said, just as much to herself as him, then she made quick work of her jeans and jumped onto the bed. There weren't any nerves that couldn't be quelled by a kiss, or at least that was the solid bet she was about to make.

"Got it." He hauled her up against him. Slowly, thoroughly, and very quietly, he led her in a sweet, slow tangle of limbs as they made out.

And then, with a tug of her bra strap, making out shifted into serious foreplay. Someone-is-going-to-orgasm-and-its-going-to-be-Tasha kind of foreplay. So much for this being something she was going to do for him.

His fingers teased her, not just exploring like the last few times he'd cupped her flesh, but testing and pushing at her limits until she was shamelessly grinding on him. She might even come like this. And she wanted to ensure he came with her.

Watching his face, she reached between them and slipped her fingers under the waistband of his underwear. She found his flesh, hard and hot and straining for her touch.

They jockeyed for position as she stroked his length and he bared her breasts. His mouth dipped to her collarbone, then her swollen skin, her tight nipples. As her back arched, she lost her hold on him and twisted again to find it.

"Okay, you win," he panted as she lined them up, legs to legs, chest to chest. She loved the feel of the hair on his body, light and crisp. And his hands, which seemed to be every-where, were quickly figuring out all the erogenous zones in her body, from the small of her back to the underside of her boobs, and then higher, along her neck.

She'd never known her neck to be that sensitive, but the way his tongue curled and teased at her skin made her shake and whimper and need unspeakable things.

His fingers tangled in her hair. He cradled the back of her

head as he kissed her again, his cock rubbing between their bare bellies, then he sighed and tipped his head back. Oh, the sounds he made—quiet but barely restrained, choked but raw—lit her up.

He bucked into her touch as she tightened her grip. He lifted his head enough to give her a sloppy, lusty smile, then he rolled his neck back again. She pressed against him and kissed that long stretch of muscles and tendons, tight beneath his skin. His pre-come slicked the inside of her hand and he moved faster, whispering her name and groaning over and over again. She watched his face as he came undone for her, then she turned her attention to her hand, covered in his release.

"Wow," he said on a rough exhale. "That was…"

"Yeah." She grinned. *So hot.*

And because she was a mom, she had a package of baby wipes handy. "They're cold," she whispered as she handed him one of the damp cloths.

"It's all good." He hissed at the first touch, then quickly cleaned up his belly before setting the wipe aside and taking her in her arms again. "Now it's your turn."

She wasn't going to argue with that. He kissed her neck, and her legs fell open. God, she wanted him so much. His hands, his body—

"I want to taste you, and I want you to come on my tongue," he whispered against her lips as his fingers grazed the tops of her thighs. Back and forth, back and forth. Gentle touches, making her sizzle. "Is that okay? If I lick you until you come?"

"Is that okay?" She laughed. "Uh, yeah."

"How do you like it? Fast or slow?" he asked huskily as he palmed her ass, pulling her on top of him.

She shivered under the hot weight of his perusal. He

caught her wrists in his hands and tugged them over his head, planting them against the wall.

Oh.

"Like this?" she asked breathlessly, looking down at him.

"Yeah, I want you on top." He licked his lips, giving her another slow, lusty look. "But you gotta tell me what you want first."

"Slow, long licks," she breathed, adjusting her hands higher on the wall. She needed a headboard for this, but Matt seemed to have a firm hold on her.

"Here?" He swiped around her navel, then down the soft swell of her lower abdomen.

"Mmm. Lower." She rocked her hips as her legs scrambled on either side of him, trying to get purchase on the mattress.

"Closer?" He brushed his lips against her mound.

"Yep, definitely—ahhh…" Her fingers tangled in his hair as his tongue slid against her slit. "That's the spot."

"Secret. Soft. Spot." He licked her until her legs shook, slow, luxurious swipes that scrambled her brain cells and turned her into a quivering mess of need.

"Suck," she whispered. "My clit."

He did that slowly, too, only speeding up once she began babbling words too filthy to properly recognize. She was shameless in her desire for him, and she didn't care.

When her orgasm began to build, it was her favourite kind. Slow and steady in its rise, a heady tug from her clit to her womb that grew tighter and more demanding until—boom— the feeling exploded inside her and she tumbled down.

Literally and figuratively, because Matt had her. He held her so tight as she curled against him, his arms bands of steel, and it was *so* tempting to fall asleep like that. Naked, wanton, and smelling like sex.

But she had a daughter just down the hall.

Alarms had to be set.

Clothes had to be rectified.

Real life intruded far too fast as the bliss receded.

"No rush," Matt murmured into her hair, but there was, of course.

She couldn't forget herself for too long. "Did you set an alarm?"

"Yeah."

"Because—"

He caught her wrist and tugged to get her attention. His eyes were warm and steady. "Ninja alarm set. It's okay. I'll be gone before she wakes up in the morning."

"You don't need to be gone." Maybe just downstairs on the couch. Did three-year-olds even think about stuff like that?

"Let's take this one hot sleepover at a time," he said with a little laugh. "Next time I can be sitting at the kitchen table nonchalantly drinking coffee."

"Or pretend snoozing under a blanket on the sofa?"

His smile relaxed, lifting on one side of his mouth. "Yeah. I like the sound of that, too."

"Me, too." She crawled off the bed and found some pyjamas, then bit her thumb as she watched Matt tug on his bright red underwear and his t-shirt. "This good?" he asked, holding his arms wide. "If she wakes up, I'll roll under the bed so fast, I promise she won't see anything."

"Except a puff of smoke?" Natasha waved to the bed. "You're perfect. And she doesn't come and find me at night. I asked her if she wanted to sleep with me the second night we were here, and she laughed at me. Rejected her mother."

Matt gasped, which made her laugh. "I'm so sorry."

She shrugged and gave him a rueful smile. "That's the price for having her go to sleep without me most of the time.

She's Little Miss Independent. Do you want to borrow a toothbrush?"

"Sure, if you've got one." He followed her to the bathroom, where she pulled out her tote of toiletry extras.

"You have your choice of silver and purple, extra-soft bristles, or a children's size My Little Pony brush that vibrates."

"Tough choice," he deadpanned. "I'll take the purple one."

"Don't say that we don't have the best hospitality here at…" She frowned. "I haven't named this place. I should do that. I mean, I'm trying *really* hard to not let myself get too far ahead on those kinds of frilly things, because a name for a bed and breakfast is useless without either beds or breakfasts, but…"

He took the brush from her and pulled her right against him. "The name is important," he said. "That's not a frill."

"You know what I mean, I don't want to get too excited and put the cart before the horse."

"I know."

She handed him toothpaste then grabbed her own brush.

They took turns using the sink, then he left her alone to pee. When she got back to her room, Matt had remade the bed and turned down the blanket on her side.

She crawled in next to him. "Hey."

He yawned.

She laughed and stretched out. "Come here," she said, holding out her arm. "You look tired and like you want to tell me all about your day."

He groaned. "Yes and no."

She got that. There were privacy concerns with medicine. "Okay, then just come and rest your weary head on me anyway."

He grunted contentedly at that, and she leaned in, brushing

her lips against his temple. She'd never had such an easy connection with a man.

The closer she got to Matt, the more she was realizing it wasn't only David who had made her jaded and cynical about love. There had been a long chain of emotionally unavailable men before him, none of whom had wanted more than her body.

And now she was all wrapped up in a man who was the last kind of guy she'd ever thought she'd be with again. A lot of men just like Matt had liked her. But they'd all left her. She hadn't been enough, hadn't been right for any of them.

Her track record should guarantee her fling with Matt would prove the same in the end.

But amazingly, she wasn't afraid of losing him.

He was the outlier element in that equation—because Matt was nothing like what he'd seemed when she first learned who he was.

"Tell me something interesting," he murmured, his eyes closed.

"Like what?"

"Whatever you want. Something that turns you on, something that freaks you out." He blinked his eyes open and looked up at her. *Give me something*, his face said.

Something was going on with him tonight. His bad shift had affected him, and her heart softened as she thought of him being that sensitive. Big, tough guy with real feelings.

"You know most of my secrets." She tried to think of a non-relationship thing to share. "Debt freaks me out. I've never owed as much money as I owe on this house. I've never owed money, really, ever. I don't carry credit card debt, I saved up to buy my car." She took a deep breath. "But this gamble? On the house? I *love* it. I thought I'd be terrified about the money, but I am stoked about the challenge."

"That's incredible." His arm relaxed around her waist and his breathing slowed. "Tell me something else."

"Uh…" She thought about how she'd blushed during sex. "I feel shy around you. Which is weird, because I am not a shy person. At all. You just make me feel all twisted up. But in a very good way."

He made a happy sound, and she pressed her lips against his hair. She should get up and turn off the light, but he felt too good against her. She'd let him drift off all the way first.

"What do you think about Escape Bed & Breakfast as the name for this place? I'm not going to necessarily offer breakfast, though. I could. But it seems lofty to call it Escape Inn when it's just two small apartments for rent…"

He didn't answer. His breath had slowed, evened out, and she kissed him again, inhaling his scent.

"Don't say we don't have the best hospitality at Escape Inn," she whispered.

One day, that would be true.

CHAPTER TWENTY

MATT LURCHED STRAIGHT up in bed, drenched in sweat. It was still dark out, and the room was quiet. His alarm hadn't gone off yet.

His heart was pounding, though. *Shit.* He dragged in a breath, trying to calm himself down before—

"What is it?" Natasha asked quietly. Her voice was low and sleep-filled.

"Time for me to go." He swallowed around his anxiety and reached out to squeeze her hip. "Go back to sleep."

She didn't say anything and he slid out from between the sheets. His chest pulled tight and he rubbed the skin, trying to make the ache go away.

Silent as could be, he found his jeans and his socks, making sure his phone alarms wouldn't go off as he tiptoed past Emily's room. Then he padded down the stairs and into the empty living room.

Not empty.

There was the red velvet sofa, now decorated with black and white cushions. Natasha's taste was impeccable. And on the opposite wall, every detail of her plan for the house carefully outlined in lists, sketches, and timelines.

He stood there for a long stretch, looking at her work. Thinking about how it made him feel.

She had dreams with a capital D.

Dreams.

What did Matt have? Fear. Regret. Anxiety.

And instead of facing all of that last night, he'd come here to bury himself in her arms.

"Is everything okay?"

He spun around. He hadn't heard Natasha come down the stairs, and now a fresh wave of those negative emotions washed over him. He looked at her wrapped in her blanket, her legs bare beneath it. "I…"

"I can put on coffee," she said levelly. "If you can't sleep."

The invitation was crystal clear. Did he want to talk?

No.

He knew that was the wrong answer, knew he should tell her something, anything, but as he stood in the shadow of her wall, all the anxiety and stress of the last eight months coalesced into a clear, punishing message in his head.

He wasn't worthy of her.

She deserved someone who could give her the moon and save the world and protect her and Emily from every bump in the road.

What did he have to offer? A guarantee that at some point, they'd go out for dinner and run into a woman he'd slept with once and never called again. Awkward family dinners with his brother and a constant reminder that Tasha had been left alone at her most vulnerable. And if Owen and his fucking book were right, probably a shit-ton of mental stuff that would only get worse before it got better.

Matt had promised Natasha he wouldn't be any kind of drama for her, but he hadn't been looking at himself when he'd said that.

He'd been so fucking cocky.

"Matt?"

Natasha put her hand on his arm and he jerked back.

"I have to go."

"It's the middle of the night, are you sure?" She didn't blink, didn't move. Just looked at him. "Did you have a nightmare?"

"I… How—" No, he wasn't sure he wanted to know how she knew. Had he said anything? Done anything to her?

"It's okay. You just seem rattled."

"Sorry."

"If you ever want to talk about anything, I can be a friend to you in that regard, too." She gave him a small smile. "You've been nothing but steadfast support to me. It's probably time I repay the favour."

His mouth was dry. He couldn't tell her and he didn't even have a good reason why. Just a feeling. A crushing sense of panic at the thought of burdening her with anything. "I'm good. But thank you."

"Okay."

It wasn't, though. This was some kind of test, and he'd failed it. He didn't know how to be a good boyfriend.

"I'm going to put coffee on anyway," she said, and something about the smoothness in her voice scratched at him. Like she was handling him.

"Don't."

The silence stretched between them, palpable and ugly. He forced himself to look at her, to look her in the eye. She was hurt. He'd done that. *Fuck.*

He clenched his teeth and shrugged. "Go back to bed."

"What's going on?"

"Nothing."

She gave him a long, slow, assessing look. Disappointment rippled across her face. "Not nothing. Don't lie to me. Something happened yesterday and—"

"Yeah. Something happened yesterday. I shit the bed at work, okay? I snapped at a patient. I was fucking pissed at her stupid fucking daughter and I didn't want her fucking death on my hands. It was completely the wrong thing to do and instead of dealing with it, I came here because I wanted to fuck you and forget—" He made a fist. *Fuck.*

She gasped and her face drained of colour. "Right. Okay, yeah, I'm going back to bed. Let yourself out."

———

THE RIGHT THING TO do would have been to apologize.

Of course Matt knew that immediately on some level, but he didn't really, truly get it until he was parked in front of his apartment building in Pine Harbour.

"You are a fucking idiot," he said out loud. Then he punched his steering wheel.

It was still dark out.

Had she actually gone back to bed? He didn't want to risk waking her up if she had, but on the other hand…

He pulled out his phone.

Matt: Fuck, I'm so sorry. No justification for that.

As soon as he sent it, bubbles appeared as she composed a reply. It took forever for them to turn into a real message, and when they did, it was short. Whatever she'd written, she'd edited it down into a clear, neat reply.

Natasha: Let me know if you want to talk about it.

Jesus, she slayed him.

**Matt: I do. But I might need a rain cheque for a
few days.**
Natasha: Take all the time you want.

It was a painful echo of Owen's advice to take some time off. Like everyone else could see that Matt needed to lie on his couch and face his fears like a grown-up. But he was not emotionally functional enough to do that.

Matt: I don't deserve you.
**Natasha: That's a really intense thing to say (and read)
at five in the morning.**
Matt: I get that.
Natasha: Are you okay?
Matt: Yeah.

No, but the real answer was more complicated, and needed to be explained in person.

Matt: I need a bit of time.
Natasha: Okay.

It wasn't the right way to end things, but he was running on empty. He grabbed his bag, locked his truck, and headed inside.

When he woke up for the second time, he was alone in his own bed.

No nightmare, no full body sweats. But no Natasha either, and he had a bone-deep ache in the middle of his chest. Not like the tightness of anxiety. This was something different and he hated it.

Owen had been right. Matt had snapped, and barely twenty-four hours after promising it wouldn't happen again.

And even worse, he'd taken out whatever the fuck was wrong with him on Natasha, who didn't deserve that. Nobody did, but least of all her, who had let him bury himself and aching need right in the middle of her heart.

He'd shown up at her house, talked his way into a sleepover, and then shut her down when she'd tried to help him in exactly the same way Owen had.

He couldn't ignore that there was something wrong with him anymore.

The rest of the day was spent on his couch. It took two false starts and three beers to crack the spine on the book, but once he started reading he couldn't stop.

It wasn't easy to see himself on the page like that. Every choice he'd made, every personality trait he'd always valued laid bare as a coping strategy to mask wound after wound.

When his stomach growled, he looked up and was surprised to find it was nearly dinnertime.

He set the book down and shook his head. Then he reached for his phone. His brother picked up on the first ring.

"Hey," Sean said. "What's up?"

So fucking much. He didn't know where to begin. "What are you doing for dinner?"

"Re-heating something. Jenna's out at a birth."

"Can I come over? I can pick up takeout from Mac's."

"Sure. Grab me meatloaf and a slice of apple pie."

"Deal."

Matt called the order in before leaving his apartment, then he bundled up. It was a cold, crisp night, but the walk would feel good.

Sean and Jenna lived on the other side of Main Street. It was a decent walk out to the edge of town to pick up food at the diner, then triangulating over to the small bungalow.

Before Sean had gone overseas, this had been their oldest brother's house. Dean had been a confirmed bachelor and a workaholic cop who didn't need more than a small two-bedroom house. In hindsight, there was a lot for Matt to unpack about his brother's choices, too.

Then he'd fallen in love, as apparently the Foster brothers managed to do despite their dysfunctions, and he'd built a bigger house for Liana north of town.

When Jenna showed up a month after Sean came home and introduced herself as his secret bride—another fucked-up Foster kid making fucked-up choices—Dean offered up his empty bungalow for her to stay in while she convinced Sean to pull his head out of his ass and give them a second chance.

Yeah, he had a lot to talk about with his brothers.

Jake, too. They were quite the dysfunctional crew.

Sean was on the porch as Matt approached. "Fucking cold tonight. Why'd you walk over?"

"Wanted the fresh air."

"Woman troubles?" His younger brother flashed an uncommon grin. "Happy to give advice in that area."

"Yeah, I've got troubles. Bit deeper than just what to do about Natasha, though, but that's as good a place as any to start."

"Whoa. All right, come on in." The metal leg of Sean's cane glinted as he moved under the porch light. It was a constant physical reminder that his brother still struggled with balance, even as he worked like a beast on his physical strength. Once a lean runner, now Sean had thick biceps and a solid wall of chest muscles. He looked every inch the personal trainer he'd turned himself into.

Reinvention hadn't come easy to Sean, though. It wouldn't come easy to Matt, either. They were stubborn, all of them.

But that needed to change.

Once inside Matt handed the takeout bag to his brother, then peeled off his outerwear.

"Can I offer you a beer?"

"Not tonight."

"Jenna bought me one of those make-your-own soda machines for Christmas."

"Christmas is still three weeks away."

"I was an exceptionally good husband and got my present early."

"Ah. Sure, make me something with that."

After Sean set what was basically just sparkling lime water in front of him, they dug into food. But each bite was hard for Matt to get down, so after a few forkfuls, he set his plate aside.

Sean noticed right away. "You okay?"

Matt took a deep breath. "No."

The story jerked out of him in fits and starts. He began with that morning, with treating Natasha badly, and worked backwards. The running, the nightmares, the extra shifts at work.

It got harder the further back he went, and when he got to those early days when Sean had come home and was living in Dean's guest room, he stopped.

"That was hard," his brother said quietly. "I was an asshole."

Jesus, no. Matt shook his head. "Not the point I'm trying to make. You were injured."

"No denying it, though." Sean took a deep breath. "You didn't come around a lot."

Matt's throat closed up. He nodded. That was true. He hadn't.

"It's okay."

"It's not."

"You're here now."

"Because I need to talk."

"Yeah? And you think I don't?"

"Fuck." Matt swiped at his eye. There was something in it. *Feelings.*

He laughed hollowly.

"What?" Sean grinned at him. "Come on, share the gallows humour."

"I might cry over you, you little shit. Fucking feelings."

"So cry."

Matt wrinkled his nose. Not yet. He hadn't gotten to the worst bit. "There was another reason I didn't come around that much when you first came home. The day we found out you'd been hurt, Jake and I drove Dean to Toronto. Did he tell you any of this when you woke up in Germany?"

Sean shook his head. "I don't think so. If he did, I don't remember."

Matt pinched the bridge of his nose, where the feelings were burning the worst. He needed to get through this like a man. *Or maybe you don't. Maybe that's the fucking problem.* "Jake called me when I was working. End of a shift. They picked me up at the hospital. Owen was my partner that day."

"What did we fucking miss?"

"Nothing. It was just one of those things."

It hadn't been the answer he'd been looking for. He'd wanted to know what he could have done differently. And then the phone rang and his world upended because on the other side of the globe, another *one of those things* had happened to his flesh and blood.

He couldn't breathe.

"Matt?"

He shook his head. "Sorry."

"Jesus, don't be sorry. Tell me more about that drive to Toronto."

Slowly, he opened his eyes and looked at his brother across the table. Sean was leaning in, his face earnest.

"I read a book today," Matt blurted out. "Well, part of a book. About depression. About not dealing well with trauma."

"Yeah?"

"I lost a patient that day. He died about a minute before Jake called me. An old army guy, really stubborn son-of-a-bitch who smoked too much and didn't take care of himself. Fred. Fucking good guy. We would transport him regularly, and it felt like just a regular call. We got him to the ER no problem, handed him over, and before we'd left the hospital, he had a sudden heart attack. Bam, gone. They worked on him, crash cart, the whole thing, but…"

"The same day?"

"Same fucking moment pretty much. I watched him die. And then Jake called."

"Shit."

"Yeah."

"That's some brutal double dose of trauma."

"I think it may have been the straw that broke the camel's back in a way. I didn't know, but Owen knew. He saw that I was spiralling into a mess, and I had no clue." Suddenly thirsty, Matt grabbed his glass and took a long drink.

"What are you going to do now?"

"I don't know. Keep reading this book I guess. I've got a few days off work. Owen wants me to talk about this stuff.

With you, with him. Fuck, I guess I'll have to have a deep and meaningful chat with Dad." Eventually. He wasn't in any hurry to negotiate the frustration that would be.

"I did that. It was good. I was angry at him for a long time, but now I just think…it is what it is. I can't change my childhood. And what I would change isn't about him. I wish I'd known Mom. That's what I would change."

"I remember her a little. She had the gentlest smile. I remember you sleeping with her in her hospital bed."

Sean gave him a sad smile. "Yeah? That's…Shit, I wish I could remember that."

They sat together silently for a few minutes. Matt picked at his food, but he still wasn't hungry. Finally he packed it away and pulled out the pie. Maybe dessert would go down better. "Have you thought about counselling?"

Sean's answer surprised him. "Every day. I did a bit in the hospital before I came home, but it wasn't the right time."

"Why haven't you done any since?"

"It's hard to find the right fit up here. Because everyone knows everyone else. Because—a lot of excuses, to be honest. But we're going to do a couples retreat for military members and their spouses when we're in Florida next month."

"Yeah?"

"Jenna's idea, to be honest. She basically said, if I want to have babies, she wants to do some processing of stuff first so we're going into that with as clean a slate as possible."

"Smart woman."

"The smartest. I tell myself every day that I don't deserve her."

"I know the feeling." Matt stretched his arms wide. "You want kids, huh?"

"Life is short, man."

"I know."

"You ready to talk about Natasha?"

He wasn't sure. "Is everyone talking about her behind my back?"

"Shit no. Everyone's talking about *you*. Jake's been really clear that we can rip on you as much as we want, but she's off-limits because you care about her."

"I do care for her. So damn much—which would be sweeter if I hadn't hurt her this morning."

"What did you do?"

"I barked at her. I told her I didn't want to talk."

"Well that was stupid." Sean shrugged when Matt frowned. "What? It is. Don't do that again."

"I need to get my head screwed on straight first."

"Before what?"

"Before…" He wasn't sure. "Before I ask her to forgive me?"

"For a fight? Dude, that's not how any of this works. You gotta talk to her. Sooner than later. Tell her everything you told me."

"Honestly, I don't know why I didn't this morning. She asked. And I pushed back."

"Yeah, you should figure out why you did that. But even if you don't, you could tell her that you know it's an issue."

No, he couldn't do that. "The last thing Natasha needs is for me to be any kind of burden on her."

His brother shrugged. "I think you may be wrong there, but I don't know her. I'd like to, though. Why don't you find a way to make this right so I can invite her and her daughter over for dinner?"

"I'll get right on that." And he would. Not just for the dinner invite path-smoothing, though.

It had only been a day. A very long, emotional day. And he missed Natasha and Emily something fierce.

But he couldn't go back to her half-cocked. He had to know that he'd be able to do what Sean said, and really open up to her.

Because if he froze a second time, he wouldn't deserve another chance to make it right.

CHAPTER TWENTY-ONE

IT TURNED OUT THAT RAGE—WHITE-HOT, are-you-fucking-kidding-me outrage—was the perfect fuel for Natasha to go job hunting.

She wasn't even sure what she was raging at, or about, but she knew she was *pissed*. And it felt *good*.

Matt ghosting on her was a big part of it. She knew something had happened, and he'd apologized for snapping, although she wasn't sure a simple sorry was enough. She didn't need drama like that in her life, no matter how good his arms felt around her.

But the vague worry she'd been chewing on about David's renewed involvement in Emily's life started to coalesce and sharpen, too. So she added another item to her to-do list on the wall.

Hire a lawyer

THAT WOULD TAKE a lot of money, no matter how she sliced it. But for three years, she'd been parenting solo, without any worry about custody issues. Now she had to face her growing concern that that might not always be the case.

Emily was her heart and soul. Of course she wanted her daughter to have a relationship with her father, but David had bailed when she was pregnant, and he'd established their default custody arrangement—it hadn't been her idea for her to do this all on her own.

He didn't get to radically change things now. Adjust, sure. But upend her daughter's life? Nope.

Mama Bear wouldn't let that happen.

So she needed to get a job, and she needed to get the apartments done, and being pissed off at the men in her life drove her out of the house and into action on both of those fronts.

They went to the thrift shop first, because retail therapy was always a good way to start the day. Most of the women's clothes were the same as the last time they'd popped in, but there was a fresh supply of children's stuff that was fun to pick through. She found a Christmas outfit for Emily to wear to David's. She didn't miss the irony of that being something she cared about.

But it was a really cute outfit.

Then they drove in a big loop, dropping resumes at all the bars and restaurants within twenty minutes.

Next on her to-do list was sourcing kitchenette materials.

"Let's go to the lumber store," she told Emily. "And we'll pick up hot chocolate on the way."

"Yay!" Emily cheered, waving her hands in the air.

Yes. Yay. She needed to take life lessons from her kid. Hot chocolate made everything better.

At the lumber yard, she introduced herself to the woman at the back counter, where custom orders were placed. They went over her detailed notes and she got a quote that was probably fair but just out of her budget. When she balked, the staff person gave her a heads up that they had a pre-Christmas sale starting on the weekend.

"Might want to think about stocking up then, it's usually our best sale of the year."

"Good to know, thanks." Tasha scribbled a reminder to herself on the top sheet of her notebook, then shoved her clipboard back into her tote bag. "I'll probably be back then."

If she could afford it.

Back at home, she worked over the numbers once more.

She couldn't really afford to hire a lawyer before she picked up another job. But she couldn't afford to wait, either. Same with the kitchenette purchases.

At some point, she'd have to dip into her savings in a big way to get all the balls moving.

But there was no such thing as reward without risk, so the last thing she did before calling the day done was she made a short list of family lawyers to call and feel out for compatibility. If David caused her any trouble, she'd need an ally in her corner who she could trust.

The next day she got her period, which explained some of the don't-fucking-dare attitude from the day before. Well, not being pregnant was a good thing. She would never again curse her cycle.

And then after breakfast, she got a phone call from a number she didn't recognize. "Hello?"

"Is this Natasha Kinglsey?"

"It is."

"This is Raj Patel from Wiarton Lumber. You dropped off your resume yesterday, and I'd like to schedule an interview for the cashier position."

"I didn't—" She cut herself off. Had she accidentally left a resume on the counter at the lumber store the day before? "I didn't realize it was a cashier position," she said somewhat clumsily. "How many hours a week is it?"

"Fifteen hours to start. Midday coverage, when we take lunch breaks and there's a rush at noon."

She quickly did the math. No tips and likely minimum wage meant that fifteen hours a week wasn't that much money. On the other hand, she'd probably be able to find part-time childcare midday at a more reasonable rate than evening or weekend care, which would probably make up the difference. She swallowed hard. "Is there an employee discount?"

He chuckled. "Doing some home renovation?"

"Something like that."

"That could be arranged. Would you be available to come in for an interview tomorrow?"

She closed her eyes and exhaled softly. "Yes, I would."

So that was two good things, and it wasn't even breakfast yet.

Letting herself be pissed was paying off.

———

BY THE FOURTH day of no work and no Natasha, Matt was ready to sacrifice himself on the altar of emotional availability.

He told Owen as much in a text, and his boss replied with a laughing animated GIF image.

Matt: I'm serious.
Owen: I believe you.
Matt: Let me come back to work.
Owen: Take a knee, man.
Matt: You're killing me.
Owen: Meet me at Mac's for lunch.

Apparently the altar of emotional availability was the diner on the edge of town. Matt found Owen in a corner booth, nursing a cup of coffee and a slice of pie.

"Did you eat already?"

Owen shook his head. "This was an appetizer. Pre-lunch sugar therapy. My ex is going south for a week over the holidays and my daughter wants to have a party at her house while she's away. My head is going to explode because it's not my call but it's a really bad idea."

"I'm sorry."

"Yeah. Well, what can you do?"

"Set up surveillance from a distance?"

Owen cracked a ghost of a smile. "Don't think that thought hasn't crossed my mind."

"Parenting is complicated shit, isn't it?"

"Hardest thing I've ever done. Seventeen years go by in the blink of an eye, man."

"Seventeen?"

"Her birthday's in January."

Matt tried to picture Emily as a teenager. Fourteen years from now, would Natasha be worried about the same thing? Emily having parties at David's cottage while he's not there? "Shit. Time flies."

"Don't remind me. A year from now she's going to be an adult and I am not prepared for that. Anyway, let's order and talk about you."

"I read the book."

"Good."

"I talked to Sean."

"Even better."

"I want to come back to work."

Owen shoved a menu at him. "Not yet."

"Why not?"

"What did you think of the book?"

Matt rolled his shoulders against the tension pulling across his chest and around his back. "It's heavy. You were right. It's me on every page. Childhood issues, messed-up relationship with my dad, medicating myself with meaningless sex for years. *Years.* It's a miracle I didn't end up using drugs or gambling, and frankly, I'm not sure I haven't misused alcohol in the past."

"Yeah. I know the feeling well."

"I know I've got some long-term work to do on all of that. Sean and I talked about counselling. I'm not messing around here, if that's your fear."

Owen waved down the waiter, some new kid Matt didn't know. "What do you want?"

"To come back to work."

"Food, Matt. What do you want to eat?"

"Oh." He scrubbed a hand over his face and thought about the menu he knew by heart. "Hamburger with extra pickles. Fries and coleslaw on the side."

Owen ordered the Greek salad, then leaned back against the booth. "You're on the schedule again starting on Monday."

Exactly a week off. "When did you put me back on?"

"Never took you off. I just told you to take a week. You need to breathe, Matt. To process and think and react and ache."

"Oh, I'm aching. I've never been more painfully aware of my own limitations. I've had enough of that, to be honest."

"Yeah, that's not going to work."

"What?"

"You cramming your days so full of work you can't sit in that discomfort and actually hear yourself think."

"I took the week. I read the book."

"There will be more books. Counselling is going to take time, too."

"I know that." He did. He knew this wasn't going to be easy, but it couldn't consume his every waking minute, either.

"Do you?"

"What do you want me to say? I like working."

"You can come back, but it's to a modified schedule. No more fill-in shifts, and honestly, I wouldn't mind you dropping to a part-time schedule for a while."

"I—" Shit. "Why?"

"Because I want you to be whole and healthy and doing this when you're fifty. Because there will be more Fred Carletons, and I don't want any of them to be your last patient."

Matt tried to swallow and couldn't. He grabbed his water. No, he didn't want that, either.

"That was a rough day," Owen said quietly.

"Yeah."

"There will be more."

Matt nodded.

"What will you do if Monday is one of them?"

Fuck. His eyes burned and he looked down at the chipped Formica table. "Talk about it."

"When? On Tuesday when you're back on the road? Wednesday when you're at work? Thursday when you've been called in to cover for someone because you live around the corner?"

He saw Owen's point. "Okay."

"Two shifts in a row. That's it for a while. Downtime in between. And keep talking. To me, to Sean, to your woman. To a professional as soon as humanly possible."

"Got it."

Owen nodded, looking at him closely. "We all know this,

but it's hard to actually apply to ourselves, isn't it? If we don't take that time regularly, and especially when we're dealing with trauma, we won't be resilient enough to deal with the blows we cannot avoid."

Matt frowned. "I'm figuring that out."

"Good."

Their food arrived, and the conversation faded. But it picked up again as their plates were cleared. They talked about Owen's new job, and Matt realized he'd also failed as a friend. "You've had a lot of change over the last six months, man. I'm sorry I wasn't paying attention to that."

Owen grinned at him. "You just did a deep dive into that book, didn't you?"

"Fuck yeah. I've got a lot on the line here." His job. Natasha. Emily. His long-term happiness and mental stability.

Natasha and Emily.

He was still piecing together everything he wanted to tell Tasha, but he was close. And at the end of lunch, Owen said something that completed that puzzle.

"Thanks for keeping me updated," his boss said. "I appreciate your trust in me. There's this unspoken idea in our occupation that we don't need to talk about all this death and pain we're exposed to, because what can we do about it? But we should talk. That's what we can do. And I want your help in setting that standard with the others, too. We need to be more open."

Words to live by.

After Owen headed off, Matt pulled out his phone.

Matt: Can I come over? I'll bring brownies.
Natasha: Is that all?
Matt: Also strong arms and an open heart. I want to

**talk. I've got a lot to tell you. But you can put me to
work, too.
Natasha: Okay.
Matt: Is that an Emily "okay"?
Natasha: Don't forget the brownies. Come after dinner.**

He didn't miss that she didn't answer his question. Maybe it wasn't okay. Maybe she wanted to give him a dressing down in person. Was that how dating went? Better to fight in person?

It would give him a chance to grovel and make up in person, too.

When he arrived, both girls came to the door, Emily in a blur of curls and squeals, Natasha looking cautious.

He stepped inside. "Hi."

She searched his face, her gaze full of questions, but Emily bounced into his arms. There wouldn't be any talking until she was asleep, and maybe that was okay.

"I missed you," he told his favourite three-year-old, not that she knew why. "What have you been up to?"

"Mommy got a new job."

"What?" He jerked his head toward Natasha.

She gave him a small smile. "Yeah. I'm the newest cashier at Wiarton Lumber. It's not really the job I was looking for, but the people who own the store are really nice and I'll get a discount."

"Hey, that's great."

"I need to find a babysitter, though, which is kind of stressful. But it's going to work out nicely in the new year because Em can start pre-school."

He set Emily down and took a step closer. "That's awesome, congratulations." He wanted to hug her. Instead, he kept his arms at his side and felt like he'd missed an awful lot in a few days.

"I'll tell you more after she's in bed," she murmured, holding his gaze.

He nodded slowly. "I can't wait."

"I'm not tired," Emily announced. She wrapped herself around Matt's leg. "Let's play ponies."

"Uh…" He grinned down at her. "Okay. And then bedtime."

She led the way upstairs to her room. Natasha followed too, stopping in front of the bathroom. "It's been a day and a half. Do you mind if I take a quick shower?"

He frowned. He'd been so focused on coming over and telling her about himself that he'd missed that she looked wrung out. "For sure. Take your time, I don't think anyone is going to be rushed through ponies."

And that was very true. Emily had elaborate plans for him. She carefully told him where to sit, then got out a big box filled with prancing pastel toys. "These are my new ponies," she said proudly. "Mommy got them."

They looked like they might be vintage, from when he and Natasha had been kids.

"This one is my favourite." Unexpectedly, it was yellow with a teal mane.

If she was moving out of the pink phase, he'd kind of miss it a bit. He grinned. "Nice."

"What do you want to play?"

"Whatever you want."

She pushed a purple pony into his hand. "You're the princess pony."

"Okay."

"You were a bad friend."

"Accurate. Okay." He cleared his throat and made the pony bob her head as he raised his voice. "I'm a selfish pony."

"You should say sorry."

He dropped back to his regular voice. "That's good advice. Who am I apologizing to?"

She wiggled her yellow one at him. "The queen."

"This is definitely accurate." He swallowed a laugh and lifted his voice again. "I'm sorry, my friend. You are the kind, benevolent queen and I was…" Thoughtless.

Emily held out her own, bigger pony. "Do you know what you did?"

Matt had to fight back a smile. "No, not really."

"You should think about what you did."

"Trust me, I am."

"Go to your room." Emily turned her pony around, then turned it back. He didn't think plastic toys could look disappointed in a person, but there it was. "And pick up all your toys."

But that wasn't the end of it. As soon as his naughty princess pony went to her room, he was given another pony, this one who had to have a whispered conversation about how the princess was doing a very good job at cleaning her room, and maybe they should throw her a party to make her feel better once she knew what she was sorry for.

Matt liked that. More grown-ups needed to be as forgiving as the plastic ponies in a three-year-old's bedroom.

By the time they were on their third role-play, Natasha was done in the shower. She appeared in Emily's bedroom door, her long dark hair loose and damp around her face. She was wearing Roots sweatpants and a faded band t-shirt.

She was fucking gorgeous.

He gave her a smile, acknowledging her presence, but he didn't stop playing right away. He liked her watching him.

"Emily," she finally said softly. "It's time for bed."

"I want five stories."

"Two."

"Two from you, five from Matt."

He laughed. "That's seven."

She frowned. "No, I said five."

"Okay, pumpkin. Do you need to go brush your teeth?"

She scampered past her mom and he stood. Finally they were alone. "Hi."

"You already said that when you got here."

"I'm saying it again."

"Hi." She smiled, but it didn't reach her eyes. That scared him a hell of a lot more than he could properly admit. He'd hurt her through his selfishness. "Full disclosure: I've had a long week, but I didn't want to tell you not to come over."

"I'm glad you did."

"Well, someone has to read her five bedtime stories, and it's not going to be me."

He smiled. "Fair enough."

By the time Emily was racing back into her room, he was sprawled in the chair beside her bed. She climbed up onto her pillow and shoved a book in his hand. "This one first. Please."

"Tuck in, then. Head on the pillow, blanket pulled tight." Once she was snuggled in, he angled the book so she could see the pages as he turned them, and he read it slowly, acting out each voice.

"Another," she whispered, and he picked one from the pile.

The third story he read more softly, letting his voice drift on the same note. By the second last page, her eyelids were firmly shut, and he read the last page quiet as a church mouse.

He tugged her blanket up around her shoulders, smoothing it over her back. She was so small and soft when asleep, such a marked contrast to her fiery personality when awake. Then he pulled her door shut and crept downstairs. He found Natasha curled up on the red velvet couch. She'd found a large crate to work as a coffee table, and a bottle of wine and two glasses were sitting in front of her. "Are you driving home tonight?"

He shook his head. "Not if you don't want me to. I'll set my alarm and get up before Emily."

She nodded without looking at him. "Okay."

She didn't look like she was in a talking mood. But if she was pouring them wine, she didn't want to just head straight to bed, either.

He thumbed through his phone, looking for the Havana song he'd downloaded. He hit play. "I listened to this on repeat a lot this week," he admitted as he held out his hand.

She looked at his outstretched fingers. "Why?"

"Because it made me think of you. And I like remembering the way you move. I missed you in my arms."

She took his hand and slowly stood.

"I missed you," he said gruffly. "So much. I have a lot to apologize for here. But first I want to dance with you. Would that be okay? And I want to hear about your week."

She stepped into his personal space, bumping her hips against his, and he said a silent prayer of thanks. His hands felt right on her waist, her smile as they danced better than any burst of sunshine on a cloudy day.

When she pushed up onto her toes and kissed him softly, he almost started crying, which was weird and disconcerting and fucking amazing at the same time.

Instead, he kissed her back. Soft and endless, until the song started all over again, and she laughed softly. "We should dance."

"And talk," he reminded her. "Tell me what's been going on. Tell me about the job."

"That happened by accident. I left a resume on the counter when I was getting a countertop quote—I'd handed a bunch out at restaurants, and it was stuck to the bottom of my notebook—and they called me the next day."

"Amazing."

"Anyway, I spent most of the week getting shit done. I crossed stuff off my to-do list like a boss," she murmured as she rolled her body to the music. "But it feels like each done thing creates three more tasks to add to the list, and it's kind of insane now. So much to do, not much time left before the holidays, and I'm not sure where to start with finding a babysitter."

"Can I help?"

She sighed. "It's fine. I'll figure it out, and the Patels are flexible about when I start. If I can't work many shifts before January when she can start preschool, it's not the end of the world."

"What else is on your list?"

"My sister is moving this weekend, and Em and I are both really sad about that. We're going there tomorrow for a last dinner and playdate with her cousins."

"I'm sorry."

"Yeah." She twisted around as the song ended, and he turned his phone off. Wine time.

Once they were settled on the couch, she lifted her glass. "To siblings and cousins."

"I can drink to that." Siblings. Fucking hell, that was a segue if there ever was one. "A lot of my week has been spent untangling my thoughts about my brothers."

Her eyebrows hit the roof. "Really?"

"Yeah." He cleared his throat. "It's complicated. I'm not sure where to start."

She leaned her head against the back of the couch. "I'm here to listen to any of it. All of it, if you want. Maybe just start at the beginning?"

Was it that simple? "I lost a patient at the start of the year. That's not really the beginning, but that's what triggered all of…whatever I'm dealing with." He told her about Fred, and it was harder than he'd expected. He got choked up around the death, and that emotional response took him by surprise because he'd gotten through telling the same story to his brother.

He took a big slug of wine.

Natasha just looked at him.

He took another drink and thought how his chest was tight, his throat was tight, and why couldn't he get on top of these feelings?

"Tell me what's wrong," she finally said. "Tell me what's scary."

Could she see the way that panic rose up from deep inside him? "Everything," he said roughly. "Everything except this, everything except you. But the rest of it is kind of fucked up."

"Oh, Matt, I'm so sorry."

He put his wine down again and shook his head. "I don't want sympathy, though. That's the thing. None of this is really that big a deal."

She leaned in and brushed her fingertips against his temple. "But in here…"

He shook his head and circled her wrist with his fingers, drawing her hand to his chest. "More like in here. Clawing fear."

She spread her fingers wide and pressed against his body. "I know what that feels like."

"Jesus, I'm sorry." He wrapped his arms around her and pressed his forehead against hers. "I don't want you to ever feel like this."

"But I don't feel it when I'm with you," she said. "Not even when you left the other day, and I was mad at you."

That made him smile weakly. "You were mad?"

"I was pissed. Men are so frustrating."

"I'm starting to see that. We're not the best communicators."

"Huge understatement. But I see you, you know?" She sucked in a ragged breath. "We're both kind of wrecks. Both sorry for the other, but maybe we shouldn't be sorry. Maybe we should—"

"Talk?"

She nodded. "And find some kind of absolution in that."

They could be refuges in the storm for each other.

He liked that idea a lot. So he dug deeper, right into the heart of the wound he'd exposed this week. "Those nightmares that I have…I run away from them. Literally, some days. I wake up in a cold sweat and I put my shoes on and run as hard and fast as I can. But I can never run fast enough."

"Are they about that patient?"

"Sometimes. Snippets of that. I re-live that morning a lot, the drive to his farm, the way I joked with him. I hear myself being casual about women, about dating and flirting, and it turns ghoulish. Ugly."

"Tell me…" she said, her voice not even a whisper. A breath.

Why would she want to know any part of that? He didn't want to know it, and he'd lived it. But she was asking. She wanted to know, and if there was anyone in the world he could trust with this secret, it was her. Even if it broke him to admit it. "I lost sight of what mattered. I missed something because I was too casual."

"I don't believe that's possible." Her words were gentle and kind and far too forgiving. "You are kind and good and giving and funny, but I don't believe you didn't do your job."

"I don't know." His voice cracked. He couldn't tell anyone

else this. "I know that by the book I did what I needed to do for him."

"But...?"

"But I can't shake the feeling that we could have done more. That it could have been prevented, that Sean—" Blood pounded in his ears. "I mean—"

"Oh," Natasha whispered. Her eyes were locked on his, her breath sweet against his face.

He felt his face drain of colour. "That's not what I meant."

"Are you sure?"

It took him a long time to swallow around the lump in his throat. "No."

"Matt..."

He shook his head. He didn't want her to say it. Didn't want her to pity him.

"It's okay to cry about your brother."

"He's fine."

"Now he is. He wasn't then. You must have been terrified."

It all slammed into him like it was brand new. He tried to clench his hands but his fingers were shaking too much.

She wrapped her hands around his and squeezed.

"I'm sorry," he groaned.

"Why?"

"I didn't want to burden you with all of this. I wanted to have this shit straight before I came over."

"That's not what I want. I want *you*."

"I'm not the guy you thought you met."

"What does that mean?"

"I want to be everything you need."

"That's not realistic. *I* need to be what I need. *You* can be what I want."

His heart pounded in his chest. "You deserve better than that."

"Do I? Do any of us? Or do we deserve to know that we are enough, without another person propping us up? That was my big realization this week. That I don't need you in my life to be happy, but I want you anyway. I want *you*, Matt. Hear me say that, and hear how good that is. I. Want. You. Just the way you are, right now, damaged and imperfect."

"Why?" It wrenched out of him, because that was a complete mystery to him now. He understood why women liked the old him, the flirt, the player. He even understood why Natasha would have time and patience for him to go through a low point, because she was kind and strong and brave. But he couldn't understand why she'd want him at his worst.

"From the moment I met you, I thought, you're too good to be true. And then I thought maybe the problem was that you're Jake's brother. Except you were again too good to be true there. Like it just didn't matter."

"It didn't."

"I know that now, but before, I thought, *How can I ever measure up to that?* I don't want you to be perfect. Don't you see how suspicious that is to me?"

Shit. No, he hadn't thought about it from that angle. "So… I'm not handling something well, and that's a good thing?"

"That sounds really horrible, but yeah, kind of. I just am relieved to know that you might find as much comfort in me as I do in you. Friendship and support—"

"Not just friendship." That distinction was so important to him now. "Right?"

"Right." She crawled into his lap and kissed him. "Not just friendship."

He tangled one hand in her hair and spread the other across her back. He'd hold on to her so damn tight. Forever, if she let him. "This week I've realized a lot of things. Had to come to terms with a lot of shit."

"It sounds like you've been traumatized. That's hard to come to terms with."

"It's not just trauma. It's also…I've had to think hard about how I feel about you. I've never let anyone get close. This is different. You are different to me. I want you, too, Tasha. So damn much, and I'm so sorry I couldn't tell you all of this the other day. But I need you to know that I see you, too. I see that you're right here, and I love how open you are with me even though a bunch of other assholes did their best to teach you men can't be trusted."

"You showed me otherwise."

"And then I misstepped."

"We do that. We're human."

He kissed her then, because he'd waited too long to do that. She tasted so sweet it made his knees weak. "That this has happened at the same time as I stopped coping in a bunch of other ways… I don't know. Maybe it happened for a reason. Maybe I fell for you because I finally let my guard down."

She gasped. "You…fell for me?"

"Too much?" he asked against her lips.

"Shut up, I'm falling for you too," she said with a sweet, unexpected laugh.

He opened his mouth and let her take over. She stroked her tongue against his, then nipped at his lips. She kissed his face and rode his body and God, he wanted to take her right there on the couch.

Relief surged through his body, hot and fast, and it felt a lot like heady arousal. Fucking hell. Fucking *yes*.

She stroked her fingertips over his face, then up into his hair. "Can I take you to bed?"

He felt big and raw and broken. Unwantable. And yet this

woman sat curled in his lap, gorgeous and kind, and she wanted to lead him upstairs and hold him against her body.

"Can you?" He laughed hoarsely. "I'd beg you for the honour, Natasha. Please, take me to bed."

And never let me go, he wanted to add.

But he'd been given enough for one night. He'd ask for forever tomorrow.

CHAPTER TWENTY-TWO

FOR THE SECOND time in a row, Natasha woke up because Matt had jerked awake beside her. But unlike the last time, when he'd rolled out of bed without saying a word, this time he grabbed his phone and, before answering it, whispered to her that he had to take the call.

"Hello?"

She listened to his side of the conversation, trying to figure out if she should get up and start coffee for him.

"Understood. I'm close by, I can respond. I'll find someone to meet me there, no need to call the OPP."

The police? That had her attention. She sat up as he ended the call.

"That was the military police. The vault alarm went off at the armouries. I just need to go over there and check it out." He grinned. "Convenient that I'm close by. Usually it takes a few calls down the list before they find someone."

"Where are the military police?"

He named a base a few hours away. "The sensor just pinged. Old building, new technology, it doesn't always work well together." He kissed her fast on the mouth. "Go back to sleep, I'll be back for breakfast."

A bleary examination of her bedside clock said it was barely three in the morning.

She tried to drift off again, but it was no use.

She grabbed her phone and went downstairs. While her coffee was brewing, she checked social media. Her sister's profile showed a green dot for chat, so she clicked on that.

Natasha: Are you awake?
Meredith: Packing up the kitchen. What are you
doing up?

She hit voice dial. "Long story," she said when her sister answered.

"A good one or a bad one? I feel like we haven't talked all week." They'd texted the day before about the new job, but Natasha had kept it brief.

She hadn't felt like talking when she didn't know what was going on with Matt. Now all these thoughts were bubbling up inside her, fast and furious. "I know. I tried to bury myself in the job hunt, but there was other stuff going on and I didn't want to burden you."

In the background, Tasha could hear her sister running water. "Are you making tea?"

"Of course I am. You should do the same."

"I put coffee on."

"Not quite the same, but okay."

"I wish you were here."

"We're going to have to get used to doing this over the phone. Tell me what's wrong. What did David do?"

"It's not David this time."

"Oh no, what did the cute firefighter do?"

"He has a name."

Meredith laughed. "I'm aware. What did Matt do?"

"Nothing, really. We had a…non-fight? Just a thing that happened." She considered how much of Matt's story to share with her sister. "He has some job stress, like a lot of first responders do. And he didn't know how to share that with me. He's just…not perfect. And apparently that's hard for him to realize." She laughed out loud. "Actually, I'm more fine with it than he is."

"None of us are perfect."

So far from it. "Right? And all of us have scars, isn't that what you said?"

"Yep. You know, I like the guy, but I'm glad to know he's been knocked around a bit, too. It puts you both on an even keel. You live life harder than anyone I know, and you deserve someone who does the same."

"I'm not sure I am at the moment."

Meredith clucked her tongue. "Okay, your coffee is clearly not inspiring you to have faith in yourself. Make tea. I'll wait."

She put her phone on speaker. "I haven't even had the coffee yet."

"Fine, pour that, give it a go."

Natasha laughed and grabbed a mug. "Shouldn't you go to sleep?"

"In a bit."

"Are you okay?"

Her sister sighed. "I am. You know how excited I am about the move. But this is the house I brought my babies home to from the hospital. I just scrubbed seven years of fingerprints off the trim around the kitchen door, and I thought…what am I doing?"

"Showing up for the fight?"

"Shut up. Do not turn my advice around on me."

They talked for another fifteen minutes, and just as Meredith announced her tea mug was empty, Matt knocked at the front door. "I have to go," Natasha said as she went to open it for him. "I'll see you tonight for dinner."

"Your sister?" Matt asked as she hung up the phone.

"She was packing and I couldn't sleep, so…yeah. Middle of the night sister chat. Everything okay at the armouries?"

He nodded. "I gotta say, it was nice dashing over there from here."

"You can stay here more often," she murmured. "If it's convenient."

He unzipped his winter coat and cupped her face in his hands. "I want to stay here a lot. And not because it's convenient. I want to stay here even when I have to work at the other end of the peninsula the next morning."

Her heart skipped a beat. "Well, Emily's going to be gone for two nights around Christmas, if you're interested in an extended sleepover—no pyjamas allowed."

"Sounds like a plan." He hung up his coat. "Do you want to go back to bed? Or should we make an early breakfast?"

"I'm not tired," she said quietly.

"And we have a lot to talk about still, too." He gestured to the kitchen. "Lead me to the coffee."

"I'm not sure you've finished your story about your brothers," she said after pouring him a cup.

"My brothers?" He barked a laugh. "Oh, last night. Yeah, I, uh, may have lost the train of thought there. Okay." He took a deep breath. "I've realized I have a complicated relationship with my brothers. With my father, too. Him first, then with them. We're best friends in theory, but we keep secrets from each other. I was thinking about you and your sister, and how close you are. We aren't close like that. It took me forever to tell

Jake about you, and not because I didn't want to. It just didn't need to come up."

She nodded slowly. "And by comparison, I told Meredith about you at the first opportunity."

"Right."

"Wow, that's kind of a heavy realization."

"Yeah. We want to have a good relationship with each other, you know? So it's weird. And it was the same, frankly, when Jake was going through his thing with you—we had no idea."

She winced. "Yeah?"

"He didn't tell us anything. He told Dani's brothers, because he thought he owed them an explanation. But confiding in each other for emotional support?" He snorted. "Yeah, that's not a Foster thing. But on the other hand, when Sean was hurt, there was no question about the fact that Jake, Dean, and I were all in that together. Jake and I drove Dean to the airport and he flew to Europe not knowing what he'd find, but he knew he had to go and sit with Sean, or bring his body home."

"You guys can't talk about your feelings, but you'll carry each other's bodies?"

"That's it in a nutshell."

"Wow."

"Yeah." He glanced at his watch. "Deep thoughts for five in the morning."

"We need pancakes to go with this conversation, don't we?"

"Extra syrup. And maybe bacon."

She pointed to the fridge. "Get on it, mister."

———

THE REST of December swept by in a blur. Natasha found a local daycare provider who would take Emily three days a week, starting immediately, so she started working at the lumber store. On her second day, she used her employee discount to place a big order, everything she'd need to put in the kitchenettes in the apartments, and tile for the bathrooms, too. It ate a big chunk of her budget, but once she had the kitchens built, she could take pictures of the studios and get her listings live online.

Coming this spring! Modern, cozy weekend getaway spaces.

SHE COULDN'T WAIT.

The cashier job proved more similar to bartending than she'd first expected. Because they primarily served contractors, she saw a lot of regular customers—and it paid off in a big way that she could remember what they'd come in for before. Plus she learned a lot about renovation trends from their conversations with Raj, which he happily included her in. She'd been agonizing over how to refinish the staircase to the second level on the apartment side until a contractor dropped a tip about his favourite wood paint. "A quick sand, then primer and two coats, and voila, you've got a brand new staircase that will look good for a decade."

Done. She picked up the paint before she left that day.

In general, her shifts went by quickly, and left time for her to do work at the house as well before she picked up Emily from daycare.

Matt slept over twice, and came for an early dinner before his Wednesday night parades at the armouries.

It was all in all an exhausting but rewarding routine she'd stumbled into.

But she was still looking forward to a few days off around Christmas, especially because a wicked winter storm was brewing out there.

As the temperatures dropped overnight the night before Christmas Eve, the wind howled and seemed to hammer the house from all sides. Tasha tucked Emily into bed, then took the baby monitor to the apartments. She'd already assembled the cabinets for the kitchenettes, and her countertop chunks had arrived earlier that day.

It was pretty straightforward—one piece of butcher block for the cabinet beside the sink, another to turn into a high island with legs she'd found at a recycling store. She finished the downstairs unit, then headed upstairs, where it was colder, and her fingers stiffened up as she got the screws and drill ready.

As she worked, she realized it wasn't just cool up there—it was pretty damn cold, and getting colder.

She ratcheted the last screw into place, then crawled out from the lower cabinet and ran her hand over the ancient register.

The air coming from the furnace wasn't hot at all. It felt like the air conditioner was on—except she didn't have AC.

Something was wrong.

Damn. She looked at the still-to-be-assembled island parts and decided that was as much as she could do tonight. She collected the baby monitor, her phone and her keys, and made sure the back side of the house was locked up before she went through the interior door into her own kitchen.

It was just as cool on this side of the house.

Double damn. Wincing at the thought of an emergency

repair visit, she searched for the name of an HVAC guy and placed the call anyway.

"Lot of calls tonight," the guy who answered the phone said. "I'm not sure how long it'll take for her to get there. Would you rather wait until the morning, or be on the overnight list? It's a bit cheaper to have a daytime call."

"Okay, let's do that."

"Bundle up under blankets," he said cheerily. "She'll call when she's leaving the previous customer."

Great.

Natasha knew what call she had to make next, and it physically hurt her. *Be brave*, she told herself. *Be fearless*. Hmmphf. When it came to her judgemental ex, she wasn't there yet.

David answered on the third ring. "Hello?"

"Hi, sorry for calling so late." It wasn't that late. Barely ten. He was probably still drinking wine after a lovely dinner in his always-perfectly-heated condo.

"What's wrong?"

Damn it, that was not how this conversation was supposed to start. "First of all, everything is fine. But I might not be able to drive Emily to Collingwood tomorrow to meet you at the cottage. My furnace just decided to act up, and now I need to wait for a repair person to come on Christmas Eve, so…"

"Act up?"

"It stopped working."

"You don't have heat right now?"

"Uh…" She wiggled her fingers in the air. "I mean, I did until like an hour ago, so the house is fine. I'll put Emily in my bed and we'll be fine under the blankets together."

"You don't have any heat?" He repeated the question, which was unnecessary. She'd answered it.

"This literally just happened, and you were my second call after the furnace people. So—"

"We'll pick her up first thing."

"You don't need to come that early. Or I can bring her after the appointment."

"First thing, Natasha. I don't want my daughter to be cold."

Oh, he did *not* just say that. "Obviously, I don't want her to be cold either. We have warm clothes and blankets. It's fine."

"Is it? The weather is terrible up there right now. What if your pipes freeze?"

Jesus, could that happen this quickly? "The repair person is coming as soon as possible." Except that was a lie. Natasha had pushed it back until tomorrow to save a few dollars. Her stomach sank. "Look, I just wanted to give you a heads up. Let's not make this into a thing."

"A thing like, my daughter needs a home with reliable heat and real furniture?"

She hung up the phone. She was shaking with rage as she switched to text messaging.

Natasha: Per our phone call, I would underline that I have given OUR daughter a loving, safe home every single day of her life, and your new interest in parenting needs to be grounded in an understanding of MY constant care for her. Do not ruin her Christmas by making this a judgmental pissing match. Please let me know what time you'll come tomorrow to pick her up.

He didn't reply.

She wasn't surprised. She stomped upstairs, carefully picked up her beautiful baby, and carried her down the hall to her own room.

It didn't take long to get warm under the covers. It took

much longer to fall asleep, her mind racing with what challenges the next day might bring.

***

FOR THE FIRST time in a year, Matt's partner on a shift was his sister-in-law, Dani.

Which meant he had to field a hundred inappropriately nosy questions in between calls. But it also meant he had lots of food to eat as she bugged him about Natasha while they stretched their legs in the break room of the station in the early hours of Christmas Eve.

"I'm just saying, I think I should invite her out for a girls' night," Dani said.

He stabbed his fork into a bowl of meatballs. "These are great. What spice did you use?"

"Can I have her number?"

"No."

"It's not like I'm a complete stranger." Dani had been the first responder when Natasha had wiped out in a snow storm —the same night everyone had found out Jake's former fling was pregnant and the big question was, might he be the father? "I want to meet her again, properly this time."

"And I want you to leave her alone."

"I bet she'd like to share a bottle of wine with me."

Natasha probably would—at some point. "Can you give me space to explore this relationship in privacy, first?"

"Of course." Dani tried to look hurt, but failed. "Come on, we have so much in common."

Matt choked on his next bite of meatball. Yes, they did.

"I didn't mean it like that."

"I know." He sighed. "Soon. Okay? I'm going to her place for a couple of days, and we'll talk about it then. But I don't know when she's going to want to start hanging out in Pine Harbour, and frankly, I'm in no rush either. I like having her all to myself."

"Don't be creepy and controlling. Girls' nights are essential to life."

That was a fair point. And with Natasha's sister moving away, maybe Dani's forceful brand of love might be an entertaining alternative to sister time. Not a replacement, but… He held up his hands. "How about this. I'll give her your number, and we'll see what she does with it. Deal?"

"Deal." Dani grabbed another Tupperware container from her bag. "And give her these cookies."

"Who's trying to woo her here, you or me?"

"Maybe you should bake her cookies."

Actually, maybe he should.

He'd already bought both Emily and Natasha more Christmas presents than Tasha would probably think is appropriate. But if he made her something, that would be her favourite gift of all—and soften the reaction to the spoiling he was going to do no matter what.

He should have thought of that before Christmas Eve.

Dani eyed him suspiciously. "Are you going to tell her you made these cookies?"

He opened the container and grabbed one. He shook his head after tasting it. "No way would she believe I made them. But I am going to make her something. Anyway, enough about me."

"Never."

"Let's talk about—" The radio squawked to life, and they were both spared the rest of that conversation. They shoved their food away and headed for the ambulance bay.

They were flat out until the end of their shift.

He went to his apartment, and before he got in the shower, he sent Natasha a text.

Matt: Happy Christmas Eve. Done my shift. What time are you taking Emily to her dad's? I need to grab some sleep, but I don't want to miss any time together.
Natasha: About that…

His heart sank as he watched the bubbles appear on the screen.

Natasha: So my furnace is broken. I'm waiting for a repair person, and David's coming all the way here to pick up Emily. Christmas may need to be postponed, because it's really freaking cold here.

He was already pulling on his coat.

Matt: I'll be there in thirty minutes. Hang tight. I'm so sorry.
Natasha: No, it's okay, get some sleep.
Matt: I'm honestly fine, and I bet you could use some moral support right now.
Natasha: I won't say no to that.
Matt: Good. I also have cookies.
Natasha: Even better. I could use them more than Santa right now.

When he arrived, the house was cool, but not freezing, and Natasha's smile was bright if a bit forced. "Hey," she said as he gave her a quick, one-armed hug.

"Merry Christmas no matter what," he murmured.

She nodded.

He held up the bag in his other hand. "I brought presents. I thought I'd leave Emily's here for her, but since she hasn't left yet…"

Natasha's face softened completely, even as she gave him a reproachful look. "You didn't need to do that."

"I wanted to."

"We got you a little something too, but it's a token. I hope you didn't go overboard."

"Let's focus on the cookies. Which are, by the way, from Dani, who is desperate to invite you out for a girls' night, and I need to get that bit of news out of the way before we focus on making a chilly Christmas super awesome."

Natasha laughed. "Okay."

"The cookies are really good. We worked together last night and she made them just for you. But I ate two because I'm a terrible person."

"You are anything but." She held out her hand and he passed over the tub of cookies. She took a bite out of one immediately. "Delicious," she pronounced.

He leaned in and kissed her. "Yes you are."

That got him a real smile.

He followed her into the kitchen where Emily was colouring in a notebook on the floor. He liked that his coming and going was now so normal to her that she just looked up and gave him a big grin before going back to her work.

The oven was on, which gave the kitchen some warmth.

"I'm making a big breakfast, since for once the fact that this ancient oven spills out heat is a good thing." Natasha said. "Bacon is on, and I'm about to do up some scrambled eggs and toast, too. Are you hungry?"

"Always." He sprawled out on the floor next to Emily. "I can source electric heaters if need be, too. Jake has a bunch for work sites, and he won't be using them this week."

"I hope it won't come to that." She frowned. "But thank you."

He tapped his finger beside the colour book. "Hey, Miss Monkey… Merry Christmas."

Emily flashed him another quick look. "Merry Christmas," she repeated.

"I hear we're having a big breakfast."

"Mm-hmm."

They coloured together while Natasha finished cooking, then they ate picnic-style, right there on the kitchen floor. Once they finished, he quickly did the dishes while Natasha wiped Emily's hands and face.

Then he crouched in front of the three-year-old. "Do you want your present?"

"A present?" She clapped her hands. "For me?"

He dropped his voice to a conspiratorial whisper. "And I have one for your mom, too."

Emily leaned in, eye to eye with him. "We have a present for you."

"Where is it?"

"Upstairs." She disappeared, rounding the corner in a flash before he heard footsteps flying on the stairs.

He got up from the ground and grabbed his bag of gifts.

Emily returned with a small, square box.

He held out one of her presents. "You go first."

She set his aside and ripped into the paper. This one was for her to share with Natasha. Matching aprons, and Emily held up her mother's first. "This is too big for me," she said solemnly. Then she spotted the matching fabric, now on the floor. "Oh! This one is *little!*"

Natasha, silent beside him, reached out and took her apron —pink, like Emily's, with Kitchen Boss stamped on the front. "Oh, Matt, these are awesome."

"Emily's says Kitchen Boss in Training," he explained.

"We need to get you one, too."

"Kitchen 2IC?" He grinned as she gave him a blank look. He tapped on his chest. "As a sergeant, I'm second in command of a platoon. 2IC."

Her eyes lit up. "Yeah, you could be my Kitchen 2IC."

He'd order an apron as soon as they had her furnace sorted out.

"Next present," he said, handing over the next one for Emily. She ripped into this one with even more abandon, and hugged the stuffed moose tight to her chest.

"Now it's your turn," Natasha said. She swiped the small box Emily had brought downstairs. It wasn't wrapped, just secured together with ribbon, and the box itself was beautiful —a faded, vintage world map print all over it. "This is something we saw and we thought of you immediately."

She handed it over. Her hands were shaking, and he caught her fingers with his. A little squeeze to say that he saw her, that he knew this was a weird first holiday together, and he didn't have any expectations.

He carefully worked the ribbon open, then lifted the lid.

They'd found him a leather passport wallet.

He lifted it out of the box and realized it wasn't empty. Inside was a notebook, carefully trimmed to be exactly the size of a passport. He paged through it.

Each page was coloured by Emily, and Natasha had written neat, careful words on some of them. *Paris*, said the first page. *Peru*, said another. *South Africa, Australia, Hong Kong...*

He kept flipping until his eyes blurred.

Then he cleared his throat. "I..." He lifted his head and looked at Natasha, who searched his face, her eyes wide. "Can I kiss you in front of Emily?" he asked under his breath.

She laughed and nodded.

He swept her into his arms and pressed a hard, grateful kiss to her lips. She curled her fingers into his shirt, right against where his heart was pounding a mile a minute.

"We haven't talked about travel again," she whispered against his mouth. "But I saw the wallet and wondered if maybe you wouldn't have one, and might like one..."

"I love it. And I love what's inside it more." *I love you*, he wanted to add, but a knock at the door interrupted them.

He let her go, and while she was answering the door, he crouched down to show Emily how much he liked the present.

"I drew this," she said as she pointed to the pictures. "And this is a tree."

The green squiggle was the most beautiful drawing he'd ever seen in his life. "I'm going to keep this forever."

Natasha returned with an HVAC tech in tow. "It's in the basement," she said, "This way."

He glanced up. "Do you—"

She gestured to Emily. "Can you?"

He nodded. Of course he could. He'd do whatever she needed here.

They disappeared, but they weren't gone long. And when they came up, there was no hiding how devastated Natasha was.

She took a copy of the invoice from the tech. "Thanks. I'll be in touch after Christmas."

"Don't let it go too long," the other woman said, and Natasha jerked her head in acknowledgement.

Shit.

She glanced at Emily. "Baby, can you go and grab your stuffies for the trip to your dad's?"

Emily scurried off, and Matt waited until the tech let herself out before instinctively taking a step closer to Natasha, wanting to at least give her his touch in comfort. "What's the verdict?"

She bounced up and down on her toes, anxiety rolling off her in waves. "Well, the current issue is the internal thermometer. She cleaned it off and said it should start up again in a few minutes. But I have a much bigger problem. She says the blower motor needs to be repaired, and given the age of the furnace, that might just be pouring money down the drain and I should consider replacing it entirely." She shook her head, her face crumpling. "I thought the furnace was fine when we moved in, but there's no way around it, I need a new one, and before winter is over. Fuck, Matt, I can't afford that."

He pulled her into his arms. No, he imagined that she couldn't. "We'll figure something out," he said softly into her hair.

She stiffened. "No, I can't—"

Shit. "*You* will figure something out," he corrected. "And I'll be here for you, as a sounding board. A friend."

Her chest shook against his as she dragged in a ragged breath. "This is the worst Christmas ever."

"You haven't opened your presents yet," he said lightly. "And even though I haven't slept yet, and my girlfriend is distraught, selfishly, this is the best Christmas I've ever had."

"What?" She jerked her head up and looked at him, her forehead knitted together in concern. "No."

"Yep." Which was a super fucked-up realization. "We never really did Christmas in a sentimental way growing up." He made a face. "I haven't told you a lot about my dad. He leaves much to be desired in the care and affection categories of parenting."

"Those are the primary categories."

"Yeah." He shrugged. "Tonight, after a nap and once we're well into a bottle of wine, I'll tell you more about my rough and tumble formative years in the Foster house. But the point right now is that while the furnace news is shitty, you did something amazing for me. So, let me try and salvage the day for you."

Emily came hurtling back into the room. "I have my bears. And Daddy's here."

"What?" Natasha whirled around.

From the entranceway, a male voice called out. "The door was ajar."

She leapt out of Matt's arms and he took a big step back, too. He hated that they both had the same reaction but he flashed her a reassuring smile anyway.

So he was about to meet the asshole who left Natasha alone and pregnant. Great. Maybe it was going to be the worst Christmas ever, after all.

CHAPTER TWENTY-THREE

DAVID HAD DELIBERATELY LIED to her when he said he was three hours away, since he somehow, magically, got to Wiarton two hours after he texted. Natasha clenched her jaw, letting herself process that realization.

Did he not trust her to tell him the truth of the situation?

She had nothing to be ashamed of here. And for now, the furnace was working again. Sort of. Tentatively. Guaranteed to break again before the season was out, but whatever. Her ex didn't need to know that.

Maybe she didn't tell him the whole truth, but she was as straight-up as she needed to be. And beyond that, her life was none of his business. She kept her nose out of his insanity. Why couldn't he return the favour?

"Merry Christmas," she called out as Matt gave her a look she couldn't quite figure out. Sometimes she really hated her compulsive need to be the better person.

I'm sorry, she mouthed to her boyfriend—and how wrong was it that she hadn't had time for that lovely new term to settle in before this rude interruption? This wasn't how she wanted him to meet David.

Matt just shrugged. And then he smiled, his eyes warm, and she felt it to her core.

With a nod, she moved into the living room, where David was standing looking at her wall of ideas. It was the only thing he could look at, other than the red velvet couch, because the room was otherwise completely empty.

"Nice place," he said completely without humour.

Out of the corner of her eye, she saw Matt sizing him up. In comparison, David was sleek and urbane to Matt's honest country boy looks. But the starkest difference was in how they interacted with those around them—David hadn't even acknowledged Matt yet. He never cared about who a stranger was. Everything was always about him.

"It's a work in progress." She turned sideways, including both men in her gesture. "Matt, this is Emily's dad, David Costello. David, this is Matt Foster. My boyfriend."

"Emily has a lot to say about you," David said, holding out his hand.

Matt closed the distance and took it.

Natasha imagined she heard bones crunching, enjoying the testosterone show-down a little too much. Matt had David beat in every single way that mattered, and a bunch that didn't.

"She says you don't like tomatoes," Matt responded. If Natasha were to say that it would sound bitchy, but Matt pulled it off as charming, an invitation for David to bring a bit of self-deprecation to the table.

Her ex didn't, of course, but he offered a ghost of a smile.

Natasha realized he was alone. "Is Sable in the car?"

"No. Uh…" He made a face. "She made me drive up on my own, first thing, to get Emily. She had some shopping still to do, so she'll meet us at the cottage."

"She *made you* get up early?"

"Woke me up at six with a thermos of coffee." Another faint smile. "She said if you needed our help, I needed to be early."

Huh. Maybe the Selfie Queen was more than just nice enough. "Well, tell her thank you. I appreciate it."

He turned to Matt as if she hadn't said anything. "Are you helping Tasha with this…house?"

"She's more than capable on her own," Matt said, his words just tight enough for Tasha to know he was clipping them. But he still sounded affable and easy-going. It was a mask, she realized suddenly—one he probably had to use all the time at work.

One that had slipped recently, because of stress. Well no shit. Nobody liked to have to constantly pretend.

Just then the furnace kicked in, like the tech had promised it would, and Tasha's knees threatened to give out. "Ah, the furnace is back online. I'm sorry about the panic in that regard. I should have waited to call you until after I had the appointment. I could have driven her to you after all."

"Listen—" David looked down at Emily, twirling on the end of his arm. "Is two nights enough time to…" He glanced around her empty house. "Do whatever you need to do? I need to get back to work on the twenty-seventh, but I could take Emily to Toronto. Sable has the week off between Christmas and New Year's Eve."

Panic flooded Natasha's chest. She wasn't ready to be separated from her daughter that long. Not yet. Not ever. "I'm fine."

"You don't have any furniture, and you called me last night, freaking out because your house didn't have any heat. Are you sure you're fine?"

Where was Sable to put him in his place when Natasha needed her? "One thousand percent fine. Okay, you guys should go. See you in two days. Have a *wonderful* time, baby girl." She crouched down and held her arms out. Emily flew in for a hug and Natasha tried to block everything else out. Skinny little arms around her neck, sweet kisses on her cheek. Nothing else mattered.

As she helped Emily into her snow pants, Matt gestured to her wall of ideas. "It's pretty impressive, isn't it?"

"It might be if I knew what it was," David said.

"Renovation plans." She stood up and patted Emily in the direction of the front door. "Put your boots on."

Matt shot her a quick look.

Was she telling David the whole plan? She was genuinely torn. She wanted to show him she had a plan, but she also didn't want to open herself up to criticism from someone whose opinions didn't matter.

Actually, no. She didn't want to show him she had a plan. She wanted to show that she had vision.

And not for him—his opinion of her no longer mattered.

For herself. Because she was proud of what she was doing here.

"I have two rental units on the back of the house," she said. "Small studio apartments, really. Not small by Toronto standards, though. I'm renovating them. That's why I don't have much furniture on this side. Most of my energy is being poured into those."

David looked at Matt, and in that moment, she wanted to punch him so hard, right in the mouth. It didn't matter what another man thought.

He glanced at the wall again, and finally to her. "Rental units, eh? You used to talk about having an inn. Is this the more realistic version of that idea?"

She laughed. "No. This is the first step in the very realistic plan to eventually get to that inn. But thanks for the vote of confidence."

"I—" He cut himself off and nodded. "Okay. See you in a couple of days."

They followed him to the entranceway, where Emily was still tugging on her second boot. Matt got a hug goodbye, then Natasha got another before Emily put on her coat and mitts and hat.

By the time the door shut behind them, Natasha felt like a wrung-out dishcloth. But at least she could be grateful that she had Matt at her side and the hum of her furnace—

She cocked her head and swore under her breath. "Did the furnace die again?"

It did.

"It mother-fucking-did," she whispered. "On Christmas Eve. After I paid—" She swallowed a cry as Matt pulled her in close for a hug.

"I don't think I've heard you swear quite like that," he said softly. "I'm sorry. We'll fix it."

She laughed slightly hysterically. "How?"

"I can go down and see if I can figure out where the ther-mometer is inside it. Or…here's a radical thought. It's going to warm up tonight. The house is fine to get a bit cool. How about I take you back to my place? It's warm and I have a big bed."

"Your plan is to distract me with orgasms?" She gave him a wide-eyed look. It wasn't the worst idea, but she needed to get her furnace fixed. She couldn't just hide out under his covers, no matter how nice that sounded.

"No distraction. Just a bit of dedicated care while we figure out a plan. Plus you still need to open your presents."

Another laugh burbled up from deep inside her. He'd brought her presents, and she'd forgotten all about them. She took a deep breath. He hadn't slept after his shift yet, and the thought of his bed sounded pretty good to her, too—with or without orgasms. "Can we save those for after a nap? I want a do-over on Christmas Eve."

"Abso-fucking-lutely."

———

WHILE NATASHA WENT upstairs to pack a bag, Matt jogged downstairs to look at the beast that was distressing his girlfriend. He didn't know shit about furnaces, but a quick Google search explained that a failing blower motor would make the furnace turn off instead of overheating. While he was down there, it fired up again, worked for a few minutes, and shut off.

Back upstairs, he found Natasha putting away the dishes he'd washed.

"I heard it come back on," she said. "I guess it's going to just cycle like that until I fix it?"

He held up his phone. "I did a quick search and that sounds about right. But it is working, at least intermittently."

"Fine, take me away from this madness. I'll buy you a coffee on the way because you must be exhausted."

"I can sleep when I'm dead," he joked.

"Or in an hour, with me…"

"Oh, that's a much better plan. Lead on, gorgeous."

They took his truck. He liked seeing Natasha curled up on the other side of his cab, her bright eyes flashing at him from under a brimmed toque. It was a bright day, the sun glinting off the snow as he drove up the steep hill out of town.

Rocky outcrops on either side of the highway marked the shift in geography. Wiarton, at the base of the peninsula, was a dividing point between his world and the rest of the province.

It was also an invisible but palpable line to cross with Natasha.

Their entire courtship had been in her space. Now he was bringing her home, to a place where she'd invested some hopes and dreams in the past, however fleeting, and had them dashed.

He reached across the console between them and took her hand.

She squeezed back. "Did this disrupt any family visiting before you were going to come to my place tonight?"

"Nah. Dani's sleeping today, because she's got another shift tonight, so Jake will take Calvin to my dad's for a visit. Sean and Jenna might meet them there, but we're not doing a family meal until next week when Dani's off and Dean and Liana are back from Nashville. I wasn't kidding before when I said Christmas isn't really a thing for us. If it weren't for the wives, us guys would just exchange a group text and be done with it."

She looked out the window. "I miss my sister more than I thought I would today. She always went all out with the decorations. I'm glad Emily's getting that with her dad this year."

A different kind of tension pulled at Matt's chest. He didn't want to overstep, but he hoped that this time next year, they'd be decorating her house together from top to bottom. "I will do my best to make tonight as festive as possible. It may require a fair bit of improvisation, but I can be a creative guy." It started to snow as he pulled into the parking lot of his apartment building. "See? I live in a snow globe."

"Pretty," she said with a real smile.

Only on the outside. His apartment was as basic as it could be, because he literally just needed a place to store his shit and be horizontal every sixteen to thirty-six hours. He'd never thought about bringing her here before. Hadn't wanted her to see the starkness of what he was—and wasn't—splayed out like a tableau. The old Matt would have felt super self-conscious about Natasha sizing up his space and finding it wanting.

He'd wanted to be something better for her, in a way he'd never cared about before with any other woman.

But now he knew he could show her any and every part of him and it would be just fine.

They climbed the stairs, then he ushered her inside first before setting down their bags—her overnight clothes, his tote with her presents still in it, and his present from them, the passport he wanted to talk to her about later that night, over a bottle of wine and under whatever twinkly lights he could commandeer.

"So this is your bachelor pad, eh?" She turned in a slow circle, taking it in just as he'd expected. "Wow. Barbells stacked in the corner, big-screen TV taking up literally half the wall."

"I know. I'm a cliche."

She stopped in front of him and pressed her hands to his cheeks. "No you aren't," she breathed. "You surprise me at every turn. Even when it's discovering that you are such a completely conventional country boy."

He grinned. "Want to make out on my navy blue comforter?"

"You know it." But she didn't really feel the bright, false confidence she projected, and he saw right through her.

"Hey, it's going to be okay." He shrugged out of his coat and pulled her close for a soft, gentle kiss. "I'm tired, how about you?"

"Exhausted." She sagged against him.

"Presents after our nap, okay?"

"Whatever. Just peel me out of these clothes and tuck me in right next to you."

He did just that. As she stretched out, her head nestled on his pillow—a Christmas gift in and of itself—he grabbed his phone to set his alarm so they didn't sleep the entire day away.

He showed her the text message group chat Dean had started an hour ago. "See? I told you this is how we do the holidays."

She laughed and rolled onto her back. He fired off a couple of messages to his brothers, then set the phone on the bedside table and joined her under his navy blue cliché of a comforter.

"Christmas is looking up," she murmured as she melted into his arms.

If by Christmas she meant his erection, that was accurate to the nth degree. But now that he was horizontal, he was also exhausted, so he kept his dick in his shorts and just kissed her, over and over again, until they were both warm and giggly.

Sex could wait. Right now they had cuddling, and that was everything.

Cuddling is everything was his last thought before he fell asleep.

His unconscious self was more mercenary, though, and when he woke up hours later, both of his hands were down the back of Natasha's panties and he was holding her tight against his body, her legs spread on either side of his rigid thigh.

From the way she was nuzzling his neck, he was pretty sure she was horny, too.

And he would have done something delightfully filthy about both of their needs if his alarm hadn't gone off at the same moment as a happy knock sounded at his door.

He grabbed at his phone first to silence it. There were a bunch of text message alerts, too.

He stumbled out of bed to tell whoever was at the door to go away, Merry Fucking Christmas-style, before realizing that the most recent message in the group chain was related to that.

Sean: Supplies left at your door as requested. I knocked just to be a dick. Merry Christmas.

He scrolled back up and read the rest of the messages, then grabbed a hoodie from the chair in the corner and tossed it at Natasha. "Put this on."

She zipped it over her bare breasts and climbed out of bed, gasping when her bare feet hit the floor. "Holy cold! Where are my—"

He knelt in front of her and tugged a clean pair of his wool grey work socks onto her feet. "There."

She laughed at him. "What is going on?"

"Christmas surprise. Come on." He led her back into the living room and then held up his hand. "Close your eyes."

She grinned and did as instructed, standing in the middle of his apartment in nothing but his sweatshirt and socks. Insanely gorgeous.

He opened the door, expecting to see a box of stuff. There was that, but…

Sean and Jake had outdone themselves. *Fucking perfect.*

"Matt?"

"Yeah…" He stared at the Charlie Brown Christmas tree in front of him, already on a stand. How was he going to get it inside? "Ignore any noises you hear for the next thirty seconds, okay?"

"This is really assuming a level of trust I'm not sure we've discussed," she said with a giggle. "But sure."

The tree brushed the doorway with a quiet rustle. Needles dropped everywhere, but he didn't care. He dragged the cardboard box in, too, then shut the door. A quick check inside the box showed everything he'd requested and then some. Jake had probably taken the Christmas lights off his own tree.

"Keep your eyes—"

"Closed, I know," she murmured as he moved around her. He grabbed one of the strands of lights and plugged it into the wall before stringing them haphazardly up and over his TV.

Next from the box was a dubious sprig of greenery that he was ninety-seven percent sure was not mistletoe, but it was a close enough approximation for his purposes. He shoved that into the DVD stand next to the kitchen door, and then swung past where Natasha was waiting so he could kiss her before finishing up.

"Still closed?" she asked, laughing at him.

"One more minute."

"Sixty, fifty-nine, fifty-eight…" As she counted backwards, he jammed the Santa hat on his head and shoved the USB stick into the side of his TV.

Sean had downloaded a video of a burning fireplace. Apparently his brothers were more festive than he'd ever given them credit for.

"Eighteen, seventeen, sixteen…"

He grabbed her presents, shoved them under the tree, then stopped in front of her and hit play on the Christmas music on his phone. "Open your eyes," he said as the first few notes of Silent Night started.

She blinked her eyelids, then focused on him first before her gaze jerked to the TV behind him, and then slid to the ugliest Christmas tree she'd probably ever seen. "Oh."

"Merry Christmas, Tasha."

Her eyes sparkled suspiciously as she poked at the white fur trim on his hat. "Look at you," she breathed. "My real-life Santa."

"I ordered us our own little Christmas and my brothers made it happen. That was the, uh, unexpected tumble out of bed that interrupted our dirty wake-up."

"You are forgiven." She glanced around. "They all did this?"

"Well, Dean is in Nashville, so it was just Sean and, uh, Jake. Yeah."

"Wow."

"They know how important you are to me," he added.

"This is so sweet." She unzipped her—his—hoodie and leaned in, brushing her lips against his jaw. "Really thoughtful."

The tip of her tongue found his skin and electricity jolted straight to his balls.

Oh, God. "Anything for you," he said thickly.

"Mmm. I don't know. It's Christmas and Santa has a long night ahead of him. I think it should be anything for *you*, don't you agree?"

He hefted her in the air and she shrieked, but when she slid back down his body, her legs wrapping around him at just the right spot, the lusty sigh came back.

It had been a long day. And she was right. He did have a long night ahead of him. They could both use some restorative affection first.

He turned and lowered himself onto the couch, holding her against him the whole time. When he sprawled his legs and arms wide, she stayed clinging to him. They were down to their underwear, except his hoodie hung off her arms and he was wearing the Santa hat.

"I don't have any condoms close at hand," he growled.

"We don't need them for this," she said, reaching between them. "You like my hand, right?"

Fuck, yeah. "Damn straight I do."

She licked her lips and looked between them.

"I want to make you happy," she said softly, then looked at him.

Yeah, he wanted her mouth. But he wanted something else even more.

"I want to be inside you." A rough, hungry admission that was one hundred percent true.

She climbed off him, all long limbs and loose smiles. He watched from beneath hooded eyes as she jiggled her way to her bag and produced a string of condoms.

Excellent. He'd burn his way through all of them tonight.

When she turned back to him, she stumbled to a stop.

"What?"

"Stop looking at me like that," she said huskily.

"Never."

"It's indecent."

"That's me."

She shook her head slowly. "No. You're the best man I've ever met."

"Take off your panties."

With a grin, she hooked her thumbs under the cotton and wiggled free. Gloriously bare, she sashayed back to the couch and resumed her position straddling him. This time when she reached for his straining erection, he said nothing. They had everything they needed now.

She freed him from his briefs and stroked his length firmly. Her touch made him groan and sent more blood to his already throbbing cock. He was more than ready to surge into her, hard and fast, but having her rub and slide against him was the sweetest kind of torture.

He cupped her breasts with his hands, played his thumbs against her nipples. Two could play the torture game, and he could up the ante with his mouth, too. He sucked on her until she fisted her hands in his hair and tugged him off.

"Enough," she said as she gazed down at him, her eyes glassy and her mouth swollen.

When she rolled the condom on to him and rose up on her knees, he had to fist his hands into the couch cushions to keep himself from squeezing her hips and pulling her right back down again.

"This is what you want?" She rubbed him against her slick entrance. "Like this?"

"I want you." His voice was hoarse. "Every way. Any way I can get you."

"You've got me," she whispered as she brought him into her body.

She was tight and hot, a sweet, agonizing glove he had to work his way into. It took three slow thrusts until he was fully buried inside her. Countless more, each one a little less controlled than the last, each one making her tremble and shake and grind against him. Sensations overwhelmed him and his thoughts scattered as she rode him roughly.

He found her breasts again. Like in his sleep, holding her possessively felt right. Handfuls of Tasha for the rest of his life. That's all he wanted. Maybe more kids if she was game. A dog.

A white picket fence she'd long sworn off.

This was everything he wanted. The best gift in the world.

"Fuck, Tasha," he growled, which was a long way off from the sweetness rioting around in his head. "I…You…"

"Come," she urged.

He crushed her against him and took her mouth as they came together. A kiss, a promise, a plea. He couldn't tell where he ended and she began, and he knew he'd never want to have it any other way ever again.

CHAPTER TWENTY-FOUR

"CHRISTMAS STATUS CHECK?" Matt asked into Natasha's hair.

Post orgasms, they'd stretched out on his couch, her on top of him, both naked. He'd lost the Santa hat somewhere along the way but it had done its job.

"Hungry," she mumbled.

He'd been going for happy, but he could work with hungry, too. "Food first, shower second? Or food first, sex again, decorate the tree, maybe shower last?"

She laughed and lifted her head. "You're insatiable. I like it."

He stroked her cheek. "For you? Yeah, I am. It feels like we never get enough time—and I get why. Obviously. But the long-distance thing makes the time that we have together…special."

"For me, too." She twisted her head and kissed his fingers. "Food first. Let's play the rest by ear. But decorating the tree is definitely happening."

Once they untangled their bodies, she tugged on his sweatshirt again, then grabbed her discarded panties from the floor and stepped into them.

"I like you in my clothes," he said as he zipped up the hoodie.

"This is going to smell like sex."

"Good." He kissed her hard on the mouth. "Food options. Let's see what we've got in the Christmas box."

There was another tub of cookies, half a fruitcake, and a box of chocolates. He handed the chocolates to her and carried the cookies and cake into the kitchen.

"Before we do a head-first dive into dessert..." He pulled open his freezer. "Steak? Stuffed chicken breasts? Stew from..." He scraped a bit of ice off the container and looked at his handwriting. "Four months ago. Still good."

"You made stew?"

"I love stew. One pot can feed me for days." He grabbed a second serving and ran them both under hot water to release the frozen blocks. Then he added them to a pot on the stove with a bit of water and got that warming up. "Toast with that?"

"Please." She sat at his tiny table and watched him with what felt like wonder—not that he was doing anything impressive—as he put bread in the toaster and pulled dishes out of the cupboard.

"Now the tricky thing, Ms. Bartender...I don't have much to offer you in the way of drinks." He nodded toward the fridge. "I think I have a can of Heineken in there, which we could split."

She got up and instead of going to the fridge, disappeared into his living room. She returned with a nice-looking bottle of red.

He burst out laughing. "You packed wine?"

"I have my priorities straight, don't you worry. Do you own wine glasses?"

"Yeah, I'm not a total caveman. I just haven't used them recently." He pointed to the top cupboard, then watched as she stretched up on her toes to get them. Condoms and wine. She was something else.

When the stew had warmed through, he split it between two bowls and they sat next to each other with a plate of toast between them. They ate slowly and talked about all sorts of things. Natasha grabbed her phone and showed him pictures Sable had texted her of Emily opening way too many presents.

"I'm glad I saved the ones I have for her until she gets back," Tasha said, chewing on her lower lip. Then she took a deep breath. "Oh, speaking of dysfunctional families, my parents sent an email wishing us a merry Christmas, which I suppose is better than absolutely nothing."

"Where are they?"

"RVing through Arizona." She shrugged. "They're basically going through a second youth, and don't really want to invest time in being grandparents. They used the excuse of not approving of my pregnancy to fuck off, but they weren't great with Mer's kids, either."

Matt lifted his glass. "To dysfunctional parents."

"And may we not be them." She tapped her glass against his lightly.

"I'll drink to that."

She watched him over the rim of her glass.

"What?"

"Nothing."

"Not nothing," he said softly.

She laughed and shook her head. "No. Just a weird memory that roared back with a vengeance at the weirdest time."

He held her gaze because he wasn't afraid of anything. "What was it?"

"After we knew for sure that Jake wasn't the father of my baby, he said that a real man would step up, even if he hadn't wanted the pregnancy in the first place. And he said something like, 'A lot of men don't think they want babies. My brothers are all like that.'"

Matt swallowed hard. Thanks a fucking lot, Jake. "That was four years ago. And someone else's assessment of me, not my own words. But he was right about what a real man would do. And if it had been me instead of Jake four years ago, I'd have wanted your baby even if it wasn't mine. Emily is amazing."

Her eyes glittered. "I know. That was a weird tangent, sorry."

"Don't be. It's Christmas. The holidays are emotional, or so I hear. I've been emotionally unavailable my whole life, so this is new and fascinating to me." He scooted his chair back from the table and turned it so he was facing her, nothing in between them. "I never thought about having kids or being a parent before I met you. I spent my entire adult life avoiding second dates. Commitment wasn't anywhere on my radar. But that's all in the past. Okay?"

"Yes." She leaned in and kissed him. "Thank you for not freaking out."

"I'm good. What other hard topics should we cover? Or are you ready to talk about this morning?"

"Which part?"

"All of it."

"Sometimes I really don't like my ex," she admitted.

He resisted the urge to agree with her. David was arrogant and awkward, at least around Natasha, and the way Matt saw it, he'd made that bed for himself with poor choices. The natural consequence of abandoning a woman to raise your child by herself is that woman not liking you, and not wanting you in her house.

"But then there's another part of me that worries that he might be right. That I'm in over my head. Because when the furnace stopped? That felt true. And then I get angry about *that*, because fuck him and his judgement."

"This is your first real speed bump as a homeowner. It's natural to worry about how you'll sort it out. But you will."

She bit her lip as she looked at him, her eyebrows pulled together. "I spent more than I should have on my construction supplies. There were some good deals, and I had an extra discount, and now…suddenly I'm perilously close to running out of money. If I don't get the units up and running soon, I'll suddenly find myself in a financial hole every month. I—I have never been reckless with money before, but I've never owed money on this scale, either."

"You said you loved the challenge of all of this. Is some of that waning?"

"I guess. That was before it got real. Now I'm back to being terrified. Last night I thought, maybe I should try and sell it."

"Wow. Really?"

She shrugged. "I feel like I've bitten off more than I can chew, and doing a quick flip of the house would cut my losses. Sell the potential. I don't know. If I can get it sold at a profit, with the work I've put into it and a new furnace, someone else with more capital might be able to do what I was thinking without the stress of riding it so close to the line. I don't know if I want that extra pressure." She licked her lips and dropped her gaze.

"What?"

"Wrong thought, wrong time."

"No, never. You can tell me anything."

She lifted her eyes, glittering with unshed tears. "It might be easier for me to move closer to David."

That punched Matt in the chest. Hard. He wanted to tell her no, that she should stand her ground. The asshole didn't want her or Emily three years ago. He'd had his chance to have them close. Now Matt wanted them, and he'd do whatever it took.

Except he wouldn't tell Tasha how to live. Or where to live.

He loved her enough to let her make whatever choice she needed to make for her daughter, or herself.

He opened his mouth to say something—anything—but nothing came out.

"I know that's not the right answer…"

Did she? Good, because he hated it and couldn't say that out loud.

"Matt…"

He re-focused on her face as the first tear rolled down her cheek, fat and full of sorrow. *Shit.*

"What if I make a bad decision out of stubborn pride or spite, and it ends up hurting Emily?"

He squeezed her arms and shook his head. "You are an amazing mother. You would never hurt her. Trust your gut."

She blinked solemnly and more tears fell.

He took her face in his hands, wiping away each tear, drying her cheeks. "I have all sorts of selfish reasons to say you shouldn't move, but I can think of one really good reason that has nothing to do with me. Your dream matters, Tasha. It really does.

"Remember what you said to me. You are all that you need. You are stronger than strong. You will slay this dragon. But you are not alone. You could do this on your own, but you don't need to. I have your back."

"I know you do."

"And I know people."

"No, Matt, I can't…" She trailed off.

He knew she wanted to figure it out all on her own. But she had a boyfriend who had her back, and he came with brothers who loved nothing more than leaping into the fray. It was a Foster trait, for better or worse. "Just promise me you'll think about it. That's all."

"Okay," she finally said. "It's not that I want to sell. I just don't want to be selfish, either."

"You're not. You deserve happiness." *Let me be your happiness.* "And this house is the first step in your master plan for world domination. Don't let a speed bump derail that."

"Right." But she whispered it like she really wasn't sure.

He kissed her. "You're going to be just fine."

"I want your confidence," she said with a little laugh.

He stopped and pressed his forehead against hers. "You know what? I don't have a lot of confidence right now. But when I told you about my troubles at work, you had faith in me. Even when I don't have that faith in myself. This is the same thing. Let me be your biggest cheerleader."

Her eyes, big and dark and wide, searched his face.

Matt had never let anyone in like this. A friend to share dreams with, a lover to confess one's biggest fears. It would be foolish to fall in love with a woman who just told him she might leave him, but for the first time in his life, Matt didn't care if he was being a fool.

And he wasn't going to passively wait for her to figure out how he felt, either.

"I love you, Tasha," he said quietly. "And that's the scariest thing I've ever said in my entire life. I promise I won't ever hurt you like David did. I'll never make you doubt yourself."

She slid her hands over his forearms, her fingers shaking as she leaned in and kissed him, a barely open brush of lips and tongues that felt raw and eager and vulnerable.

Perfect.

He kissed her back, then hauled her into his lap. She wrapped her arms around him, a lamprey eel again.

He couldn't ever forget how much she needed him to be a rock she could cling to. "I've got you," he whispered into her neck. "Forever."

CHAPTER TWENTY-FIVE

NATASHA FINALLY OPENED her presents from Matt on Christmas morning, while he proved he could make a mean cafe au lait and wicked cinnamon French toast.

"I could get used to watching you cook," she said from her perch at his tiny table. "Although the kitchen space leaves something to be desired. Of course, I'm not one to talk."

"What do you want to do with your kitchen—eventually?"

"I'd knock out the wall between the kitchen and the living room, and make it one big eat-in space. The long-term plan would be to turn my side of the house into a bed and breakfast, and I'd live somewhere else. I don't feel comfortable with Emily coming home alone to a house with short-term tenants, honestly. Is that too paranoid?"

He shook his head. "Nope."

"So by the time she's old enough to walk home on her own from school, I'd like to have a different house of my own, and be using the current house as a mini-inn. Practice for a full-fledged inn property in the country."

"Amazing. So the big eat-in kitchen would be for the two rooms upstairs?"

"And open to the self-contained units, too."

"Genius." He pointed to her presents. "If you don't open them soon, I'm going to think you don't want to open them at all."

She picked at the paper. "We just got you a used leather passport wallet."

"Which I love. And Emily filled it with drawings which will one day be worth millions, so…honestly, my gifts will be dismal disappointments."

She laughed.

"Open them," he said warmly. "Or there's no French toast for you."

Taking a deep breath, she peeled the paper off the first present, a thin rectangle that weighed more than it looked like it would. Inside she found a plain grey-blue cardboard box. She wiggled the lid off, and inside that found a dark black-brown leather-bound book.

"What is this?" She asked as she picked it up. It was heavy but slim. Quality paper, excellent construction.

She opened the cover and gasped at the embossed inscription on the first page.

ESCAPE INN WIARTON
GUEST REGISTER
PROPRIETOR, NATASHA KINGSLEY

"You…"

He grinned. "I took a chance that you'd go with your heart's true desire over what was practical."

"I thought you were asleep that night."

"I was drifting off. But it stuck with me. It's a good name."

"Wow." She ran her fingers over the letters. "Well, I guess I can't sell the place now."

"I hope you don't."

Oh, Jeez, there was a big lump in her throat now. She swallowed around it and blinked hard. "I love this." She set it aside and crossed the tiny kitchen to kiss him. "It's perfect, thank you."

"Merry Christmas," he murmured. "One more to go."

"'Kay." She topped off her coffee, then reached for the second gift. This one was light as a feather, even though the box was bigger than the first. She ripped the paper away and found a cardboard box, clearly recycled—unless Matt was giving her a box of protein supplements.

And he wasn't. Inside that, there was a soft bit of fabric.

Two bits.

She burst out laughing as she held them up. Matching underwear, his and hers, pink with avocado dancing across the fabric. "For you and me?"

He wiggled his eyebrows. "Indeed. You already saw my intended Christmas underpants, so...I ordered these. And they had women's styles, too. We don't ever need to tell Emily that the matching apron gift gave me such an inappropriate idea."

There wasn't any part of him that was inappropriate. She stood up, peeled off her panties, and pulled on the new pair.

She twirled around for him, and when she stopped, he was right in front of her.

"They're amazing," she said softly. "And so are you. Thank you, again, for turning my blue Christmas around." She laughed as she threw her arms around his neck. "You really are something, you know that?"

He hugged her back. Simple, loving, kind.

"I..." She choked up again, because this wasn't easy. It was nearly impossible. But he was the best thing to happen to her since Emily, and he needed to know that. "I love you, too, you know," she whispered against his cheek. "And it's scary for me, just like it's scary for you."

"Maybe it doesn't need to be scary anymore, if we're in this together," he said, his voice warm and sure.

Wouldn't that be something?

After breakfast, they piled back into Matt's truck and headed south. Away from Pine Harbour, away from his bachelor pad, and back to real life.

The house was cool but not uncomfortable with the sun streaming in the windows. With steaming take-out coffees in hand, they walked through the rental units as Natasha reviewed her plan and tried to figure out how she could get them up and ready as fast as humanly possible.

"The thought of buying beds right now makes me want to throw up," she admitted. "I can't skimp there, but they're so expensive. All of the furnishing stuff is going to quickly add up."

"Can't you go minimalist? Only buy half of it at first and sell the places as Spartan?"

She laughed. As if.

But wait.

Half.

"Oh, Matt, maybe that's *it*." She pressed her lips together, trying to quickly do the math. It was too complicated for her head, so she grabbed her notebook. "If I only finish one of the units…" She scribbled the costs on a new sheet of paper. "Some of the contracting costs will be higher since I'll have to start the other side as a separate project, but the furnishings are literally half the expenses, so if I can space those out while I get some revenue coming in…"

He leaned on the other side of the kitchen island, looking at her sheet. "I don't get it."

"*Half.* I only need to rent out *one* of these spaces as soon as possible. The other one can wait a bit. So that's just one bathroom I need to renovate, not two, and there's the money for a new furnace." She wrote a big flourishing line under the numbers. "Right there. It affects my income projections for the next…six months? Maybe even a year, but I can break even on one unit and pick up more hours once Emily starts school. Even do some bartending again. Malcolm would have me back. *Yes.*"

"This is a good plan?"

She leaned across the island and kissed him. "This is a great plan. I don't know why I didn't think of it sooner, but it doesn't matter." She clapped her hands on the butcher-block counter. "Amazing. Of course the answer isn't all or nothing. The answer is to keep moving forward with *something.*"

He rubbed his knuckle against her chin as he gave her a look that warmed her right to her soul. "Smart."

"Thank you. I don't know that I would have figured this out without your support and positivity. I might have collapsed into a weeping, despondent pile."

"But you'd have been a cute despondent pile," he murmured. "And then you'd have picked yourself up and found the solution in the end."

His love was such a gift. She smiled at him. "Okay, now I need to find a contractor who can do a simple, single bathroom as soon as humanly possible." She took a deep breath. "But that can be tomorrow's problem. Let's go build a blanket fort in my room so we're cozy tonight."

———

THE DAY AFTER CHRISTMAS, when everyone else was

sleeping off turkey or snagging Boxing Day deals, Natasha did the grown-up thing and spent a painful chunk of her savings on a new furnace. It would be installed two days later, and the sun was shining enough to keep the house habitable until then with the occasional anemic push from the failing blower motor.

This was a decision that was immediately tested when David returned with Emily mid-afternoon.

"I've been thinking," he said after she'd hugged Emily and their daughter sprinted upstairs to introduce her new stuffies to the rest of the gang.

Natasha regretted having let him inside, but the last thing she wanted to do was stand around with the door open when her house barely had any heat to hold on to in the first place.

"Not really necessary," she said. Maybe snarky. Maybe she didn't care.

"Hear me out."

She took a deep breath. "What?"

"Emily could come and stay with us for a few months."

"No."

"While you fix this place up."

"No."

"Because—"

"I said no, and that's final. This is not a discussion I'm going to have. Not now, not ever."

"We had a great visit."

She knew their daughter was upstairs and could hear them, so she grabbed his hand and dragged him—possibly with more strength than she'd ever mustered before in her entire life—into the kitchen.

"There is so much wrong with this idea I don't even know where to begin," she whispered in a hiss. "Did you say anything to her? She's *three*."

"No. I thought we should discuss it first."

"We are not discussing this. You're suggesting something I am not okay with, on any level. It doesn't matter that she's living in a fixer-upper. It doesn't matter that my furnace blew up. I provide for my daughter, and you never have, in all the ways that count. You had a nice *visit*. Get it? Visit. That word is key, and you are fucking insane if you think—"

"She's my daughter, too." And there it was. The glint of danger she'd feared since he'd popped back into their lives.

The blood in her veins turned icy cold. "What are you suggesting?"

"I could sue for custody."

Five words, and her entire world spun on its axis. Blood pounded in her ears and she actually saw red.

"Try it." She'd burn his misguided idea to the ground. "Go ahead and sic your lawyer on me. But by the end of it, the court will make you cover every single last penny of my legal fees, because you have abdicated your responsibility from day one. Day one, David. I wanted you to be her father. I wanted you to be there for all the dirty diapers and middle of the night feedings. I wanted someone—anyone—to hold my hand as I pushed your daughter into this world, but you were nowhere to be found. So fucking try it."

He blinked at her.

Good. She was fucking done with not being crystal clear on this point. "I'm glad you are learning to love Emily, but we both know that you do not want to be a full-time parent to her. I do. I always have. So back off."

Another blink.

She kept going. "You will always be her father, regardless of how much time you spend with her. And you have a choice to make about how you want to live *that* role. Do you want to be fighting her mother? Do you want her to grow up knowing you judge me and my decision-making skills? Or do you want to be grateful for the time you get with the most beautiful little girl in the entire world, who is that way because of how I raise her?" She paced away, then stalked back. "Well?"

He cleared his throat. "You make some valid points."

Oh for fuck's sake. "No fucking shit."

"Stop swearing, Natasha. It's not necessary."

"Yeah, well, I'm not fucking sure it's not. Will you just be straight with me? What's going on?"

"Sable wants a family."

That knocked the wind out of her. "What?"

"I mean, she wants a baby. Of her own. Our own."

"Oh."

"She doesn't want to take Emily from you. Neither of us do. But you've been right all along. I don't know how to be a single dad. She's had to push me to step up, and…"

He trailed off. But she could see it now. If he had a child with Sable, she would do all the parenting.

Good lord, Natasha had dodged a bullet.

She took a deep breath. "Are you sure…It is none of my business what you and Sable decide to do as a couple. But you cannot use Emily as a trial run. You cannot use her to prove to Sable that you're Dad of the Year when you aren't."

"That's not what I'm doing." But his cheeks darkened.

"Maybe it's not the whole thing, but it's part of it."

"I shouldn't have said anything." His jaw flexed. Great, now he was defensive.

"I like Sable," Natasha offered more softly. "She is genuinely kind and good with Emily. If you are serious about having a full-time family with her, take some time to think about what that would mean. She deserves a full-time partner who wants the same things she does."

"I'm doing my best, which you may not think much of, but

—" He cut himself off this time, more decisively. "I'm not going to sic my lawyers on you. You're right."

She took a long, wary inhale. She knew this stage in a David argument well. He'd try to save face by doing something reasonable, in the hopes of sweeping his offensive behavior under the carpet. "Good."

"I'm going to offer them up instead. Let's craft a clear custody agreement about Emily. All in writing, so there's no doubt about how much Sable and I respect you as a mother." He stumbled on those words, and she wasn't sure he meant them. "I'll foot the bill, of course."

That wasn't how good legal representation worked. She shook her head. "I'll have my own lawyer work on it, too." Dignity was damn expensive, but she'd make it work.

After David got home he would surely send a silky email, using all the right words, and pretend he hadn't threatened her with a custody battle.

Pure bullshit.

But she didn't care, because she'd stuck up for herself and her daughter. She was slaying dragons left and right.

———

THE DAY after her furnace was installed, Emily went back to daycare and Tasha went to work at the lumber store.

The Patels were happy to hear she'd be open to more hours, and told her to use any of the contractor connections through the store to get a good deal on the bathroom installs she needed. So she told herself she'd ask the next contractor who walked through the door about their availability.

She was not expecting that person to be Jake Foster. Apparently the universe was committed to throwing a third dragon in her path this week to slay.

Everything happens in threes, she thought.

"Hey," he said, stopping a few feet short of the counter. He looked older than the last time she'd seen him, but happier. The few lines on his face looked good on him.

She smiled, because she could. She'd wondered what this moment would be like, seeing him again, and it turned out it was almost nothing. A whisper of regret from her past, that was all. And now that he was in front of her, the sharp contrast between him and Matt—and the intense connection she'd only ever had with Matt, from day one—was so stark it physically pained her that she'd let Jake ever be an issue. "Hi," she said softly. "Long time no see."

"Yeah. I didn't realize you were working here."

"Started earlier this month."

"I don't come in that often, I guess. I'm usually further up the peninsula."

"Makes sense." She suddenly remembered the Christmas decorations. "Hey, I should say thank you for the Christmas tree. That was a fun surprise. It meant a lot to Matt."

He shrugged. "It was a fun assignment. Sean took the lead. He even stole my fruitcake."

"Ah, that was yours?" She grinned. "It was delicious."

He laughed and rubbed his jaw. "I guess I deserve that."

She shook her head. "No. Nothing like that. Anyway, what can I do for you?"

"I'm here to pick up an order. I called it in first thing this morning and spoke to Raj."

She pulled out the stack of contractor orders, and there was Jake's, third from the bottom. "Got it. Here you go." He handed over his credit card, and she swiped it, then handed over the invoice and stamped it as paid. "It's palleted up for you, just pull around to the side and give them this order number."

"Thanks." He stopped, then glanced around.

They were alone, but this was her job. Whatever he wanted to say could probably wait. She searched for a non-rude way to push the conversation to a close. "I'll see you soon, maybe?"

"That would be good. Dani has been bugging Matt for your number."

Natasha laughed. "He'd said something about that. He gave me cookies she baked, but I didn't know if she was just being nice."

His eyes went soft. "Dani doesn't do anything just to be nice. She, uh, has some thoughts about how I could have been kinder to you. Back when you were pregnant."

That was not what Natasha had been expecting to hear. "Really?"

"Yeah. I think…" Okay, they were doing this now.

She took a deep breath, bracing herself.

But he shook his head. "No, never mind. Now is not the time or place, but just know, she's definitely Team Natasha. Womanhood and sticking together, that sort of thing. Which of course, I'm fully supportive of."

Natasha burst out laughing. "Okay. That's the weirdest pitch for me to hang out with your wife, but it worked. I'll get in touch with her. Matt says she likes girls' nights."

"Yeah." He grinned widely. "She does. Even more so since becoming a mom."

"You have a boy, right?"

"Calvin." He pulled out his phone. "He just turned one before Christmas."

"Cute."

She grabbed her phone. "Here's Emily. She'll be four in June."

"She's adorable."

And that was that. He headed back outside to pick up his

order. She didn't realize until after he left that there was zero weirdness for her about him having a child with another woman. He'd never been hers to lose, and she'd known that for ages, but it still felt good to have it confirmed.

Third and final dragon slayed, and it wasn't even lunch yet.

CHAPTER TWENTY-SIX

ON THE FIRST parade night after the holiday break, Matt got to the armouries early, because he only had to drive four blocks. He'd been at Natasha's house for dinner first, and headed out when she marched Emily upstairs to have a post-spaghetti bath before bed.

He'd go back to her place tonight after the Army got their pound of flesh from him for weekly training.

He wasn't the only one in early. Some of the most senior NCOs—including his brother Dean and Ryan Howard—were in for an O-group meeting before training began.

Matt checked in with his officer and gave a verbal report of how many members of their platoon he was expecting to show and explained the absences reported so far. Then he decided to go and grab a coffee because he had time, but Ryan stopped him on the way out.

"Matt," the DSM said, holding out his hand.

"Sir."

"Shit, you know I hate that." Of all the non-commissioned officers, only the sergeants major were called sir. And the rest of them enjoyed doing it a bit to get the ribbing in.

"That's why I remember to do it every time." Matt grinned. "What can I do for you?"

"I know I covered it last time, but we've got another Mental Resiliency session tonight and I'm going to be in and out of exercise planning meetings all night. You don't get to dodge it this time, sorry."

"Actually, that's fine." He didn't miss the look of surprise on Ryan's face. "I've had some, uh, stuff come up at the day job. Owen Kincaid's got me thinking about how a lot of this is more relevant to me than I wanted to admit."

"Owen's a smart guy."

"He is."

"Listen, you know my door is always open on that score— or any matter."

"I do, sir. Thank you."

It had been a while since Matt had taken the course for leading the professional development sessions on mental readiness, so after the training night started and his troops were tasked off, he grabbed the notes from online and got himself squared away in a classroom upstairs.

Like the book on male depression, the teaching slides described Matt—and his brothers—on every page. He also saw his issues at work.

He was a pro at compartmentalizing his stress.

He just couldn't ignore the boxed-up shit for too long.

When the troops filed in, he shoved away those personal reflections and took them through the slides. It was a textbook perfect lesson, but one that was not connecting with them. He could see it in their blank stares and shifting body language.

He could see himself, and his resistance to all of this until it was almost too late.

His throat tightened up, and he firmed up his jaw. *Damn.*

"All right. Let's set aside the slides with the canned

language, and get real." He turned off the projector and paced back and forth, waiting until he had everyone's attention.

He made eye contact with every troop in the room before continuing.

"Here's the thing," he said thickly. "All of you are going to need this shit at one point or another. Every single one of you will be in a place where your emotions run high or you're blindsided by conflict, trauma, injury, or stress. And you know how I know that? Because it happened to me. I want to tell you a story. And I want you to know before I start that this is a hard thing for me to share, because I don't like to think of myself as being weak. But the thing is, it's not weak to recognize stress inside your body. It's strong."

As he said those two words, everyone shifted. It wasn't what they had expected him to say. Maybe someone else. Maybe Sgt. Major Howard, but not Sgt. Foster. They were listening now because he was shocking the hell out of them.

"As I'm sure you are aware, a year ago my younger brother was injured in Iraq. We are all grateful that he survived, that he is home again and doing well. What none of you know is that the same day I found out Captain Foster had been hurt, I lost a patient at work. And I didn't have a chance to deal with that death. He was a soldier, too. Retired guy, long history of service. Did three peacekeeping tours overseas. Kosovo, Bosnia. Life-long smoker, had chronic bronchitis. And a couple times a month, I'd be called out and we'd take him to the hospital.

"I know that COPD kills people. I knew he was sick. But he was as alive as you or me when we picked him up. When we arrived at the hospital, I joked with him about picking up women. And in the half-hour or so it took us to do our paperwork before we headed out, he had a massive heart attack and died in the emergency room.

"I didn't see it coming. That's the shit that will fuck you up, boys. Something in your life will blindside you. Your woman will cheat on you. You'll be in a bad car accident. You'll lose a job and slide into debt. You will lose a loved one, a friend, a neighbour. Have a house fire. And in our line of work, you will see people get hurt, see people die, or worse."

"Nothing's worse than seeing someone die," a young corporal interjected.

Matt didn't bother to jack him up for interrupting. This was too important. "It's not about better or worse. It's all about what gets under your skin, what gets in your head. And that's going to be different for each of us."

"So what happened to you?" Another corporal asked.

"I got nightmares. Panic so real it felt like my chest would crush in on itself. I stopped hanging out with friends and my brothers. I poured myself into work so I wouldn't need to be alone with my thoughts. I, uh… conflated what happened to my brother and what happened to my patient. I felt guilt so ugly, so deep, I couldn't name it. I still do, I gotta be honest with you. This is some fucked up shit."

"You don't look fucked up."

Matt looked at the young woman's name tag. "No, Barro, I don't. I look like I've got my shit together, don't I? And most days I do. But my supervisor—he's ex-infantry too—he saw some subtle shifts in my personality. He called me on it, and gave me a good book to read about depression."

Every spine in the room straightened.

He nodded. "Yeah. That's not a word we talk about a lot. There are other ones, too. Anxiety. PTSD. You're going to hear people talk about mental injuries, and that's what these all are, but I dunno…I think it's good to talk about depression the way we do everything else. To use the word and name it. I'm struggling with *depression*. And it completely blindsided me."

"So..." Another troop started and then stopped his question.

"What am I going to do?"

"Yeah."

"Go see a doctor at some point. Talk to my girlfriend about it—a lot. Talk to my EMS partner and boss about it, especially when I feel it affecting me at work. Focus on a good work-sleep-exercise balance. And I'm going to talk to a professional about it as well. The key takeaway for you guys is that I ignored all of the early warning signs. So don't be like me. Don't be stupid. Treat your minds like they're any other part of your body and don't hurt them."

———

HIS TRUCK HADN'T EVEN HAD a chance to warm up, that's how close the armouries was to Natasha's house. That's how quickly he could get back to her after a night of work.

Natasha was in the living room, staring at her idea wall when he pulled up. He watched her through the window as he parked, hopped out, and headed up her front walk.

She was working so hard to get everything done and watching that—this late at night—did something weird to him inside.

Stopping, he turned around and jumped back in his truck. He drove around the block and hit the drive-thru at Tim Hortons. He got two different herbal teas and a twenty-pack of Timbits, fuel for a late-night planning session.

When he arrived back at her house, she was in exactly the same position, still wracking her brain for how to best tackle her mile-long to-do list.

He jogged up the steps and knocked quietly.

It wasn't until she opened the door that he realized his heart was pounding and his chest was tight.

"What's wrong?" she asked, her eyes wide as she looked at his face.

"Nothing." He stepped inside and stopped. "I mean, I didn't think anything…"

She took the tea and donut holes from him and set them aside. Then she closed right in up against him and kissed him. Warm caresses to his wintery cold skin. A sweet balm to his broken soul.

"I was fine," he said, his voice cracking. "I was. I am. I just… Something snuck up on me and I didn't realize it." He barked a laugh that sounded weird to his own ear. "I came straight here, and I saw you in the window. You are so beautiful. So fierce. Focused and gorgeous and strong. So I thought, I should go and get you tea, because I know you like that."

"Thank you." She whispered it against his skin. Soft and sweet.

His hands clenched on her hips and he closed his eyes. "I told a room of young guys about my shit tonight."

"Oh, wow." She breathed in, and he tried to match her inhale and exhale. He failed. "How did that feel?"

"I thought it was good." But she was looking at him like he'd seen a ghost and his chest was doing that fucking thing it did where it screamed like a canary in a coal mine that he was not fine, not good, not okay. "But maybe it was scarier and harder than I thought."

She nodded. "Maybe. And then you got me tea?"

It wasn't possible to hold her tight enough. He wanted to get her anything and everything she needed to make her dreams come true. Tea was nothing.

She unzipped his coat and he hung it on one of the hooks just inside the door. He'd installed them two days earlier. A row up high, where he put his coat. And a little row down low, for Emily.

He hauled Natasha against him again and kissed her.

"It's okay," she whispered, her lips not leaving his. "I'm right here."

"I don't want to talk about the Army." He took a ragged breath, then another, this one smoother. "Not tonight. I did a thing, it had a delayed effect on me, but now that I've got you in my arms, it's better."

"Okay." She squeezed her arms around his neck. "Hugs are always good, though."

"Always. And now I want to talk about why you're up late staring at your idea wall."

She sighed and stepped out of his arms. "I was actually trying to distract myself. My current problem isn't reno-related."

"What happened?"

She shrugged, but she didn't meet his eyes. "Tea first?"

"Tasha." He stopped again and bent down enough to meet her eyes. "What happened?"

Screwing up her face, she took a deep breath, then gave him a small, sad smile. "David sent me an email blowing off his next weekend with Emily."

"What?"

"Said something work-related came up, but I don't know." Her mouth tightened up, and he could see the pain in her eyes.

Fuck. "I'm sorry."

The corners of her mouth turned down. "Yeah, me too. I really am, because…" She dragged in a breath. "For Emily, first of all. He had a nice run there of being dependable. And this doesn't mean he isn't necessarily dependable—"

Matt begged to differ.

She caught his expression and gave him a look.

He raised his hands. "I know, not my place. I just don't like to see you like this."

She picked up her tea and paced towards the couch. What a night of rocky feelings.

He followed, not sure what else to say.

"He's always had a way of running roughshod over boundaries," she said. "And I let him get into my head when I knew better. He's not going to ghost completely, I don't think, but I need to be more cautious about trusting him to commit to a schedule. And I shouldn't make plans based on that promise. Lesson learned."

"This was next weekend?"

"Yeah. And I agreed to cover three shifts at Bailey's, which would have gone a long way to pay for the tiling of the bathroom."

"I'm sorry." Matt scrubbed his hand over his face. "Can I help?"

She shook her head. "There's nothing to be done. I'll call Malcolm and apologize. I should never have agreed to take the work."

But he knew she needed the money, and not just for renos. She didn't make much at the lumber yard, and paying for childcare out of her earnings had to be making a big dent. Working when David had Emily would have helped her out a lot. "I could take care of her."

"I can't ask you to do that."

"I'm offering. You're not asking. You just need to say yes— if you're comfortable with it. And if you aren't, that's okay, too."

Her mouth flapped open, then shut. "You aren't working that weekend?"

"I don't think so, and I can probably trade the shifts if I

am." He grinned. "It may mean I need to show up the night before and fall exhausted into your bed."

She gave him a weak laugh. "Right."

"But I can sleep on the couch. I'll make a big production of it." So far, Emily hadn't noticed that he was there each night, and he was gone before she woke up in the morning.

Natasha frowned as she searched his face. "She might need cuddles at night."

"I can cuddle. I can also make secret midnight hot chocolate—with teeth brushing afterward, of course—and read endless stories."

"This is a huge favour."

It didn't feel that way to him. "It's not. You need help. I love you. I'm here in whatever capacity you need me. It's the same thing any friend or your sister would offer."

She cut him off with a kiss, first a gentle brush of her lips against his, then when he tugged on her hands, she climbed into his lap. More kisses, always more. Never enough.

"You can trust me with her," he whispered against her mouth.

"I know."

"We'll have fun."

"It'll just be this once."

"It doesn't need to be." He wanted to be a part of their lives. He wanted to be someone she could lean on, could depend on to help her out. And if she needed to work more to get her dreams done, he wanted to be the guy she could trust to always be there to read stories to her daughter.

She leaned into him, giving him her weight. It felt like a gift.

Let me be your rock, he thought, and not for the first time. But it was the first time he'd felt like that when out-of-sorts himself, and it grounded him. "I'm yours," he said gruffly. "To lean on and ask favours of and share Timbits with."

"They're all the way over there." She nodded toward the front door.

"I'll get them for you." He shifted out from beneath her and fetched the treats. "Chocolate?"

She shook her head. "Honey dip."

He found one and fed it to her. She offered him a chocolate one and he gobbled it up, licking the icing off her fingertips, too.

"It's hard for me to lean on anyone, you know," she whispered softly.

"I do know." He stretched his arm out across the back of the sofa. "Same for me. We're going to have to figure this out together, because I want to be there for you."

"Same," she murmured.

He ate another donut hole. "I love you," he said quietly as she picked another Timbit for herself. "I don't know what I thought love would look like if I ever stumbled into it, but it wasn't like this. It wasn't tea and donuts and confessing frustration at the end of a long day. And that makes me a total idiot, because this is actually amazing."

"Stress eating is amazing?"

"Reward eating," he corrected. "Because you're handling stress like a rockstar, and I came here instead of driving home tonight, where I'd have felt like a caged bear and had no idea why. But you saw something—"

"You were white as a ghost," she said softly.

"See? I didn't know."

"It's nice to have someone to catch you," she breathed as she nestled in tight. "I'd written that off as an option for myself."

"I'd never even put it on the options list."

"We are quite the dysfunctional pair, then." She laughed and nudged him. "Shall we go to bed?"

Yeah, this was love. And it *was* actually amazing.

———

AT THE END of the following week, Matt arrived at the Kingsley residence at eight in the morning, following his shift. He had breakfast with Emily, who thought it was hilarious that was actually his dinner. Then he crawled into Natasha's bed—alone—and passed out for seven hours.

It was the longest stretch of daytime sleep he'd had in a year.

It felt glorious.

When he woke up, the room was pitch black. He fumbled for his phone and checked the time, but he still had an hour before Natasha had to leave for her Friday night shift at Bailey's.

He ground the heel of his hand into his eye as he woke the rest of the way up.

She'd bought blackout curtains. That's what was different. He hadn't noticed when he'd fallen asleep, so maybe she came in and closed them after he was out.

His mouth tasted like an animal had died in it, so he got up and used the washroom. His overnight bag was downstairs, but he didn't need it—he had the purple toothbrush she'd given him that first time. She'd put it in a cup in the medicine cabinet, and he'd been using it for weeks now. Heading into months, really. And he liked that.

Downstairs, he found Emily playing with her ponies on the couch. "Good afternoon," he said.

She laughed. "Good morning, you mean."

"It is my morning, yep."

"Mommy's making you soup for *breakfast*," she said, giggling again.

"Is she?" He turned toward the kitchen, where he could see the edge of Natasha's body swaying in front of the stove. "I'll go help her."

She was listening to music turned down low, and she glanced over her shoulder at him as he approached. "How'd you sleep?"

"Like a baby. Did you buy blackout curtains just for me?"

She blushed. "It was the least I could do since you agreed to watch Emily this weekend."

A purple toothbrush, a pair of curtains. It wasn't much, but it felt like everything. "I really appreciate that. It was...unexpected. I thought I'd slept really well because I was in your bed, surrounded by your scent. But maybe it was the curtains."

"I like the more romantic reason better," she whispered.

He kissed her quickly. "The curtains? That's true romance. That right there is why I love you."

"Good, because I'm making you really cheap tomato soup for dinner, so..."

He blew a raspberry on her neck. "I love that, too."

CHAPTER TWENTY-SEVEN

ONE OF THE givens of living in rural Ontario was how far everything was from everything else. This rarely bothered Natasha. She loved her Jeep and enjoyed cranking up the radio.

Her drive to Bailey's had been lovely. She'd grabbed a coffee to go and watched the sun set as she'd headed south-west to Port Elgin. But now that it was the middle of the night and she was exhausted, the drive back seemed endless and horrid and good Lord she didn't want to repeat it tomorrow night.

This was her last weekend of picking up bartending shifts. It had to be. She needed to get her ass in gear with the apartment listing and sell the shit out of it to people from Toronto who would pay top dollar for a hipster weekend getaway on the edge of pristine wilderness.

When she finally got home, Matt was waiting for her. She'd texted when she'd left the bar, and he'd been busy since then.

"I ran you a bath," he said as he took her coat. "Do you want anything to eat before I tuck you into bed?"

She shook her head. "But maybe check on me to make sure I don't fall asleep in the tub."

He laughed.

She wasn't kidding, and maybe he picked up on that, because he followed her upstairs, collecting each piece of discarded clothing as she stripped down. He disappeared momentarily with the pile, and came back with a towel.

"Gold star service tonight," she observed.

He sat on the closed toilet seat and leaned forward, his elbows on his knees. "You had a long night. A bit of tender care is deserved."

"You were on kid duty," she protested.

"Easy peasy. We played a bit, watched some videos on my phone—I apologize in advance for her new interest in tobogganing, I may have started a thing—and then it was story time."

"Whoa, go back to the tobogganing. What happened?"

"I showed her some videos I took of the snow mountain a couple of Army guys made in the park in Pine Harbour. We plow the snow from the parking lot into the grassy area, and then..." He grinned. "We sculpt some pretty good slide runs out of it."

Tasha wasn't sure how she felt about Emily swooshing down an icy slide run. "Interesting."

"I wouldn't suggest taking her this year. But next, maybe. We'd get her a helmet."

And full body armour. "Okay."

His smile turned bashful. "There weren't any kids in the video. It was just the guys from when we did it last year."

"Have you done it yet this year?"

"They did. I was, uh, busy."

"Here?"

"Working, probably. And if I was hanging out here, I

promise that is a thousand percent where I'd rather be. Not plowing snow into a sledding hill for other people's kids."

She sank under the bubbles. But she had him take care of her kid tonight. Wasn't that kind of the same thing?

When she pushed herself back up, her head breaking through the warm water, he was looking at her.

"What?"

"This—you, Emily—is better than anything. This is what I want. I had a really good time with her tonight, and I'm glad I get to spend the entire weekend with her. With you both. Besides, I get rave reviews for my storytelling skills, which is good for the ego."

That reminded her… "Oh yeah, apparently I read the troll's voice wrong in her favourite book?" She flicked bubbles at him. "You set a high storytelling bar."

"You can't pin that on me, little girl," he growled the exact line she was talking about, and she burst into a peal of laughter.

"That's pretty good. I don't do it anything like that."

"What do you do?"

"You can't pin that on me, little girl," she said, deepening her voice a register.

Nope. Not even close. "That's generic bad guy. You need to add some moss and grit. You live under a bridge, come on."

She tried again and got through three words before dissolving into giggles.

Matt looked pleased with himself. "It's my high school drama career finally paying off."

"You did drama?"

"Of course. Theatre girls were easy." He covered his head as she flicked more bubbles at him, his entire body shaking as he joined her laughing.

"I was a jock in high school. Track and field, volleyball, basketball. I kind of expected the same of you."

"Nope." His eyes darkened as she stood up, water sluicing over her breasts and down her legs. "I would have been if I'd have gone to the same school as you, though."

He held up the towel and she stepped onto the mat, letting him wrap her in the terrycloth.

She yawned.

"Okay, my sexy volleyball player, it's time for bed."

She didn't bother to protest.

In her room, she pulled on sweatpants and a t-shirt, then crawled into bed and collapsed against his inviting form. "Don't let me sleep in, though," she said softly as her eyes drifted shut. "I have a lot to do tomorrow."

"What's left on your list? Can I help with something?"

She mumbled something incoherent even to herself into his armpit, so she rolled onto her back and tried again. "Furniture shopping," she said with a sigh. A mental image of her shopping list swam before her eyes. "I need a funky couch, a bookcase, and a nice set of bedroom furniture."

"We could go out together, take Emily, make it fun."

"The problem is I don't even know where to go. There's a really specific look that works for these short-term rental sites. Funky, modern, bold. I'm not sure I'll be able to find what I need unless I take a trip into the city." Which would take more time and probably more money than she wanted to spend.

Matt was quiet for a moment. "How modern?"

"Not cold. It has to be warm. Clean lines, wood."

"Something like my stuff?"

She thought about that. Not his man-cave-esque couch, but his bedroom furniture was great. "Yeah. I like your bed. Where did you get it?"

"Uh…" He scooted down a bit so they were eye level to

each other. "I ordered it online. But I was thinking you could…borrow it."

"What?"

"If for no other reason than you'd have furniture in the unit tomorrow night."

"Oh."

"Would that help?" He searched her face, his gaze careful. "I mean, there are other reasons, too."

Taking a deep breath, she pushed herself up. She was wide awake now. Both of them sat cross-legged on her bed, neither of them speaking.

It was not a simple offer. If Matt brought his bed over to her place, he wouldn't have one at his place. "Borrowing" something would be tangling them together further, and de-tangling that at the end of the usage period would hurt.

Unless there wouldn't be a de-tangling.

He scrubbed his hand over his jaw and gave her a sheepish look. "Is this the wrong time for this?"

She glanced at the clock. "Nah. All reckless relationship conversations should happen at two in the morning. What could go wrong?"

"You could tell me that you don't want my stuff in your house." Zing.

She wasn't going to do that, though. "Your pants are currently on my floor," she whispered. "I like your stuff."

"If my furniture is in the apartment behind your house, I won't really have a bed to sleep on at my place."

"You sleep here a lot as it is."

"Because I like sleeping with you. And you bought me blackout curtains, which I don't want to be too presumptuous about the meaning of, but—"

"Presume." She grabbed his hand. "Maybe it's time to sleep in and not worry about crawling out at dawn before Emily wakes up. It's not like she's old enough to understand what you sleeping over means."

"I want to help here. With the apartments and childcare and cooking dinner. Something that you brought up at Christmas has been on my mind. About having kids, and I want to set the record completely straight on that point."

She sank back on her heels, her eyes widening.

He leaned in, his gaze burning. "Tell me if you don't want me to be a permanent part of your life. That's okay, of course it is. But if you wonder if I dream of a future with you, I can tell you all about that."

"Tell me." Two words on a breath. Another one. "Please." Her heart pounded in her chest, sleep now the last thing on her mind.

"You want to know if I want babies?" Matt took both of her hands in his. "I want a daughter. I want bobbing curls and fierce questions. I want to be a man she can go to when she has a scraped knee, or nightmares, or a fabulous story to tell. I would happily make her a big sister as many times over as her mother wanted, or never at all if that was how it worked out. I want to be a dad so much it hurts, Natasha, and that started the day I met Emily. I want to be one of her dads. I don't care about hypothetical babies, but I'd cut off my right arm for your daughter."

"She loves you," Tasha whispered. "So much."

"I love her too," he said gruffly. "With my whole heart. It's layered right on top of the complicated love I have for you."

"Complicated?"

"Do you know how hard it is to want to give you the moon, and not be able to? To have to hold back because I know you're not ready? I want to be everything you need. I want to be a part of this. Share this burden. I want to be your best friend. I want to be your lover. I want to be your husband, someday, when you're ready."

"I'll be ready soon."

"Because I know it'll take time—" His mouth dropped open, and his eyes went wide. "What?"

"I love you. I'm terrified, but I love you with my whole heart."

He tumbled her backwards in a wild tackle that matched her wild heart, then kissed her fiercely. When he pulled back, his mouth was wet and his eyes so bright she thought they might catch fire. "Excellent. Stay here."

"Matt—"

He pressed his finger to her lips. "Stay. Here. Please?"

She nodded mutely and he kissed her quickly again before dashing off the bed and out the door. His footsteps were heavy on the stairs, then silence for a minute.

More footsteps, and then he was back on top of her, his face pink with excitement. "Hi," he said, his grin goofy and sexy at the same time.

"Hi." She laughed.

He crowded against her, urging her arms up around his neck, and he kissed her. The familiar hunger was tinged with something new. Relief, maybe. She certainly felt that. Delight that they were finally on the same page, too.

But she tasted something else in his kiss. Not caution. Something else like that, though. Against her cheek, his hand trembled.

"I bought you another Christmas present, and then I chickened out of giving it to you," he said. "Because we're grown-ups, and rings have particular meaning, and I don't want to rush you at all."

Her heart stopped at the word ring.

"Tasha," he murmured, kissing her again. "Shh, it's okay."

"I don't know…" She did, of course. Deep down.

"One thing at a time," he said softly. "Consider this a promise that one day, when you're ready, I'll get down on one knee."

She twisted her head to the left and looked at his hand. At the world's thinnest twist of hearts and glittery stones. "Matt, what did you do?"

"It's a promise ring. Honest to God, that's what it's called. I don't know what it says about me that Facebook ads seem to think I'm a lovestruck sixteen-year-old kid, but just before the holidays I saw this pop up and I thought, I want to give that to Natasha. And then I told myself that was insane. But I ordered it anyway, and it's been in my bag ever since."

She blinked again, trying to take it in. Two hearts…no, three hearts. Two hearts in the form of an infinity symbol, and another one, the glittery one, wrapping through them.

Her and Emily, forever. Matt embracing them both.

It was a pretty big promise.

She burst into tears.

"I shouldn't have done this at two in the morning. Or this soon. Or in general. Okay, let's walk this back—"

She grabbed him and pulled him down on top of her, silencing him with a kiss.

He wasn't allowed to take it back.

———

THE NEXT DAY, Matt made breakfast for his girls. Then he started a group chat with his brothers.

Matt: Who's around today? I need help moving some furniture.

**Jake: I can help. Are you finally getting rid of your
ugly couch?**
Matt: You're fired.
Jake: No, seriously. What are we moving?
Dean: I'm free.
Matt: Good. I'll need some trucks, too.
Sean: I can drive.
**Matt: Awesome. We can probably fit it all in the
two loads.**
Dean: It all? What are we moving? And to where?
Matt: Everything. To Natasha's house.

It took another ten seconds for his phone to start ringing. Well at least they called him instead of each other.

He ignored Jake's call and answered Sean's instead. "Hey."

"You're moving in with her? I still haven't met this woman."

"We'll fix that soon. Like, today. You can meet her when you bring my stuff to her house."

From across the room, Natasha's head jerked up and she gave him a wide-eyed, *what are you doing* look.

He winked at her and she blushed.

Sean laughed in his ear. "Okay, fine. What time are we meeting at your place?"

"I don't know. We could have sorted that out via text but you all decided to call me instead." There was a beep in his ear. He glanced at the screen. "Dean's turn now, gotta go. I'll text a time in a few minutes."

He ended that call and answered the next. "Hey to you as well."

"I'm not going to say you're moving too quickly—"

"Good, because I'm really not."

"Isn't this a little out of left field?"

"Only because I didn't think she liked me this much. I took an opportunity, man. I love her, and she'll have me here, so…boom. Done."

"All right. Liana wants to know what kind of wine she likes."

"Red. Or a good bottle of whiskey if you have it."

When he hung up the phone, Tasha had her hands over her face. "Oh my *God*," she groaned. "Are we going to have a spontaneous housewarming party this afternoon? You're telling people to bring me booze?"

"They asked. And of course we aren't doing a house-warming party today. You have work tonight. We'll have the party tomorrow afternoon."

She groaned again and then lifted her head. Her eyes were soft. "I guess this is happening."

"I apologize in advance for my family."

"They love you."

"And I love *you*. It's going to be just fine."

"I'm going to hold you to that, mister." She cupped his face. "Hey, if you're bringing your bed over, maybe bring your couch too."

"You don't like my couch."

"I like it just fine for in here. For us. The red velvet one can go in the apartment for all the transient hipsters who want to give me their pennies."

"Clever girl."

He left shortly thereafter to head back to Pine Harbour. His brothers met him at his apartment building, where he backed in next to Sean.

"I only have about an hour," Jake said. "I had to leave Cal with Dad, and you can imagine how that's going to go when we hit nap time."

"Then let's get to work," Dean said, slinging an armful of bungee cords and tarps into the back of Sean's truck.

It took them forty-five minutes to get his couch into Sean's truck and fit a couple of bookcases around it. Then they dismantled his bed and loaded that into his own vehicle.

"Do we need to fit the dresser in there?" Dean asked skeptically, looking at the overflowing bed.

"Nah. Strangers don't need to move in to Natasha's apartments, they just need a bedside table, and I'll come back and grab that tomorrow. Or..." He dug out his spare key and handed it to his oldest brother. "You and Liana could pick it up before you come over mid-afternoon."

"What's happening tomorrow afternoon?"

Matt looked at all of his brothers. "It's time for you guys to meet the woman I love."

Dean held out his hand and they clapped their palms together before he was yanked in for a hug. Then Sean mauled him, a rough embrace that Matt felt right to his soft feelings place inside.

And as those two headed for their cars, it was Jake's turn.

"About tomorrow..."

He waved his hand as his brother trailed off. "Nah. Come. Please. We're all good. Natasha told me that you came into the lumber store."

Jake laughed. "Dude, I wasn't going to say I wouldn't come. I was going to ask if I should bring any power tools."

Matt nodded as he screwed up his face. Shit, he fucked that up out of the gate. "Right, that's better."

Bumping his shoulder, Jake kept chuckling. "But good to know that's where your mind went a little bit."

"I just overthought things for a moment. Tasha's a little overwhelmed with the suddenness of all of..." He gestured toward the full trucks. "This. Not us, but the influx of Foster stuff and Foster brothers and Foster...noise."

"Well, I have to go get my kid, so that's one less bit of noise today. And tomorrow, I'm serious. If there's anything I can do to help with the renovations, just let me know."

Matt hadn't talked about the work Natasha was doing in anything but the broadest, vaguest of terms. He didn't waver from that now. "I'll ask her about it. Thanks."

———

MATT TEXTED before they left Pine Harbour in a convoy of furniture-laden vehicles. Natasha would have been stress cleaning her house if there was anything in it.

There wasn't, so she took Emily on a quick beer run instead. Matt's brothers were coming over, or at least the two she hadn't met yet.

"Maybe we should get snacks, too, baby, what do you think?"

"Can we get cookies?"

Maybe they'd had too many treats lately. "For tomorrow. We're going to have a little party with Matt's family."

"What kind of party?"

Natasha swallowed hard and glanced at the ring on her right hand. "A welcome to our little family kind of party. Matt's brothers are all kind of like uncles to you. And there will be a little boy there, too."

"A baby?"

"A toddler. Smaller than you, though."

"Babies are cute."

She smiled to herself. "Yep."

The beer store was on the other side of town, a mini stand-alone store. She pulled up right next to the door and left the engine running to keep Emily warm. She loved living in a small town for a lot of reasons, and that was high up on the list. Inside, she paid for a two-four at the cash while keeping an eye on her car.

She loved small town life, but she could thank her time with David in the city for her wariness.

Speaking of him… Once she was back in the car, beer safely stowed in the trunk, she pulled out her phone, because she hadn't heard from him since he cancelled that weekend's visit.

**Natasha: Hope that work emergency got sorted out.
Can we confirm your next weekend with Emily?**

To his credit, he responded right away. Less to his credit, it had a sarcastic bite, but she'd started that.

David: Your genuine concern is appreciated. At work today, in fact. But I've blocked two weekends from now off in my calendar and will take her no matter what.

It took three attempts to get a be-the-bigger-person response just right.

Natasha: Thank you. Please keep me posted.

Then she put her phone away and went to the grocery store to get cookies. For today *and* tomorrow, because these were stressful times.

When they got back to the house, Matt's truck was in the drive, and another pickup was parked on the street.

She pulled in behind Matt and unbuckled Emily. "Shall we go see what's going on?"

Emily looked at the front door nervously.

"It's okay," Natasha whispered, as much to herself as her daughter.

The door swung open, and there was Matt. Big and smiling and far too handsome for his own good.

Natasha took a deep breath and grabbed the beer.

Emily had run up to the porch, but lingered there, shooting glances backward. Matt didn't urge her inside, even though it was cold out. He crouched down at her level and waited for Tasha with her.

"I thought I should get some beer," Natasha said when she joined them. "And then we hit the grocery store to stock up on stuff, too."

Matt stood up and looked her straight in the eye. "That was really thoughtful." Not *you didn't need to do that*, because she did. And he got that. "Come on. We've already moved the red couch to the apartments, making room for the bachelor pad explosion."

That made her laugh. "Excellent."

Inside, she found two Foster brothers, immediately recognizable as relatives of Matt and Jake. "Hi," she said to both of them.

Matt took the case of beer from her and gestured. "Natasha, these are my brothers. Dean…"

She shook his hand.

"And Sean." The younger one stepped forward, his cane moving fluidly with his body.

"Nice to meet you both."

Matt stowed the beer in the kitchen while she was saying that. "And this is Natasha," he said as he returned quickly. "Who stole my heart over a cupcake."

She laughed and beamed up at him. "I think that was actually Emily."

"Yeah, a little bit." He scooped up her daughter. "Hey, should we bring in the new couch?"

"Okay," Em whispered, burying her face in Matt's neck.

"How about we get out of your way and put that beer in the fridge?" Natasha offered, taking Emily from him.

And that was that. The guys went back to work, bringing in Matt's couch first, which really was excellent and better for family lounging than the red velvet one. Then they took his bed around the back and into the more finished of the two units.

When they were done, they gathered in the kitchen. Sean waved off the offer of a beer, but Dean took one and so did Matt.

There was no grand inquisition. Neither of them even looked at her funny. They were kind and entertaining and good with Emily.

"That's a pretty nice space you've got back there," Sean said. "And Matt says you aren't looking for long-term tenants?"

She nodded. "The business model for short-term holiday rental is pretty attractive. More risk, but better reward if you work it hard enough. I never wanted to be a landlord, either."

Dean nodded. "Being a landlord is stressful."

"Yeah. And honestly, I didn't even think about that seriously. My background is in hospitality and tourism."

The conversation slid from there to cooking and the dinner they needed to make before she headed to work that night. Matt's brothers left quickly after that, promising to be back the next day with their wives for a longer visit.

Once they were alone, she went around back and looked at Matt's bedroom furniture set up in the apartment. She'd ordered new bedding, crisp white hotel linens, and she squinted, seeing the room finished.

It was perfect.

Now she just needed to get the bathroom done and all those little touches wrapped up, and she could start renting it out.

Back on her side of the house, she found Matt and Emily curled up on his old couch with a storybook. She leaned against the kitchen doorframe and watched them, her loves.

Once Emily was done and went to play with her toys, Matt got up and gestured at the wall. "You know… When we finish the apartments, and the big idea wall is done, we can bring in my TV."

"The big-ass bachelor-sized television?"

"No?"

She grinned at him and twirled in a circle. "Who says the planning stops with the apartments?"

"You'll want another project," he said softly. "Of course you will."

"I've got big dreams." Boy, that felt good to say. "Long-term dreams."

"I'm in. I can't wait to get started on the next Escape Inn."

She laughed, feeling giddy. "Oh God."

"That's what you mean, right?"

"You knew that when you ordered me the guest register. Escape Inn Wiarton. Nice pun, by the way."

"Where's the next one after that? Escape Inn Port Elgin, Escape Inn…"

She knew exactly where she'd look next. "Pine Harbour."

Matt pulled her in close, and she knew that was the right answer. And maybe the next house would have room for a big idea wall *and* a TV.

CHAPTER TWENTY-EIGHT

NATASHA'S PHONE rang at ten o'clock that night, while she was mid-pour on a tray of pints for a celebrating women's curling team.

In the past, she'd always turned the ringer off while working, but this was only Matt's second night alone with Emily. So as soon as she was finished with the tray of drinks, she grabbed the phone, ready to call him back.

But it wasn't Matt. It was David.

She didn't bother to leave behind the bar, she just hit the call button. He picked up on the first ring.

"Sorry about the late hour," he said.

"It's fine. What's up?"

"I can come up tomorrow and take Emily for a day or two. I can use vacation time to make up the lost weekend. I shouldn't have cancelled."

Natasha leaned against the bar, truly stunned. "What?"

He sighed. "Especially after you reamed me out for overstepping. I just got lost in this project, but we wrapped it up today and I want to make it up to Emily. And…to you."

She wouldn't give him a cookie for essentially doing what he'd said he'd do in the first place, but there was something in his voice that softened her heart a little. "We're having Matt's family over for an informal get together in the afternoon tomorrow. Could you work around that?"

"Sure. I can take Monday off. Pick her up at three tomorrow, bring her back the same time the next day?"

"That works." She paused. "She starts pre-school on Tuesday. Do you think you could take her backpack shopping? We were going to do that on Monday."

"I can do that."

When she hung up the phone, she stood there looking at the dark screen for quite a while, until Malcolm came out to tell her the kitchen was closing up. She went up on her tiptoes, raised her voice, and announced it was last call for food.

Her boss, and her friend, was looking at her with curiosity when she rocked back on her heels.

"What?"

"You've changed."

"Stress will do that to you."

"Stress doesn't usually make you...content."

She laughed. "Is that what I look like? Content?"

"Don't knock it. It's a good look."

She took a deep breath. "Yeah. I guess it is. And I suppose I am. I'm going to miss it here, though."

"We'll have you back any time. Kick the new bartender to wait service."

She pushed at his shoulder and he held out his arms. Leaning in, she gave him a tight hug. "Thank you," she whispered. "For everything."

"You've been one of the most reliable employees I've ever had. The thanks are all mine. Now get out of here." He pulled an envelope from his back pocket. "Your final pay, in cash. Vacation pay and a small bonus are in there too, because you're going to do great things and I want you to remember me fondly when you do."

She took the thick bundle, trying not to get choked up. "That's not necessary."

"Yeah, well…" He shrugged. "I think it is. So there."

So there.

"Now get out of here. Go home to your baby and get an extra hour of sleep tonight."

"Are you sure?"

"I'm going to hit on the curling team. If we're lucky, we'll close the place down together."

She held up her hands. "Fair enough. Best of luck."

When she got home, Matt was passed out in her bed. She crawled in next to him and he slung his arm over her, mumbling something about trolls.

THE NEXT MORNING sped by in a blur of Natasha trying to make her house look absolutely perfect in a casual, it's-always-been-like-this kind of way.

Which was ridiculous because two of Matt's three brothers had already been there the day before, but she didn't even try to talk herself out of the ridiculousness. Some things just needed to be given a white flag of surrender, and neurotically wanting to impress her boyfriend's family was one of those things.

Matt found her in the apartment. He was carrying the baby monitor. "Emily's playing in her room," he said, wiggling the device. "I wanted to ask you something."

"Okay." She stepped back from the bookshelf. She'd been collecting hipster-ish decorative items for the last month or so, and she liked what she'd done. A typewriter on top, some nicely bound hardcovers in a few stacks on the shelves, and a couple of decorative pottery pieces for balance. "I think this is missing something, but I don't know what."

"Jake wanted to know if he could bring power tools today."

"What?" She did a visual run-down from top to bottom. Maybe a generic picture frame. Too late for today, but— "Wait, *what?*"

She whirled around and Matt gave her a sheepish smile. "Hi."

"Matt…"

"Is this our second fight?"

"No." But she crossed her arms over her chest anyway. "Maybe. What did you do?"

"Nothing. I swear. I haven't told any of them anything about the renovations."

She let her arms swing loose at her side. "Then why does Jake think that I need power tools kind of help today?"

"He knows you're doing this on your own and he was just offering to help. It's kind of a funny story, actually."

She looked at him in disbelief.

He soldiered on. "He brought up today in a vague way, and I thought maybe he was offering to not come, and I told him that was silly—"

"That is silly."

"Right." Matt cleared his throat. "He thought so too. He wasn't offering that. He was offering help."

"I don't need help."

She could tell it was taking all of Matt's self-restraint to not look at the door to the old, ugly bathroom behind him.

"Well, okay, I need to figure out what I'm doing with *that*," she said. "But not today. No tools." She marched past him and tugged the door to the bathroom shut. "And the tours of this space won't include the bathroom."

He held up his hands. "Your call, absolutely."

She marched right back to him and kissed him hard on the mouth. "Thank you for telling them nothing."

"Just so you know, he's going to find a way to offer help again."

"And I'll find a way to dodge around it." She lifted her chin defiantly, and Matt kissed her there, and then on her neck, and behind her ear.

Then he brushed his lips against her temple. "You are fierce and gorgeous. You can do anything. But there's nothing wrong with a little nepotism to get you a deal on some sub-contracting work."

She poked him in the belly button. "Can you go to the store and buy some fresh flowers?"

"Of course." He kissed her quickly. "I love you."

"Love you, too," she murmured as he pressed the baby monitor into her hand. She turned around, doing another visual sweep of the space.

She loved it. They were almost ready for photos to go on the rental site. She just needed the bedding to arrive. And people might not book it without fancy bathroom shots, but she was willing to gamble and make the listing live without those.

Maybe.

A decision for tomorrow, either way.

When Matt got back from the store, his arms were full of flowers. Four mixed bouquets, which split up into every mason jar she owned and still filled a big water jug, too. That went on the kitchen counter, and the mason jars went over to the apartment.

"Now we really need to get it shiny tomorrow for photos," she said. "Wouldn't want to waste these gorgeous flowers."

He caught her by the waist and spun her around. "If the only thing they do is make you smile today, they aren't wasted. Put on music and we can dance."

"Your family will be here soon."

"So? They can see us dancing." He brought their bodies together, hip to hip, thigh to thigh, and kissed her.

"Music," she whispered.

"I'm good." He swayed, rocking them to a silent beat, and she let him lead until Emily's feet hit the stairs. He kissed her knuckles as she slid out of his arms, making her melt all over again.

"Mommy!"

She cleared her throat and fought back a smile. "Yeah, baby?"

"People are here."

Which meant Emily had been playing with her ponies in Natasha's room—her and Matt's room, now, her skipping heart reminded her—so she could see out the front window.

Tasha didn't mind that. "Okay," she called out as a knock sounded at the door.

Showtime.

She got to the door just as Emily was turning the knob. "Maybe let Mommy..." she murmured, but it was happening.

Her three-year-old was welcoming guests to their house, and okay, that was adorable and fine.

Everything was fine.

Except she was flustered from Matt's silent dance in the kitchen and the flowers and everything.

"I'm Emily," her daughter announced. "Hi."

Tasha pulled the door open and found Jake on the other side. Beside him was his wife Dani, who had their son in her arms. "Welcome," she said. Then she smiled. "Come on in."

As soon as they were inside, the couple traded armfuls. Jake took their kid, and Dani grabbed the bag he'd been carrying. "Hi," she said, stepping forward, letting Jake deal with the snowsuit-clad child. "I brought wine. Red, white, and sparkling."

They were going to be best friends.

"I've got six kinds of cheese and extra large wine glasses," Natasha said. "Follow me to the kitchen."

Matt met them in the doorway. "Hey, drinks!"

"For ladies," Dani said, giving him an innocent smile. "Wait until the others are here, and we'll see who all is drinking. There may not be enough to share."

He raised his hands. "No drama. I'm no threat here."

Tasha laughed. "Wow."

Dani winked. "This is going to be fun. And I love your house, by the way."

"It's a work in progress." Something she'd be saying over and over again, she was sure.

"But amazing bones. What a good find." Dani held out the options. "What do you want to open first?"

"We can start with the white and go from there."

"I like the way you think."

Another knock sounded from the entranceway. Matt got that one, and from the exponential increase in volume, she guessed the other two couples had arrived.

Dani gave her a sideways grin. "They're all great."

Sure, but one of them was a famous country music singer. In all of the chaos of the weekend, she'd forgotten that bit. It seemed quite removed from her quiet romance with Matt, but

Dean had been Liana Hansen's bodyguard two years earlier, and they'd fallen in love.

So now a Nashville celebrity was in her house, which meant that standing next to Jake's wife sharing wine like besties was no longer the weirdest thing about this afternoon.

She swallowed a big gulp of wine. "I'll go say hi."

Dani held out her hand for Natasha's wine glass. They were definitely going to be great friends. Weird and wonderful.

"Hi," she said, and the whole exchange of pleasantries started over again.

"We brought Tennessee whiskey," Liana said, holding out two gift boxes. "But honestly, I'm more of a tequila girl if we're talking about the hard stuff. Probably neither of them are appropriate for this afternoon, but we'll have to do this again without the men and children and then we can truly get to know each other."

Natasha's cheeks pinked up. "That sounds awesome." She took a deep breath. "Can I get you something a little less potent to drink right now?"

Sean's wife, Jenna, a midwife, declined wine because she was on call, but Liana said she would join them.

"Jenna, can I get you water or juice?"

"Water would be great."

"I want milk, Mommy," Emily interjected.

"Lead the way, baby."

After Natasha handed glasses all around, she hoisted Emily up onto the counter and gave her a plastic cup. Then the guys joined them, and there were eight adults and two kids—Calvin got a cup of milk, too—squeezed into the kitchen.

"We weren't sure we'd ever get to meet you guys," Dean said from his post right behind his fiancé. One of his arms was wrapped around her waist and she was leaning fully against him. "I mean, before the wedding, of course."

"Oh, have you set a date?" Jenna asked, pulling out her phone.

Natasha was momentarily amused that Mrs. Cargill's gossip had been somewhat accurate, and the date was still up in the air. Or had been until recently.

"We're thinking about Victoria Day," Liana said in her southern lilt. "My band will get a kick out of the May Two-Four nickname for the long weekend, and we can play up the Canadian details. That's if it works for y'all."

Sean nudged his wife. "Jenna's the only one who schedules that far in advance, probably."

"I'm booking the weekend off right now," she murmured. Then she lifted her head and looked at Natasha. "How about you? Will you be renting out the units by then?"

How about her? She'd barely met these people and they were asking about her calendar for a family wedding.

"Uh…" She smiled. "I'm sure it'll be fine. Yes, we'll be renting them out then, but, uh…it'll be fine." Slick, she was not.

But then Matt was beside her, sliding his fingers through hers and giving her a gentle squeeze, and it didn't matter.

"How are the renovations going?" Sean asked.

Natasha gestured at the definitely-not-renovated kitchen they were standing in. "This part hasn't even started yet."

Everyone laughed. It wasn't that funny, but they were kind.

She pointed at the interior door to the apartments. "We can go take a look if you want to see? They're works in progress. One has more work done on it than the other."

"Are they the same size?" This time it was Jake asking questions. Of course he was, he was a builder.

But Natasha wasn't intimidated by him, his job, or their

history. She knew her house inside out now. "Upstairs is a bit smaller, because of space taken up by Emily's bedroom, but downstairs has this little hallway, so it's pretty close." She let them into the first apartment. Matt's bed was set up in the sleeping nook of the studio space, and the red velvet couch was front and centre, facing the door, with her homemade coffee table with hairpin legs in front of it.

Liana let out a wolf-whistle. "Hello."

Natasha grinned. "Thanks."

Jake did a slow prowl, looking at her paint job, the new trim she'd installed, and the floors she'd painstakingly refinished. "Very nice," he finally said.

"What's through this door?" Dean asked, pointing to the bathroom.

"Part of the work in progress—the bathroom. But I haven't started in there yet."

Jake glanced at her, then at Matt. She didn't blink.

Finally he nodded again. "Looking forward to seeing it when it's all done, then."

But as everyone else filed upstairs, following a climbing Calvin and a very concerned Emily, Jake hung back.

"Hey," he said. "If you need anything, let me know. No pressure, but the offer stands even if you don't need it right now."

She could say no again. But she'd done that once already, and actually, she did need something. "Do you know any plumbers who might be available sooner than later? And a tile guy? I can afford to pay a bit more for expediency."

He poked his tongue into his cheek as he glanced back toward the bathroom. "Can I take a look? How big is it?"

"Sure." She led him to the bathroom and he peeked inside.

"What are you thinking? Tub or shower?"

"Whichever is faster to install in here. I'll do the opposite upstairs, probably."

He nodded. "Smart. Okay. Yeah, I can find you a guy. I'll make some calls, but then I'll put them in touch with you directly and you can deal with them from there."

"Thank you." She meant it to her very core.

He gestured around her first rental space. "This is great. Good job. I wish I'd thought of it, to be honest."

"Maybe I'll let you be a silent partner on my next project."

He laughed.

She wasn't kidding. Escape Inn Pine Harbour would need a good contractor.

———

DAVID AND SABLE arrived as everyone was leaving. Natasha thought about offering them the same tour she'd given Matt's brothers, but decided she didn't need to open herself up to that kind of punishment.

"How was the drive up?" she asked politely as Matt helped Emily into her coat.

"Pretty good," Sable said.

And the conversation ground to a halt there.

Great.

After a quick last hug and kiss, Emily was out the door. Matt closed it behind them and gave Natasha a *look*.

"What?"

"That was a roller coaster of a day," he said, advancing on her.

"It was."

"And it's done now."

"I know."

"Aww," he said, catching her by the hips and holding her

close. He kissed her lightly. "Come on, let's have a shower. You may feel better about everything when you're squeaky clean."

"I'm not in the mood for sex right now."

"Who said anything about sex? I'm talking about the world's greatest shampooing and totally platonic back washing."

She arched an eyebrow at him. "What do you know about platonic back washing?"

"Zero experience. But I have a lot of enthusiasm and outside of technical skills, I've found that carries me a long way in general. Probably true for being your faithful and agreeable eunuch in the shower."

"Nobody said anything about a eun—"

"Manservant. Naked butler. Take your pick."

She was laughing now, even though her heart hurt. "Naked butler has a certain ring to it."

He took a deep bow, all of his muscles rippling. "At your service, Ms. Kingsley."

She sighed. "I think I only drank half a glass of wine today. How do you feel about getting a little tipsy?"

"I feel great about that." He grabbed her hand and tugged her into the kitchen. The bottle of white wine was half empty and the red hadn't been touched. "Which do you want?"

"Erm…"

He opened the fridge. "Wait. I have it." He pulled out the bottle of sparkling wine Dani had brought. "Let's drink this."

"The white is already open."

"And it will keep a day or two." He started to unwrap the foil. "Let's celebrate. First family get together done. Civil child transfer accomplished. And other than the bathroom and a few details—I haven't forgotten the picture frame—the apartment is *done*. You are a goddess and I want to drink this out of your belly button."

"How about a flute?"

He winked at her. "We can negotiate the details as we make our way through the bottle."

"Your brother is going to help me find tradespeople for the bathroom."

"Good. More reason to break out the bubbly. Let's keep listing the good news."

"We're going to be drunk before dinner, aren't we?"

"And how."

She reached out and grabbed the front of his shirt, tugging him in for a kiss. Not a light one, either. A full-on passionate reason to celebrate. "I love you," she breathed when they came up for air.

He twisted the cork out of the bottle with a resounding pop. "I know."

It took them two hours to empty the bottle. Then they ordered dinner to be delivered from the pub, and once it arrived, they ate it on the floor in the kitchen.

"Maybe we should bring your table here," Natasha said as she stole one of Matt's fries.

"Or we could buy a nice big dining room table for the living room. Fill the space between the couch and the kitchen."

"I don't—"

He pressed his index finger against her lips. "My present to you, since I've just moved myself into your house."

She needed more wine. "Okay."

"And I'm going to start helping in other ways, too. Fair warning."

"We can argue about that when we're sober," she whispered.

"What are you thinking now?"

"I want to do tequila shots."

Matt groaned. "I started this, didn't I?"

"You did." She laughed. "I'm so sorry."

He dug out the bottle Liana and Dean had brought and she found shot glasses.

"You don't have limes, though." He grabbed the salt shaker. "Do we need this, bartender?"

She inspected the bottle. "I'm guessing this is a hundred bucks a bottle. This is going to be straight up. You ready for this?"

"No. Pour them anyway."

The first went down easy.

"Another?"

"You know it."

The next one made her head spin, and she grabbed the front of Matt's shirt again. His mouth was wet and red and she wanted his tongue in her mouth like whoa.

"Easy," he said as she tried to climb him.

"I love you. Did we celebrate that earlier? With the bubbly?"

"I think so."

"One more shot."

"Ah…"

But she was already pouring them. This one was a little heavy on the pour, which was fine. The hundred bucks a bottle tequila was fine shit.

"Bottoms up," she said, lifting her glass in the air. "And then you can take me upstairs and discover the hot pink thong I've been wearing all day."

He waited a beat, then tossed the shot back.

She followed suit, and as soon as her glass hit the counter, he had her up and over his shoulder.

"Matt Foster, put me down."

"In a minute."

She shrieked as he carried her through two doorways and

up the stairs. How he managed to do that without whacking her head on anything, she wasn't sure. But the next thing she knew, he was dumping her on the bed.

"Get naked," he growled.

"Demanding." She laughed as she tugged him down, too. "You first."

He unzipped his fly and shoved his jeans down his legs. She would never tire of this unveiling. His long, muscled legs, lightly dusted in soft hair. The powerful flex of his thighs, the tight nip of his body at his hips.

The thick, straining erection between his legs.

"Touch yourself," she whispered before peeling off her shirt. She watched wide-eyed as he worked his hand up and down his shaft. "That's gorgeous."

"Pants off," he reminded her. "I want to see that pink thong."

"Yeah. Sure." She worked at her fly, which took more effort than she'd have expected—thanks, tequila. Then finally crawled off the bed and kicked her jeans free. After she got naked, she climbed onto the bed again, perching between his legs.

His eyes were liquid heat as he watched her watching him. He lifted his hand away from his cock and it flexed in the air, bobbing and growing under her perusal. "You want this?"

"So much. I want it all." *Put a baby in me,* she wanted to say. Thanks, tequila. Again.

By the end of the night, it might slip out, and she was just drunk enough to think that might be okay. She stroked her hand over his calf, and just up onto his thigh. He lifted his leg.

She kissed his knee as she watched his fingers drag back across his hip, his belly, then around the base of his erection.

So big.

So heavy and masculine.

Scootching onto all fours, she drifted her mouth higher up his thigh. He smelled good. The booze made her head swim, or maybe that was just him.

Her gaze zeroed in on his hand. He was moving it faster now, his index finger knuckle rocking over the sweet spot just beneath the head.

"Do you want to take over?"

She shook her head. "You keep doing that. Ignore me."

"Hard to ignore how good your breath feels."

She exhaled as she smiled, and his skin tightened up. Goosebumps and flexing muscles. She licked a line along the edge of his groin, then over his balls and up the underside of his cock. He tasted like clean musk, like sex.

"I love you," she whispered before she took the thick, straining crown in her mouth.

His taste exploded on her tongue and her head swam. She wanted to ride him, but the condoms were…somewhere. So she swallowed him instead, licking and sucking at his length as he moved beneath her.

"Come here," he whispered.

But when she pulled her mouth off him, the whole world tilted on its axis.

And then she hiccuped.

He started laughing, and she rolled onto her back.

Clumsily, he followed her, pressing one of his heavy, muscled legs between hers.

"Oh God," she whispered, rocking against his thigh. Another hiccup shook her body.

He laughed harder.

"I'm so drunk." She groaned and flopped back, barely missing kneeing him in the junk.

"I know, baby, me too." He kissed her head. "We'll pick this up again in the morning."

That made her groan again. "The morning."

He chuckled. "Yeah. It's the thing that comes after the night."

She closed her eyes and pressed her face into his chest. God, he smelled so good. "I don't think I'm going to like the morning."

CHAPTER TWENTY-NINE

MATT WAS up for a solid two hours before Natasha stirred. He did a short workout, then grabbed a shower and made coffee before grabbing a book and curling up next to her in bed.

She slept until nine-thirty, and when she finally woke up, grumpy-faced and beautiful, he was waiting beside her with an extra-big cup of coffee and a gentle kiss on her pouting lips.

"Do you want pancakes?"

She gave him a wide-eyed look. "I don't know."

"How about a bath?"

That got a very slow nod before she gingerly took a sip of her coffee. "Mmm. Good."

"I've never seen you hungover before."

"I haven't been that drunk in forever." She managed a half-smile. "It was fun, but…ouch."

He grabbed the painkillers he'd set on the bedside table. "What can I offer you?"

She took two Tylenol, washed it down with more coffee, then handed back the cup and curled up under the blankets again. Bath might wait a while longer. "Thank you," she mumbled from under the bedding.

Matt grinned. His pleasure. "How much of last night do you remember?"

There was a long, pregnant pause. "Uh," she finally said, her voice muffled. "All of it?"

"Are you sure?"

"Why, what did I do?" She yanked the blankets down and gave him a stricken look. "What did I say?"

"Nothing bad," he assured her. "Not bad at all. But…we got a bit dirty. And then we gave up on the dirty, because tequila."

"I think I remember that."

"And then when you were falling asleep, you got a bit sweet, too."

She frowned. "I did? I don't remember anything after I started hiccuping."

"Aww, that's too bad." It had been adorable. Nuzzling, kissing, the world spinning around him as she brushed her lips against his ear and confessed—

"Did I say something about wanting another baby?" she whispered.

He grinned. "Yeah."

She reached for her mug and took another ginger sip of her coffee. "Okay."

"And I liked it."

"Oh my God."

"Don't freak out."

"Too late."

He crawled under the covers with her and set her mug aside. "Come here."

"I'm never drinking tequila again."

He kissed her head. "You know what I'm going to say, right? We'll do this at your pace. But that was really sweet. Remember that. You shared a little secret with me and I loved it. That's all."

There were some things they needed to do before they talked about babies for real.

They needed a dining room table.

The apartments had to be finished.

And he needed to make her some more promises. Grown-up ones.

———

MATT WAS a half-hour early for his next shift. He headed for the break room first to put his sub in the fridge.

Owen was waiting for him. "You're early."

"Indeed I am."

"Got a few minutes to talk?"

The old Matt would have a snappy response here. Something about having an endless capacity for talking like a good little EMT. He could feel it rising inside, but instead of it exploding out without thought, this time he caught it. He was getting better at that. "Sure," he said. Soft, reasonable. "What's up?"

A whole new Matt.

"Just wanted to check in and see how everything's going."

He told his boss about the move to Wiarton. "That's why I was early. Wasn't sure about the weather on the drive, but it was fine."

"Well, congratulations."

"Thanks. Actually..." Matt glanced around, making sure they were still alone. "I could use a favour."

Owen grinned. "Deja vu."

"Yeah. You know, that course got all this started. That's the week I met Natasha and her daughter. Which brings me to this. She's in the middle of renovating her house, really close to the end. And I want to help get it done. So I know you're already accommodating me six ways from Sunday, but I was wondering if I could put in a last-minute request for another week of vacation."

Owen laughed. "Man, if you are voluntarily offering to take some down time—even if it's to renovate a house—I am all over that. Yeah, sure, as long as it's not in the next week."

"Two or three weeks from now."

"Consider it approved. Get me the exact dates at the end of your shift, okay?"

"Deal."

Owen held out his hand. "And Matt—I want an invitation to the wedding."

"You got it." Matt clasped his friend's hand and shook.

———

DEMOLITION STARTED the first week of February.

They backed Matt's truck up to the back door and hauled the old tub out in pieces, hacked to bits with a reciprocating saw he borrowed from Jake. Then the old flooring and tiles came out by the shovel full. Natasha filled buckets and he carted them out to the bed of his truck, emptying them onto a tarp.

It took an entire day, with a pause for Tasha to pick up Emily from daycare and another at dinner.

The next day, the plumber came to move some of the rough-in pipes.

The day after that, Matt picked up a new bathtub and they got that into place all by themselves.

"Holy crap," Natasha said after they wrestled it into place. "I can actually see how it's going to come together."

"Tomorrow, we put up the new drywall." Matt slung his

arm around Tasha's waist. "And tonight we sleep like the dead."

"I'm so glad we're having someone else do the tiling," she whispered. "I have DIY limits."

By the end of Matt's week off from work, they'd done all the walls, patching, and painted too. The tile work started next.

He did two night shifts back-to-back, and when he woke up from his morning nap after the second one, Emily was sitting on the bed next to him.

"Hey there, Miss Monkey," he said groggily. "What time is it?"

"I don't know."

"Mm-kay." He reached for his phone. One in the afternoon. He'd slept long enough, because he'd get a full sleep that night. "All right. I'm up. What's going on?"

"Mommy said I should play in my room and be quiet." She walked a pony onto his chest. "But that was boring."

He laughed. "Well, sometimes I need to sleep, but this time it's okay."

"Do you want to play ponies?"

Natasha appeared in the doorway. "Emily!"

He waved his hand. "It's fine, I'm up." He swung his legs out of bed and stretched. "How goes the work in the apartments?"

"It's all done. Well, grout tomorrow, but the tiles are all up. Do you want to come see?"

He grabbed a pair of socks and a hoodie, pulling those on over his sweatpants and t-shirt. "Are beavers frisky? Hell yeah."

She giggled. "What does that mean?"

"It's from a book Dani's reading. I'll tell you about it later." He glanced at Emily. "Not for little ears."

"What's not for little ears?"

He picked Em up. "Don't you worry about it. Want to go see a pretty new bathroom in the apartment?"

"Okay."

Natasha beamed as she led the way, then presented the bathroom with a flourish—and it was totally deserved. She'd picked a really clever tile design, mostly big, white rectangles, but with a vertical stripe of tiny glass squares. It was modern and bright.

"Wow," he said as he took it in. There was a matching tiny backsplash behind the mini sink—a total deal she'd scooped from the clearance bin at work. And the floor had a line of the glass tile running around the perimeter, too. "This is *slick*. I'm…speechless."

"I know," she whispered. "So I think I can take pictures tomorrow and get the listing up."

That's exactly what she did. Matt kept Emily busy as Natasha spent an hour on the phone with her sister hashing out the best language for the listing—"Do you think that will grab someone's attention? What's another word for cozy that doesn't sound claustrophobic? Should I use the word romantic since Valentine's Day is coming up? Right, I guess that would work year round, wouldn't it?"—and then his phone vibrated.

Natasha: Does this link work for you?

He clicked on it, and it pulled up a listing on a vacation rental site.

Matt: It does. That place sounds amazing. Should I book a night?

She appeared in the doorway of Emily's room, grinning. "Don't you dare. They take a percentage of the sales."

"But maybe if I book it right away, then it'll tell them that it's a hot commodity."

Laughing, she flopped on Emily's bed. "That's not how it works. But…yay! It's done! It's live!"

Emily crawled on top of her. "Way to go, Mommy."

"Aww, thank you, baby."

Matt scooted over to the foot of the bed and wrapped his hand around Tasha's calf. He squeezed, and she smiled down at him.

"Thank you, too," she said softly. "For everything."

"You worked hard for this. We should celebrate."

"How about we wait until I get my first booking?"

He hesitated. What if it took a while? But he had faith in her. "Deal."

It took five days.

By the fourth day, Natasha was a stress ball, and she'd gone back to her wall of ideas. "Maybe I should try finding a longer-term tenant," she said, her arms tightly crossed in front of her body.

Matt stood behind her and hugged her. "Have some faith," he murmured into her hair. "Maybe it's the low season."

She huffed a frustrated sigh.

But the next morning her phone vibrated, and when she checked it, she shrieked.

Matt and Emily both jumped.

She pressed her hand to her mouth and waved her phone at Matt. When he took it, he saw a booking request for three nights, arriving on Valentine's Day.

"Calling it romantic paid off, eh?" He picked her up and swung her around before handing her phone back. "Go on, confirm the booking."

She did that, dancing on the spot. "I have to call Meredith. She's not going to believe this."

"Yeah, she will." Matt laughed. "She's your biggest fan. Or one of them, anyway. She has competition here."

"Eek!" Natasha dialled her sister's number. "Mer! Guess what?"

She told her sister about the booking. "Yes, I'm putting on the kettle. Of course I am. It's tea—" She stopped and looked at Matt. "Oh my God. A *kettle*."

"What?"

"Mer, I have to call you back. Make tea, this will just take a few minutes." She ended the call. "I didn't get a kettle for the kitchenette in the apartment."

"I'll go and get one for you."

"Do you mind?"

"Not at all. And I can pick up something special for dinner, too. What do you want?"

"Cheesecake."

He cupped her face. "You've got it, rock star."

————

AFTER HAVING a long-distance cup of tea with her sister, Natasha put on some music and had a dance party with Emily in the kitchen before going to her wall.

She already had a pre-guest-arrival list, but she wanted to triple-check it. And she should write her welcome and instruction emails in advance so she could have Matt beta-test them by pretending he was arriving at the house.

Once she was done that, she did a walk-through of the apartment. The crisp white bedding and perfectly folded towels in her brand-new bathroom made her so happy.

Chocolate, she realized. It would be a nice touch in both the bedroom nook and on the coffee table. She texted Matt.

Natasha: If you haven't left the store yet, can you pick up fancy chocolate, too?
Matt: Yep, still shopping.

Still shopping? How long did it take to pick out a kettle?

He texted fifteen minutes later that he was on his way home. Since the grocery store was a block and a half away, she kept a eye out for him. If he'd spent that long at the grocery store, he'd probably need help with bags.

But when he pulled up and got out of his truck, he only had one bag of groceries—and in his other hand, he had a gallon of paint.

She held the door for him, and he stopped to give her a kiss before setting the paint down on the front step.

Then he gave her the bag of groceries. "Put this in the kitchen, then come back out."

"Oh-kay…" She gave him a curious look but he wasn't giving anything up.

She did as instructed, stowing the cheesecake and chocolate on the counter. Then she pulled on her boots and coat and headed outside.

Matt was unloading lumber from the back of his truck.

"What…?"

He stopped and turned around. "Hey." He held up his hand. "I also got a kettle. It's on my passenger seat."

"Okay."

"Ah… And I stopped in to see Raj Patel while I was out. I used your employee discount. I hope you don't mind."

She walked down the steps, trying to figure out what his madness was all about. "What did you do?"

He closed the gap between them. "I bought wood."

"I see that."

"I want to build you a white picket fence." He gestured at the snow-covered front yard. "Not now. I'll put the wood in the basement until the ground thaws. See, it's a bit of a tradition in my family that the men build houses for the women they love. But the woman I love already did that. You built a home for Emily, and let me crash land in it. So I want to add a fence, and hang a tire swing in the big oak out back for your daughter, and promise to be a part of every project big or small you dream of in the future."

She was crying. It wasn't even adorable tears, she was full-on bawling.

And Matt wasn't done. "I know this isn't what you were looking for. But it's what I want with you. It's what I want with Emily. I want a yard we can play soccer in, where she can kick the ball as hard as she wants, and it stays safely enclosed. I want a border around our space that says, inside these pickets is a family."

Inside these pickets is a family. She couldn't breathe.

His arms slid around her and she buried her face in his neck. "I want that."

"Me, too," he whispered. "I want to build this for you so you see it every day and know that no matter how bruised and jaded and broken you might feel, because life is rough, that I want to build castles in the sky for you. That I see how hard you work, and I appreciate you, and I want to honour you."

"Matt…" She needed a fucking tissue. She swiped at her eyes with frozen fingertips. "That's the most beautiful thing anyone has ever said to me. You make me so happy, you big dork. A white picket fence?"

"Yeah." He carefully touched her chin, lifting her face. "Happy is my middle name. Last and final version. And I was wondering if maybe you and Emily wanted to adopt it as a common middle name. Natasha Happy Kingsley, wife of Matt Happy Foster, who is the proudest step-dad in the world to Emily Happy Kingsley." He stepped back, pulled a ring box out of his pocket, and lowered to one knee. "I didn't get this at the lumber store."

"What are you doing?" She whispered. One of the more ridiculous questions she'd ever asked, but she was awestruck. "You already got me a ring."

"This one is more than a promise. This one is a vow." He opened the box and pulled out a diamond solitaire. "Natasha, will you marry me?"

"Yes," she said through fresh tears. "I'll marry you tomorrow if you want."

"You have guests arriving in a few days, maybe we should wait." He slid the ring onto her left hand, then stood up. "I was thinking maybe Christmas Eve. Here. With our family. I can make stew and you and Emily can decorate the cupcakes."

CHAPTER THIRTY

THE WAITING ROOM looked like Natasha's hipster rental units. Matt even took a picture of the bookcase decorations in case his fiancée wanted to steal some ideas from his new therapist.

As the quiet clock on the wall ticked to the top of the hour, the inner door opened and a man stepped out. A big guy with a gentle smile. "Matt?"

"Hi. Yeah, that's me."

"I'm Vic. Come on in."

There was awkward paperwork first, then Vic leaned forward. "You said in your email that you're recovering from some trauma."

Matt swallowed. "That's right. Last year I, uh, had a pretty shitty day at work."

"You're a paramedic?"

He nodded. "I lost a patient at work, and it stuck with me."

"Then that's where we should begin. Tell me about that day."

Matt repeated the story that now slid out of him in a rush of words, not quite easy, but no longer traumatizing to recount. "It was just bad timing, really, that Fred died at the same time my brothers were trying to get ahold of me. And I conflated the two events in my head."

"And what happened next?"

An exhausted, worried drive to the airport. No news until the next day, when Dean finally arrived, and then waiting. Endless waiting. Weeks went by before Sean came home, broken and angry.

The therapist looked at him as he drifted to another pause. "He's okay now," Matt finally added. "Happily married, in fact."

"But what happened with Fred?"

"He died," Matt said, confused.

"Was there a funeral?"

A dull roar started somewhere in the back of Matt's brain.

"Matt?"

He gritted his teeth. "I don't know," he said thickly. "Fuck, how did I not know?"

"You were understandably occupied by a family tragedy."

His ears were ringing and he shook his head. Fuck. More than a year had passed. A year of running and working and nightmares—

He froze.

His hands were tight balls of fury in front of him and his vision blurred.

There was a grave in his dreams.

"I thought it was Sean." His voice cracked. "I had nightmares. Have. Still, sometimes, but not that often."

He'd been living with Natasha and Emily full-time for weeks now. Spring was trying to come to the peninsula, although winter was doing a good job of fighting to maintain its hold, too. He'd only woken up in a sweat twice, and both times, Tasha eased him back under the covers and held him as he talked about his brother.

But he didn't talk about Fred. Not enough.

"I don't even know if Fred has a grave." He looked up at Vic. "Maybe he was cremated."

"Who would know?"

"The Legion, I'd imagine."

Vic nodded. "How does that sound as a bit of homework for this week? Find out what sort of memorial there was. Next week we can talk about how it might feel to go to the grave, or see his ashes."

"It would be good." Matt didn't need to talk that through. He knew.

"All right."

Matt nodded. "Yeah. Shit."

Vic smiled. "Welcome to therapy, Matt. I think you're going to do some good work in here."

He left the office through another door that dumped right into the parking lot. Before he left Owen Sound, he stopped at the big grocery store and picked up everything he'd need to make his girls dinner.

The next day it rained. Heavy, relentless. A fitting backdrop as he drove north to Pine Harbour. The Legion opened after lunch, so he went to Mac's first and texted Tom and Sean to see if they wanted to join him.

They both showed up ten minutes later, Tom in his park ranger uniform, Sean in sweatpants and a t-shirt with his new elite athletics coaching logo printed on it.

"What's with the unexpected visit?" Sean asked after grabbing a menu.

Matt told them about his first counselling appointment, and his mission.

"We'll come with you to the Legion," Tom said.

Matt pointed to his uniform. "Don't you have to go back to work?"

"I've got a phone. They can call me if they need me. This is important." Right on cue, his phone vibrated. He glanced at the screen, typed back a response, and put it away. "See? All good."

Matt's leg shook restlessly as they ate. He pushed his foot into the ground, telling himself this would be fine.

Maybe he should have brought Natasha along for the drive, but she had a shift at the lumber store, and he didn't want to wait until they both had a day off together. Now that he'd realized what he needed for closure, he was grabbing it with both hands as soon as possible.

They walked over to the Legion once it opened. Matt introduced himself to the bartender and explained why he was there.

"Fred Carleton?" The guy nodded. "Yeah, I remember him. I'm not sure if there was a funeral."

Shit. That hit Matt in the chest like a sucker punch.

"There are a couple of guys who usually come around in the early afternoon to play cards. Sit down, have a drink, and I'll flag them for you."

Tom and Sean asked for pop, but Matt went for a beer. "I may end up on your couch at the end of the day," he warned Sean.

"Jenna's sleeping off a long birth this afternoon, so you'll need to be quiet, but sure."

"Dude, of course I get that."

"I know but..." Sean grinned. "She needs all the rest she can get. She's pregnant."

"Fucking eh, man!" Matt clapped his hand on Sean's shoulder and squeezed. "Good job."

Sean laughed. "Thanks."

The outside door swung open, and two older men stepped inside.

One of them was his father.

"Uh…" Sean sat up straighter.

So did Matt. Then he stood up. "Dad," he said. "I didn't know you came in here."

The Colonel shrugged. "I like to play cards, so I pop in from time to time. What are you boys doing here?"

Boys. Sean cleared his throat at that, and Matt expected their father to grump about the reaction, but instead he nodded his head.

"Sorry, Sean."

Would wonders never cease.

Matt was going for it. "Dad, did you know Fred Carleton?"

"Yep, sure did. Not as well as the others, but he was a regular here before he got sick."

"I, uh…" Matt's throat tightened up. "I was wondering if there was a funeral or anything. I missed it, and it's been weighing on my mind."

The Colonel frowned, then waved over the other man who'd gone to the bar. "I think that was around the time Sean was hurt, wasn't it?"

Matt rubbed his chest. "Yep. Same time."

"Jim, what did you guys do for Fred Carleton's memorial?" His father gestured to Matt. "My son here was wondering." He looked back at Matt. "You knew him through work, did you?"

He nodded. He wasn't going to share the details with Fred's friends.

Jim, an older man, slight and slim, pulled up a chair and sat down, so then their father did the same.

"We had a lunch here a few days after he died," the veteran

said. "Said a few words in his memory. That was it. Often is the way."

"So there was no funeral?"

Jim shook his head. "His ashes went to his niece, I think. I'm sure I could find out."

"I don't want to put you out." Except he did, he really did. "But I would appreciate that enormously. I'd like to find a way to say goodbye to him."

"Well," Jim said slowly. "I don't know if it would be the same, but we did up a plaque for him. It's in the back." He stood up and nodded his head. "Follow me."

There were a few dozen plaques lining the walls. How many times had Matt been in this Legion hall for a stag and doe or a fundraiser, and he'd never noticed the solemn commemorations to the members who had died?

Fred's was near the end, but not the last one. The Legion had lost a couple other members in the intervening year, it looked like.

Matt stopped and just looked. It had his name, his rank at time of release, his years of service. His birth date. And the date of his death.

What a shitty day that was, Matt thought.

Not at the start, though. They'd laughed and joked and shared stories.

If Matt was going to die, he'd want the hours before his death to be like that. Talking about women and military service and professional duty.

He'd talk about Natasha. About Emily. About cupcakes and taking chances.

"I wish I could tell you about my life now," he said quietly, looking at Fred's picture. "It's so different, man."

But he couldn't because life was finite and fragile.

He stood there for a while longer. It didn't magically lift his guilt, but it did help sort some of his feelings out. Definitely gave him some new things to talk to the therapist about.

And more than anything else, it made him want to go home and tell Natasha about his day. To wrap his arms around his woman and hold on tight.

EPILOGUE

December, again

THE DAY BEFORE CHRISTMAS EVE, Matt worked a half-shift, as a favour to cover Owen because his daughter had an emergency.

He rarely pulled any extra shifts these days. He was too busy renovating the new Escape Inn, on the outskirts of Pine Harbour. If they kept to a good schedule, they might open in time for Valentine's Day. He liked to joke that Natasha might have a boutique inn empire at this rate, and she liked to joke that he hated sleep.

She wasn't wrong. But he was getting better on that score every day. Balance and purpose in his life really helped.

So did doing little things to make his fiancée happy—like picking up a newly cut Christmas tree the day before their wedding, so it would be as fresh as possible.

Except that wasn't such a little thing.

And Natasha freaked out when she saw the one he'd picked. "You have got to be kidding me."

Matt glanced behind him, following her gaze to the tree in the back of his truck. "What?"

"That thing is not going to fit through the front door."

"Ah, sure it will."

"Matt!"

"What?" His grin was so big he thought it might split his face open. Okay, so the tree was a bit big. Even bundled, it wasn't contained in the bed of his pickup. It bulged proudly, promising thick green branches to hold the Christmas ornaments he'd been buying every time they stopped at a thrift store together over the last year. "I want to have a nice big tree. It's an important date."

"There won't be much room for our guests since the tree is going to take up half of the living room."

"I had a different idea. Let's put it in the back hallway, outside the downstairs apartment. Next to the stairs. I think everyone would fit in there, and that would be a nice place to exchange vows."

"Did you just rewrite our entire wedding plan?"

"Maybe."

She kissed him hard on the mouth. "I love it."

———

NATASHA'S SISTER and her family arrived that night, checking into the upstairs apartment. Shortly after they arrived, Matt's brothers came over to take their brother to the pub for a final drink as a single man.

Meredith gave Tasha an *are you freaking kidding me* look, and as soon as the Fosters were out the door, she told Dan he was on bedtime duty for all three kids.

"We have sister things to talk about," she said. "Over tea."

"I've missed you," Natasha said, laughing as she was dragged into the kitchen.

"You never said Matt's brothers were all equally hot."

Because they weren't, but she didn't think Meredith cared about Tasha's opinion on the matter. She forced herself to stop giggling. "They're all married."

"What? So am I. Dan's definitely there in whatever firefighter-sandwich fantasy I might innocently have."

"There's nothing innocent about you. And I didn't need to know that about Dan, either."

"He looks great in yellow and red."

"Please stop. Also, none of them are firefighters." She hesitated. "There is one coming tomorrow, though. Matt's boss. Don't grope him."

"I make no promises. What's his name?"

Natasha wiped happy tears from her eyes. "Owen. And he's lovely. Don't scare him away."

Of course Mer was all talk. The next night, Christmas Eve, she was the picture of sweetness as Natasha's maid of honour. "None of this matron crap, right?"

"Never," Tasha promised her sister as they finished getting dressed with Emily in the downstairs apartment. "You look beautiful. And very maiden-ly."

They were all wearing lace. Meredith and Emily were both in red—Emily's dress with a pink ribbon around the waist—and Natasha was in white.

Their wedding might be small and intimate, but her dress was gloriously formal. It even had a little train, which she would bustle up immediately after the ceremony.

A knock at the door interrupted their tearing up. Dani popped her head around the door. "Calvin's ready," she said, ducking into the room with her son.

He was dressed in a tiny tuxedo.

"And everyone is outside."

Nerves fluttered to life in Natasha's chest. "Okay. We're… ready, I guess. If Matt's out there?"

Dani nodded, her eyes wet. "He's grinning like an idiot."

"Then let's do this. Em, take Calvin's hand. Dani, you can start the music."

Her new sister-in-law left, and then she heard the first strains of "Carol of the Bells", the song she'd decided to walk down the aisle to. Or really, out the door to.

Meredith went first, opening the door, and this time leaving it open. Then Emily and Calvin followed her, hand-in-hand. Her daughter had sprouted up in the last year, now proudly four-and-a-half.

She was going to make the best big sister.

They would tell her tomorrow morning.

Tasha pressed a hand to her still-flat belly, then took a deep breath and stepped up to the doorway.

Everyone in their family was there. Meredith and the kids had stepped up the staircase, moving out of her way. In front of them stood Matt, on the bottom step. Gorgeous and strong in a black suit.

He held out his hand to her and she crossed the small landing to join him and the minister who had agreed to marry them.

"My bride," he whispered.

She smiled and took a deep breath. "My husband."

———

AFTER THEIR VOWS, and a long, glorious kiss, Matt took Natasha's hand and led everyone back to their side of the house for a dinner he'd made with his own two hands.

Except for dessert—that was all his wife's doing. She'd put

herself in charge of the drinks, too, which meant she kept getting dragged from his arms.

He didn't mind, though. He had the rest of his life to hold her, and she was in her element as a hostess.

And it meant that he could spend time with their guests—and notice when things were wrong. Tom kept checking his phone, and after the third hostile shove of the device back into his pocket, Matt sauntered over with two beers.

He held one out to his friend. "Here."

"Thanks."

"What's wrong?"

Tom wiped his face. "Nothing."

"Are you sure?" Matt gestured for the kitchen, and his friend—always in control, always stoic and reserved—stormed past him.

Okay, so not nothing.

He followed Tom through the door to the back of the house and found him pacing in front of the giant Christmas tree.

His friend swore under his breath. "I didn't mean to bring down your night. That was a really nice wedding."

"You aren't doing anything to my night, it's fine. What's going on?"

"Chloe's pregnant," Tom growled.

That's what he was blowing up his phone over?

"Chloe who you hooked up with once before she rejected you?" If Tom was having misplaced jealously over an old fling, Matt didn't have time for that.

The growl got worse. "Chloe who I've been sleeping with for a year."

Ah. Not misplaced, and not jealousy. "Okay, well, congrats on keeping that a secret. And why are you pissed? Is it yours?"

"Yes, the baby is mine. Except she's taken off. She left me a note that she doesn't expect anything from me. And now she's not responding to any of my text messages."

Oh, good Lord. "You probably said the wrong thing and she's reacting with pregnancy hormones. She'll be back after the holidays and you can make it up to her then."

"No. She won't. Her apartment is empty. She's gone, and I don't know where or why."

Well, shit. "This sounds like a problem for Dean and Zander."

A muscle spasmed in Tom's jaw. "No. We're not telling anyone else until we track her down."

Their brothers were the security consultants, but Matt sensed that this was not a time for logic. "Okay. We'll figure it out."

"I mean—" Tom swore under his breath again. "Jesus. Even though it's unexpected, this baby would be loved, you know?"

Oh, Matt knew. But now wasn't the time to get into that. "Yeah, for sure. It's just, ah, maybe she thinks she's not ready for a baby?" He was out of his depth here. "Maybe she should talk to Natasha. And she'd keep the pregnancy a secret, of course."

The door opened behind him as he said that, and he turned around.

Owen was glaring at him. "How did you know?"

Tom frowned at Owen. "How did *you* know?"

"Who are you talking about?"

"Who are *you* talking about? I'm talking about Chloe."

Fuck. Matt held up his hands. "Okay, one at a time. I mean, I don't know who's drama is bigger here, but please tell me you aren't talking about the same woman."

Owen was still giving Tom a terrifying look, but he shook his head. "No. Sorry. Not the same woman."

Matt wasn't sure he wanted to be in the middle of any of

this, but hey, he'd never been a friend one would have confided in before, so he wasn't going to knock that he had two buddies sharing secrets.

Except it was his wedding day, so they should make it quick. He wanted to get back to his bride. He turned to Owen. "Who did you think he was talking about?"

"It doesn't matter. I overreacted."

Tom laughed. "Welcome to the club."

"Is someone else…" Matt trailed off as Owen's eyes blazed with fury. Pregnant. Someone else was pregnant.

And Matt was pretty sure it was Owen's eighteen-year-old daughter.

———

———

THANK you for reading Matt and Tasha's story! If you want to be the first to know when the next Pine Harbour books go up for sale, join my newsletter!

SIGN UP HERE: www.smarturl.it/ZoeYorkNewsletter

When you sign up, you'll get an email from me with an update of what I'm currently writing, and what's coming next! If you'd like a sneak peek at Owen's book (Reckless at Heart, The Kincaids of Pine Harbour #1), or Tom's book (Love on the Edge of Reason, Pine Harbour #8 - the last book in this series!), turn the page.

I would love to hear from you on Facebook, too. Here's my reader group: www.fb.com/groups/WardhamAmbassadors

~ All the best, Zoe

Love on the Edge of Reason (Pine Harbour #8)

Tom Minelli doesn't know why Chloe Davis has fled Pine Harbour, but she's pregnant with his baby and he wants her back. Not just back in town. He wants Chloe back in his life, and not as the casual hook-up friends they were before. But finding her proves harder than he expected—and when he does track her down, she drops a bombshell on him.

Love on the Edge of Reason is the final book in the Pine Harbour series, but the standalone romances with men in uniform continues with Reckless at Heart, book #1 in the new Kincaids of Pine Harbour series.

Reckless at Heart (The Kincaids of Pine Harbour Book #1)

"Daddy, I'm pregnant."

The last three words Owen Kincaid ever wanted to hear from his teenage daughter. He knows how hard it is to have a kid when you're still a kid yourself. He did it, and now eighteen years later, history is repeating itself. To say he's beating himself up is an understatement. The last thing he needs is to fall head-over-heels in lust with his daughter's midwife.

Kerry Humphrey hates her new client's father. She has no reason to hate him, except for the fact he's tall and brooding and always there, hovering in the background of appointments. And the crackle of chemistry every time their eyes meet. She hates that, too.

Everything about their attraction is ill-fated. But it won't go away. Maybe, for one night, they can be… Reckless at Heart.

Coming in 2019!
For more information, visit my website: www.zoeyork.com
Or sign up for my newsletter: www.smarturl.it/ZoeYorkNewsletter

ACKNOWLEDGEMENTS

aka The People Who See Me, Warts and All

First nod must go to Kristi Yanta, who has edited five of my Pine Harbour books now. None of them have been easy, but this one took the cake. She held my hand through three brutal drafts and still promises to come back for the last book in the series (and the start of the next one, because I'm a glutton for punishment).

This series guts me in a way nothing else I write does. These characters are alive and real in my heart, and I want to capture every tiny part of their

The Viking gets a mention here, too, because every minute that I was writing this book was also a rocky period personally —for him, and for us. But he never wavered in understanding that no matter what else was going on, I needed to write. Sometimes it wasn't much. December and March were gong shows. But once the storm was over, and I picked up my computer again, he brought me endless cups of tea and rubbed my arms and handed me tissues.

I told him that it took twice as many words as usual to convince myself that my characters could have a happy-ever-after ending, and that was really hard to realize. I know a lot of my readers sometimes feel the same way, that what we read between the pages is a stretch from reality. But I hope this book shows that we all have a story—just some have a lot more words than others.

I'm also thankful for my assistant Lori, who designs the most beautiful release week graphics for my books, and keeps my Facebook page updated when I'm locked in the writing cave. And in general is always there to listen and support and make me more tea.

Tea. Yes, if you were wondering, I am Meredith. Right down to being the small-town girl who left Bruce County to live in the city. I like being close to a Starbucks, but the county will always have a special place in my heart.

And a huge thanks to Bonnie, who got the copyedits on this turned around faster than I thought humanly possible.

Other grateful notes:

Jessica A, for reading this book in broken parts and pointing out where my characters were being stupid.

Liis M., who lives in Port Elgin for real, and posted on Facebook about her kids playing hockey on her driveway while she watched them—wrapped in a parka. I went back to the scene where Natasha was watching Emily play and changed it from what I'd originally written (tricycling) to playing hockey. I love my real life reader inspiration for scenes!

Speaking of which…

Mandy R., who tagged me on Twitter to ask why romance heroes (especially in Pine Harbour) always wear #blackboxerbriefs. Well, Mandy, Matt most certainly does not. #pinkavocadotrunksforlife

And finally, a grateful nod to the early ARC readers who caught the last handful of typos: Liis M., Carissa R., Beverley H., Wendy F., Mel K., Terri S., Gi P, Ariana B, Elizabeth C.

As always, I appreciate my tribe more than words can say.

~ Zoe

ABOUT THE AUTHOR

Zoe York lives in London, Ontario with her young family. She's currently chugging Americanos, wiping sticky fingers, and dreaming of heroes (mostly) out of uniform. She also writes erotic romance as Ainsley Booth, because who needs sleep?

www.zoeyork.com